THE Maverick MEETS HIS Match

ANNE CARROLE

Hearts of Wyoming series

Book 1: *Loving a Cowboy*
Book 2: *The Maverick Meets His Match*
Book3: *The Rancher's Heart* (coming 2016)

Table of Contents

Chapter 1

Ty Martin had never regretted the choices he'd made, until now. Shading his eyes against the sunlight glinting off the dial of his Rolex, he checked the time. Twenty minutes until life changed. Maybe temporarily. Maybe for good.

Or bad.

Tamping down the unease that always came with loose ends, Ty moved past the corrals where the cowhands were topping off the water troughs. Heads popped up like jack-in-the-boxes, but no one acknowledged him. Not a word, not a wave, not a nod. Instead, they stared as if he were some curiosity on parade.

Ty tugged the brim of his Stetson lower. At least being an outsider would make decisions easier.

Without breaking stride, he swept by the barn where the stalls were being mucked out and moved on past the low building that served as an office for the livestock rodeo company he would now head. Dust kicked up as he went, coating his custom-made alligator boots and threatening to settle on his black dress pants.

A steer bellowed in the distance, part of the ranch herd that had been brought in for culling.

He scanned the side parking area for a gray pickup truck. Silver metal glistened just a few feet away from his black BMW. At least he wouldn't be the last one to walk into the lawyer's office.

For most of his life he had run from anything to do with ranching, working his way through law school, scoring a job at a land development firm, and fighting his way to a partnership—only to eventually walk away. And now, here he was, heading up a livestock operation. A rodeo livestock operation.

Just a year. That's what he had promised. Just enough time to decide the fate of the company that bore another family's name. And they would hate him for it, or at least one person would hate him for it, if she didn't already.

He clicked the remote in his pocket, and his car hummed in response. A few more steps and he pulled open the door. Semi-cool air blasted his face from the side vent, carrying with it that new-car odor. He slipped onto the sun-warmed leather seats, extracted a pair of Oakley shades from the center compartment, and opened the sunroof as he closed the door.

It was too damn hot for May in Wyoming, he thought, removing his suit jacket and hat and laying them on the passenger seat. He buckled up, popped on the sunglasses, and shifted into reverse. Gravel crunched under the tires.

Mandy Prescott would fight him despite this just being business. He might understand why the old man had worked it this way. She never would.

It would be easier if she wasn't so damned attractive, and stubborn. A challenging combination he'd found tempting in the past. But the fact she was J.

M. Prescott's granddaughter had kept Ty's pants zipped. He'd realized early on dallying with Mandy was not an option unless he was prepared to marry her. And that would never be the case—with any woman, but certainly not with a hardheaded, determined woman like Mandy, no matter how much she tempted him.

Ty shifted the car into gear. Of course, now that J. M. Prescott was gone, maybe a little fling with Mandy, if she was as inclined as she'd once been, would be just what he needed to fight this strange feeling that had come over him since JM's passing. Like something important had seeped out of him, slowly, almost imperceptibly, but steady enough to leave an uncomfortable void.

Yup, Mandy Prescott's feminine charms could be just what the doctor ordered, despite her current disposition toward him, because if life had taught him two things, it was that anything was possible and nothing was certain.

* * *

Mandy Prescott misstepped on the tan carpet of the law office's hallway almost causing her to stumble. Ty Martin stood in the conference room doorway, looking like he'd strode out of an Old West wanted poster, given his six-foot height, the stubble shadowing his firm jaw, and the black suit jacket outlining his broad shoulders. Dark eyes peered at her from under the brim of a Stetson pulled low enough for the back of his ebony-colored hair to feather the crisp white collar of his shirt. Neater than an outlaw, maybe, but no less threatening.

"I didn't know Ty would be here, did you, Mandy?" her mother whispered, leaning closer as they walked and bringing a whiff of Chanel No. 5 with her movement.

Her heart pounded hard against her ribs, like it wanted out.

"No."

Brian Solomon, the family attorney, had said only the main beneficiaries of her grandfather's will would be in attendance. To her that had meant family. But there was Ty, leaning against the doorjamb with arms crossed and an annoying smile gracing a face she'd once found attractive.

Devils were always tempting.

"Ty." She nodded, barely able to get the single syllable past her dry lips as she stopped outside the doorway.

"Mandy." He touched the brim of his hat. "Mrs. Prescott."

"I've told you, it's Shelia, Ty. Mrs. Prescott makes me sound old." At forty-eight her mother was still an attractive and vibrant woman. Dressed in a tailored black sheath, her blond hair meticulously styled in a bang-less page-boy, Shelia Prescott exuded quiet elegance. It was a wonder she'd never remarried, given it had been over ten years since Mandy's father had died.

"Sheila it is." The lines around Ty's eyes crinkled as his smile broadened and he trained those dark orbs on Mandy. "I was worried about you, Mandy. Thought you might not be feeling well since you've yet to meet with me about the Greenville rodeo."

"I've been busy." She hoped he didn't miss the

edge in her voice. After all, her grandfather's funeral had only been a few days ago. The grief was still raw.

Of course, with Ty everything was business. That's what her grandfather, J. M. Prescott, had liked about him. Because that's the way her grandfather had been.

Nothing personal, just business.

She'd had to swallow a gallon of pride when JM, his health deteriorating from cancer, had installed Ty Martin as head of the family's rodeo stock company just a few weeks before his passing. Temporarily, her grandfather had said. Nothing personal. But it had felt personal. Very personal.

For ten years, since her father's untimely death, she'd made it her mission to be ready to lead the company when her grandfather retired. All through high school and college she'd worked after classes and every weekend, missing football games, dances, proms, just about any social occasion. Extracurricular activities had been raking out stalls, training horses, loading trailers, and organizing rodeo events. Every college course she took, even attending business school, had been with one goal in mind—to be ready to lead Prescott Rodeo Company. The few guys she had dated had either been rodeo hands or rodeo cowboys, but none had understood her drive or tolerated it for long.

She'd been the only Prescott interested in running the company, much to her grandfather's disappointment, apparently, given the "temporary" hiring of Ty Martin— an arrogant man, full of himself, and as strikingly handsome as Michelangelo's stone statue of Apollo, and just as cold. A man who was a lawyer by degree and a land developer by trade. A rancher's son who, at the first opportunity, had gotten as far away from herds as a prairie dog facing a stampede. Just like he'd gotten far away from her ten years ago.

Nothing personal.

"I think I'll freshen up a bit," Sheila said, taking a step back. "Before the reading of the will starts."

"I'll come with you," Mandy offered. Anything not to be left alone with Ty. Not now. Not here.

"Stay, dear, in case Brian comes in. He'll want to get started right away, and I'll only be a minute." Sheila smiled at Ty before she turned and continued down the hall toward the restrooms at the far end. Mandy didn't follow. After what her mother had said, she'd be admitting she didn't want to be alone with Ty, and she wasn't about to give him that satisfaction.

Still leaning against the doorjamb, he shifted slightly so she could pass, pushing back his hat and flashing that disarming grin of his. A grin that had surely lured more than one woman to a broken heart—including Mandy. But that was long ago.

"So maybe we should talk about it now. While we're waiting," he said as she slid by so close she could feel the heat of his body, smell the fresh scent of his soap. It distracted her. She didn't want to be distracted. Not today.

"About Greenville?" Mandy shrugged in an attempt to look unruffled despite the churning inside her, like beaters in a mixing bowl of nerves. It was a good thing she hadn't had time to eat. She hadn't had time to change, either, having worked with the parade horses that morning. She still wore her dirt-speckled shirt, faded jeans, and had pulled her long brown hair back in a pony tail to keep it off her face. She must have looked a dusty mess and clearly not her mother's daughter.

She hadn't even changed her scoffed barn boots and boots were her one and only fashion obsession. She had ones made of leather, python, lizard, and caiman. She had red ones, white, gray, brown, black, tan, honey, and even a purple pair that she bought on an impulse after a really bad day. Snip-toed, rounded, pointed, and squared. Embroidered, embossed, distressed, and inlaid. Every famous maker, several no one ever heard of, and, of course, a number that were custom made. Most fell into the cowgirl category, but there were a few that were spiked heeled and knee high, and one dominatrix-style thigh-high black pair she'd bought to impress a certain cowboy she'd been dating—but never had the courage to wear. That was the extent of her fashion sense, or lack thereof, depending on how one felt about her taste.

Not that it mattered what she wore and she certainly didn't care about impressing Ty.

She circled the oval wood table, putting it between them, and looked at Ty through the narrow space framed by two chrome pendant lights dangling from the high ceiling. She'd been in the long, narrow conference room once before, ten years ago, but she remembered nothing about that day. She'd been crying too hard. "What do you want to know?"

Mandy pulled out one of the table's black leather chairs and sank into it, taking refuge in its overstuffed comfort as she set the large purse she carried on the floor.

"Everything," he said, still standing in the doorway like some gatekeeper controlling who entered and exited. "What stock you're pulling, how many of the crew you're using, your expense estimates, how much you expect to make on the event."

This from a man who knew nothing about supplying stock. Those beaters inside her whirred faster.

"Everything," he repeated.

"You can get that from Karen, our admin."

Ty's mouth drew in, and his eyes narrowed as he stepped into the room, covering the distance to the table in two long strides. He placed his hands on the table's polished surface and leaned forward until he was mere inches from her face so that he blocked out everything around her. Even with that strong jaw of his clenched, he was still too attractive for her own good. She tightened her grip on the chair arms as her pulse quickened, determined to meet his steely gaze with a glare of her own.

If he was trying to intimidate her, it wouldn't work.

"Here's the thing, Mandy. I want the information from you. And I want you to go through it with me, number by number." His tone was matter of fact, even if those tantalizing lips of his had flatlined.

"I need to understand the business if I'm going to lead it. And you're the best one to show me."

She could feel the blood pulsing at her temple, which meant she was on her way to an epic headache. Breathing deep, she cocked her head to get a better bead on his arrogance. "Here's the thing, Ty. After today, I expect the family to own the required shares to vote you out of your role." She prayed she was right. "And you won't need to understand anything about the business."

Leather creaked as Ty folded his long, lean, undoubtedly buff body into the padded chair while his dark eyes scrutinized her, as if her words puzzled him. She thought she'd been pretty darn straightforward.

Six tension-filled beats of her heart passed before he finally spoke.

"I guess we'll just have to wait and see about that."

At that moment JM's nephew and Prescott's livestock foreman, Harold Prescott, sauntered in, escorting her mother back from the ladies' room. Weathered and graying, Harold was all cowboy, long and wiry with a conversational repertoire of a bronzed cowboy statue. Not that it mattered, since Harold dealt primarily with the animals and was as loyal as they came.

Mandy took a calming breath as greetings were exchanged and the two sat down, her mother next to her, and Harold on the other side of her mother. Taking pains not to spare Ty another glance, she looked past him to the doorway in search of her younger brother. Tuck was never one to worry about what time a clock chimed, so she was relieved to see him enter with Brian.

Except for the blond hair, Tucker Prescott was the spitting image of their late father, with his blue eyes and high-school-quarterback looks, though genes were all the two men shared. While her father had been deep into the business before his death ten years ago, Tuck preferred to ride in rodeos rather than stock them, adding to JM's dismay. Tuck maintained he didn't want to end up like their father, working too hard and never enjoying life. Instead, Mandy had taken up the mantle. Or tried to.

After giving both women a peck on the cheek and greeting Ty and Harold with a handshake, Tuck sank his long-limbed body into the chair next to Ty and across from his mother. Brian too went out of his way to shake everyone's hand before settling into the head seat.

Mandy struggled with the unsettling prospect that Ty Martin might still be leading her family's business after the reading of the will. Her leg jiggled seemingly of its own volition.

Had it come to this? Had JM held such little faith in her abilities?

It was hard to keep the doubts at bay when her mind replayed snippet after snippet of failures. And her grandfather's corrections. Like the time she'd underbid a rodeo and her grandfather had docked her salary the five-thousand-dollar difference to make up for it. The time she'd brought too few rough stock to an event and her grandfather had to call in favors from other rodeo suppliers. The time she'd understaffed a rodeo and her grandfather had to hire temporary chute help from among the contestants. But she'd learned from those mistakes. She hadn't repeated them.

What of your successes, Amanda Prescott? Those should count too, she reminded herself. How about wooing the largest rodeo within the Montana circuit and raising two National Rodeo Finals broncs, one of which achieved ProRodeo Riders Association horse of the year? What about hiring away one of the top pick-up cowboys in the business, increasing attendance by promoting the matchups between cowboy and the particular livestock, and bringing every rodeo in on budget for the last two years?

She shifted in her seat. Maybe Ty had been left some small remembrance, and she was fretting for no reason. Anything was possible.

"Now that everyone is here, we can get started." There was an uncharacteristic officiousness in Brian's voice as he shuffled through sheets of paper. Distinguished, late fifties, impeccably groomed, Brian had been the family lawyer for the past ten years. He read off the standard opening paragraphs of the will, which stated this will superseded all other wills and that her grandfather had been of sound mind. Mandy half listened. The other half of her mind was working through the odds of her taking over Prescott Rodeo Company given Ty's presence. So far she hadn't been able to get above fifty-fifty.

"I've a copy of the will for all of you, so I'll just provide a summary of the pertinent facts. First off, your grandfather made a number of bequests."

Brian proceeded to rattle off the cowhands who had been with Prescott Rodeo Company from the early days and the generous sums attached to each of their names. He ended with Mrs. Jenkins, JM's housekeeper, who had come to work for him after Mandy's grandmother had passed a few years ago.

It wasn't clear where Mrs. Jenkins would end up now. It would depend on who would get her grandfather's ranch house, Mandy supposed. Her bet was on Tucker.

"The real meat and potatoes of J. M. Prescott's will has to do with Prescott Rodeo Company, and everyone at the table today is concerned by virtue of the contents of that document," Brian explained.

As if synchronized, all of them turned their

attention to Ty, including Mandy. Ty's smile was closed lipped, his dark eyes never flinching under the scrutiny.

Beneath the table, she felt her mother's cool, soft hand close over hers. A squeeze followed. It was her mother's way of telling her to stay calm. Mandy squeezed back. Her mother didn't remove her hand.

"As a privately held company, your grandfather had more flexibility to do as he saw fit than if it was a publicly held company. And JM took advantage of that fact, as you will soon learn." Brian raised his gaze from the sheaf of papers he held. "I feel obligated to tell you all that I do not countenance everything he did in this document, but I don't think any of you can question whether he was in his right mind a month ago when he drew up this new will. I'll also caution that I am a fairly good lawyer, so I don't expect there will be grounds to break his will."

Sheila squeezed Mandy's hand harder. This was going to be worse than she ever imagined. She couldn't bear to look at Ty. If the man had duped her grandfather, she might not be able to do anything about it.

"Mandy, you and Ty Martin have been named as trustees of the scholarship fund named in your father's honor for a worthy student from the local community college who wishes to go on for a four-year degree. I believe, Ty, you were the first recipient of that scholarship."

Ty nodded.

Maybe that was why Ty was here. Nothing to do with PRC directly. Of course, that would make sense. Mandy began to relax. She was worrying about nothing. She might have to see Ty more than usual, but that wouldn't be as horrible as him running her company.

She met Ty the summer following her father's death, her life having been upended by that catastrophic event. In what would become a tradition, her grandfather offered the recipient of the scholarship a summer job helping out. She remembered stumbling upon Ty in the barn, his shirt off, as he cleaned the stalls. It had been hot, and the flies were biting as her seventeen-year-old self had sauntered in to fetch a bridle out of the tack room. She'd wanted to take a dip and planned to ride out to the creek that ran through the western side of the ranch.

She'd been stopped in her tracks by flexing muscle and slick flesh. With dark, cropped hair, angular features, and a lean, lanky body, it had been crush at first sight. And he'd barely noticed her as he cleaned out the barn stalls. As she'd scooted into the tack room to catch her breath, she'd vowed to make him notice her—and soon. Little did she realize what a mistake she was making.

"In addition, Sheila, JM left the Prescott ranch land and ranch herds in your trust for Mandy and Tucker, who hold equal shares of the ranch enterprise, which, as you know, is a separate entity from Prescott Rodeo Company. He made provisions for Prescott Rodeo Company to continue to lease from the trust the portion of land it uses for its enterprise at reasonable fees. The will grants half of those rent monies to you as income for as long as you live and the ranch stays in Prescott hands. There are provisions, should the company change hands, for you to continue to receive a stipend from the proceeds of that sale equivalent to the projected rental stream, as if the company continued to lease the land from the trust."

"JM was always generous," Sheila said as she dabbed a hankie to her glistening eyes.

During his lifetime, JM had provided for her mother, given she was his only child's widow and the mother of his grandchildren, but now her mother would have her own income, making her an independent and well-to-do woman. As to the company changing hands, that would never happen as long as Mandy had breath left in her.

Brian laid aside the sheet of paper he'd been reading and turned his attention to the next page.

"Harold, you are bequeathed shares equal to nine percent of Prescott Rodeo Company and, at a minimum, your current salary for the rest of your life, whether you work or not, to be paid out of company funds."

"I know. JM told me. And of course I'll be working as long as the young'uns need me to." He spared a smile with a nod in Sheila's direction as if the two had already spoken about it.

"Of course we need you, Harold," Mandy piped up. People were the fabric of the company and, regardless of who was running it, Mandy would let nothing destroy that fabric.

"Tucker, you inherit a twenty percent stake in the rodeo business. JM wants me to note that it could have been more if you'd been willing to help run the company."

"So he told me," Tucker said with good-natured resignation. "I'm okay with the way things are."

Brian raised his gaze and stared at Mandy a moment too long for good news. Her heart sputtered in her chest like an engine choke that couldn't take hold.

JM, it seemed, had spoken to everyone but her about the contents of the new will.

"I guess I should mention that before JM made this will, he also completed a transaction with Mr. Martin here. Ty currently owns twenty percent of Prescott Rodeo Company, bought and paid for under terms advantageous to Prescott, I might add."

Mandy couldn't stifle the gasp that left her lips, even as her mother's hand tightened its hold. It was just as she'd suspected. Ty had wormed his way into her family's business for reasons that eluded her. Tension pressed in on her chest, making it hard to breathe. She couldn't, wouldn't, look in his direction. But she could see his hands, half-fisted, on the table. Large hands. Masculine hands barely weathered by the outdoors but no doubt used to doing dirty work.

"I imagine you all must be wondering what has happened to the other fifty-one percent." Brian stated the obvious. "Mandy, you will receive twenty percent of the company outright, bringing you equal to Tucker and Ty. But because Mandy is willing to take over the business one day…"

Mandy clenched her teeth and braced for bad news. Brian had used a future tense in talking about her taking over.

"The remaining thirty-one percent will also go to Mandy, from which she will receive the dividend stream…"

Mandy let out a breath of air in relief. She would have controlling interest. And the authority to hire—and fire.

"And Ty Martin will hold the voting rights to those shares."

And just like that, her empty stomach turned over. She swung her gaze to Ty, whose face was grimmer than she expected for someone who had just been handed the keys to the company. If looks could kill, she meant hers to strike him dead.

"What do you mean, the voting rights are held by Ty?" her mother asked.

"Just what I said, Sheila. JM had this block of stocks issued as a separate class, so Mandy will get the dividend stream, but the voting rights fall to Ty for a period of time."

Ty leaned forward, his Stetson dipping lower on his brow, shadowing his eyes. Definitely an outlaw. "Mandy, it's only for a limited time."

"What do you mean, a limited time? How long?" she snapped as she grappled with the emotions whipping through her. Anger at Ty, frustration with Brian, and betrayal by her grandfather, the man she loved and admired and had tried so hard to please.

Brian looked at the assembly. "May I have a moment with Ty and Mandy alone? The major portions of the will have been read. What I have to say really just concerns them. You can get copies of the will from my secretary."

Harold and Tuck stood up in unison. Apparently neither wanted to be in the room when the bullets started flying. Mandy held on to her mother's hand even as Sheila rose.

"I'll be right outside, dear," her mother whispered. "Hear what Brian has to say." Mandy felt the warmth of a quick peck on her cheek as Sheila drew her hand away.

Mandy waited for the door to close, her leg

jiggling beneath the table. At the click of the latch, she let loose.

"You low-life lizard." She grounded out the words through a jaw held so tight it ached. "You clawed your way into my grandfather's good graces so you could steal the company from his family. And in his ailing health, he handed you voting rights to fifty-one percent of the company."

Her worst fear had come true.

Ty leaned back in his seat, drilling her with his hard, stoic gaze. If he thought he could shut her down with a stare, he was about to find out how mistaken he could be. She'd have her say. By God she would have her say.

"JM made those terms so I can make decisions unimpeded over the next year. And I only bought into the business because he needed capital to acquire more bulls in hopes of getting a supply contract with the American Federation of Bull Riders—an opportunity that could help future prospects of the firm."

Mandy was well aware of her grandfather's plan regarding the AFBR, since *she* had suggested it as a way to improve their bottom line. But she had no inkling he had sold shares in the company to raise capital to buy those five young bulls in their corral—and to Ty Martin, of all people.

"Given the credit crunch, we thought this would be a better way to fund," Brian offered. "And Ty, who, I'm pretty sure, had no intention of owning a rodeo company anytime soon, agreed. It was generous of him."

Mandy rubbed a hand across her eyes and wondered if the world had gone mad. Generous of Ty?

He was buying into one of the most respected rodeo suppliers in the business and now had the majority vote. How did that make Ty generous?

"As for the time period, this is where your grandfather recently changed the will." Brian shifted his gaze to include Ty. "And this is where I parted company with him regarding the terms. I want you both to know that up front. I do not approve of these terms. Absolutely I do not."

Panic rose up inside of Mandy as rapidly as flood water from a hurricane. This was going to be bad. Very bad.

Chapter 2

Ty rubbed the back of his neck. He didn't like the sound of things. JM may have been the smartest businessman he knew and his mentor ever since Ty had won the scholarship, but that only meant JM wasn't above doing the unexpected now and again. "Why don't you just tell us what this is all about, Brian?"

Mandy scowled and glared at him, her pretty green eyes narrowed in accusation. She hadn't always been so pissed off at him. No indeedy.

He still remembered the first time he saw her ten years ago. She'd slipped into the barn and, as he shoveled out an especially large pile of manure, she walked past him. He turned to catch the back of a pair of long shapely legs, a tight butt in cut-off jeans, and a mane of wavy brown hair floating down her back. He'd made a mental note to find out who she was, and find out he did.

"Well, JM has a deal he wants offered to you both." Brain shifted in his chair as if trying to get comfortable. It was a bad sign when a lawyer squirmed in his seat. "Previously, Ty was to run the company for one year. In that time he would assess the firm's future prospects and determine next steps. But in accordance with the new will, Ty has the option of extending his stewardship to a total of two years with Ty continuing to have complete authority to determine the company's future, or whether it even has a future. At the end of Ty's tenure, if the company isn't sold, control would revert to you, Mandy."

Mandy's gasp was loud and deep as she slapped a hand on the table, creating a distinctive smack.

He could understand her reaction. This two-year amendment was a new wrinkle, even to him. At least the two years was an option. He could still exit after a year. By then he should know what was best for Prescott and what he wanted to do with the rest of his life.

His tenure at the land development company had left him well-off but with a bitter taste in his mouth. It would take him some time to set up a rival company. Prescott could hold the key to that, or at least the ranch could. If he could get agreement from the family to develop that property, he'd make a name for himself. Because if the rodeo company sold, there'd be little reason beyond sentiment to hold on to the ranch. Selling the ranch could make the Prescott family not just well-off, but wealthy. And Ty even wealthier.

Not that he wasn't looking forward to managing the rodeo company for a period. He needed a break given the corporate politics he'd been embroiled in the past few months, which had almost broken him. And then had come JM's death.

He was counting on hard physical labor to get him mentally back on track. Different work from lawyering and negotiating land deals. Work that involved his hands as well as his head.

"And Ty, there's a bonus in this for you as well," Brian added, spearing Ty's attention. "But there is another option, along with conditions, for the both of you to consider."

"If it means I can run this company sooner, I'll do anything. Anything," Mandy said with a determination that almost made Ty laugh. As nicely as she filled out a pair of jeans, and it was very nice indeed, Mandy Prescott was a handful. While he was looking forward to being involved in the business, managing Mandy was not likely to be one of the highlights, considering she thought he was the devil incarnate. Unless, of course, they could come to some mutually beneficial terms that involved the bedroom. That would certainly turn the dynamics favorable.

He enjoyed a challenge, particularly when the effort was worth it. And he had no doubt with Mandy the effort would be well worth it. The hardest decision he had ever made with regard to a woman was when he'd walked away from Mandy ten years ago.

He could still see the hurt in her eyes, the tear that had traveled down her cheek, as he'd denied every instinct and told her no.

It had been the right decision. But it hadn't been an easy one.

Brian stroked his chin. "Well, Mandy, that statement will surely be tested."

"What does grandfather's will say?"

Mandy looked ready to jump right out of her seat.

"Just remember, I'm only the messenger." Brian looked back at the paper in his hand. "The will states that if you agree to marry Ty Martin and he agrees to marry you…"

Ty felt like he'd been hit with a stun gun as Mandy surged out of her chair.

"Marry? What is this? Some cruel joke?" She whirled around and faced Ty, accusation in her eyes.

Ty was thinking the exact same thing. He held up his hands in surrender. "Believe me, I'm just as shocked as you are."

Brian signaled for Mandy to sit down. "Just hear me out. I know neither of you are interested, but I have to read it out nonetheless."

Mandy thudded back down in her chair. She was one peeved female, and Ty couldn't blame her. What was JM thinking? Marry Mandy? She hated him, and while he did have plans to change that, it wasn't in exchange for a wedding ring.

As Brian read out the legal language that specified the terms, Ty could feel the pressure on his ribs increase like one of Prescott's two-thousand-pound bulls had just sat on his chest. When Brian finished, he looked up.

"Ostensibly, what it means," Brian explained, "is that, assuming you married, cohabitated, and stayed married for at least six months, thirty-one percent of the company represented by the remaining shares would be split so that, Mandy, you would get sixteen percent additional with voting rights, and, Ty, you would get fifteen percent with voting rights. This would make Mandy the majority stockholder, though neither of you would have the controlling interest individually. Being married, however, your combined stock holdings would result in a controlling interest."

"Hah, he must of been out of his mind," Mandy

said, crossing her arms under those nice breasts of hers, her foot jiggling like it was preparing for lift off.

Ty had to agree with her assessment, even though JM must have drawn up that provision right after he'd asked Ty to buy into the business, serve as Mandy's mentor, and determine what was best for the family's financial future. JM had not seemed the least bit addled. Physically weak from the rapid advance of cancer and the treatments, but still mentally sharp.

Brian shook his head. "No, he was not. I won't go into everything, but among other precautions, legal and otherwise, your grandfather had a preeminent psychiatrist attest to the soundness of his mental state."

Mandy shook her head as if she could make the provision disappear. Ty sunk back in his chair and stretched out his legs. No cause for alarm. This woman wanted nothing to do with marrying him, even if he did manage to get her into his bed. Right now that prospect wasn't looking too good.

Still, it hadn't taken but a second for his mind to leap from marriage to having sex with Mandy, especially given she looked damn attractive all fired up. Images of taking her to bed, running his fingers through that hair, and finishing what they'd started ten years ago crowded his mind, making his groin pound. He gave a mental shake in hopes of getting rid of those images.

Nope, they were still there.

Mandy leaned forward, breasts resting on the table as she bit her lip. She had very kissable lips, as he remembered. And breasts. "Why would my grandfather think I would ever agree to such a thing?"

Ty sure had no clue what the old man could have

been thinking, because not even the promise of additional stock, which surely would be worth a nice chunk of change, would be enough to get him to the altar. Why JM thought either of them would consider such a life-changing step was the wonder.

"Because Ty has a mandate to assess the long-term viability of the business, and according to the provisions of the will, Ty retains the voting rights of the remaining thirty-one percent of shares for up to two years, at his option, if you don't marry."

"I don't understand."

Ty did, and Mandy wouldn't like it. But business was business, like JM always said.

Brian cleared his throat as if the words had gotten stuck there. "With fifty-one percent of the stock between what he owns outright and the voting rights JM has assigned over to him, Ty has the votes and the mandate to sell the business if he feels the financials warrant that step. And up to two years to do it. That is, *if* you don't marry."

Mandy's face turned a chalky shade of pale. The chair she was sitting in seemed to swallow her up as she drew back into its leather embrace. He could see the import of Brian's words sinking in as her jaw tightened, her eyes rounded, and her lips thinned.

"You wouldn't."

Ty hardly felt like giving her an explanation now, but there would be no good time to explain, no time when she'd want to hear what needed to be said.

"Your grandfather was worried about having enough money for the family over the long haul. I think the recent downturn in the economy fueled that concern. He asked me to analyze the rodeo operation and determine if the operation could provide enough income for the family through the coming years, given the investments that would be needed in livestock, and the state of the industry, and…" Ty looked straight into her eyes. Sometimes the only way to say bad news was directly. "And the quality of the leadership. If I think there is too much future risk, I am to sell before Prescott's reputation can be tarnished." He took a hard swallow. It was the truth, but no doubt a harsh one for Mandy to accept.

He'd hoped to serve up the idea of selling the company as an opportunity when and if the analysis warranted it. But maybe it was better she knew the truth from the beginning, considering he would be probing pretty deep into Prescott's business practices.

He watched her face as she processed the news, saw her eyes turn glossy as tears filled them. Hell. He could handle anything but a woman's tears.

It wasn't but a heartbeat, though, before she faced him squarely with the fierceness of a warrior ready to battle and with the tears, gratefully, at bay. "Does that include the ranch land?"

It was almost a relief to see her back in fighting mode instead of silenced by an unintended blow. He preferred her like this, he realized. Strong and resilient. JM would have been proud of his granddaughter's spirit.

"Planned communities are sprouting up here in the West, and though the housing market has been hurt across the country, Wyoming is in better shape than most states," Brian began. "There could be a small fortune to be had for the ranch. And if the rodeo company is sold, the need for the land will be negligible given the meager return on investment on cattle herds. From the figures I've seen, it's the rodeo company rent that makes the ranch profitable. But selling the deeded land of the ranch would be at your and Tucker's option. The company would be Ty's decision."

She cast her eyes downward and shook her head.

"The ranch piece is something for me to look at, Mandy, and for you and Tucker to consider." Ty knew from experience that money could do a lot of persuading, and a land deal this size could mean real wealth for the Prescotts. And a coup for him and the new company he planned to form.

"You're a developer though. That's what you do. And that must have been why he picked you." Her monotone couldn't disguise the cracks of emotion in her voice.

"That was one reason."

And the other was that JM knew Ty would be objective in his assessment, wouldn't let sentimentality, or his own interests, interfere with the cold, hard facts. Ty had built his reputation on being cool and detached when it came to making profitable business decisions. And that's why he was also no longer at the land development firm. Some people didn't want to know the truth. Some people preferred to make deals based on connections, paybacks, and, worse, gut instead of reason.

Head bent, Mandy continued to stare at the table's polished surface as if the answer was written in the grain of the wood.

Brian cleared his throat again. "Should you consider marriage instead, JM expected Ty to use a prenup to protect his own assets. The provisions of JM's will would protect Mandy's interest. If you decide not to marry, JM has granted Ty a sort of consolation gift for all he's asking of you, Ty."

"Isn't it enough he can sell the business? Why does he need a consolation prize?" She jerked her chin in his direction as if there was some question as to the "he" she referred to.

"It's a gift, Mandy, not a prize. Ty, under the circumstances I outlined, if you decide not to marry but instead to just manage the business, you would receive JM's ranch house and the surrounding hundred acres of land. The boundaries of these acres are prescribed in the will and would be taken from the deeded ranch land held in trust for Mandy and Tucker." Brian looked up and met his gaze. "I guess he felt you needed a little piece of Wyoming to call your own."

Mandy gasped. "That's prime land. We have barns and corrals on that land. It's Prescott land."

"You and Tucker would still have over 30,000 of deeded and leased acres if you decide to hold on to it," Brian noted.

"But he'd be living in *my* grandfather's house. That belongs in the family."

"I guess he hoped you two would marry so it would indeed remain in the family. If you marry, the ranch house is a wedding present to Mandy, so if you choose the marriage option, regardless of what happened after you married, that house would be yours, Mandy."

Mandy's green eyes shot fire in his direction. Too bad all the passion was anger.

Hadn't been that way ten years ago. Not that time at the creek.

Not that she didn't have good reason to be worked up about this will. If it was a surprise to him, it must have been a shock to her—a damn unpleasant one.

How many times had he told JM how much he loved his house, wanted one just like it, never dreaming of such generosity, never expecting it? JM had apparently divined the truth. Ty hungered after a place where he could have a few horses, despite his decade-long aversion to anything having to do with his family's ranch. But he never mentioned those things with a thought that JM would or should do something about it. Ty was more than financially capable of providing a house and land for himself. That he hadn't was another matter.

Still, he had questions. "So as long as the marriage lasts a minimum of six months, I wouldn't get the house, but I would still get shares equal to fifteen percent of the company, even if we divorced after that time period?"

"Yes," Brian said with a reassuring nod.

Mandy shook her head. "How can you even conceive of such a sham of a marriage?"

"I'm just trying to understand the options. If I had an interested buyer, I might be able to complete the analysis and sale of the rodeo company, if warranted, within six months. So, Brian, why the marriage provision, since the six months timing wouldn't necessarily prevent the sale of the business? Course it would get me out of Mandy's hair faster, and, Mandy, you'd be able to keep closer tabs on me." He couldn't quite keep the smile off his face.

Mandy stared at him. He could see the pulsing of her clenched jaw, no doubt from grinding teeth.

"I absolutely refuse to consider such a thing. End of story." Mandy wrapped her arms around her trim waist in a hug. She probably could use one right about now. "The company is profitable. I'll stake my future on that."

Ty didn't think it was the time to remind her that his mandate wasn't to determine if the business was profitable but whether it was likely to provide enough profit, under Mandy's leadership, to sustain the family, meaning Sheila, Tucker, and Mandy, for the next twenty years or longer. JM was worried about his family's future, not their present.

"I'm just trying to understand his motivation for making such a strange provision. You have to admit it's a doozie."

Brian nodded. "I wish I could shed light on what he was thinking. I asked him several times, but he wouldn't answer. However, in studying this provision, I can only guess he was trying to play matchmaker."

"Matchmaker?" He and Mandy spoke in unsettling unison.

"Whatever gave him the idea we were a match?" Mandy questioned, glaring at Ty with a look that could wither a steel rod. As if it was somehow his fault.

Ty searched his mind to see if he'd ever given the old man any ideas in that direction. He'd asked after Mandy whenever he'd see JM, but that was just being polite, as anyone would have been. He may have commented a time or two about what a pretty granddaughter JM had, again just being nice, making talk. He certainly never admitted he was physically attracted to Mandy. That would have just been awkward. Ty might have added his two cents about her most recent boyfriend, Mitch Lockhart, not being worthy of someone like Mandy, but then he was just agreeing with what JM had already said. As to marriage, he'd always deflected any talk about marrying by saying he'd never find a woman who was beautiful, smart, and as driven as he was, someone who would understand and support his work ethic. Nope, he'd never given JM a hint he was in any way attracted to Mandy Prescott, much less interested in marrying her, because he wasn't. Not Mandy, not any woman.

"I was wondering the same thing," he added.

"You know it wasn't *my* idea. I don't even like you." Mandy swung her attention back to Brian, leaving Ty to absorb that statement. Why did it feel like someone had just dropped an ice cube down his pants?

"This is ludicrous." Mandy charged ahead. "How could you let him write such a thing—or believe we'd even consider it?"

"As I said, don't blame the messenger. You have until Tuesday to think about it."

"You have my answer now. It is no." With that decision, Mandy rose and slung her large leather satchel over her shoulder. She brushed her hands down her jeans as if she could get rid of the whole discussion. "I've got a rodeo to put on this weekend, gentlemen. I'll be seeing you."

"Wait," Ty said, also rising. No way could he let her leave without clarifying things. "Regardless of this provision, I'm heading up the company, at least for the time being. So I think the phrase is *we've* got a rodeo to put on this weekend."

If he didn't assert authority immediately with Mandy, he knew it would only get worse between them. "So, when we get back to the office, you will meet with me, you will show me the plans for this weekend's rodeo, what stock we're pulling and why, cost estimates, and profit potential. And just so you know, I've already had Karen book me a room at Greenville since I will be overseeing the operation, as I will all the rodeos going forward."

She looked at him as if he'd lost his mind. "Don't think I'm going to train you."

"If you want me to release the money for the event, I need to review your plans." She needed to understand who was boss. He could almost see the wheels turning in her head as she struggled with his edict. She had to know he'd bench her if she balked at his requests. If she was smart, she wouldn't test him.

"I still need to clarify a few things about the terms of the will," Brian said. "For one, cohabitation means not only living under one roof, but sleeping in the same room whether on the road or in the ranch house, and you can't be away from each other for more than twenty-four hours at a time. Essentially, he wants you together during those six months." Brian looked from Mandy to Ty. "Not that it matters, since you both seem set on not doing this."

"Does he dictate where we take our meals and how many showers we must take together?" Mandy said in a voice filled with fury, though Ty kind of liked the shower image.

"No," Brian answered.

"That was a rhetorical question, Brian." She shook her head, and it seemed as though some of the steam had come out of her as she sighed. "I don't know what got into JM at the end, but thinking Ty and I are in any way a match is just too ludicrous to contemplate. I don't have to wait until Tuesday. You have my answer now."

With her large purse slung over her shoulder, she moved toward the door, ready to escape.

The whole scene would have been pretty entertaining if his bachelor status wasn't part of the ante. Still, it was kind of ironic that all these years he'd avoided Mandy out of deference to her being JM's granddaughter, and here JM was giving his blessings for what could be six months of guilt-free sex.

"I can't accept it until Tuesday. So you both should plan to be back in the office at two o'clock on that day." Brian nodded. "And I'll have a judge and the license ready. You both need to take a blood test today, which I've arranged at the clinic around the corner." He looked at his watch. "At three o'clock. Plenty of time to make it."

"But I said no." Mandy waved her hand. Ty couldn't help but feel sorry for her. She reminded him of a caged animal that had been pacing far too long and not getting anywhere.

"I can't accept your answer now, as I said. And if you don't want to jeopardize that outright grant of shares equal to twenty-percent of the company, Mandy, you must satisfy these simple requests for getting a blood test and giving me your answer on Tuesday." Brian strode toward her and handed her what appeared to be a copy of the will. He held out one for Ty to take. Ty grabbed it, interested to read it for himself.

"You can have another lawyer look it over," Brian continued. "But I advise you to do now what is outlined in the will, Mandy. And that means getting a blood test. I've already done the paperwork for the license. You both need to sign before you leave." Brian held out a silver pen.

Mandy froze as if a doe in the sight of a hunter's gun. She probably felt like she'd been a target lately, what with her grandfather's passing, Ty taking over, and now this ridiculous provision. And Ty hadn't exactly made it any easier by pulling rank. But he was responsible for the company now. He took the responsibility seriously.

"Mandy," Ty said, using the same low, controlled voice he would use with a spirited horse. "Let's just sign and get the blood tests. We both know it's not going to happen, but there's nothing to getting a blood test." Ty took the pen and signed the paper Brian held. He handed the pen to Mandy.

"Ever pragmatic, aren't you, Ty?" She nabbed the pen from his hand, and her fingers swept over his in a delicate brush. An odd jolt ricocheted through him. What was that about? Too much thinking about having sex with her, no doubt.

Mandy took a minute to read over the papers before she signed and handed them back to Brian. Straightening, she whipped her hair over her shoulder in defiance. She looked stunning, even when she was mad—especially when she was mad. Her curvy chest heaved under her black top, drawing his attention to a spot he'd no business looking at. Of course, if they were married…he gave a mental shake.

This would get him nowhere fast. JM's

proposition was unacceptable. *Working* with Mandy a full year in a "no touch" zone would be difficult enough. Six months living together would be torture if she held out for no sex. Of course, if he could convince her otherwise…maybe. As long as they both agreed to a divorce at the end.

"Fine, blood tests. I go first."

Ty stepped to pull open the door to the hallway. "Then my office for our first meeting since I got here two weeks ago."

"Or what?" she challenged.

"Or he can fire you, Mandy," Brian called from behind.

"He can't. I'm a shareholder."

"He can, and he can keep you from running the business for up to two years if he chooses," Brian said.

"Let him try."

Ty struggled to keep the smile from his lips but failed. This was going to be some year.

Chapter 3

Sitting in her cubicle in the cramped space that served as Prescott's headquarters, Mandy reviewed the revised budget yet again, going through each line item, trying to see it through Ty's eyes, except she couldn't fathom what a man who knew nothing about putting on a rodeo would see there. Yet he would be the ultimate arbiter.

She glanced at the closed door of the only office in the small building. It had served as her grandfather's office. Ty now sat behind that desk.

Life could be cruelly unfair.

Mandy's cubicle faced that office door, the half wall providing just enough space for a counter to hold her computer and two old pictures—one with her smiling father, mother, grandfather, a young Tucker, and her teenaged self at some rodeo event long forgotten, and one of her and her father at one of her barrel racing events. Two upper cabinets formed the right wall she shared with the cubicle belonging to Karen, their office manager, with two long file cabinets tucked under the right wall's counter space. The back half wall, which she shared with Harold's cubicle, was covered in cork, and she'd hung pictures of her horses and bulls interspersed with the faded ribbons from her barrel racing days. She really should take those ribbons down, but they reminded her of going to rodeos with her father as he worked them and she competed in them. Happier days, days free from worry as to the future. Little had she known.

She hated the idea that Ty was sitting in her grandfather's office and that he was heading her company, and yet she was working late to give him the budgets. Her gaze fell on the black-and-blue spot on her arm where blood had been drawn. The whole idea of marrying Ty Martin was just too ludicrous to endure, but she had dutifully gone for the blood test.

Her headache only slightly eased after the day's events, she glanced at the closed door. What did Ty think of such a preposterous proposal? At the reading of the will, he'd actually seemed to be considering it, and he'd gone for the blood tests.

She picked up the revised budget sheet and scanned each line item again until she got to the personnel line. Kyle Bradshaw, the most recent recipient of the James Prescott Memorial Scholarship and a part-time employee of PRC since he was fifteen, had asked for Fridays off during the summer, their busiest time, so he could take a summer course. Of course, she'd granted it. Kyle, his father, and his brother all worked at PRC off and on as the ranch season allowed and the whole family had been at her grandfather's funeral, though she hadn't had the opportunity to say more than a few words to them or half the crowd of guests who had attended.

She changed the personnel figure to reflect Kyle's absence and hit Print for revision number four. She'd have to change around the personnel duties as well. Flipping to another screen, she deleted Kyle's name beside the feeding-and-watering duty and replaced it with her name. Added to her event duties, it would make for a very long day. No matter. She'd been short-handed before, and Ty certainly couldn't complain about the salary savings. She flipped to still another screen and made a note to hire a temporary replacement for Kyle, hopefully by the next rodeo event.

Maybe she should put Ty in for feeding-and-watering duty. He'd said he wanted to learn the business. No better place to start. The thought brought a smile, but another moment's consideration had her thinking better of the idea. She needed everything to go well at this first rodeo since her grandfather's passing, and if she had to pull double duty, so be it. She hit the Print button and sat back.

She wished life was as easy as hitting a Print button. Her whole world had been thrown off its axis today. And the guy in the office held her future, and her happiness, in his oversized hands.

Retrieving the sheets of paper from the printer located in the copy room, Mandy stood outside of the office door ready to knock. Only she didn't. Instead she slipped the papers under the door and walked out into the sunlight of the early evening, headed toward the barns.

Retrieving her saddle from the tack room, Mandy walked on the gravel path toward the paddock where Willow, her favorite riding horse, and some of her best broncs peacefully grazed. A horseback ride would be the best momentary antidote to that unnerving provision and the news that Ty would be running PRC for the foreseeable future.

Looking out over the acres of dusky-green plains toward the mountains that stood sentinel in all their purple glory against a peacock-blue sky, she was grateful that at least the ranch wasn't in Ty's clutches.

Why had JM drawn up such a preposterous will?

JM had already named Ty acting president before his death, which assured Ty could temporarily run the company, so it wasn't for business reasons. And if her grandfather was so concerned about her ability to lead the company, why had he proposed something that would have handed over the firm after only six months?

Matchmaker. Had her grandfather harbored hopes of her and Ty being together? Had he learned about that summer when she had been seventeen and Ty nineteen, and she'd practically begged Ty to make love to her—and he'd walked away. Even now, that memory singed her cheeks with humiliation.

She'd been young, still feeling the loss of her father, and vulnerable. And Ty had been confident, smart, and ready to accomplish all the things she hoped to do. He'd also captured much of her grandfather's time and attention during that summer. Looking back, she recognized she'd been desperate for someone to notice, to care.

Still, those seeds planted a decade ago had run deep, because, try as she might, she'd never been able to ignore Ty's appeal, at least his physical appeal, despite the rumors of his less-than-generous business practices and playboy lifestyle. Even today, of all days, her pulse had raced in his presence. She could say it was because she'd been angry at him, but that wasn't the whole truth.

"Mandy," a sharp, low voice called from behind her. "Where are you going?"

She swung around as a fistful of irritation punched her stomach.

Ty strode toward her clutching the sheaf of papers. Still in black dress pants and white shirt with the sleeves rolled up, he looked as out of place as a sleek Rolls-Royce at a NASCAR race. So how come her heart took an extra beat as she watched his long legs close the distance between them? "I need to go over the Greenville Rodeo plans with you."

"You have the reports."

Without the cowboy hat, Ty looked like a corporate CEO. Something she shouldn't find appealing at all, so why was her whole body tingling?

"I have questions."

"I'm going for a ride." The five o'clock shadow on his face gave him a bad-boy appearance. She'd always had a soft spot for bad boys.

"Fine, I'll ride with you."

"Alone." No way did she want to share any more air with Ty than was absolutely necessary.

Ty placed his hands on his hips and looked at her as if he could give her a spanking. "It may be past five o'clock, but we either talk in the office or on horseback. But we talk now."

A half-hour later, mounted on Willow, Mandy headed due west toward the mountains at a leisurely pace at odds with her churning insides. Ty rode alongside her on one of the parade horses, since the remuda of working ranch horses were either earning their keep on the range or grazing in one of the northern pastures. The ranch horses were kept separate from the rodeo parade horses since the former had to be trained cutting horses and the latter had to have gentle dispositions to carry riders of varying skill.

Wheatgrass danced in the gentle breeze that blew off the mountains and swished against the legs of the horses. Mandy resisted the temptation to nudge Willow into a gallop, knowing Ty's gentle, aging mare wouldn't be able to keep up. Her day had already been spoiled. Might as well listen to the man.

"You said you have questions."

"God, it's beautiful out here," Ty said, twisting in the saddle, no doubt to get the full view of nature's vista.

"You were raised in this county."

"I haven't seen it on horseback for many years."

"That's nothing to be proud of. Surprised you can still ride."

Ty shook his head, his ebony hair brushing against the back of his collar as a dark lock fell in sullen carelessness over his brow. Life would be a lot less complicated if he wasn't so darn good looking.

"I've been busy."

"Me too. And your question?"

"Well first off, it seems like you are hauling a lot of livestock for a weekend rodeo."

Mandy shifted in her saddle to see if he was serious. He looked serious. "We only buck a horse or a bull twice during a weekend event. Any more and we risk the animal getting complacent and stalling in the chute. This is a popular rodeo and will draw lots of cowboys. As it is, Rustic Rodeo will be helping us out with some of their stock since they are Colorado based. JM set it up with them a while back." If he knew anything about running a rodeo, which he clearly didn't, he wouldn't have had to ask.

"Speaking of cowboys, why would we sponsor a rodeo cowboy?"

There was only one cowboy they were sponsoring, and that was Mitch Lockhart. Her grandfather hadn't liked it, but he'd approved it. That was before Mitch had dumped her.

"Publicity?"

Ty's eyebrows arched as if he was having a hard time accepting that explanation.

"I'll have Karen notify him that we are ending sponsorship." She should have done it the moment Mitch had walked out the door, but she hadn't had time to think, with all the curveballs coming her way.

"And I see we are going to be short a rodeo hand?"

"Kyle Bradshaw is taking a six-week summer course and needed Fridays off. I think we can cover for him until I can find a replacement. We can usually find one of the competitors who is looking to pick up some money."

"Why did Kyle sign up for the course if he knew it met on Friday?"

Ty obviously didn't believe in providing flexibility for a valued employee. She shrugged. "He's a good worker, and half his family works for us off and on, and he's this year's scholarship recipient. I made an accommodation."

"Without talking to me first."

"It was before the will was read."

"So you didn't expect me to be here."

"Exactly."

Ty had nudged his horse so he was riding close beside her. He looked good in the saddle, even if he was in a dress shirt and pants. At least the man wore cowboy boots, fancy ones. The mare, being well over fifteen hands, often carried the rodeo chair at an event because tall men looked good on her—Ty was no exception.

Over the years, she'd seen Ty at fundraiser events or at the yearly scholarship awards, which he attended at JM's invitation. He was either in a tux or dark suit, and the moment he walked into the room, her pulse sped up and she broke out in a sweat. She'd always made sure someone was with her when she greeted him, to avoid an awkward moment. Of course, he usually had a well-endowed woman glued to his side.

There may be no accounting for biology, but marry him?

She'd told herself she'd do anything to get back her company. That was before she knew what "anything" was. How could she consider marrying him knowing how her body sparked in his presence and the extent of his deceitfulness? Six months. That would take them through the end of the rodeo season and into the fall, where things slowed considerably as they geared up for the National Rodeo Finals in December, the biggest event of all. If she agreed to such a crazy stipulation, she'd be free of Ty and the threat of a sale right before the NRF. But was that enough incentive to put herself through the torture of living with a man she despised—and her body craved?

"Guess there was a lot in that will that came as a surprise," he said, breaking into her thoughts as an animal, no doubt a prairie dog, skittered in the grass.

No sense denying it. By virtue of that will, her grandfather was the third rider on the trail. "It was definitely a shocker, for me anyway."

"You think I knew what he was up to?" His eyebrows arched. "Marriage is not on my radar screen for any reason." He shifted in the saddle, clearly uncomfortable with the thought. Which brought a smile to Mandy's lips.

"Not even for love?"

Ty scowled and rubbed the back of his neck like he could dispel the thought. "Don't believe in love—not the romantic kind, anyway. Marriage is like any other partnership, just with some side benefits."

"Sounds like you."

"What the hell does that mean?"

"Well, in order to believe in love, you'd have to have feelings." Score one for her.

"Just because someone doesn't show them doesn't mean they don't feel."

She turned just enough so he was in her line of sight. "Lust, Ty, doesn't qualify as an emotion." And score another one.

He pulled up his horse.

She reined Willow to a stop and twisted in her saddle to look behind her.

For a guy who was always so controlled, a surprising amount of fire flashed in his eyes. She'd made him angry. Good. At least it qualified as a reaction from Mister Calm, Cool, and Collected.

Turning back around, she nudged Willow into a

trot and headed toward the hills. She heard the clacking of hooves behind her and knew Ty was following. The breeze whipped across her face, tangling with her hair. It felt good to ride, even with Ty in pursuit.

Suddenly it dawned on her—they were riding toward the creek. Originating in the mountains, the rivulet cut across the western edge of the flatlands, so there was no way to avoid it and only a few places to cross it—like where she'd tried and failed to entice Ty that fateful day.

She slowed Willow to a walk and pondered whether she should turn back. Before she could decide, Ty was beside her. He sat the saddle like he'd been born to it—because, as a rancher's son, he had been. She wondered what had made him become a company man. Maybe he just loved the real estate game. No harm in that. She loved rodeo.

"Let's keep the discussion on the will," he said, maintaining pace. "JM did give you a way to get me out of here in six months. I just want to be sure you're dead set against it. Otherwise, I'd reconsider my stance if we could come up with a way to make it work for both of us."

Would he seriously contemplate marriage? To her? Impossible. Unless he had a way to circumvent the provision. After all, he was a lawyer, though he'd made his fortune on land deals, courtesy of JM's connections.

"Have you read it through?" She obviously hadn't had time to take it to an attorney and wouldn't know who to call, given Brian had always taken care of Prescott business.

"I have."

"Please tell me there is an escape clause."

Ty shook his head, and the lock of ebony hair swished across his brow. He had thick hair that felt silky to the touch, if she remembered correctly.

"No. Not in the sense of voiding it and still getting Prescott in six months. JM had obviously done a lot of thinking about this. Even down to the details of the prenup. If we entered into the marriage and didn't follow every provision, the payoff is voided. We'd be back to me heading up the company for a year, at minimum."

"Is there nothing to be done?" Even the beauty of the mountains and the feel of the breeze against her skin couldn't stem the hope leaking out of her.

"It would depend upon us. If we decided to marry, all we need to be certain of is that we'd both walk after six months, because there's nothing keeping us from divorcing after that time. We'd still get the shares. Nothing keeping us from making the marriage a real one during that time either."

She shifted so she could see his face. The smile he flashed brimmed with illicit promise, stopping her heart for a beat. With his dark eyes glinting in the rays of the sun streaming just over the mountains, he looked more devil than angel. A handsome devil built for sex, and just sex. The thought caused a volcano of lust to erupt inside of her, spilling its heat into her veins.

He reined in the mare and cocked his head like he noticed the sizzling flush engulfing her. Lord, she hoped not.

"You know we'd be good together—at least in that way. I'd even let you do the seducing…"

The arrogance. "From what I hear, you don't put up much of a fight with anything that wears a skirt." *Except me, ten years ago.*

He laughed as if he was pleased with her description. "Well, I don't need that hundred acres or the ranch house, nice as it was of your grandfather to gift it to me."

A hawk circled overhead, silhouetted against the deep-blue sky and setting sun.

"Don't you have your family's ranch anyway?" *Then leave mine alone.*

"Hardly. My brother, Trace, owns that. And it's not exactly profitable, I might add. He'd have been better off letting me develop the land before the economy tanked, small as it is."

"You put everything in dollars and cents, don't you? Even your own heritage. Maybe Trace prefers scratching out a living on the homestead rather than selling off family history just to gain a buck."

Apparently for Ty, there wasn't any reason to do anything but the almighty dollar. And this was who her grandfather wanted her to marry. Who her grandfather had given the keys to the company. Who her grandfather had trusted to make the decisions about Prescott's future, including if it even had a future. And who her body wanted with frightening insistence.

A tick appeared in his jaw. "Let's keep things on topic, Mandy."

"As I see it, you take the ranch house or you take half the remaining shares. Either way, I lose. I'll wait the year."

"Could be two years." He was back to cool,

implacable Ty. Caught on a breeze, the wayward lock of his hair blew across his brow. She'd love to really mess up his hair, run her fingers through it. Instead she watched as he finger combed it in place.

"Is that the creek up ahead?" he asked as a sliver of blue came into view in the distance.

She wondered if he even remembered that day, a day she would never forget.

"Yup."

"I hadn't realized we'd ridden so far. Race you." With that he took off on the mare, only it was more of a lope than a gallop, given his horse didn't often go above a trot.

She fought the urge to ride in the opposite direction, like he'd left her that day, but then she'd be admitting to herself, and him if he remembered, that the day had mattered to her. She lightly kicked Willow into a gallop and, with the wind sounding in her ears, quickly overtook him.

She pulled up just shy of the bank, not wanting to risk Willow's legs to uneven ground. Water gurgled below them. The drought had taken its toll, and the stream was but a thin ribbon winding through the encroaching banks. Right now it looked barely knee deep.

The slash of water against the brownish-green land, along with the smoky-purple of the mountains and the setting of the fiery sun in a blue sky, was a testament to Mother Nature's handiwork. A stand of cottonwoods provided shade along the bank. And there was that large boulder jutting out into the water. Funny how she had come to the exact spot.

"I have very fond memories of this place," Ty

said, walking his mare up to stand alongside her. He leaned forward to rest his arms on the horn of his saddle.

Could he be referring to that time? Her memory of that day was far from fond.

"Aren't you anxious to return to your real job rather than traipsing around ranches and rodeos? Being away even a couple of weeks, I'm guessing, is killing you. To take a leave of absence for a year must seem the equivalent of a prison sentence, regardless of whether you are doing it for the right or the wrong reasons." She prayed her assessment was correct. She was having a hard time getting through a day. How would she get through a year?

"I made a commitment to JM. One I take seriously and wouldn't have made if my circumstances hadn't allowed me to fully meet that commitment. I wouldn't count on less than two years unless I sell the company. I'll do what I think JM would have wanted me to do. So if you want to run Prescott in six months *and* keep the ranch house, seems the solution is easy." There was that devastating smile again. "We'll probably end up in bed together anyway, even if we don't marry. Marriage would be in keeping with your grandfather's wishes, is all."

His audacity was only equaled by the smug smile on his face. Yet she feared his prediction had more truth to it than was good for her emotional health.

"Just so you'd get an additional fifteen percent of the company, and I'd come away without *controlling* interest. And what's to say you wouldn't sell the business within that six months' time frame anyway. Where would I be then?" Willow stretched her neck for some grass, and Mandy gave a tug on the reins, then lightly petted Willow's neck. The horse's weight shifted, but Willow obeyed.

"A very wealthy woman. But it won't be easy, especially at this time, to find a buyer in six months, if the analysis warrants that. But I won't lie to you. It is possible."

"So why would I marry you? It's like you're asking me to prostitute myself to save the ranch house." Although at the moment, staring into the eyes of tall, dark, and handsome, the prospect wasn't as insulting as it should have been.

"How about the fact you'd still hold the *majority* of shares and, with the family votes, you'd have *de facto* controlling interest? And marriage has its benefits." His gaze traveled from her eyes, down her throat, past her neck, to the top button of her shirt…and back up again with an intensity that made the beats of her pulse reverberate clear to her heart. "Just to be clear, I'm not asking anything of you. I didn't write this will. I'm only exploring options. But I can guarantee you a pleasurable time if you're open to it."

He sat back in his saddle. "Think about it, Mandy. Six months, you'd be head of Prescott Rodeo Company. I could accept marriage as long as it's understood we divorce at the end of six months. And you agree to a prenup, of course. I just think it's something you should consider."

The man was an arrogant, egotistical sidewinder who brought out the worst in her. Except for that long-ago summer.

She looked past the creek, over the plain, and

toward the point where the land sloped gently up to the foothills. This was her land. PRC was her company. And this was her life.

"It will be a cold day in hell, Martin, before I'd marry you, much less sleep with you."

He arched an eyebrow as if he doubted her.

There was only one thing to do to preserve her sanity. Reining Willow to the right, she gave a light kick. Her horse lurched into a gallop, heading north up the stream and away from Ty, away from the creek, away from bad memories, and overpowering lust. Mandy gave the horse its head, leaving, she hoped, Ty in the proverbial dust.

Chapter 4

"Well, I can think of worse things," Sheila said as she poured Mandy another cup of coffee from the glass pot.

Dawn was just breaking over the eastern sky, streaming dusky light into the oversized kitchen of Mandy's mother's house. Granite counters gleamed, stainless steel appliances shined, and the travertine-tiled floor glistened in the light. Though Mandy lived in her mother's house, somewhere along the way she'd stopped thinking of it as her home. More like a way station on the road to her real life. Yet she hadn't taken any steps to find her own place since getting her master's degree in business. Maybe because it would mean leaving the ranch—the one spot where she belonged.

Dumping two teaspoons of sugar and at least a quarter cup of cream into the strong brew, Mandy took a huge gulp hoping the caffeine would jump-start her body—and her mood. Given her sleepless night, she'd barely been conscious enough to shimmy into her jeans and the white shirt with the embroidered PRC logo of a riderless bronc in midkick.

Sitting at the kitchen-table with the list of the

rodeo livestock and entrants spread before her, Mandy inhaled the coffee's nutty aroma, one of her favorite scents. "Worse things than marrying a man I don't even like?"

She hadn't expected Ty to follow her last evening—and he hadn't. She'd ridden far upstream and then crossed over and rode toward the foothills, trying to distance herself from their conversation, but she hadn't been able to get him out of her thoughts. His arrogance had unsettled her like the sight of a fox unsettled a hen. When she'd returned in the half-light of dusk, the mare was safely in her stall and Ty, gratefully, nowhere in sight.

Her mother laughed, more like a giggle. "Honey, have you looked at him? He's a hunk. Twenty years younger and I'd throw my hat in that arena, for sure."

Mandy pushed away her plate with the remains of a half-eaten scrambled egg and tried to hide her shock. Even though her slim mother looked full of youthful vigor, it was downright weird to think of her having *those* thoughts about any man. Sheila had never even dated, at least to Mandy's knowledge, since her father died, though surely there had to have been men who'd been interested in such a vibrant, still-beautiful woman. Her mother seemed content with her female friends and volunteer activities. The only man she'd ever seen her mother with on a routine basis was Harold, and that was because Harold was always around.

This morning, her ever-perfect mother was decked out in designer jeans and a western shirt, as if she was going somewhere. Given it was six o'clock in the morning, Mandy chalked it up to Sheila always looking pulled together. No one would ever catch her mother in a robe and nightgown outside of the bedroom.

"Mom, what are you saying? You think I should consider an arranged marriage? Because that's what it would be. Something right out of the Victorian era."

"Well, given how you're married to the job, this may be the only shot I'll have at grandchildren," Sheila said as she scrubbed the fry pan in the sink. Mandy couldn't help the eye roll. Like most single women in their twenties, she was used to having her lack of husband and children pointed out to her. But this time, she felt a little twinge at the prospect of never having a child. After hearing that one of her best friends was pregnant, she'd found herself eying babies at the mall with not a little bit of envy. She chalked it up to hormones.

"This marriage is not happening, and even if it did, it would certainly not include children." With Ty? Never. He was so not father material.

Mandy scanned the list of cowboy names, happy not to see Mitch Lockhart on the list. Didn't mean he wouldn't be there. Since the roster wasn't yet full, cowboys could sign on at the last minute. She was already dreading this weekend given this would be the first rodeo without her grandfather and the first rodeo with Ty in charge. All she'd need was Mitch to show up to have a fiasco trifecta.

"Apparently, Ty is your grandfather's choice," Sheila continued. "JM knew how to pick 'em. After all, he picked me for your father."

Mandy swung her head around so fast she felt a little dizzy. "What? That's not true. Daddy picked you."

"Your grandfather introduced us. And told your father right at that introduction I was the one he was going to marry."

Looking over her shoulder, Mandy watched as her mother washed and then dried her hands on the checkered towel hanging on the oven handle, adjusting it so it hung just right after she finished.

"Are you saying Daddy didn't love you when he married you?"

Sheila smoothed her hands down the front of her stylish jeans. "Of course not. But your father wouldn't have given me a second look if it wasn't for JM." Sheila motioned toward Mandy's plate. "Is that all you are going to eat?"

"I'm not hungry. The coffee will keep me going." Getting up, Mandy grabbed her plate and scraped the half-eaten egg into the garbage can hidden behind a cabinet door by the sink. Her mother's cooking was a benefit of living at home. She just didn't have much of an appetite. She placed the scraped plate in the dishwasher and returned to the table to gather up her papers. "Why do you say daddy wouldn't have given you a second look?" Her mother had been and still was an attractive woman by anyone's standards.

"Your father was a bit of a playboy back then. He seemed to like buckle bunnies and models. Much like Ty, if the gossip is true," her mother said, placing the remaining uncooked eggs and bacon back in the refrigerator and closing the fridge door with a firm press. "Given my height, no one would call me statuesque, that's for sure. But your father, out of respect for JM, started dating me, and, well, soon there were no more models or rodeo girls in his life. Just me."

Mandy sat back down and tried to process this new revelation. Surprised as Mandy was, she had to disagree. "This is so different. Daddy wasn't trying to take over your family's company. And we're talking marriage here, not courtship." Her foot jiggled.

"Your grandfather was just making your arrangement respectable."

"And binding."

"For six months. And stop shaking your foot, dear. It's not ladylike."

Mandy curled her right leg around her left. Her mother had been trying to cure her of her nervous habit for years, to no avail.

"No court would deny you a divorce if you wanted it once the will was entered into evidence," Sheila said "These days marriages can be about as lasting as a date, so why not, is all I'm saying."

"Ah, because I despise the man."

Sheila shook her head. "Mandy, I'm your mother. I know you better than you know yourself. You do not despise that man. You are attracted to him. And on some level, I think you respect what he's accomplished, when you can stop envying it." An image of Ty riding the mare, dressed in slacks and a white shirt, his jaw darkened by a five o'clock shadow, and a lock of hair falling across his brow flitted across her mind, causing a tingle low in her belly.

"I'm not envious of Ty Martin. I might concede to a little lust, but not envy." Never envy. What did she have to be envious about? Ty wasn't married, didn't have children, and though he might be well-off, Prescott Rodeo provided all the money Mandy needed. No, she was not envious.

"Fine, I won't argue. I just think you should consider it. After all, JM went to a lot of trouble to draft this provision. He obviously thought it was best for you, Ty, and the company."

Mandy sank her head into her hands. "That's what I don't understand. I don't understand any of it. Did he think me so incapable he had to go through all of this?"

Her mother's warm hand rested on Mandy's back. "I don't think his motive had anything to do with your capabilities. I think he was concerned about the shenanigans the other stockmen might pull. And he was concerned about your happiness. He thought Ty the solution to both, is all."

Mandy wished she could believe the part about it having nothing to do with her capabilities. As for Ty being the solution, that marriage provision in the will made him the problem. She shuffled the papers before her into a semblance of a pile. Last evening Ty had asked her to consider marriage and told her they were going to wind up in bed together anyway. If she agreed, she'd be playing right into his hands. "JM put up his ranch house for me to lose if I don't marry, in addition to the threat of Ty selling the firm. He's put me between the proverbial rock and a hard place."

If anywhere felt like home, it was her grandfather's house, built just up the road. It had always been full of people coming and going, even after her grandmother passed away.

Shelia leaned over and picked a stray hair off Mandy's sleeve. "JM must have seen that spark of attraction between you two. He thinks he can fan it, even from the grave. And he's willing to put up

Prescott shares and the ranch house. That must mean he's pretty certain of the outcome."

Mandy shook her head. Obviously, her grandfather had been losing it toward the end. Engaging in fairy-tale notions that weren't based in reality. "JM was wrong. There is nothing I find admirable about Ty Martin."

Her mother's smirk poked her like a cattle prod.

"All right, except maybe his body," Mandy relented. "You happy?" It was way too awkward speaking about lust with her mother, of all people. "And Ty Martin has never given one hint he's attracted to me, other than as a way to pass some time."

We'd be good together.

"Really? I don't think you've been looking too hard then."

Mandy sighed. Her mother was just being a romantic, a perspective Mandy didn't share. "How can I give up controlling interest in the company and endure a sham of a marriage just to save the ranch house? No, JM has actually made it an easy decision. One year, even two years, is not such a long time. I'll just have to tolerate having Ty around until then."

I can guarantee you a pleasurable time if you're open to it.

Sheila slipped into the chair beside her. "Can you? From what you've told me, Ty's going to have full authority to sell the business if the numbers don't work. I don't care much if the business is sold, except for the fact I know how upset you'd be."

"If I am to believe Ty, and I don't entirely, we'd be well off if we sold out. But it's not just about me or you, Mom. What about everyone who depends on

Prescott for their paycheck? For several families, we are their livelihood. Fathers and sons and even daughters. We're like a family at Prescott. And Daddy? It was his dream to have a premier stock company. What about that dream?"

Sheila shrugged. "That was your father's dream. You could make your own dream. But if you really are against selling, then I think you should consider doing what JM proposes. It's obviously what he wanted you to do. Wouldn't it make it tougher for Ty to find a buyer if he only has six months?"

"I don't know if I could marry a man I don't respect, much less like, even if it is only a few months." Mandy closed her eyes, hoping she could block out the whole idea. "And he could still sell it within six months anyway. Then what? The best this marriage may allow is for me to keep tabs on him. It's not enough."

"Mandy, look at me." Mandy opened her eyes and stared at the familiar gentle smile on her mother's face. It was the same smile her mother used when telling Mandy she'd feel better soon or getting a B in math wasn't the end of the world. "You'll be working with him for even longer if you don't marry him. Suppose you do fall for him, you fall for each other? If you think there's any chance you two will have an affair of some sort, why not go with this proposal?"

We'll probably end up in bed together anyway, even if we don't marry.

By the time he'd uttered that sentence, she'd been ready to wrap her fingers around his throat and squeeze. True, she doubted she'd be able to spend a year or more working with the man, but not because she was tempted by him. Because she didn't like what he stood for. So how could she stand six months living with him?

"I'm not worried about falling for a man I don't like." Even if she had a history of falling for the wrong kind of guy.

Her usual type was a guy with a ready smile, easygoing attitude, and no thought of the future. Unfortunately, that combination usually came with a dearth of ambition and a wandering eye.

Regardless, she would never lose her heart again to a man as cold and arrogant as Ty Martin. Six months. That wasn't enough of a reason to do it, and there were 180 reasons, called cohabitation, not to do it.

"What are you worried most about?"

"Losing Prescott. That's all that matters to me."

"Well, why not go with the marriage and at least lessen the odds of selling? And there's always the potential for using womanly wiles to change the course of events." Shelia cocked her head to the side and winked.

"Shouldn't marriage vows be taken seriously? I never thought you'd encourage me to be a loose woman, Mom."

"I'm just trying to be practical about this."

Mandy rose and hugged the papers to her chest.

"Would you place your cup in the dishwasher?" her mother asked.

Mandy dutifully complied. Returning to the table, she gave her mother a kiss on the cheek and caught a whiff of her mother's Channel No. 5. "I best be going. They're leaving at seven."

"I know. I'm coming with you," Shelia announced.

"To see us off?" That would explain why her mother was so put together at this ungodly hour.

"No, I'm coming to Greenville with you."

Mandy leaned her thigh against the table. "Why?" Sheila hadn't come on a rodeo excursion in the two years since Mandy had returned from grad school.

Her mother bit her lip. "Because I want to. Because Harold wants me to." Her mother brushed a wayward strand of hair behind her ear.

"What does Harold have to do with this?" Mandy said, crossing her arms and pressing the papers to her chest.

"Harold and I are…well, we are a couple. Have been for a while."

How many shocks could she stand? "Come again."

"While JM was alive, we were discreet. But now, well, there's no reason to be."

Mandy felt like the floor had shifted under her boots. Discreet? She hadn't had a clue. And apparently, neither had her grandfather. "Grandfather wouldn't have approved?"

Sheila lifted her chin. "Neither Harold nor I wished to cause him any consternation on that score. He was good to both of us. I think, on some level, he may have suspected. But I never wanted him to think I wasn't in love with your father. I always will be. Just, Harold has a place in my heart too. We plan to marry after the season."

Her mother and Harold? "He's so different from Daddy." Her father had been a hard-charging stockman with focus and determination. Harold was laid back, content to be second banana.

Sheila shrugged. "At this time in my life, maybe I need a man for whom I'm the center of his world, and not some rodeo company. Not that your father wasn't good to me. He was. And at that time, I was happy to raise our children and be his wife. But now, well, I'm happy to have a man who thinks I'm everything—and who wants to be the center of my world too."

Mandy gulped and tried to process. "Does Tuck know?"

"Yes, dear. He…well, let's just say he found out. I'd planned to tell you once we'd decided to marry, but…well, then your grandfather took a turn for the worse, and it seemed best to wait a bit. Now that we'll be staying together in Greenville…"

Her mother and Harold shacking up in a hotel room. Mandy blocked that thought as Sheila stood, rubbing her hands over and under each other, hope in her eyes.

If Harold made her mother happy, who was she to interfere? "You deserve a good man, Mom. And Harold is one."

A smile beamed across her mother's face, creating a warm glow. There obviously was real love there. Who knew?

"Thank you, honey. That means a great deal to both of us. And you deserve a good man. Better than that tie-down roper Mitch Lockhart."

Given Mitch had chosen her grandfather's funeral to dump her because he needed "breathing room," code for dating other women, she couldn't disagree. He'd used her for sponsorship money, and she, if she was brutally honest, had used him for sex.

"Give Ty a chance, Mandy. You might be surprised."

Her mother had no idea how wrong she was.

* * *

Walking around the outskirts of the arena, Ty looked out on the sizeable Greenville rodeo grounds and listened to the tinny sounds of work that permeated the early morning air. He'd flown his plane, a Cirrus Gold, down to Greenville, Colorado, so he could arrive early, before Mandy and the crew.

He wanted time to familiarize himself with the venue and meet with the committee members, seeing he was the new kid on the block. The large, round arena, built on cinderblocks, sat to the right, and to the left was a field of campers parked in haphazard fashion. Those campers were likely filled with sleeping cowboys and cowgirls ready to enter the night's events.

Ty spotted the livestock trailers of the subcontractor, the Rustic Rodeo Company, in the distance. Given they were Colorado based, that didn't come as a surprise. The owner, Stan Lassiter, had been the only person JM had mentioned as a potential buyer of Prescott, which could make for an interesting weekend.

The acrid scent of manure filled his nostrils as he strode on past the stable area filled with competitors' roping and barrel horses, but with plenty of stalls left for the broncs. Mandy had said that often the horses were just pastured, but Greenville, apparently, was a first-class operation with its own barns. A few cowboys were about, feeding their horses and mucking out stalls. Ty touched the brim of his hat in acknowledgement and turned toward the arena and the chutes, where workers were hammering together the pipes that would secure the horses.

There was a lot more to putting on a rodeo than he'd imagined when he'd been a mere spectator. But the burden JM had placed on his shoulders wasn't what was occupying his thoughts this morning, though it should have been.

Try as he might, he hadn't been able to get JM's provision and last evening's ride with Mandy off his mind.

Last night they'd ended up in the exact same spot he'd left her years ago, and he wasn't at all certain it was by accident. And if it wasn't an accident, that meant she remembered. And if she remembered, it meant they had some unfinished business.

He'd never forgotten the image of her emerging naked from the creek, her long hair damp and clinging to her shoulders, a smile on her sweet face and desire in her green eyes. Her lissome seventeen-year-old body was wet with rivulets of water streaming down perfect white breasts, over rosy nipples, down her flat stomach to the apex of her legs and the damp curls that guarded her virtue. He'd been so turned on he'd frozen in place until she stopped before him…and begged him to make love to her.

Only then did the earlier morning conversation with her grandfather echo in the far reaches of his brain, telling him Mandy was off-limits and anymore encounters behind the barn or anywhere else would spell the end of Ty's future.

He had jumped back on his horse and ridden like he was being chased by a herd of stampeding cattle, just as she had ridden away yesterday in the full-out panic of a person who knew that if she didn't leave, they would do something they wanted to do but shouldn't.

The more he thought about it, the more potential he saw to finish what they'd started ten years ago. However misguided JM's matchmaking intentions, JM was giving Ty his blessing to have a relationship with his granddaughter. Marrying Mandy could mean six months of sex with a woman he'd always craved, and then walking away. Six months of a woman who, even at seventeen, could bring a man to his knees with a kiss. And no one would get hurt.

Ty entered the arena gates and headed down the cinder-block alley to the contestants' entrance. He wore his Prescott T-shirt, informing people with a glance that he was with the show, and he passed a worker or two checking on the railings. He climbed the cement steps to the alley behind the metal-framed chutes. This was where JM always stood, watching over his livestock and the cowboys who rode, or tried to ride, them. This is where Ty would be tonight—not as a spectator but as one of the owners. He had to marvel at the change in his circumstances in just a few weeks.

Greenville was a sizeable rodeo to tackle the first time out of the gate, one that attracted a lot of talent. He'd be ready for it. He grabbed on to one of the railings and gave a shake, testing its sturdiness. He continued down the walkway, testing the railings of each chute and familiarizing himself with how the chutes worked when moving livestock in and out. If Mandy agreed to the marriage proposition, in six months he'd make sure to leave her financially well-off, either from the sale of the business or profits from a stronger enterprise, fulfilling his promise to JM. Ty could move on, having secured a larger stake in either the sale or the ongoing business and gaining some experience in a different industry. Hell, he might even decide to become a stock contractor in his second career.

Ty stopped at the last chute and leaned against the railing to look out over the arena. If he played things right, this could all be a win-win for everyone involved. Maybe even convince Mandy to allow him to develop the ranch.

He'd taken a quick look at the books before he had turned the accounts over to the financial firm he'd hired to run the numbers. PRC turned a modest profit, and JM and the rest of the family had made decent money from it. But whether Mandy could sustain the business and whether operating it would provide the best return on investment versus the alternative of investing money from a sale into land development, for instance, was the question he'd been tasked with answering.

Because if Ty didn't think Mandy could assure Prescott's place in the industry—and that meant holding on to contracts, expanding and improving the bucking bulls to be competitive for the AFBR, and going toe to toe with competitors to get in on the big events—JM had instructed him to sell the enterprise and do it before the Prescott name lost any of its luster.

Ty heard the clang of boots on the walk and felt the slap on his back before he could turn around. Stan Lassiter wasn't heavy, but his height and barrel stomach made him appear big and formidable. Ty had met Lassiter at JM's funeral but knew him mostly by reputation, a reputation as a cagey stock contractor with a winner-take-all business strategy. And JM had warned Ty not to trust him.

"Thought I'd find you here," Lassiter said, his voice sounding like pebbles in a ceramic cup.

"Stan." Ty straightened and slid his hand over Stan's for a firm shake.

He'd let Stan do all the talking. Ty had learned long ago that, with some people, not saying much could elicit a lot more information than leading the conversation.

"Was hoping to speak with you." Stan was dressed for work in a plaid shirt, denims, and scuffed boots. Most contractors were hands-on kinds of guys, like JM had been, and Stan was no exception.

"About what?"

From under the shadow of his hat brim, Stan scanned the arena. "Mandy with you?"

"She's coming with the livestock. I got here ahead of them."

Stan nodded as if he agreed with the decision. He stuck a boot up on the metal railing and hunched his frame over the top bar. "Word is you're running Prescott now."

"Temporarily." Ty eased back against the rail so he could see Stan's face. He could tell a lot from a man's facial expressions.

Stan averted his gaze and focused on some imaginary spot in the center of the arena. "Until you sell, you mean? I'm letting you know I'm interested.

"In what?"

Stan scowled. His brown eyes widened. "In buying the damn company. And the sooner the better. Every day JM is not here to run it is another day a little value is lost. He was Prescott Rodeo Company, and Harold's not enough to fill his shoes."

"What about Mandy?" Ty pushed off the railing.

Stan snorted and drew his bushy graying brows into a *V*. "This business is no place for a woman. A very young woman at that. This is a tough industry, with lots of facets. I've seen her work the chutes, and I've watched her at meetings with her grandfather, and she's in over her head."

Something flared inside Ty, bringing with it a need to defend her. "She's a good businesswoman, Stan," he said, resting his clenched fists on his hips. "Has some viable plans for the company's future." JM had told him that expanding into the AFBR had been her idea. But having a good idea wasn't the same as making it happen.

Stan leaned back and looked at Ty with cold, ash-gray eyes. "If that were the case, why are you running the company and not her? JM was a smart man, one whose judgment I respected. Word is you're now a partner with controlling interest. He wouldn't have done that, given it to someone outside the family, unless he wanted to sell it."

"I am a partner," Ty allowed. He wasn't about to admit to more.

Stan's eyes narrowed. "You're not a stockman, Ty. And odds are you don't want to be, or you'd have bought Prescott outright from JM. All I'm saying is that I'm interested. But now, while you've still got contracts and before Prescott loses its good name. JM was the brains and the shine of Prescott. Without him you've got nothing."

"I'll keep that in mind."

Stan looked frustrated as he let out a sigh. "I'll tell you something, Ty. Something I don't have to

67

share, but I will. Already rodeos are calling me and asking if I can take them on if they pulled out of Prescott." He arched his eyebrows, waiting for Ty's reaction.

Having learned the lessons of hiding his feelings early in life, Ty held his face expressionless. "Thanks for the heads-up."

Stan ran a hand through his hair. "Think on it. But not too long. Once the rodeo committees get jittery about a supplier, that supplier isn't going to be worth much. I'd like to do right by JM's family, but if the company loses value, I won't be charitable about the price. So maybe you and I should catch up later and have a drink while you're here."

"Maybe." Something about Stan Lassiter rubbed Ty the wrong way. He couldn't put his finger on why, but just like JM, Ty didn't trust him. In any event, Ty wasn't about to appear too eager for the sale. In truth, he needed to see the numbers before he took any steps. Until then, there was no sense in fanning rumors of selling and getting rodeo organizers more nervous than Stan suggested they already were.

Clearly waiting for a reaction that Ty had no intention of giving, Stan stared a bit longer.

"I'll see you around," he finally said and thrust out a hand. Ty shook it with a firm grip.

After a slight hesitation, Stan turned and ambled away with an arthritic gait that no doubt came from being in the saddle too long and stepped on one too many times.

Ty looked back at a group of rodeo cowboys huddled at the far arena gates, and took a deep breath. He wouldn't be surprised if Lassiter was initiating those calls to the rodeo committees. JM had warned him about that. It was one of the reasons he'd asked Ty to step in. Ty may not have supplier experience, but he had a reputation of being a tough businessman. Yet determining what was right for Prescott, for the Prescott family, for Mandy, would not be easy. But he'd promised JM he'd do his best to ensure the family members would have the means they needed for the future, whether from company income or proceeds from a sale, and he would keep that promise. And he'd start by finding the head of the Greenville Rodeo.

Chapter 5

Mandy watched Ty kick up gravel as he cleared the pens behind the arena and walked straight toward the stable area where she had been currying her horse, Willow. When his text message said he would travel separately, she'd hoped that meant he'd arrive later, much later. Seemed like he'd actually arrived early. She wondered why.

Working for Ty was going to be the hardest year of her life. Maybe two years. The thought brought a lump to her throat.

She followed Ty's movements as he drew closer.

He was decked out like he was ready to work. No suit jacket today. Just washed-out denims, worn in interesting places and anchored by an ornate silver buckle he'd likely picked up at one of those little touristy stores that dotted the county roads, and a black Prescott Rodeo T-shirt stretching over his torso, revealing his gym-ripped biceps. His boots were polished, embroidered black leather, and a clean black cowboy hat covered his thick dark hair.

Tanned, taut, and no doubt talented. He strode toward her with that determined, long-legged gait of his, like he meant business. Personal business. She wondered what he thought about her leaving him last evening at that same spot by the creek and if he even attached any significance to that spot. She wondered, too, if he would continue the conversation from the evening before or accept her decision. As her body temperature kicked up a notch with his every step, she wasn't certain she wanted him to accept her decision, since the idea of marrying him had dusted up thoughts of what that would entail. Touching, kissing, and... Her heart thumped hard against her chest.

Control, that's what she needed. If she was going to get through these next months, this next year, she needed to control her thoughts, her impulses, her mouth, and, most of all, her attraction to him.

She took a deep breath.

"So you're here," Mandy said as he drew close. She threw the currycomb into the box of brushes that sat on the ground next to the stall door, causing a clattering noise. Willow shifted her weight at the sound, and Mandy patted the horse's satiny neck in reassurance. Remember, control, she told herself.

"I told you I'd be here," he said. She felt a flutter in the pit of her stomach as he ambled toward her. Knowing she watched a man who held her future in his hands was surely the source of that flutter and not that he looked like a western-wear model.

She pulled on the reins that tied Willow to the post outside the stall to assure they were secure. "It appears you beat us."

His smile didn't quite reach his eyes. "I flew down. Wanted to get the lay of the land."

Of course he flew. She'd known he owned a private plane. Made her shudder just thinking about one of those little puddle jumpers. "And how does the land lay?"

He stopped mere inches from her. So close she could feel his breath on her lips as he looked down into her eyes, like he wanted something from her. Something not business related, but that was just silly. She took a step back.

"Introduced myself to Guy Lager."

Guy headed up the Greenville Rodeo committee and was the one who signed the contracts and checks.

Mandy had called Guy yesterday to put him at ease. He'd told her he had confidence in her, but that didn't mean he did.

"Did he share any concerns about the rodeo now that JM isn't here?" Asking cost her some pride, but she needed to know for the sake of the business. She squared her shoulders for the blow.

Ty nodded.

"Let me guess. You told him you were running things, and his issues disappeared."

Ty shrugged, as if he couldn't help how the man felt. Mandy turned away and grabbed the saddle that had been resting on a hay bale. She didn't want Ty to see how irritated she was. Or how hurt. She'd known Guy Lager a long time.

She swung the saddle up on the mare. The bay horse took a step back. A pat on Willow's rump, and she settled. Mandy threaded the cinch through the O-rings, her back turned to the man who so easily upset her equilibrium.

"Don't you think we should have talked to Guy together? I am the Prescott in Prescott Rodeo Company now. I do know the man."

Ty stepped beside her and swiped a hand across his jaw. She swore that man had a jawline chiseled from canyon rock.

"I would have done that if you were here. I thought catching him first thing was more important."

No, Ty thought his being there first was more important.

She had too much to do to tussle though. It had been hard enough organizing everything this morning without JM at the helm. She'd done it tens of times before, but this morning was different. She'd never realized how her grandfather's presence had made her more confident in her decisions. Luckily, the crew had pulled together and got it done, like the family they were. She was thankful for that family.

That family had gotten her through the death of her father, when JM, devastated as he was, had discouraged any sign of grief and buried himself in his work. She imagined they would get her through this too. She was counting on it just as they counted on her to help with a small loan when needed, provide a recommendation when they graduated college or were looking for different work, or find a relative a job during hard times.

She pulled the cinch strap tight and wove it once more through the O-rings. Willow stepped back as Mandy gave several tugs to assure the mare hadn't puffed out her stomach.

"Is Guy good now?"

"Yes, but if Guy's concerns are any indication, we've got to hit the road, Mandy, as soon as we get back. We'll visit the key rodeo committees in person to let them know we're in business, before our competitors place doubt in their minds."

Our competitors? "I'd already planned to do that with a few of the large Texas rodeos. Karen's making the appointments."

"Good. Tell her to add me into the mix."

"If you're so intent on selling, why bother yourself?" she said, snapping out the words.

Ty shook his head at her like she was a child who wasn't listening. She was listening. She just didn't like what he'd been saying. And her question was a legitimate one.

"I've told you. I don't know yet which way makes sense. Until I do, I intend to do everything in my power to make sure the company remains viable."

"That way you'll get the best price for it—and for your share of it. Isn't that right, Ty?"

He held up his hand as if surrendering, but he didn't fool her. He was well aware he held all the cards. A hand of four aces, in fact. He was in control of everything. She kicked at the dirt, and dust sprayed on his shiny, no doubt new, Tony Lama boots.

Ty glanced at his boots and then lifted his gaze to stare straight into her eyes. He had intense brown eyes, and those eyes held her like he'd placed his hands on her body. "You think what you want, Mandy. I doubt anything I say is going to change your opinion. But the bottom line is that either way, we need to hold on to our customers."

Our customers again.

She swung up on Willow. She needed some space.

"Where are you headed?" he asked, his hands resting on his hips.

If he understood rodeo, he'd know. "We're moving the stock into the pens."

"You brought a horse for me, I hope." Sun glinted in those eyes of his, creating a disconcerting sparkle.

"Was I supposed to?"

"Mandy, I'm taking over JM's role. That means I'm involved in everything to do with the rodeo, including work behind the chutes."

She tugged lightly on the reins, holding Willow in place. "We can't have two bosses behind the chutes." She'd been running the crew for the last two years. She thought it was her grandfather's way of breaking her in. Apparently not.

"You're still the boss of the crew, but I'm going to oversee things, just like JM did. And my presence will back you up as you earn the men's respect."

"The men respect me." But even as she said it, she knew it was false. They respected her as a woman, as JM's granddaughter. But not yet as head of the company. As one of the few women in the rodeo stock industry, she'd have to prove herself worthy—to the men and herself. Because Ty's presence meant she hadn't proved worthy to her grandfather. The hurt was still raw...the knowledge still stung.

She let out a resigned sigh. "Harold's unloading the parade horses. He'll mount you on the mare from the other evening."

"Lead me to Harold, and I'll choose my own horse."

Mandy nudged Willow into a walk. This was going to be a long weekend.

* * *

Ty observed the unloading of the steers from atop

a bay gelding that seemed to have a little more kick in him than the horse last evening. He didn't want to calculate how many years it had been since he'd worked with livestock.

Once he'd headed off to college, he'd been pretty much persona non grata around the old homestead. Neither his father nor his brother, Trace, seemed to expect much from him, and he hadn't been inclined to give much, since he saw a different future for himself. After his father died from a sudden heart attack, the will was read, and Trace was left the ranch. All Ty was left were memories, and not necessarily good ones. His father's will stated that Ty was taken care of by virtue of JM's scholarship and the education it had bought.

Ty had been determined to make sure his father was correct, and he'd never had cause to look back. Until now.

"Hey, cowboy. You're doing pretty good." Harold Prescott, mounted on a fine-looking black horse, had shouted that review from across the fenced alley where the bulls paraded. It was only half a compliment, Ty knew. The undertone of surprise was the other half.

He nodded an acknowledgment and looked around to locate Mandy. She'd turned her horse around and was trotting back toward the pens, probably to check on the animals. Unfortunately, he couldn't help noticing every rounded curve of her body, including her fine butt glued to the saddle. Maybe he just needed to get her out of his system. Given he might have to suffer through two lust-filled years, maybe he should find out for sure if there could be anything between them.

It didn't take long to pen the bulls. Harold knew what enclosure suited which bull. Ty guessed bulls were a lot more like people than most folks realized. Some didn't mind sharing—others needed to be left alone.

Ty definitely fell in with the latter bunch as far as people were concerned. Yet here he was, managing a group of cowhands who had known each other for decades or whose family members had worked here for as long.

No doubt the rodeo hands had all heard about the will by now. JM had told him nothing much got by the crew. They would know he was now the boss, not Mandy, even if she was still managing the day-to-day operations, as she had under JM.

He still couldn't figure out why she'd gotten upset that he'd resolved Guy's concerns. What did it matter why Guy was upset or why he had calmed down? The fact was, Guy was no longer anxious about the rodeo operation, and that was a good thing.

The horses were moved more gingerly than the bulls. Some were led by their halter rope, and for that, Ty's horse worked well, seeming to enjoy taking the lead, particularly when a mare was involved. The crew worked seamlessly, having undoubtedly been doing this too many years to count. While Ty typically gave orders rather than took them, for the moment he sublimated his own need to take charge and waited like every other cowhand for Harold to sort out the livestock and Mandy to determine what animal went with what cowboy.

He might have been wrong about the men respecting her. They looked to Mandy, as well as Harold, for their orders and followed what was said without comment.

He watched as Mandy, sitting atop her horse, pointed to the bunch of steers still on the truck and the crew went into action, herding them through the chutes to one of the larger pens. Her booted foot in the stirrup, her long legs wrapped around the belly of her horse, her focus was on the animals. His gaze traveled up to her tight waist and the fluttering of her cotton shirt due to the cooling afternoon breeze. The top buttons of her blouse were open right above her breasts, and the fabric had flapped over to reveal the beginning swell of her bosom, exposing a slip of white lace from her bra. He wanted to bury his head inside her blouse and plant a kiss right on that creamy skin. He raised his gaze to the indent of her throat, glistening with moisture. And kiss there too. And then up to her lips, pursed in concentration as she watched over the operations. And definitely there.

The idea of marrying held more appeal than he'd ever thought possible. As long as it would be just for six months, of course. Too bad she wanted nothing to do with him and didn't much like him, or so she said. Yet, they would have to work together as a team if Prescott was going to be successful, at least in the short term. When it was over, he would start his land development business, alone.

As the thud of horse hooves, the bellowing of steers, along with the snorting of the bulls and the occasional shouts of the cowhands, filled the dusty, humid air, a sense of isolation crept over Ty despite the hubbub around him. While he might pretend he belonged to this rodeo community, reality was, he didn't belong anywhere.

* * *

Two dozen cowboys, along with Mandy's mother and Harold, stood among bales of hay, folding chairs, and work stools in the small tent designated for the event crew. Flies buzzed, and scents of horse, manure, and hay mingled with wafts of fried burgers and chili emanating from the hospitality tent next door as a country tune played in the background.

Clipboard in hand, Mandy gazed at the somber faces of Doug McClane, Slim Matthews, Patrick Saunders, Neil Tanner, Keith Bradshaw—Kyle's brother—and the rest of the crew gathered at this, the first rodeo since JM's funeral. She wondered how they would respond to the change in management. How should she present the fact that Ty was the boss but she was in charge, at least in her mind she was.

Movement near the entrance caught her eye, and she watched Stan Lassiter enter and stand to the side of the tent flap. She felt a headache coming on. Stan Lassiter was only assisting at this rodeo, yet he had decided to accompany his contingent to Greenville instead of sending one of his foremen. More than likely he had come to undercut her with the rodeo committee for next year. Stan certainly wasn't above such a tactic, and it was no secret he'd been after JM to sell once he learned JM was ill. If only Stan wouldn't make Ty aware of his interest.

She closed her mind to the thought of Prescott livestock being merged into the Rustic Rodeo operation. All the work Harold had put into the breeding program could end up benefiting a rodeo supplier who had never sent one horse or bull to the

NRF in the last five years, while Prescott had sent at least one every year for the past twenty.

It was her show, and the humming birds flapping in her stomach didn't help. Nor the fact Ty had situated himself on a stool right behind her as if he was grading her. He'd changed into the white dress shirt that proclaimed Prescott Rodeo on the back. The shirt was required attire for all employees who would be front and center at the event. He'd rolled up the sleeves, exposing hair-brushed forearms, like most of the cowboys did when the weather was humid, making him look more like one of the crew than suited her.

He hadn't said a word to her when she'd come in. He may be able to ignore her, but she had a hard time ignoring him, considering all she could think about were the pros and cons of marrying him. And that was not a healthy place for her mind to go.

Seeing the last cowboy enter the tent, she stepped forward to speak just as Ty rose from his perch, a hand anchored on each hip.

"This is a difficult time for the Prescott Rodeo family," Ty announced. "As many of you may know by now, JM left the overall running of the rodeo to me on an interim basis until Mandy is ready to take the reins."

She felt her cheeks heat and her temples pound.

"Mandy and I will be operating Prescott Rodeo as a team," Ty continued. "Mandy will continue to run the logistics as she did when JM was in charge, and I will take over JM's role on the business end, such as contract negotiations and the like. If you have any questions or concerns, see either Mandy or me, and we'll do our best to give you the answers."

The pain in her head arced as Ty looked at her expectantly, like he was waiting for her to add something. There was much she wanted to add, but she'd save that for Ty. Right now, it was more important that the crew saw them as working together, however much of a fantasy that was.

"Let's bow our heads and say a prayer in honor of JM," she said, taking the high road.

As she recited the words to the cowboy prayer, her thoughts turned to past rodeos when JM would lead them in prayer. She wanted to believe that he would walk through the tent flap and upbraid them for starting the meeting without him, ending this nightmare his death had trapped her in.

She blinked back a tear as the prayer ended. Hoping no one would notice, she picked up her clipboard from the bale of hay. JM had been a stickler for details, and he'd taught her to be the same. She went through the rosters for each event, making sure that Harold, as the chute boss, knew who was riding what, and what calf or steer was to go with each contestant in the timed event. Besides the shadow of JM that permeated everything to do with the rodeo, she was supremely aware of Ty sitting behind her on a stool, no doubt evaluating everything she did.

"Doug and Slim, you will be timing the tie-down roping event. You have your positions marked in the arena?" she asked.

Gratified that both men nodded, she moved on. "Harold, you're operating the chutes for that event. Were you able to test the chute operation?"

"I also tested them," Ty answered as Harold nodded.

"Great," she muttered, trying to hide her surprise at Ty's sudden interest in all things rodeo.

Clipboard in hand, she continued down her list. She checked that every committee person had a mount for the parade. She assured that the pick-up men and bull fighters knew the order of the less experienced bull riders. Finishing her list, she removed several sheets of paper from the clipboard and handed Jace Parish, the announcer, the information on each Prescott horse and bull that was being used.

"Stan, do you have your list available for Jace?" Mandy asked, acknowledging for the first time Stan's presence.

Stan nodded and ambled over to Jace, with a single sheet of paper in hand. She'd done this rundown dozens of times before, but JM had always been beside her.

"Everything square for you?" She turned to the representative for this rodeo's major sponsor, an auto dealer. If the money sponsor wasn't happy, the rodeo committee wouldn't be happy.

"Yes, ma'am," responded the middle-aged man with a serious face. He wore dark-blue denims and a pressed chambray shirt, looking like a dude-ranch cowboy. No participants were allowed behind the chutes if they weren't in cowboy dress, PRRA rules.

"Any questions?" she asked the rest of the group, wrapping up. Several cowboys had already checked their watches a few times. She'd gone over by almost ten minutes in her quest to be sure everything was locked down tight in this, their first rodeo since JM's passing.

"Have you got the names of the clubs we need to

recognize tonight during the grand parade?" Jace asked.

Even though Jace's boyish face held an encouraging expression, heat climbed her neck. She'd forgotten to give him the list. "Yes, right here," she said with a grimace, pulling out the sheet from her clipboard. If those clubs weren't announced, the rodeo committee would have her head. Giving locals recognition was part of the fabric of the rodeo communities. She handed the sheet to Jace. At least someone had her back.

"Anything else I may have forgotten?" she asked. No sense standing on pride. She wanted this show to be the best, and she needed those in the room to do their part. If they knew about something amiss, she wanted to give them the opportunity to tell her. She looked from weathered face to weathered face.

Slim Matthews stepped forward. "Who are we taking orders from? You or Ty?"

Mandy opened her mouth to speak, but from behind her came Ty's voice.

"Both of us. I am not expecting Mandy and I to have any conflicts," Ty said.

She turned around to face him and fought not to roll her eyes as Ty rose off his stool.

"You a rodeo operator?" Doug McClane asked.

Ty pushed up his rolled-up sleeves, and his posture went ramrod straight, almost as if he was readying for a fight. His smile had vanished, and his eyes had narrowed. "No. I've worked cattle before, but I'm a lawyer by training. And the one JM asked to lead this company while Mandy comes up to speed."

A murmur went through the gathering. Lawyers

were about as respected as used-car salesmen in these parts.

"Any other questions?" Ty didn't look eager to entertain any more, and the men must have gotten the message, as a number of heads shook.

Harold stepped forward. "This rodeo is being dedicated to JM, so in his honor, let's put on the best rodeo these people have ever seen." With that the crew departed quickly, as if someone had yelled fire and Harold ushered Sheila out of the tent. Mandy breathed a silent sigh of relief while she sorted her papers, trying to ignore Ty, who was standing mere inches from her. The meeting hadn't gone as smoothly as she'd wanted, but it was over, and the difficult facts of JM's will had been announced, though not by her.

Relief was short lived when she noted Stan hanging by the entrance as if he wanted to talk to her. Hopefully he wouldn't have the poor taste to bring up the topic of buying the company in front of Ty.

"Ty, you got a minute?" Stan asked, crossing his arms over his barreled belly.

Mandy held her breath.

"Sure, what's up?" Ty said, not moving from his spot behind her.

Stan shrugged. "Just wondering if we can meet at the bar tonight. Thought I might be able to give you some rodeo insight, you know."

"Appreciate it, Stan. But can I take a rain check? I've promised Mandy I'd buy her a drink tonight. First rodeo since JM passed, and all."

"Sure. Understand." Stan's cool gaze settled on Mandy. "I know this must be rough for you, it all being so recent." He gave a nod as if he'd done his duty by acknowledging her. "I'll catch you, Ty, tomorrow night." Stan edged his bulky frame through the entryway and escaped into the forming crowd.

"I'm just curious. What did I say when you promised to buy me a drink?"

"Yes, of course."

She shook her head. No way did she want to spend any more time with Ty than was absolutely necessary. "I've got a rodeo to put on. I'll be dead on my feet after I see that the animals are all fed and bedded down for the night. It will be late. Thanks but no thanks."

She turned to leave and felt Ty's firm fingers grasp her elbow. "Wait."

She spun back to look into his eyes. She couldn't guess what he had to say to her or what he thought would change her mind.

"We've got some decisions to make before Tuesday, Mandy. We need time to talk."

"I already made my decision." Though she hadn't been able to rid her mind of the question.

Every time she looked into Ty's dark, dangerous eyes, she couldn't help but wonder what it would be like to wed the man. What would it be like to finally feel all the power of his body against hers? Heck, what would it be like just to feel those demanding lips again?

Though he'd only been nineteen during that fateful summer, he'd been far more experienced than she in the loving department. There had been nothing tentative or naïve about his kisses. Or his touch. And with her, he'd found ample opportunity and an eager partner. But that was then. She was older, and hopefully wiser, and a lot more demanding in her own right.

She just wished she didn't feel an electric zing ping through her when he was in sight. If there wasn't that ludicrous provision, and the fact he was ready to sell her company, things might have even happened naturally in the one-night-stand department. But only one night. Just to see.

"There's no decision until Tuesday. And I think we owe it to JM—and ourselves—to give it the weekend. Once we make a choice, there's no going back. Don't tell me you're afraid to have a drink together."

She shrugged out of his grasp, hoping to break that potent spell that wrapped around her whenever he was near.

"Not afraid. Just not interested."

"Most women I know would be interested."

"I'm not most women."

"Not often someone offers you a company in return for a six-month relationship." He stood there, sleeves rolled up, arms crossed over his chest and an amused expression on his face, like this was some game. Fine hair dusted his forearms, and a five o'clock shadow outlined his jaw. She should be appalled at his arrogance, but instead she was rattled by the fact he actually wanted to get married.

"Why do you want to discuss it? To get more company shares? Is that what you want from this?" There had to be a money angle to this self-proclaimed bachelor's sudden interest in getting married.

He didn't answer right away. Instead he stared at her as if he expected her to guess the answer to that question and leaned forward so his lips were a whisper from hers. The heat of his breath teased across her mouth, causing a little shiver of recognition. She resisted the urge to step back even as her pulse ticked at her temple like a time bomb's clock on a short fuse.

"I want *you*, Mandy. In my bed and happy to be there. That's what I want."

He lowered his face, and his lips swept across hers.

Like a match igniting a brush fire, heat zinged through her body in a rush. She felt light headed as his arms encircled her and his hands pressed against her back. His tongue touched the seam of her lips, and they parted like he'd pressed some automated opener. He tasted like coffee and man, and she felt her body melt like she was the wicked witch in the *Wizard of Oz*. If he hadn't been holding her, she'd be a liquid pool on the dirt floor. His hands rubbed her back, and the hard bulge in his pants rubbed her crotch. His tongue invaded to dance with hers while his warm lips swirled over her mouth, making her give more than she'd intended. Even at nineteen, he'd held a black belt in kissing. Like two people going over the edge, they were free-falling together.

Her mind struggled against the need his wonderful mouth called forth. This wasn't a dream. This wasn't a fantasy. This was her life. She needed to stay in control of it.

Summoning all the willpower her weak body could muster, she pushed away. And stared into startled eyes filled with desire, passion, lust. She took a step back, amazed she had brought forth all that. And not at all surprised there was no tenderness, no emotion, no affection to go with it.

"I've got to go," she managed to say. "Parade's starting. You'll need to mount up too."

He took a step toward her, crowding her. "Just promise you'll keep an open mind, Mandy. Six months. And that kiss was a testament that it would be six very enjoyable months. We're goddamn combustible."

Chapter 6

The sounds of the crowd roared in her ears as Mandy stood at the timed-event end of the arena near the hazers' chute and checked her roster as the next rider and horse got ready. How she could even function after that kiss was a wonder. Her body still tingled. She was playing with fire, allowing him to kiss her. But she hadn't really allowed—he'd taken, just like he'd take her company if he had a chance. Question was, would that six-month stint her grandfather devised derail Ty's chances? It was still hard for her to fathom that her grandfather had put the family's ownership of Prescott in jeopardy.

She glanced over to where Ty was standing with Harold near the bulldogger chute, talking to the cowboys who had already competed in the steer wrestling event. He stood shoulder to shoulder with some of the biggest men on the circuit, and if she hadn't known better, she'd have thought he was one of them, albeit on the slender side. As if he knew she was watching him, he looked up. From across the chutes, she felt the heat of his gaze warm her like a hot glue gun had spread its mixture all over her, bonding her in place. He winked, and a smile lit across his handsome face like he knew what she'd just been thinking. She quickly looked away, toward the hazer getting set in the chute.

I want you, Mandy.

Ten years ago he hadn't wanted her. She'd humiliated herself asking, begging almost. So what had changed? Nothing. Except now he had a chance of owning more of the company. Rich as he was supposed to be, why was that even an incentive? And he was fooling himself if he thought he could change her mind about developing the ranch. Her grandfather had locked that up in a trust that would require her approval, and she would never give it. Besides, much as Tuck didn't care about the company, he loved the ranch. Young men could be swayed by the almighty dollar, but she was certain it wouldn't sway Tuck.

And where was her brother? He was on the roster to compete in saddle bronc tonight. Mandy watched as the steer left the chute pursued by the hazer and bulldogger in a wave of dust. Three point six seconds. Not bad. The crowd clapped its approval.

Early this morning Tuck had sent her a text message saying he'd arrived and needed to talk with her. And here it was well into steer wrestling, and he'd yet to appear. She'd head to the locker rooms to look for him, but she didn't feel she should leave any event while it was going on. She had too much riding on this rodeo. She took out her silver-rimmed phone and texted him, then shoved it in her pocket to wait for the vibration. Instead, a hand touched her shoulder. She jumped.

"Hey, big sister, how's it hanging?" Tucker beamed his trademark thousand-watt smile at her.

Lean, lanky, and laid back. That was Tucker Prescott. And handsome, if she did say so herself, with his blue eyes, rangy build, and blond hair. He was just twenty-two, and Mandy still thought of him as young, but the buckle bunnies who trolled the rodeo grounds certainly didn't agree.

"Hey yourself. Where have you been?" she said, talking close to his ear so she could be heard over the announcements. The little squirt had on aftershave. Did he think the bronc would care? She almost laughed.

Tucker pushed back his hat. "Around. Checking things out. Trying to learn a few things."

That sounded mysterious—and not at all like Tucker. "What's up?"

"Is Ty around?" he asked, surveying the area.

"He's hanging out with Harold at the bulldogger chute. Says he wants to learn. And by the way, why didn't you tell me about Mom and Harold?" She swatted at his chest.

"'Cause Mom asked me not to. She said she'd tell you herself. Besides, I wasn't supposed to find out. I just did. Just like I've found something else out I wasn't supposed to."

"What?"

A cloud of dust blew up as a cowboy wrestled his steer to the ground. He didn't get a good one, however, having broken the barrier. Mandy hoped no one else did that tonight. People didn't enjoy watching a bunch of bad scores.

"Stan Lassiter wants to buy Prescott."

She shrugged. "That's not news. He was after JM to sell."

"What's news is I saw Ty meeting with Stan this morning. Early. Before you guys even got here. Alone. They shook hands."

Needles of fear shot through Mandy. Was that what Stan's request to talk had been about? Was it a drink he wanted with Ty or celebrating some secret agreement?

Ty hadn't wasted any time. Was his plan to distract her by sleeping with her while he worked a deal to sell the company out from under her? Only way to find out was to confront the bastard. Guess she'd be seeing Ty tonight after all, but it wouldn't be to get a free drink.

"Was it just what you saw this morning, or did you hear something too?" Some verification would be nice before she stormed after Mr. Martin.

"I've been asking around today. Several guys in Stan's crew confirmed he'd told them he hoped to have a verbal deal before Greenville was over."

"Over my dead body." The sharks were circling, and JM hadn't been buried a week yet.

Tucker smiled. "There's worse things than being made a rich woman. Why do you want to run this outfit anyway?"

"Why don't you want to, Tuck? It was Dad's dream. Somewhere over these last few years, it's become mine. I want to build something. Something enduring. Something to be proud of."

"A perfect life is one free of responsibilities." Tuck shrugged. "But I'll support you in your dream as long as you don't try to curb me following mine."

She nudged him in his bony ribs. "As if I could. But seriously, I know you aren't interested in the company, but you'd never consider selling the ranch land, right? Word is, Ty is hoping we'd agree to develop it if the company was sold."

"Not the ranch. Where would we live?"

"Well, I guess we'd have money enough to live anywhere we want."

Tucker shook his blond head. "No place I'd rather be."

"It's not very profitable without the rodeo business. The land is probably worth more than we'd make out of it." She had to be honest.

"If we sell the business, it won't matter. And if we don't, it won't matter. The ranch is not for sale."

She could have hugged him. "Glad you feel that way. Now if only I can save the business."

"Mom told me about Grandpa's will. I wouldn't do it, Mandy. Selling the company is not the worst thing. Marrying someone you don't like—that's got to be hell on earth."

"That's what losing Prescott would be to me, Tuck. Hell on earth."

* * *

"Did we fill the arena tonight?" Harold asked as the four of them—Harold, Sheila, Mandy, and Ty—crowded into a booth in the hotel lounge while a DJ spun a combination of country and rock tunes for the lone couple slow dancing on the small wooden dance floor in front of them. Ty had managed to sit next to Mandy, while Harold and Sheila sat opposite.

Despite the dearth of people on the dance floor, the bar was crowded, mostly with cowboys, barrel racers, and the groupies that Ty had recently learned, courtesy of Tucker, could be found at most rodeos.

"Numbers are preliminary, but looks like we almost sold out," Mandy announced.

Not exactly the tête-à-tête he'd envisioned when Mandy had backtracked and taken up his offer for a late-night drink. Ty had hoped to use this opportunity to make his case. Especially after that kiss they shared. But here he was with her mother and Harold in attendance.

Harold had ordered a beer, Sheila had asked for a cosmopolitan, he'd gotten a jigger of scotch, and Mandy was nursing a soda. Guess getting her drunk and providing a little seductive encouragement wouldn't be an option as long as she had a rodeo to run. He admired that about Mandy. She knew her priorities, understood responsibility.

"Parade went a little long tonight," Mandy added.

"Had some trouble getting Guy a mount he liked. He finally agreed to the mare. I think he wanted a splashier horse."

Mandy's eyebrows rose, showing off her green eyes under the low light of the table lamp. She had the prettiest eyes. Unusual color, flecked with brown, always watchful.

"Bet he hasn't ridden since last year's rodeo," she said.

Harold snorted as he reached for a nacho covered in cheese from the plate Ty had ordered. Mandy followed, her delicate fingers snagging one just as her mother piped in.

"Those aren't healthy, dear."

"I worked plenty hard today. I'm entitled." She

popped the nacho into her mouth. As she savored the chip, a look of sheer ecstasy covered her face, presenting an erotic image. Ty could feel his pants tighten.

"You definitely deserve it," Ty whispered in her ear.

Mandy swallowed and turned to look at him, one corner of her mouth upturned in a mischievous smile. "I agree."

"What do you agree with?" her mother asked. Sheila took a delicate sip of her drink and stared over the glass rim, expecting an answer.

"That I deserve to indulge myself." Mandy gave a slight toss of her head. The tawny mane of hair fell carelessly down her back. The word luscious came to mind. Meaning the hair and the woman.

"There are healthier ways to indulge. Heaven knows you've bought enough boots. That's an indulgence that only hurts your pocketbook," Sheila said, then turned her attention to Harold, who had asked her a question about their room.

Ty had checked out Mandy's red pointed-toe boots when they'd been in the arena. They were hard to miss. Much about Ms. Prescott was hard to miss. Like the way she filled out her shirt, the pockets making nice frames for the nipples that were poking through at the moment.

Ty moved his thigh next to hers as he leaned closer to her ear. "I have a few ways I'd like to indulge you," he whispered.

She pulled back to look at him, and the sleeve of her shirt grazed his hand. Her eyebrows were raised, but that didn't disguise the interest beaming from her eyes. "I'd be happy to elaborate," he said.

"Elaborate about what? That crazy will?" Sheila said from across the table. She'd taken another sip of her drink, and Ty wondered if she might not be feeling its effect. "You two do make a cute couple."

"Mother." Mandy's tone held censure.

Ty grasped Mandy's hand in his. It was soft and surprisingly warm. "I agree." She tried to pull it away, but he held firm.

"So you're not opposed to the idea?" Sheila asked. Her smile held satisfaction.

"Not if it's for six months." Ty patted Mandy's arm. This time she tugged harder, and her hand slipped from his grasp as a slow tune wafted from the speakers. Sitting next to her, the desire to get closer reared inside of him.

"Care to dance?"

Mandy looked at him like she'd wanted to do anything but dance with him. Well, he had some other ideas in mind.

"I think it would be an interesting experiment, this marriage," Sheila opined.

Mandy gave a shake of her head and turned to Ty. "Sure," she said answering his question.

Ty downed the last of his scotch. Heat slithered down his throat. It wasn't the smooth scotch he was used to, but it would do. Maybe it would take the edge off of his damn desire for her.

Rising, Ty moved out of the booth and held out his hand. This time, she took it willingly, and he led her to the dance floor. In her jeans, red boots, and white top she looked like a sexy advertisement for America. Two more couples had joined the dancing, and it almost seemed crowded on the small floor.

Ty wrapped his arms around her and pulled her close. Close enough he could feel her breasts rub against his chest. Close enough he could feel other things rub. Her hands rested on his shoulders, and she gazed up at him. A shot of lust barreled through him like a torpedo through waves. They fit damn well together. He began to sway to the music. Mandy followed.

He rubbed his cheek against her ear, and he breathed in the scent of roses. Her scent. "You haven't even mentioned that kiss, Mandy," he whispered. "Maybe we should talk about that."

She pulled back and stared at him like he'd just waved a red flag in front of her face. "Why did you meet with Stan Lassiter this morning?"

Just like that the mood of the room shifted with the force of tectonic plates. How the hell had Mandy found out about his meeting with Stan? Judging by the *why don't you drop dead* look on her face, she suspected the worst.

"Stan simply expressed his interest. An interest you are no doubt well aware of." How had he suddenly been put on the defensive?

"Was he inviting you out tonight for a drink or to celebrate a deal?" she asked as her breasts rubbed the pockets of his shirt. Ten years ago, her breasts had been small but perky. Now they were firm, curvy, and sufficiently prominent without being so large as to seem unnatural. Ten years ago, her kisses had been shy and sweet. That kiss earlier had been demanding and consuming. He liked consuming.

He shifted his hand so his thumb slid under her shirt and rested against her warm skin. She was soft underneath her clothes. Soft and warm.

"Stan's let me know he's interested. And I'm bound by the trust your grandfather placed in me to explore all options. But JM also asked me to help you through this transition, if selling doesn't turn out to be the best option. So I intend to do that too, whether you want me to or not."

"I'll fight you anyway I can if you try to sell. However little faith JM had in me, I'll prove him wrong—all by myself." Her eyes glistened in the low bar light, and he couldn't be sure it wasn't from tears.

Ty wished he could erase that pain rather than be the one causing it. But that wasn't the hand dealt him.

"The way he bragged about you, I doubt it was a lack of faith in you, Mandy, as much as it was an understanding of the industry and what it could be like for an inexperienced woman."

"I'm capable of running things. JM may not have been comfortable with the idea of a woman at the helm, but this is the twenty-first century. And I know more about Prescott, rodeo, and livestock than you'll ever know." She stomped her foot on the dance floor, causing a smack.

"I've no doubt you do. I hope selling will prove unnecessary." He gathered her closer in his arms in the hope of coaxing her to continue dancing.

"Will you promise, in writing, not to sell before the end of six months if I marry you?" she whispered in his ear.

Ty tucked a strand of her soft, silky hair behind her ear. No doubt about it, even with her jaw bunched and her eyes boring into his hide, she was a beautiful woman. And those green eyes gave away every thought in her head. She'd actually been considering marriage. Guess she was willing to do just about anything to keep Prescott Rodeo.

Too bad he was such an honest guy.

"You know I can't promise that, because I made a different promise to JM. But I will promise that I'll do my best to help you keep the business viable. Whether the company is sold or kept, it's in my best interest and everyone's best interest to do that." Ty moved her across the dance floor further from their booth. He hadn't intended to be so blunt, but in his experience, truth was the best anecdote to wishful thinking.

She stared, her chest rising and falling seductively in deep breaths, just like he imagined would be the case when he made hard and fast love to her.

"Has Stan made you an offer?"

"I'd liken it to our situation, Mandy. Stan's in the courting stage, so to speak."

"How is that anything like our situation?"

"I'm trying to court you."

She scowled. "You haven't been trying to court me, Martin. You've been trying to get me in your bed. Big difference."

He shook his head. "No. I've been trying to marry you. That's the big difference."

"So you can have your cake and eat it too…"

He arched his eyebrows. Now that was an intriguing metaphor. She blushed—an angry blush.

"You know what I mean."

He stroked his thumb across her smooth back. Just touching her had him hot. He could just imagine what he'd feel if he were inside of her. "What I know is that we have an opportunity to enjoy each other for half a year, at which time you would get to lead the company if I don't have a better deal on the table by then. Worst case for me, I'd get a larger share of Prescott. So, if selling is such a bad idea…marry me."

The last two words almost caught in his throat. He'd sworn he'd never say them. Now here he was, asking a woman who didn't even like him. Desire and money were potent motivators for sure. Made men do crazy things. He was apparently no exception.

"That's some proposal."

"Seems your best play." He counted on her preferring honesty to sweet talking. "I'm willing to abide by the provisions of that bizarre will. But I'm a realist. We will end up in bed. Married or otherwise."

"You're awfully sure of yourself," she challenged. She lifted her hand to smooth down her hair and then returned it to his shoulder. Despite the air-conditioning, the room felt warm.

"We've been circling around each other for ten years now. It's time we tested out what we'd be like together. Hell, marriages have been based on a lot less than the physical attraction we have—and don't go spoiling my sense of your integrity by lying about what you feel. Your lips didn't lie."

She swallowed hard and rested her chin on his shoulder, facing away from him. The fact she didn't snap right back or refute his assertion about their sexual attraction, he'd take as tacit agreement.

"Can you think of a good reason why we shouldn't marry temporarily?" he said against her ear. He hadn't closed deals by laying back.

She lifted her head. "You'll get more shares in the company, and I might never be rid of your interference. If you agreed, in writing, not to sell Prescott, however, I'd be much more interested in marrying you."

Ty released a smile. This was the oddest negotiation he'd ever been involved with. "No deal on that score. I gave JM my word. I owe it to him to do the best thing for the family. Besides, sounds a little too much like blackmail."

"Then guess you'll have to be content with getting the ranch house." The way she scowled, he knew she hated that idea almost as much as she hated the thought of marrying him.

"I told you before, I'm not interested in the ranch house, Mandy. I'm interested in us being together after all this time." He held her closer, tighter. He could feel every inch of her body against every inch of his. Damn she felt good in his arms. She'd feel even better in his bed.

"Just for another notch on the old belt?" She looked up at him and thrust out her chin. He admired her fight, but she was choosing the wrong battle.

"Don't sell yourself short. You're a woman I find…challenging. And desirable."

She blushed, the color suffusing her cheeks with a rosy pink glow, making her look like a cute little Kewpie doll.

"As for the company," he continued, "after the six months, I wouldn't own enough shares to sell it or block you in whatever you wanted to do, even if I could make a case that I had ideas for a better use of capital."

She picked at something on his shoulder. "I don't trust you, Martin," she finally allowed.

"No kidding."

"I guess that's been obvious." Her eyes shimmered in the light, like pools of deep water under the moon. There was something about this woman. Something that challenged him to dig deeper, try harder.

He reached for her hand on his shoulder and folded her fingers into his. She was soft and warm, and another jolt of lust zinged him. "I promise I'll always be straight with you."

He ran his thumb over her smooth warm hand, making lazy circles. She had pretty hands, small boned and surprisingly soft.

She didn't pull her hand away. "Being married doesn't mean I'd go to bed with you," she said.

If she was asking him to gamble on whether she'd succumb in six months, those were odds he'd gladly take. He was marrying to have a woman he'd wanted for ten years. A woman who had been forbidden fruit by virtue of her being JM's granddaughter. Now JM had, in effect, given his blessing. And for just six months. And with an added bonus of stock. Hell, why wouldn't he take that gamble? Because there was no way Mandy was going to be able to hold out for 180 days—and nights. He'd make sure of that.

"I'll take my chances. Consider if you have more to win or lose if we married. I think the answer will be obvious."

The song ended. The dancers were leaving the floor, but Ty stood holding Mandy.

She looked up at him as if she was searching his face for an answer to her dilemma.

"I doubt it," she finally said.

But he heard a distinct quiver of uncertainty in her voice. He'd take that as progress.

* * *

Mandy slid onto the red faux-leather seats of the booth at the local café, where her two girlfriends sat across from her, eyeing her as if she had some strange disease. Maybe she did.

She'd texted them Monday morning on the way home from the rodeo and asked them to meet her at their regular spot. She needed a reality check, and she couldn't think of any better people to give it.

"Thanks, both of you, for coming on such short notice."

"You got our curiosity up for sure," Libby Cochran said, her blue eyes sparkling with impending motherhood, an event she'd announced at their last dinner.

Mandy had met Libby when Libby had interviewed for a public relations job for the Western Stock Show in Denver, where Mandy had represented Prescott Rodeo on the event committee. It turned out Mandy knew Libby's dad, since Prescott Rodeo had bought several pickups from his dealership. As they had gotten to know one another, they found they had a lot more in common than either might have guessed, particularly in the family dynamics department. Even though Libby had eventually turned down the position, they'd become friends.

If Libby was Mandy's newest friend, Cat McKenna was her oldest. Cat's family had been ranchers for generations, and the two girls had grown up together at county 4-H events, showing off their heifers. Mandy had seen Cat through some difficult times, what with a relationship gone bad, a father who disowned her, and a little boy to care for. But Cat had eventually come home and, with her father's passing, was running Pleasant Valley Ranch, or at least trying to.

Mandy had introduced Libby to Cat, and they hit it off. The three friends had been meeting periodically for a "girls' night out" at the local café ever since. Tonight, all three dressed in jeans. Mandy had thrown on a balloon-sleeved turquoise shirt that matched the dyed leather turquoise insert in her squared-toe Tony Llama boots. Libby's top was a blousy pink number, while Cat's sleek designer logo shirt was in keeping with her high-end taste.

"Does this have something to do with your grandfather's will? Did you find out the business is insolvent or something?" Cat bit her lip and squinted her brown eyes as if trying to puzzle out the why and wherefore of the evening.

There would be no way either of them would guess what Mandy had to discuss. And they had to be wondering about the emergency that placed them all here on a Monday night with only a few hours' notice.

"It has everything to do with my grandfather's will, unfortunately. And no, the business isn't insolvent."

At that moment, a perky young waitress appeared at the table, pad and pen in hand.

They each gave their order, familiar with the menu, seeing as this had become a regular meeting spot to reconnect over a burger and a glass of beer—or in Libby's case now, a soda. Libby was the only one who was married, having tied the knot in late winter with a handsome bronc rider she had been married to briefly five years earlier and divorced forty-eight hours later—but that was another story.

As the waitress strode away, Cat leaned in, flipping her long brown hair over her shoulder. "So tell us."

"First, I want to know how you're feeling, Libby."

"Fine, just fine. The morning sickness has finally left—although it should have been billed as all-day sickness. But tell us your news."

"And your father? How's he doing?"

Libby huffed and blew a strand of her pageboy length blond hair from her face. "He's coming along. Chance is doing well on the circuit. We're all good, Mandy—now dish."

"And little Jake? How is he doing, Cat?" Jake was Cat's son, a cute, active four-year-old who made Mandy's maternal instincts pop whenever she saw the little imp.

"Good. He misses his grandfather though. Strange as it may seem, Jake had become my father's reason for being. Life certainly takes strange turns."

That was an understatement.

"And are you still going ahead with that adverse-possession lawsuit?"

"There will be time to talk about my issues another day. You didn't call us here on a Monday night to find out how we are doing. You could have done that over the phone."

The waitress was back with a cola and two bottles

of craft beer, which she set on the table. Mandy took a swig, enjoying its yeasty taste. She hardly knew how to begin.

"The will was read on Thursday, right before we had to leave for a rodeo. It is a complicated document, but essentially…" Mandy did her best to explain it all. Libby and Cat had tons of questions, but in the end, they seemed to get it just as the plates of burgers arrived.

"I can't believe your grandfather is trying to arrange your marriage. With a guy you hate," Libby said. "Although I guess it's just as bad as a father arranging a divorce from a guy you love."

"They say love and hate are very closely related," Cat offered.

"Not in this case."

"Well, I seem to recall a teenager who thought she was in love with Ty Martin."

"A lot has changed in ten years, Cat. And no one is talking about love here. This would be strictly a marriage of convenience for just six months. And I am only considering it to get my company back and keep it from being sold."

"But you said he could sell it in six months, regardless, if he has a buyer."

"Well, that's the gamble I would be taking. Given how tight credit is, I think I have good odds of keeping the company. Has to be better odds than if he has a year." Or two.

"Then why are you hesitating? If you hate him"—Cat put air quotes around the word "hate" as she spoke—"wouldn't that make it *less* complicated? Just divorce him after six months, since you said that was what he wants as well."

106

Mandy took a deep breath. These were her dearest friends. She would have to be honest. Cat, for sure, would know if she wasn't.

"I may not like him, but strange as it is, I find myself still physically attracted to him. I don't know if I can hold out for six months. As part of the conditions…" She paused, not sure how to present the terms of the will. She would just say it out loud. "I have to sleep in the same room with him, and I can't be away from him overnight. Basically, we have to be living together."

Libby's mouth fell open, and Cat chuckled.

Libby recovered first. "Well, take it from me. Even living at Chance's in separate bedrooms, while I was taking care of him after his accident, didn't change the inevitable,"

Cat shook her head. "And I can't imagine anything would stop me if I was twenty-four seven with someone I was attracted to. Although I'd like to try that experiment with the right person."

"Cody Taylor popping into your head?" Mandy teased.

Cat smiled. "Oh yeah. But he's the one who hates me, so that's a nonstarter."

"You tell your mama this?" Libby asked Mandy.

"I did. And surprisingly, she's encouraged me to go for it. For some strange reason, she seems to like Ty, and she doesn't see anything so awful in this. I think she fears this is the only way I'll ever get married."

"Well, you have to admit your choice in men hasn't been the best, not that I'm one to talk." Cat grimaced. "Maybe your grandfather will have a better batting average."

"Highly unlikely. But if I did do this, how can I have any self-respect?"

"Well, what's more important, your pride or your company? Because that's what it comes down to, doesn't it?" Libby said. "Pride can be a big obstacle. I know it was for Chance. I'm just glad he overcame it." Libby's smile broadened.

"So you have to decide tonight?" Cat asked.¬

"Two o'clock tomorrow I have to be in our lawyer's office either ready to get married or ready to give my company over to Ty for up to two years, shorter if he sells it."

"That's some dilemma—either marry a man you don't love but would like to go to bed with or stand to lose your family's business," Libby said.

Mandy shook her head. "And what hurts the most is that this was all my grandfather's doing. My grandfather, who loved me and loved the company. It boggles my mind."

"Why do you think your grandfather chose Ty and asked him to look into selling the company?" Libby took a big bite of her hamburger. Considering petite Libby ordered not only a deluxe hamburger platter but a plate of onion rings and a milkshake, it seemed she was already in the "eating for two" mode, even if she was only three months along.

"That is a million-dollar, or more, question. Our lawyer thought he was trying to play matchmaker, which is such an absurd idea. As for selling, I can only assume he had no faith in me."

"Well, I can relate to family having no faith in you. That's pretty much how I was raised," Cat said, taking a swig of beer. "But surely you already proved yourself to your grandfather, and if he had such little faith, why did he allow you to run the company in six months if you married?"

"It makes no sense," Mandy agreed. "But regardless of why he did it, what am I to do about it?"

"I'd do whatever I had to do to save our family ranch. Kyle Langley, my lawyer, keeps urging me to sell it, but I want it for my son."

Libby patted her barely round stomach. "I can understand that now."

"But I don't have a child—not that I don't want one but…my mother may be right about my marriage prospects. I seem to scare men away. Maybe I should just let Ty take the company, sell it if he finds a buyer, and take the money and start running the ranch for a living." Life would be easier if she could convince herself not to care.

Cat snorted. "There is no money in ranching, let me tell you. And it's damn hard work. Sometimes I question what I'm doing trying to keep it, considering I know next to nothing about running a ranch because no one ever thought enough of me to teach me."

"Truth is, I know and love rodeo, not ranching. They are two different animals—literally."

"I think you have your answer," Libby said. "And worst case, you'll have a little fun while you're saving your company."

Mandy grimaced. "That's what my mother said."

Chapter 7

Mandy waited outside the door of Brian's office, her heart pummeling her rib cage. She was really going to do this? It was still a question. She glanced at her mother, who stood with Harold, watching her as if she were a horse ready to bolt. A realistic fear given how she felt.

"Honey, you don't have to do anything you don't want to." Her mother was dressed in a stylish lilac sheath. "I know I was encouraging you, but now that you've decided, I'm having second thoughts myself. What was JM thinking, Harold?"

Harold shook his Stetsoned head. For the occasion, he'd donned the same dark suit he'd worn to JM's funeral, probably the only suit he owned. "Damned if I know. This is the darnedest thing I've ever heard of. Sounds like something out of the Middle Ages. Ty's all right, I guess, but why JM wanted you to marry him in order to run the company, I don't understand."

"By the way, Harold, I didn't get a chance to say congratulations. Mom told me."

A slow smile slid across his weathered face. "Thank you, Mandy. Guess that's gonna make me some sort of in-law to Ty." His expression turned determined. "I can have a word with him if you want."

"I appreciate the offer, but it's not like this is a real marriage. I mean, a lasting one. Six months it will all be over, and this will just be a footnote in my life." Some footnote.

"I don't know, honey," Sheila said. "Marriages are supposed to be happy occasions. You look like you're going to another funeral, not your wedding."

Mandy straightened her shoulders and smoothed the skirt of the pastel-blue jersey dress she'd pulled from her closet. Certainly not the Cinderella dress she'd imagined for her wedding. And not the groom either.

This isn't a real marriage.

What it was, however, had yet to be defined. An affair? An arrangement? An agreement of the personal kind? None of them sounded honorable or even decent.

An indecent proposal, concocted by, of all people, her traditional, conservative grandfather.

"I'll be fine. It's not like he's evil or anything. I just don't trust him with the company."

Not a very flattering portrait of the man she was going to wed.

There was still time to back out.

The door opened.

"I thought I heard voices." Brian poked his gray-haired head out of the door. "All set?" He eyed her like he too expected her to bolt. "He signed the prenup, and I gave him your signed copy."

Mandy nodded, feeling both a sense of dread and, oddly, anticipation. "I'd like to see Ty first. Alone," she said, looking at her mother and Harold.

"Traditionally, it's bad luck for the groom to see the bride before the ceremony," Shelia said, placing a protective hand on Mandy's forearm.

"This is hardly a traditional marriage, Mother." And it wasn't like her luck could get much worse.

With an accepting nod, Shelia walked through the doorway, Harold following, as Brian disappeared inside, presumably to fetch Ty.

Mandy worried her lower lip as she waited, her hands clasping and unclasping. She could still turn around and walk away.

Ty stepped out into the hallway.

He was dressed in black, with a starched white shirt. But it wasn't an ordinary suit. Ty wore a tuxedo—and wore it well. The expert tailoring emphasized his broad shoulders, while the jacket skimmed along his torso and nipped in at his waist. The trousers fell loose and long over black shoes. A lock of dark wavy hair had settled across his brow. He looked like he'd stepped out of the pages of a bridal magazine's photo shoot of the perfect groom.

As his gaze danced over her, the smile that spread across his face paid her a compliment like no words ever could.

But what intrigued her most was the gorgeous bouquet of flowers in his hands. Beautiful red roses, baby's breath, and purple orchids. The sentiment behind it dried her mouth.

"You look beautiful, Mandy." His fingers fondled a strand of her hair and then freed it to swing against her shoulder. "Stunning."

The look of pleasure in his eyes made her believe him, made her feel, in that moment, beautiful.

"For you." He held out the bouquet. "I know there are many things missing from this ceremony. Hell, I don't even have a ring to give you, but I wanted you to at least have beautiful flowers."

She reached for them. A tingle flitted through her as her fingers scraped his hand, reminding her of the swirl of his thumb over her hand after he'd asked her to marry him. She brought the bundle to her nose and took a deep breath of rose-scented air. Her favorite fragrance.

"Thank you," she said with heartfelt sincerity. It was a sweet gesture—and so totally unexpected it made everything she was going to say more difficult.

He looked at her, the smile fading as his thumb stroked down her cheek, bringing with it a pleasurable shiver. She wished she didn't respond this way every time he touched her.

"You're not having second thoughts, are you?"

"No. Not really," she lied. "But I did want to be sure we understand each other. Marriage carries certain expectations," she began. "And I want...I want to be the one who decides if and when...those expectations are met." She looked up at him through her lashes.

He took a step back, as if to see her more clearly. "Of course." He sounded offended.

"It's just...this is not a real marriage. There's no love between us. We don't trust each other..."

"I'm attracted to you. And if you're honest with yourself, you're attracted to me."

"For you, that's enough, I'm sure." She couldn't disguise the edge in her voice. "But it's not for me. Sex isn't just about pleasure..."

"It will be pleasurable. I can promise you that."

She ignored the kick of her pulse. "It's about feelings." And she counted on his role as arbiter of her company's fate to keep at bay whatever misguided feelings she may have once had for him. She'd been too young to understand what it meant to be in love, and yet, no other man had ever elicited the depth of feelings he had that fateful summer.

"Like with Mitch Lockhart?"

What did he know about Mitch Lockhart? And why did he care? "I don't need to defend my previous decisions. But I do need to explain this decision so you're realistic and not under any illusions."

"Shoot."

"If you think I am doing this for any reason other than to become the head of Prescott Rodeo Company and keep it from being sold, you are wrong, Ty. You gain regardless. I risk…everything that's dear to me, everything I've fought for. My heritage, my company." *My self-respect.*

He curved a finger under her chin and tilted her face up so she could see him. It was too easy to get lost in those dark, intense, intriguing eyes.

"And just so *you're* realistic, I play to win. So there's no way we're not going to bed together. It's not a matter of *if*—it's only a matter of *when*. I can be damn irresistible."

With a smile that gave truth to his words, he stepped back and held out his arm.

"We'll see," she said, hoping her voice held more conviction than she felt at the moment. Placing her hand on the wool sleeve covering hard bone and muscle, her legs weak, she walked with him into Brian's office to become Mrs. Ty Martin.

* * *

"You really didn't have to do this, Mom."

Mandy sat next to Ty and across the linen-clad table from Sheila and Harold in a booth at the Cattle Baron's Grille in the historic Cheyenne hotel of the same name, and tried to ignore the warm thigh pressed against her leg and the flush of her body in response.

The thigh and the heat it was generating belonged to the man she had just pledged to love and honor *till death do us part*. Hypocrisy slammed into her with an uncomfortable thud. She was now a card-carrying member of *the ends justifies the means* club, and she hated herself for it.

And she hated that Sheila had insisted they "celebrate" the occasion. Mandy didn't feel like celebrating. She felt like crawling back under the covers of her bed and never coming out. Only now her bed would include the tall, dark, and handsome man next to her and be located in her grandfather's ranch house, which she hadn't stepped foot in since his death.

She wanted to cry. But instead she picked up her fork and stabbed at the Caesar salad she'd ordered, her stomach in knots.

"It was nice of both of you," Ty said, including Harold in his thanks. Ty, along with Harold, had ordered the Cowboy Ribeye. Out of the corner of her eye, she watched him cut a substantial piece of meat off the bone and pop it into his mouth. Obviously *his* appetite had not been affected.

"Well, even if this isn't…well, traditional, we should commemorate the occasion." Sheila took a dainty bite of her salmon.

"Why? We all know it's just a sham." Mandy felt peeved—at herself, mostly, for having succumbed to her grandfather's misplaced wishes. "I just want my company back."

A frown creased her mother's creamy white brow. "Let's have a nice meal and not spoil it by talking about that confounded will. You've taken the necessary step, so it's time to move forward."

"You both headed out tomorrow to Texas?" Harold asked, apparently ready to change the subject.

"We're heading to Abilene first. Right, Mandy?" Ty seemed totally unaffected sitting in the elegant dining room in his tux like it was the most normal thing in the world to have just gotten married on a Tuesday by a judge to a woman he couldn't claim as more than an acquaintance and who, he had to know, despised everything he stood for.

Not that he didn't look good in his tux. He'd drawn the stares of several women in the room when he'd entered. Wasn't the bride supposed to be the center of attention on her wedding day? Only Mandy wasn't dressed as a bride, didn't feel like a bride, didn't want to be a bride. Well, not today anyway.

"Right, Mandy?" Ty repeated. She felt more pressure from his thigh.

Nudged out of her dismal thoughts, she nodded.

"Say hi to Lyle Thorton. Hear his wife had a bad bout of arthritis after Houston's rodeo," Harold said.

Mandy nodded again and took the tiniest piece of lettuce into her mouth, hoping her stomach would accept it.

"I'll be worried about you up in that plane the whole time you are gone," Sheila said, taking a sip of the champagne she'd insisted be poured for all of them. Mandy hadn't touched hers, but maybe she should. If this wasn't a reason to get drunk, what was?

"It's the only way we'll be able to see all the committees we have to see and still make the rodeo in Washington this coming weekend," Ty said. "Mandy's not worried, are you?"

Again she lied, nodding even though she was petrified to get into that puddle jumper of his. She'd never seen his plane, but how big could a two-seater prop plane be? This week had been nothing but a nightmare, and it would only get worse. From flying in that plane to introducing Ty as the head of Prescott to sleeping in the same bedroom with the man, her life for the foreseeable future would be nothing but one long bad dream.

But only for six months. And she'd have had to do the first two things regardless. The last had been her choice, and it was too late to second guess her decision now.

Ty reached for his champagne glass, and the sleeve of his black tuxedo softly brushed against her bare arm.

"I'm an experienced pilot, Sheila. I'll take good care of your daughter."

Sheila turned to say something to Harold, and Ty leaned toward her, his warm body touching hers, to whisper in her ear. "I'll take very good care of you, if you let me." A slow heat spread through her starting at her toes and climbing up her body to nestle right between her thighs. She crossed her legs.

After taking another sip of champagne, Ty set his glass back on the table.

"How difficult is it to fly a plane?" her mother asked.

Mandy reached for her goblet. Maybe the champagne would calm her stomach. Tipping back her glass, she felt the bubbles tickle her lips

"Takes training. Key is knowing the right switches to flip," Ty said.

The waitress interrupted to check if there was anything they needed.

Ty leaned in again, this time pressing his torso against her as he whispered, "I'd like to flip your switches."

A flush engulfed her. She had another sip of champagne.

"Dessert, dear?" her mother asked as all eyes, including the waitress's, turned toward her.

She shook her head.

"Oh, we have to have something," her mother chided. "They just got married today," she told the waitress.

The waitress looked from Mandy to Ty—and stayed looking at Ty—as she said her congratulations. Ty did that to women. Attracted them. And she, damn it, was no exception. This time she took a *gulp* of champagne.

"I'd go for some cake," Harold spoke up.

"Cake all around. And coffee," Sheila ordered. "No fuss, though. This is just a celebration for us," she told the waitress. Looking at Mandy's barely touched salad and the half-filled glass of champagne, Sheila frowned. "And my daughter's not finished with her salad yet, so leave that plate," she said as the busboy the waitress had signaled over began clearing.

"You need to eat something, Mandy. You barely ate breakfast this morning," Sheila said above the clacking of plates being cleared.

Mandy felt a funny swaying in her head. Maybe she should eat something. "I'll have the cake."

From under the table she felt Ty's hand on her thigh. She should remove it, but the swaying in her head prevented her. She turned to look at him and felt a little dizzy again as she stared into dark lust-filled eyes at odds with his amused grin. Under the table, his hand brushed the hem of her dress up her thigh and then landed back on bare flesh. Her legs uncrossed.

His thumb swirled over her skin, focusing her attention on that spot on her inner thigh, worrying that he would move it even higher. Then what would she do?

"You're going to love dessert. What follows the main event, Mandy, is always the best part," he said. The heat flushing through her body had her wondering if he wasn't right.

* * *

Married. Certainly not where he had expected to find himself, Ty thought as he gazed into the steamed glass of the bathroom mirror. He wiped off the fog, creating a watery space, and glared at the somber face that stared back at him. What had he been thinking? Problem was, he'd let his dick do his thinking—and that had never worked out well for him.

He and Mandy were sharing a bedroom, like the will said, but not a bed. They'd wrangled over whether to use the ranch house's guestroom, which Mrs. Jenkins had already made ready for them, with its king-sized bed and its own bathroom situated next to her grandfather's room, or the smaller bedroom down the hall with twin beds and a bathroom shared with a vacant room on the opposite side.

With arms crossed and heat in her cheeks, Mandy had been adamant it would be the twin beds. After dinner and several glasses of champagne at the Cattle Baron's Grille, he thought she'd be primed for tonight. He'd been wrong.

He'd given in on the bedroom issue, for this evening at least.

Tomorrow they'd hit the road to meet with the various rodeo committees and offer assurances. They'd be staying in hotel rooms. He had to get lucky and have at least one place where they would have a room with a single bed. He'd make sure of it.

Tonight he'd just have to steel himself to frustration. Not quite how he would have guessed his wedding night would go, but then he'd never imagined it. Mandy must have. Every woman he'd met had thought about her wedding day at some time. Getting married in an office with only Brian, Shelia, and Harold to witness and before a strange judge must have been quite a letdown for her. He swiped a towel across his chin and secured a larger towel around his waist.

He'd always slept in the nude. He had no plans on changing. He'd use the towel to be discreet, but it wasn't like she'd never seen a man before. And he had no problem with her checking him out. He had nothing to hide in that department.

She wasn't in the bedroom, though the bed closest to the bank of windows had been turned down.

He went and opened one of the windows. The soft cooling breeze of a late spring evening fluttered the sheer curtains. He looked around the yellow-walled room. It was simply furnished, containing two beds with old-fashioned iron headboards painted cream and covered in white bedspreads, one maple dresser, and a small vanity in the same wood. Obviously a room meant for JM's grandkids when they were young. Not for someone's wedding night.

Why had JM put him smack-dab in the middle of such a mess? It was one thing to want financial security for your family, but a whole other kettle of fish to try to play matchmaker to two people who were temperamentally unsuitable for each other.

Nothing to do but go to bed, he figured. They would be flying out in his plane at eleven the next morning and heading for Abilene, Texas, to talk to the folks there, and then they'd hit three more stops before flying back on Friday so they could make a Saturday rodeo Prescott was putting on in Washington. It would be a hectic week, but those Texas rodeos were influential. If the Texans held, they might not have to make more trips. Besides, there was an AFBR board member in Texas he'd like to see. He'd done a land deal with him a while back.

As he dropped the towel and slid under the thin cover, cool sheets greeted his hot body, hot for reasons unexplained by the mild temperature in the room. He was flying at half-mast even knowing tonight wasn't going to be that kind of night. Damn.

He'd left the light on for Mandy and was just contemplating getting up and going to find her, when the door pushed open. She stood there dressed in nothing but a pink oversized T-shirt. Those long, shapely, tanned legs made his mouth dry and his shaft harden. An image of her wrapping those legs around his waist as he took her up against the door flitted across his overactive mind.

Mandy stilled in the doorway and stared at a bare chest displaying abs that looked like they'd been fashioned from corrugated steel. He had the kind of chest seen in fitness magazines and women drooled over. Tight skin, brown nipples, and a thin line of dark hair trailing toward the blanket bunched at his waist. Staring back, he propped up on his elbow to rest his head on his hand. The movement caused well-defined muscles to ripple and the blanket to slide down to his hips. Dangerously low. Below his belly button low. He was totally nude under that threadbare blanket.

That was knowledge she could have done without, knowledge that formed a pool of moisture between her legs.

She felt light headed, no doubt the residual effect from the poor decision of too much champagne, though she'd sobered up fast enough after stepping into her grandfather's house. Too many memories.

"Make yourself at home, Ty."

The words snapped in the air with more crackle than she'd intended. Partially to dispel her physical reaction. Partially because she'd just been down the hall in her grandfather's room—remembering.

She flicked the wall switch off, killing the light. In the gray darkness, she picked her way past their two suitcases and the foot of his bed, toward her own.

"You okay?" he asked.

She flipped back the chenille bedspread and backed onto the mattress so she faced the window, not Ty. The cool sheets sent a chill through her as a slightly stuffy smell greeted her nose, probably from bedding that hadn't been used for a number of years. She'd found them in the linen closet after she'd won the battle of the beds. Now here she was spending the night in the room she'd shared with her brother when they had stayed over at their grandparents' in her younger years, when their grandmother had still been alive.

"Yes," she mumbled. Could he tell she'd been crying?

She hadn't planned on stepping into JM's bedroom, the place she had last seen her grandfather alive. But being in the house, she'd felt an almost morbid need to confront the emptiness of that room. So much had happened since his death, she hadn't had much time to grieve. The will was part of the reason, the rodeo, Mitch and Ty, the other parts, and somehow all interconnected. Regardless, she hadn't had space to be alone, to process JM's death.

The ache in her heart started the moment she'd set foot inside JM's room. It looked the same, like it was waiting for his return. The comb on the dresser, that special book on the bed stand, the corduroy slippers tucked beside his chair. Only the empty hospital-like bed suggested the truth.

During the last days of his life, she'd read to him from the pages of *Anne of Green Gables*. When she'd been young, he'd bought her the book and insisted she read it aloud to him in the evening so she could practice her reading. They'd laugh over Anne's stubborn, feisty ways. JM had said he'd chosen the novel for her because Mandy had reminded him of Anne.

She'd kept the book, and as his condition deteriorated, she'd sit and read to him as he listened with his eyes closed, a smile on his frail face. She'd just reached the part where Matthew had died...and the next day, so had JM.

Tears burned the back of her eyes. Her throat constricted. Her chest labored to breathe. She scrunched her body in a tighter curl.

She'd never hear JM say her name again, never feel his warm hand on her shoulder, never see that twinkle in his eye. She'd never again talk with him or ask him the thousand questions she'd yet to think of about running PRC. She'd never again be able to tell him she loved him.

Or ask him why he had done this to her.

To hurt her? Her grandfather had never been cruel in his life.

To teach her a lesson? For the life of her she couldn't understand what he wanted her to learn.

To break her spirit? Because that's what it was doing.

This was her wedding night. And circumstances had made it one of the saddest nights among several in her young life.

She hadn't meant to cry again. She hadn't meant to sob. She hadn't meant to feel sorry for herself. But she no longer had the fortitude to fight the loneliness and stubborn ache that continued to dog her since the funeral. She turned her face into the softness of the musty pillow and, with the escape of one muffled sob, she lost the struggle.

Ty heard the first garbled choke and prayed it wasn't what he thought. But stifled as the sound was, he knew his prayer wasn't going to be answered.

Mandy was crying.

On their wedding night.

Even if this was a sham of a marriage, each sob felt like a knife was being plunged through his gut. He was at least partially to blame, if for nothing else than being a tool in JM's crazy proposition and convincing her to go through with it.

Why had JM wanted this for either of them? That question just wouldn't be answered by any logic he could come up with.

He could tell by the dampened bursts of sound she was trying to stop the waterworks, trying to conceal them. It hit him that Mandy had hardly had time to breathe these last few days, much less grieve. And here she was staying in her grandfather's house, knowing she'd agreed to this marriage in part to keep it in the family. The memories alone had to be tough.

He counted the seconds as the muted sobs continued. He didn't get past sixty before he was out of bed, the breeze from the open window nipping at his skin as he padded the short distance to where she lay.

Taking a deep breath, he squatted on the edge of the mattress, glad the lack of light would conceal his state of undress. And the degree of his arousal. Her rose-tinged scent surrounded him.

She didn't move as he slid down next to her, spooning against her back with only the coverlet separating them. He shifted his hips so his hardened flesh wouldn't touch her. Despite everything tonight, he hadn't yet been able to tame his lust for her. The need was so strong he wasn't sure even her tears could do the trick.

He struggled for something to say that would provide comfort, but nothing profound came to him. "I'm sure this is rough for you." She didn't move a muscle as he wrapped an arm around her, careful to aim for the safe territory of her waist. She didn't answer. Only a strangled sob.

"You don't have to hide your tears from me, Mandy. You're entitled. God knows you've got enough to cry about."

He tugged her, pulling her around to face him. She didn't resist but buried her damp face in the bare flesh of his shoulder and wept.

He hugged her to him, mindful not to spook her by pulling her too close to certain parts of his body and grateful for even the thin shield the cover afforded.

"Let it out, honey. You're safe."

He felt the tremors as the sobs broke, as the tears wet his chest, as her moist breath teased his skin.

This was no time to come on to a woman, and yet, his body wasn't listening. Holding her close in his arms under the cloak of darkness in the bed's narrow confines had his veins thrumming and his blood hot. He couldn't help but note they fit damn well together.

He felt undone as Mandy tearfully quivered in his arms. He was in uncharted waters, for sure. He'd never held a crying woman. His mother had cried a lot before she'd gone to the hospital, never to return. He'd only been ten at the time, hadn't understood the reasons, and in all his father's remaining years, he hadn't enlightened Ty beyond saying his mother had been ill.

John Martin hadn't been a very open man. He'd kept things in, didn't show much emotion. Ty never could tell what the man was thinking, and the man never said.

Ty had a good idea what Mandy was thinking. That she should have never agreed to this arrangement. That she missed her grandfather. That Ty wasn't the man she wanted to marry, even if it was for six months. That she wanted her company back.

He wished he could convince her it would be worth it in the end. She wouldn't believe him, but as much as he had his own agenda for being there, it wasn't to hurt Mandy. Business-wise, he intended to leave the Prescott family finances in a strong position, whether from the proceeds of a sale or the income from an agreement with the AFBR and a stream of rodeo contracts. He was committed to making that happen for JM and for Mandy. And maybe in the process he could prove to Mandy he wasn't quite the bastard she thought he was. Maybe they could enjoy each other during this time. Leave as friends instead of enemies, laugh about having been married to each other "back in the day."

And maybe, just maybe, he'd find what he was looking for in life. Work that made him feel like a man instead of a corporate shill, and a place where he felt he belonged in this world, even if he had to engineer it himself.

"It's going to all work out," he said, brushing his lips against her hair. She had beautiful hair, full and luscious. Tawny bronze strands that shimmered in the moonlight.

Her breath shuddered as if in answer. The sobs

had eased some, alternating with short intervals of silence.

Her moist breath puffed against the sensitive skin on his collarbone, as if she was feathering delicate little kisses there. Lust wound tighter inside of him, like a hair-triggered coil.

The temptation to slide his hands under her breasts and touch the soft mounds pressed seductively against his bare skin intensified, along with the rose scent that drifted off her hair to tease his senses. Heaven help him. He was in sexual hell.

How long he held her he couldn't say. But sometime later, his body tight with unquenched need, he felt her relax in his arms. Her breathing slowed, coming in calm beats. He leaned back to view her face.

With her eyes closed, thick lashes feathered the high bones of her cheeks. She looked at peace as she slept in his arms, almost content. Whatever storm had racked through her, its effect had been dissipated, any signs erased. Her cheeks were no longer tear stained, her mouth was lax, and her body no longer trembled.

Instinctively he pressed his lips to her forehead, a kiss of affection for a woman who deserved some tenderness in her life. Something told him she hadn't had much. At least not from the men who counted. Her father had died a decade ago, and her grandfather, though a sterling man in many ways, valued being tough, not tender. Ty guessed he fell into that mold, but having been raised with those same values, he understood, perhaps more than most, the emptiness that came with it.

Gently he settled her head on the pillow and slid his arm out from under her. In her sleep, she curled up tighter, but her even breathing confirmed she had not awakened.

He slipped away to the cool sheets of his own bed. How was he going to last the week, much less six months, sleeping in separate beds?

* * *

"Did Ty say where he was going, Mrs. Jenkins?" Mandy asked the stout, salt-and-peppered-haired woman. Mandy slipped into a hardwood chair at the kitchen table, where a plate of freshly made pancakes waited.

The kitchen had always been sunny and welcoming. Not as modern as her mother's but not yet dated. The counters were granite, the appliances were white to match the white cabinets, and the floor was a white tile made to look like marble. The walls were painted a soft blue, and the bowl that always sat on the kitchen table, filled with fruit, matched the blue of the walls. Though the will said it was now her house, it would be a while before she felt like changing much.

This morning she'd awoken to an empty bedroom with two packed suitcases, and for a moment she didn't know where she was. Then it had come rushing back. She'd spent the night wrapped in Ty's arms and exhausted herself, crying like some overwrought woman who couldn't control her emotions. She didn't even want to guess what Ty thought of her. She knew her grandfather would have expected her to buck up, as he had when her father had died. She'd apparently disappointed him on many levels.

"Only that he'd be back at ten sharp to pick you

up," Mrs. Jenkins answered, turning around from the sink, where she had been cleaning a pan. She raised her gray eyebrows, obviously as curious as Mandy was. "He also said I could stay on at the same wages." Her tone held a question.

"We both would like that. Like JM, we'll be on the road so much that having someone keep up the house would be a godsend."

Relief flooded the woman's brown eyes. "I would like that. I feel so bad about your grandfather. Just six weeks ago…you wouldn't have thought."

"No one did."

"Your marriage…did he know?"

Everyone in Mandy's world must have been wondering what the heck was going on, and Mrs. Jenkins most of all if she had noticed which guestroom had been used.

"It was one of his dying wishes that Ty and I get married and…well, we've known each other a long time and figured, why not?" It sounded so lame, but at least she hadn't lied—just left out a lot.

Mrs. Jenkins turned around and began scrubbing the pan. "Oh. Well. I hope you two will be very happy." The woman couldn't even make eye contact with Mandy. "Over the next few days, I'm going to help your mother pack up your grandfather's personal things so you and Mr. Martin can settle in."

Of course, her mother would think of that. She should offer to help, but with everything going on, she could not deal with sorting through her grandfather's treasures. Last night had shown her that. It was enough she was living in his house where his presence filled every nook and cranny.

A glance at the clock said she only had twenty minutes to eat and get ready. She'd already showered, dressed in a denim skirt, cowgirl boots, and a pink cotton blouse, and looked over the names of the livestock to be pulled for the Washington rodeo. It was a small rodeo, one Prescott had been putting on for years, and one her crew could handle alone, so no fears of running into Stan Lassiter at least.

Gobbling down the syrupy sweet pancake, she chased it with a cup of strong coffee. "Thank you so much for the breakfast," Mandy said as she rose from the table and placed her dishes in the dishwasher. "We'll be back Friday evening and then heading out again early Saturday. So don't worry about us for meals." Mrs. Jenkins only worked Monday through Friday, seven to three, which allowed her to watch her grandchildren after school and have her weekends free. It was an arrangement that had worked well for her grandfather and, Mandy imagined, it would work just as well for her and Ty, if Mandy could handle living in her grandfather's house. "By the way, we slept in the guest room with the twin beds. I made the beds, and since we were only in there for one night, no reason to change the sheets."

Mrs. Jenkins eyes widened and her mouth gaped into an *O*.

Mandy hoped she hadn't blushed as she brushed past Mrs. Jenkins and out of the kitchen.

Chapter 8

Strapped into the plane's passenger seat, Mandy forced herself to breathe as engines roared to life. It wasn't just the thought of taking off in this slip of a plane that had her frozen where she sat, but the whole fiasco of the previous night.

What had surprised her was the tenderness Ty had shown. Holding her, whispering soothing words to calm her. She hadn't been emotionally stable enough to be embarrassed—only comforted. So comforted she'd fallen asleep in those protective arms of his. The thought he might have held her all night against his hard body brought a flush of heat.

She glanced over at Ty. He was concentrating on the gauge-filled dashboard, his arm muscles flexing as he maneuvered levers. Capable, competent, commanding—those adjectives described the man to a *T*.

"Ready?" Ty's smile was encouraging as the roar of the engines filled the air. When he smiled like that, broad, full, and opened mouth, the hard lines of his face softened, his eyes twinkled, and he looked almost boyish, like a kid with a new toy he wanted to show off.

She nodded and prayed she didn't look as nervous as she felt. Her grandfather had dumped her fate into this man's hands. She couldn't look weak again. She'd cried last night, and now if she showed her anxiety about flying, how could she hope he would see her as tough enough to run Prescott? It was humiliating to be so beholden to one person's opinion, and not just any person but the man who had broken her schoolgirl heart, manipulated her grandfather, and took the place, as head of the company, that rightfully belonged to her. And just happened to be her husband.

With a nod, Ty turned his attention to the dashboard and the blue sky beyond while Mandy closed her eyes, gripped the seat's arms, and held on as the plane rumbled down the runway.

She silently counted.

When she reached twenty, the plane picked up speed, but no lift off. Twenty-five, the plane rumbled faster but still no lift off. She braced. Finally, at twenty-nine she felt the blip in her stomach as they left the ground. Teeth clenched, heart racing, she willed herself to relax, starting with her face, then her arms, then her hands…

"We're up." Ty's tone held amusement.

Who was she fooling? Certainly not him. She opened one eye. Blue sky stretched out in front of her. She opened the other eye. They certainly were up. High. But the ride had become surprisingly smooth.

"Not so bad, right?" Ty seemed eager for her agreement.

"Not so bad," she lied. But they had a few hours to go and a landing to get through. She couldn't think about that or she might start panicking, and then what? Breathe.

"We don't have to stay there."

"Where?"

"At the ranch house. I haven't given up my room at the hotel in town yet. We could stay there instead, if it's too much for you. My Denver condo being on the market, that's all I have to offer. But at least it's not too far from the ranch."

Ty had put his condo on the market? Guess he must have done that before learning he'd only be at Prescott for six months.

Still, what should she say to his offer? She didn't want to stay at her grandfather's. Last night had proven she wasn't emotionally ready to do that. Yet admitting she couldn't handle it would be admitting weakness. She'd dealt with living in her parents' house without her father, hadn't she? But then it had been a sanctuary where she and her mother and Tucker could grieve in private, away from her grandfather, who had been the model of stoicism in the wake of his only child's death.

"It's not too much for me. I can handle it." She would handle it.

"It would be easier for me, if you wouldn't mind. They have a workout room there."

Ah, it wasn't for her he was doing it, but for himself. Things made sense again.

"Well, if you'd prefer."

"As long as it's okay with you."

"It's okay with me." A relief actually. "What about Mrs. Jenkins? She expects to be kept on."

"Keep her on until we know what's going to happen. The place still needs looking after."

She nodded her agreement. It was settled then. She relaxed—well, as much as she could relax given she was thousands of feet in the air.

Chimes to the tune of Trace Adkins's "Honky Tonk Badonkadonk" rang through the whirring din of the plane.

Ty cursed as he fished a cell phone out of an open compartment in the console.

"See who this is," he said, holding the phone out to her.

Mandy touched the screen until she viewed the message. "It's a text. From a Kendall? Asking why you haven't called." It ended with a <3, and the avatar showed the top half of a shapely and well-endowed blonde in a skimpy bikini. Mandy felt betrayed. But that was just silly. Foolish. But oddly true.

Intellectually, she knew this marriage was a sham with a husband she would have never chosen. Never. But that hadn't stopped the rush of anger. Odd.

Ty mumbled a soft curse, barely audible over the engines. "Text her that I'm flying and will call her when I land."

"Somehow I don't like the idea of texting my *husband's* girlfriend." She wished it hadn't come out so snarky, but there it was.

Ty glanced at her, a smirk on his face. "Jealous, wife? I did have a life before Tuesday. One with a few loose ends to tie up, is all."

She hadn't really thought about his personal life. And what he was giving up. She glanced again at the bikini blonde, definitely a different size than Mandy. More like a whole different category. Enough to make any woman who didn't wear size double Ds feel inadequate. And so like the women she'd seen him with over the years. Mandy began to type the message. "Should I say 'we land' or 'I land.'"

Ty huffed. "I land, if you wouldn't mind."

"She doesn't know about me, does she?"

"Not yet."

"Will she?"

He looked over at her, his brown eyes assessing. "We didn't talk about other relationships, but I'm willing to keep our vows for the six month duration of the marriage. If you are. I think that would be in keeping with JM's wishes. And the promise we made. Promises should mean something."

Like until death do us part?

She hadn't really thought ahead to the prospect of other men in her life, considering her relationship with Mitch Lockhart had ended. But of course, someone like Ty probably had more than one relationship to tie up. And she certainly didn't want any more gossip than this quickie marriage would already engender.

"I agree."

She ended the message with a period—no heart, thank you very much—hit the Send key, and then dropped the cell phone back into its cubby before she was tempted to press the Contact icon to see who else constituted "loose ends." He probably had similar pictures of the others. She suddenly felt out of sorts. Miffed. Annoyed. Which was just plain ridiculous, but…

"Is that your type?" she blurted out.

"What do you mean?" Ty shifted in his seat. With his aviator sunglasses hiding his eyes, she couldn't gauge his response, but she guessed this was not a topic the private Ty wanted to talk about. Too bad.

"The well-endowed piece of eye candy clad in the tiniest bikini in the picture on your phone." Mandy crossed her arms over her chest. Why was she surprised that Ty was like every other man when it came to women—superficial. Why should she have expected anything more?

"Her name is Kendall. And she loaded that picture on there."

"Is *Kendall* your type?"

"Is Mitch Lockhart your type?"

"I asked first."

"I dated her, so, yes, I guess she is my type. For a date."

"And for a wife?"

He twisted his head in her direction for a quick puzzled glance. "I wasn't in the market for a wife."

"Just a trophy girlfriend."

"What the hell is a trophy girlfriend?" Just as quickly, he returned his attention to the cloud-dotted blue horizon.

"Someone who looks good on your arm and in your bed. Not someone you have a deep conversation with or who necessarily shares your values or who you want raising your kids. You know, someone built for sex, but not much more."

"Your claws are out, Mandy. Don't tell me you really are jealous?"

Were his lips crooking up in a smile?

Like she'd be jealous of any woman Ty went out with. She had no cause to feel one prick of jealousy. At least, she shouldn't. She was trying to make a point, however, for all sensible, smart women. That there should be more to a relationship than just sex.

The irony of her own relationship with Mitch was not lost on her.

"Hardly. But do you even know her values, Ty? What does she want to do with her life? What does she feel is a woman's role in the world?"

His jaw bunched. "I don't know. But I don't know the answers for you either, and I married you."

"Very funny. Just so you know, I want to run Prescott Rodeo Company, marry, and raise my children to be good upstanding and productive citizens. And I believe a woman's role in this life is the same as a man's—to leave the world a better place than she found it—for as many people whose lives she can affect. So what does Kendall care about?"

Okay, so he didn't know what Kendall's "values" were. And yes, he'd dated her mainly because she charged his jets. But that's all Ty was looking for.

Mandy also charged his jets. More than Kendall. Much more. To his way of thinking, her curves were far more alluring—and dangerous. He liked her frankness, admired her integrity. But she was a lot more work, heaven help him. She challenged him, made him uncomfortable for reasons he'd yet to understand. He hadn't wanted to marry either woman.

So how the hell had he ended up married to the one he hadn't slept with?

"She met my requirements, Mandy."

"For a trophy. I understand, Ty. I really do."

Her smugness was damn irritating. "And Mitch?"

He heard her draw a deep breath before she answered.

"I'm not sure why you keep bringing up Mitch, especially since we are no longer a couple, unlike you and Kendall—"

"I said I'll fix that."

"But to answer your question, his goal is to get to the National Rodeo Finals. He doesn't want to be tied down with a wife and kids, and he believes a guy's role in life is to have as much fun as he can for as long as he can before he gets lassoed by some woman. Except for wanting to be in the NRF, I'd say you two had a lot in common."

She shot him a self-satisfied smile, but her leg jiggled. The woman could be goddamn infuriating. And Mitch sounded like a saddle bum. How could she compare Ty to him?

"What's this really about, Mandy? I didn't initiate the contact with Kendall. Yet you seem intent on making me pay for her contacting me."

She scrunched down in her seat as if she could hide that tall, nicely curved body of hers, and her brows knit together in a frown. "Are you sure you can break it off with her? I mean, you guys obviously have been going out, and this, this marriage is a little hard to explain."

"I won't have any problem breaking things off with Kendall." Or the three other women he dated when he was in their city. It was only six months anyway. He'd never admit it to Mandy, but she was right. They were trophy girlfriends. Though he doubted they would appreciate that description.

He'd intended to call the women and tell them he'd be involved in a business deal for the next six months. It wasn't exactly a lie, just not the whole truth. He wasn't dating any of the women with an eye on the future. If they didn't want to wait, he'd no doubt find other willing females when the time came. Somehow that thought wasn't as comforting as it should have been.

"So can I assume you won't be seeing Mitch, or anyone else, either?"

He knew little about the tie-down roper except JM hadn't thought much of him. And the guy hadn't won much, according to the Professional Rodeo Rider Association site he'd checked. Yet it was probable they would run into him on the circuit.

"I said I won't, and I won't." She lifted her chin up as if daring him to say otherwise.

Feisty woman. But he believed her. One thing he'd noted right off about Mandy. She didn't fabricate. She came right out and told you what she thought, whether you liked it or not, whether you wanted to hear it or not.

"You want children?" That was one thing he hadn't expected her to say. Or that she wanted a man in her life. She was an independent sort, like him, and she'd certainly given him the impression she liked it that way. Domesticity and Mandy was a new thought.

"What?"

"You said you wanted to marry and have children."

She stared at him like he'd grown another head. Seemed like a reasonable question to ask one's wife.

"Of course I want children."

"I thought you just wanted to run Prescott."

Her brows drew even closer together. "If a man said he wanted to run a company, would people think he didn't want to have children as a result?"

The tone of her voice had changed to a higher, louder pitch. He'd ticked her off. He hadn't meant to. "You're right. I shouldn't have asked."

"You shouldn't have been surprised." She had a

point. "How about you? You want to become a dad anytime soon?"

His first impulse was to say no. But lately, since JM had gotten sick, he'd been thinking about kids. Having them. Raising them. Maybe. But if he did, he'd have to think about settling down and getting a wife. And he hadn't met a woman yet who seemed a good fit. They all seemed to care a lot about looking good and not much about doing good.

"Maybe."

"Now I'm surprised. You don't seem like the family-man type. I had you pegged for a confirmed bachelor."

He stiffened at her verdict. It was hard to hear that judgment from someone else, even if he'd said it about himself many times. He really didn't have a clue how to be a father. A good father. He'd been on his own too long. But people change. Could happen to him. Maybe.

"Seems we are both into stereotyping people. But it's not worth arguing about, since whether we want kids or not isn't going to affect this marriage." But it was a provocative thought. Making a baby. With Mandy.

She nodded her agreement and turned her face toward the window.

She seemed more relaxed now than when they took off, when he was afraid she was going into panic mode, with her eyes clamped shut and all the deep breathing she'd been doing.

In profile, her patrician features were highlighted, like those high cheekbones, that straight nose. And then there was all that wavy hair spilling over her shoulders and down her back. She'd have beautiful children for sure.

"So that leaves just us, right now, this moment. And I say we make the best of this situation and enjoy the time together irrespective of the decisions with the business. I promise it will be enjoyable, Mandy."

She didn't respond. Instead, she kept her head turned toward the window.

Well, she might be able to avoid the topic, but she couldn't avoid the nights.

Chapter 9

"Ben."

Ty watched Mandy enthusiastically greet the middle-aged cowman who rose from behind his desk as they entered the small, paper-cluttered office in the back of the Abilene rodeo fairgrounds. The two exchanged hugs, and Mandy went right to work, asking after wife and kids and the cattle business as well as talking about the heat already roasting Abilene.

Ty waited for his introduction, feeling an unaccustomed awkwardness. He'd donned a white shirt and black jacket for this meeting, but he would have been right at home if he'd worn the T-shirt. Ben was dressed liked he'd just stepped off the ranch, in denims, a plaid shirt, and dusty cowboy boots.

"Ben Cornwall, I'd like you to meet Prescott's newest partner, Ty Martin. He's helping Prescott through this transition period."

The introduction was smooth, even if she failed to mention that Ty was running the company. And her husband.

She seemed comfortable in this ambassador role, strengthening connections with people she'd obviously known most of her life. Ty shook the committeeman's firm and work-roughened hand.

Ben gave Ty the once-over, like Ty was some heifer he was interested in buying but unsure of the price.

"You a stockman, are you?" Ben said, his hands now on his hips. The older man wasn't being unfriendly, just curious—at least, that's how Ty was going to take it.

"No. Harold Prescott is the stockman, and a better one you won't find. I'm a businessman who owes my success to J. M. Prescott's belief in me. I've stepped in to fill the gap created by his passing in order to help Mandy out. She's the one who will make sure the rodeo will live up to Prescott standards."

Ben kept his focus on Ty. "Being our event is at the end of the season, we've struggled to attract top talent. So naturally, we've had some concern about assuring a quality show now that JM is no longer at the helm." He shifted his gaze to Mandy. "It's a lot to take on if you don't have the experience."

"It is," Mandy responded, standing tall and taking the man's skepticism without flinching.

"But Prescott Rodeo Company is more than just one man, Ben," Mandy continued. "It's a family. JM made sure of that. As such, the Prescott family is as committed as ever to providing our rodeo councils the highest quality event with the best broncs and bulls. I feel fortunate JM started grooming me a decade ago. He understood he wasn't going to live forever."

Ben shook his head. "Geez, last year I'd hardly have guessed he was feeling poorly."

Mandy's throat moved in a hard swallow. "Neither did he. By the time they diagnosed it, it was too late."

Ben nodded, probably having heard that scenario far too often. "Tucker not interested?"

Ben didn't appear to notice, but Mandy stiffened. "He likes to ride 'em, not run 'em, but he's part owner. This is a family affair, as I said," she answered, gilding the truth a bit. "I didn't mention that Ty is not only a business partner but my husband."

If she fumbled those last two words, Ty could sympathize. It sounded strange to him too. He knew she'd emphasized family to stress continuity, and she'd only reluctantly included him to make that point.

Ben looked from one to the other as if trying to gauge the truth, and he blew out a breath. "Well, congratulations, you two." Ben waved a hand toward the office doorway. "Let's have a walk around outside and see if we can't find Lyle Thorton. You remember Lyle, Mandy."

"He still in charge of the volunteers?" Mandy asked, turning toward the door.

Ben nodded as he grabbed his cowboy hat from atop a pile of papers. "It'll give me a chance to show you around, Ty, even though there isn't much going on just yet. We only have a senior team roping competition scheduled in the outdoor arena for this weekend, but in another six weeks the place will be jumping with the volunteers getting things spruced up for the fair and rodeo."

As they filed out of the office, Ty reached for Mandy's hand. Her puzzled eyes rose to meet his. Well, he guessed if they were newly married, they should act like it.

Her skin was smooth and warm, and he brushed his thumb along the back of her hand. As she didn't pull her hand away, he added a little pressure to let her know he was there, with her, walking by her side. She turned her head toward him and frowned. He smiled back.

There was still tonight and one hundred and seventy-nine other nights ahead of them.

The sun was bright as they followed Ben, strolling hand in hand, across a parking lot toward what looked to be an open-sided arena. She matched his stride, and to anyone looking, they must have seemed a happily married couple.

It felt surprisingly comfortable having her small, slender hand in his, as if he belonged to someone, belonged to something. Not a familiar feeling. And one he wasn't sure he could get used to.

"This complex covers a hundred and twenty acres," Ben noted as they stopped at the entrance to the arena.

Ty scanned the impressive amount of buildings dotting the landscape. As a developer, he could appreciate the extent of the investment the county had made.

"This where the rodeo will be held?" Ty asked, turning his attention back to the empty seats that ringed about a thirty-foot show area as a hot breeze blew off the asphalt of the parking lot.

Ben shook his head. "This is our outdoor arena. Only holds two thousand. We use this for smaller attendance events like the senior team roping, but I thought Lyle might be hereabouts."

Just then a tall, thin, balding man rounded the corner.

"Thought I saw you crossing the lot," Lyle said as he drew closer.

"Lyle." Mandy said, tugging her hand from Ty's. He reluctantly released his grasp, and Mandy stepped forward to shake the elder man's hand. "How's Cora doing? Last I heard, she was laid up with arthritis after visiting the Houston Stock Show."

"That she was, but she's better now. Sorry to hear about JM, Mandy." Lyle's eyes scrunched up like he was blinking back tears as he removed his weathered hat.

"Thanks. We got the flowers, and they were beautiful." Mandy gave the old man a gentle hug. "I need to introduce you to our new partner. And my husband. He was also a good friend of JM's. Lyle Thornton, Ty Martin."

Ty shook the thin man's bony but sturdy hand.

"Ty here is new to Prescott, so I thought I'd show him around a bit," Ben explained. "Was going to take him to the barn next."

Lyle nodded and led the way with a rocking gait, across a paved sidewalk and toward one of the large buildings. Mandy had abandoned Ty to walk by Lyle's side, doing her best, no doubt, to solidify a connection.

Ben and Ty trailed behind. "The county fair goes for ten days, and the rodeo, which we are in charge of, runs from Tuesday to Sunday. It's a big event in these parts." Ben seemed eager to impress, and Ty took that as a good sign.

The barn was large and long. Stall after stall lined the linear building, and they all looked well used with scratched wood and stained concrete attesting to the number of horses that had been housed over the years.

"You have, what, about a hundred and thirty stalls in here, Ben?" Mandy asked.

"That's right." Ben smiled as if pleased she'd

remembered. "They're looking to upgrade the stalls this coming year, and it's about time. There are also plans for a new arena for the rodeo and cutting horse events located closer to the barn. We think that will keep attendance up."

"They don't like hauling in dirt to the coliseum, I'm guessing."

Ben raised his eyebrows. "That's right."

"Through here," Mandy said, waving a hand toward a large exit in the middle of the rows of stalls, "you can get to the cattle pens. As I recall, they can hold about a thousand head of cattle in those pens. More than enough for the bulls and steers we bring in for the events."

Ty took a gander at the maze of metal railings. "Was this all built by the county?"

"In the seventies," Ben said. "It's in need of a facelift now. The plan is to renovate the barns, build an arena dedicated to equestrian events, and upgrade the offices and restrooms. Still serves its purpose though. Let me show you the coliseum where the rodeo is held, at least for now."

"What are you looking at cost-wise for the renovation?" Ty asked as they walked out of the barn. He couldn't help the developer in him.

"About twenty million."

Sounded right.

Within minutes they were entering a huge concrete building. The air-conditioning felt good after the outside heat. The foursome wound their way along back corridors until they stood where the barrel racers would enter.

Looking across the arena and up at the stands, the

coliseum seemed sizeable. Ben pointed out where the pens would go and explained the need to haul in dirt. "It will be much easier if we get our own venue on these grounds. We need to have good attendance this season to prove it's worth the investment. That's why, more than ever, we need a top-notch rodeo supplier this year."

"You have five thousand seats to fill, and we're here to fill them," Mandy said and launched into her plans for the upcoming rodeo with unbridled enthusiasm, as if Abilene was the only rodeo that mattered. Ben and Lyle gave Mandy their full attention, and Ty knew the worst was over when the talk turned to *how* to make Abilene's rodeo a good one rather than whether Prescott would be running it again.

Her red lips moved with excitement, snagging his attention, as did the shiny mane of hair she flipped more than once. He'd like to kiss those lips again, run his fingers through all that hair. He'd like to feel her explode as he made love to her.

Holding her last night had been hell. Tonight, alone in the hotel room, he planned to hold her with a specific endpoint in mind.

He was not a patient man, and he'd no intention of allowing Mandy to drag out the inevitable. She may think she had the upper hand, but it had been ten years since he'd had an opportunity to play his hand. He wasn't one to miss an opportunity.

He shifted his thoughts to the two men, whose narrowed-eyed focus was on Mandy. She'd done a good job reconnecting with the two wranglers. She was definitely a people person with a knack for putting them at ease. Ty usually took a different tack in his business, making people uncomfortable. It worked in contentious land negotiations, but he sensed it wouldn't work here, where trust and familiarity were necessary ingredients.

Mandy had also impressed him, and by the interest the two rodeo men where showing, impressed Lyle and Ben as well, with her knowledge, not only of Prescott but of the Abilene rodeo venue and what would be needed to put on a successful rodeo.

He had to admit that her brand of sales was working. She seemed a natural. Like this was her calling. And he might have to pull it away from her. Seeing her in action, being with her, the responsibility sat heavier now than just a few days ago.

Ty waited until Mandy finished discussing the number of broncs and bulls needed, the number of steers required, the announcer and bullfighters to be used, and the parade details before he brought up next year's rodeo.

"We're here to assure you of our commitment to the Abilene rodeo in case you had any doubts, given the circumstances. What we'd like to know is, if we meet your expectations this year, can we count on doing Abilene next year as well?"

Lyle eyed Ben, leading Ty to believe they'd talked about next year already. Mandy looked at Ty with surprise. Hadn't she ever heard of a presumptive sale's close?

Ben's gaze swung between Mandy and Ty. "I won't lie. There's been others here already, sensing an opportunity."

"Can I ask what you told them?"

"Told them we'd think about it. You keeping the rates per animal the same?"

Ty did a quick mental calculation. If others were looking to take business, would they have offered less or equal, given the fact they thought Prescott was vulnerable? Especially if that someone was Stan Lassiter.

"Yes," Mandy answered before Ty could open his mouth.

Ben still didn't look convinced enough to give the affirmative answer Ty was looking for. They needed something more.

"We'll keep the same rate—and let you name a bull and bronc you'd especially want in the mix." He hadn't discussed this "sweetener" with Mandy because it had just come to him, but it was a winning idea.

Ben stared at him from under the brim of his hat. "Even if it had gone to the NRF?"

Out of the corner of his eye, he saw Mandy cross her arms, and the frown she wore didn't look all that agreeable.

"Yes," he said. It wouldn't cost Prescott any more, but from his meeting with Guy in Colorado, he'd learned it meant a lot to a rodeo.

Generally, a stock company could charge more for NRF-caliber horses and bulls than other equally good stock because of the fame of the animal. Not every rodeo could afford the headliners, but that didn't mean they didn't get good stock for their dollars. However, a legendary horse or bull would pull the top cowboys to compete, and that, in turn, would draw more people to the event.

"You've got yourself a deal." Ben offered his hand. Ty shook it. So did Mandy.

In Texas, Ty knew a man's word was as good as a contract. They'd saved Abilene.

* * *

After the meeting with Ben and Lyle, Ty had begged off, allegedly to buy some new boots more suited to rodeo work than to "squiring around a pretty woman," as he had put it, and Mandy decided she might as well get a manicure and chill. Ty had overstepped his bounds by offering that sweetener without consulting her, even if it did secure the business. It was a bitter taste of what having Ty as a partner would be like.

The manicure had stretched into a shopping trip for yet another pair of boots for herself—embossed tan leather, brown insets, and gold studs. Before she knew it, dinnertime was almost upon her, and she hurried back to the hotel room. She fumbled in her purse for the key card to no avail. She knocked on the door. No answer.

Apparently, she had beaten Ty back to the room. That suited her. She'd take advantage of his absence by enjoying a nice long, hot shower, if she could just find her key. She dug some more until she decided to check the zippered outer pocket. Success. She slid the key card into the slot, pushed on the handle, and opened the door.

She stepped inside, her purse and shopping bag swinging on her arm. No sign of Ty. Beds were made, suitcases and closet door closed. She strolled further into the room, spying a new pair of men's black boots by the bed. He'd gone for barn boots, an interesting choice for a man who always looked like he'd stepped out of an issue of GQ. She noted he had rather large feet and couldn't help wondering what else might be large.

A door clicked behind her. Whirling around she came face to...face with a gloriously naked Ty. She dropped the purse and shopping bag with a thud.

Bare chest, bulging biceps, and spectacular abs begged for her notice, but it was the large object dangling between his legs that captured her attention. And held it.

My god, he was hung. Beautifully, generously. Her heart hammered against her chest. Her palms leaked sweat. The back of her neck tingled.

She had no idea how long she stared. Just stared. Unabashedly stared. And maybe even drooled. She couldn't tell.

She forced herself to look up, following the thin line of hair that ran from his navel up his finely sculpted chest, to those broad shoulders and thick neck, up to the chiseled jaw and lips cracked in a cocky smile, until her gaze landed on a pair of fine dark eyes dancing with amusement.

"Like what you see, Mrs. Martin?" he drawled.

Holy crap.

She swallowed the saliva that had condensed in her mouth. "What are you doing? Where are your clothes?"

"In the suitcase, which I was coming out to get. I took a shower."

Gathering her splintered senses together, she found the discipline to turn around and face the wall. "Put some clothes on," she demanded.

"Sight too much for you, darling?" he chuckled.

Steam rose inside her as if her heated blood was letting off vapors. She heard hard footfalls as he moved toward her. Please put clothes on before she jumped his bones like her pitiful body was exhorting her to do with each breath she took.

"You should have knocked," she blurted out.

He chuckled again. "To come out of the bathroom?" She heard the click of the suitcase.

She waited, exercising all the control she could muster to keep from turning around and having another peek. The man was magnificent, and she was having a hard time fighting biology. She bit her lip in order to feel something other than lust.

She heard the snap of a waistband.

"You can turn around now. It's covered. But I'm pretty sure you've seen one before."

But never, ever like his.

She whirled around. He wore black boxer briefs that outlined the prominent ridge that had held her captive just moments before. Control. She had to exercise control. Get mad. Think about today and how he'd usurped her.

"Only fair since you've seen me that I see you. We could take a shower together. I don't mind going twice," Ty offered. He'd seen her checking him out. Maybe he was closer to sealing the deal than he'd imagined.

"In your dreams," she said, but her voice had a funny little quiver in it. "We need to talk."

"About what?" He pulled out a shirt from the suitcase he'd propped on one of the queen-sized beds. Ty thought he had reserved a king bed for their stay, but someone, apparently, had called after him to reserve a two-bed guest room in Mandy's name.

"You should have at least consulted me before

offering that option of choosing whatever livestock they wanted." Mandy threw the purse and shopping bag on the opposite bed. "We can't go offering that to everyone, or our premier horses and bulls get exhausted."

"It was only one horse and one bull. I thought it was a great idea. So did Ben." He sat down on the other bed and began to slip on the shirt, buttons open. With hands on hips and fire in her eye, Mandy stood there looking madder than one of her bucking horses, and all he could think about was stripping her naked and kissing her all over. Damn. They needed to work this out soon. He'd no intention of spending six months in frustration hell.

"That's not the point. It's how you did it. Without discussing it with anyone. Without the courtesy of discussing it with me." Her chest rose with a little huff. God, she was a well-built female. Built for loving.

"How could I consult you when I had just thought of it? You see, this is where you lose me. Good idea, good deal, problem solved. But here you are jawing about *how* it happened. Who cares?" He crossed his arms over his chest, feeling damn irritated—and horny.

Did she realize she'd worried her lip into a plump red treat he'd love to suck on? Did she know that standing there in those heeled cowgirl boots, legs spread apart in a gunfighter pose, had him imagining her in nothing else but those leather boots—and he meant nothing else.

"I care," she said, thumping her chest above her right breast. God, she had nice breasts. Round, perky, and more than palm sized.

Ty pulled a pair of pressed jeans from the suitcase and rose to step into them. "And the response to that is, why? We got what we came for. A commitment to Prescott for next year. What more do you want?" She wasn't happy, and for the life of him, he didn't know why. "You need to relax a little, Mandy." He shot her a smile. "I can definitely help with that."

She stomped her sexy booted foot. She always wore the most intriguing boots. "I want Ben and Lyle to take me seriously. To understand I'm capable of handling the rodeo." Her hand waved in the air. "You blurting out that idea made me irrelevant. How do you think it feels when people I've known all my life don't trust my abilities to deliver for them? If JM had made me the head of this company, I wouldn't have to play second fiddle."

Now she was getting him mad. Pretty as she was all riled up and passionate, he didn't cotton to people creating myths just because the truth was hard to hear. "JM knew what he was doing." Ignoring the sparks flashing out of her eyes, he continued as he tucked in and zipped up. "Like it or not, without me in that meeting, they wouldn't have felt reassured you could deliver this time, much less next time. Did you hear them ask after Tucker? They like you, Mandy, but they aren't sure about handing you the reins. At their rodeo, you're going to show them they're not risking anything by doing so. And JM knew having me along would give you that chance. This isn't about being competent. This is about trust."

She stared at him like he'd just slapped her. Probably felt like that.

Hell.

Ty sauntered forward. She just stood there,

blinking at him like she didn't want to believe what he said. But she had to know it was the truth. As he went to wrap his arms around her, she pushed her hands against his chest. He wrapped her in his embrace anyway, ignoring her weak attempt to stop him.

He held her, enjoying the feel of her curves against his hard edges, until he felt her body relax and give up the struggle.

"You were great in there today," he whispered against her ear. "You solidified a connection with those men that is going to last. They like you, honey. They just don't believe in you yet. You're something new, in a new role. They need time to figure you out, is all."

"You won't give me time," she said, her voice muffled and her breath warm against his shirt.

He looked down, and she lifted up her face. A mixture of vulnerability and hope stared back at him. He wished he could tell her he'd changed his mind. He hadn't. He'd made a promise. "This isn't personal, Mandy. You'll just have to trust that I'll keep the best interests of the company, of your family, in mind. JM trusted me. Why can't you?"

She pushed harder against him and wiggled to get free. No sense trying to make her listen. He let her loose, and she stepped back out of his embrace. God how he liked holding her. She fit him just fine. If only she'd give him a chance to show her just how fine.

"Because you gain more if you can sell PRC and convince Tuck to sell the land as well."

"It's true that I'd like a chance to develop that land, but only if it's because I can get you guys a fantastic offer. I swear I'm not the enemy." God how he wanted to kiss her. Kiss away those doubts.

"Could have fooled me," she said barely above a whisper, but loud enough for him to hear.

"Just give me a chance to prove it, Mandy. That's all I'm asking for is a chance."

He reached out and curved a finger under her chin, tilting it so her luscious mouth was in his line of sight. He'd need to get her to assess things with her head, not with her heart, before she'd trust him. But just how he was going to do that, he wasn't sure. He was sure, however, he wanted to taste her. And that heat coming from her eyes said she would let him.

Lowering his lips to hers, he covered her mouth and kissed her, long, deep, and full while his hands caressed her back, learning her curves and angles.

She returned the kiss, taking it even deeper, her tongue searching, reaching for his. God, she was a passionate woman. And there were two queen beds just waiting for them to try out—together.

Bringing his hand around, he cupped her breast through her clothes. Down soft, pliable, overflowing his palm, just as he had imagined. He began to slowly, gently knead. Her quick inhale told him all he needed to know.

He feathered kisses across her cheek, then nibbled on her ear lobe. She kissed his neck, and he felt it clear to his groin. Not to be outdone, he nuzzled the smooth silk of her throat, breathing in the sweet scent of roses, and sucked the tender area right above her collarbone as she moved her head to the side, giving him better access. All the time, he fondled her breast, covered by the fabric of her bra, with the tips of his fingers, caressing the generous swells with a gentle touch. She wasn't resisting at all. On the contrary, her eyes were closed, her lips parted.

Subtly, he slid his hips against her body, and his hard, thickened erection scraped her soft belly, sending bolts of lust and desire through him. He sure as hell hoped it was sending those same bolts through her.

"Combustible," he whispered in her ear.

Not willing to risk her refusal, he covered her mouth with his as he backed her up until the back of her legs hit the edge of the bed and she sat down on it with a plop, breaking the kiss. He moved to stand between her thighs and gazed down into green eyes wide and rounded with surprise, but not displeasure.

This was where he wanted her—in his bed. He'd waited years to finish what she'd started. And a hotel room in a strange city was as good a place as any.

"You are an incredible kisser," he said, meaning every word of it. Her legs opened so he could nestle between them. Gently he grasped her shoulders and eased her back upon the bed, relieved he didn't encounter any resistance as he covered her with his body.

Underneath him, she felt soft and supple, so at odds with the hard-shell image she tried to portray. He wanted to kiss her all over, wanted to run his tongue across her silky flesh, taste her—everywhere. He started with the soft skin of her throat, feathering little kisses as he glided his fingertips under the fabric of her top, inching it up.

"You're so soft." His heart pounded in synch with the throbbing in his pants. Sensing victory, his body clamored for more, but he had to take this slow, steady. He found her lips again and swirled his mouth over hers while his tongue pressed against the seam of her lips until she opened for him. She tasted like peppermint.

He increased the pressure as he slowly moved his

body against her, letting her feel how hard he was, how much he wanted her. Brushing his thumbs along the underwire of her bra, he found the clasp. Coaxing it open, the bra gave way, and his hand found the supple flesh of her breast as he kissed the soft spot at the base of her throat.

Sliding his lips down her neck, across her delicate collarbone, down to the berried nipple that begged for attention, he suckled. Hard. Firm.

She moaned, shifted, moaned again.

He switched to the other one, pulling the nipple between his lips until her hips bucked against him and he felt the jolt of lust grip his groin.

It had been a while since he'd undressed a woman when he hadn't been assured of the outcome. He reached for the buckle on her belt. His pulse quickened. Hot blood shot through him. She was gorgeous underneath those clothes. Perfectly proportioned, soft, and delicate. Bent upon his task, he hadn't noticed her knee until it bumped a sensitive area to turn pleasure into a blast of pain. What the...

He raised his head, perspiration trickling down his cheek. "What did you do that for?"

"Because we aren't doing it...that," she rasped out between heaving breaths. She shook her head so waves of hair swept over her bare breasts, providing a translucent curtain. Damn she was beautiful.

She pushed against his chest. "Get off me."

He dutifully rolled off her, and she jumped out of bed like he'd lit a fire under her. Maybe he had. Maybe she was running from something she was afraid she couldn't handle.

"I'm taking a shower," she said, her hand

clutching her shirt to her body. "And I'll be locking the door."

Mandy slumped against the bathroom door, her knees weak, her heart pounding. She'd almost caved, had been this close to losing control.

No, no, no. She whispered the word three times for emphasis. He wasn't to be trusted—not with her company and certainly not with her heart. Why he so easily flipped her switch she couldn't say, but it had been that way even ten years ago. Back then she'd been so sure he was the man her young heart desired. She'd told him the truth back then. She'd been a virgin and wanted him to be the first, thinking it would show him how much he meant to her.

Instead, he'd walked away, leaving her naked and abandoned. And made sure he was never alone with her the remaining few days before he returned to school. She'd pined after him the whole rest of the year, like a puppy waiting for its master's return. She'd sent him texts and e-mails, and got nothing in return. He hadn't wanted her, she realized—he'd wanted her grandfather and had used her to get to closer to JM.

His rejection had been cruel at a time when she had needed gentleness. And now, here she was, married to him. And still wanting him. Cool, objective, no-nonsense Ty Martin. And did she mention, sexy as hell? But if they ever made love, she knew she'd be setting herself up for a huge fall.

One hundred seventy-nine days to go. She feared she'd never make it without losing her mind. And maybe her heart.

Chapter 10

Abilene hadn't gone quite like Ty had expected on the personal front. Neither had Fort Worth, Houston, or Lubbock. He'd turned on the charm and let her know having sex with her was never far from his thoughts. And he'd come away empty.

Ty glanced over at Mandy, her face pressed to the plane's window as they headed back to Wyoming for a brief overnight to get a change of clothes and check on things at the office before traveling to the Washington rodeo. At least she wasn't tense anymore about flying, after taking off and setting down a half-dozen times. Given what was up ahead, her newfound ease would be tested.

Gratefully, business matters had fared better. The rodeos in Fort Worth and Houston had confirmed they'd keep their agreements with Prescott, and as two of the biggest rodeos around, that meant a lot going forward. Of course, since those rodeos used several stock contractors, given their size and length, they had less risk in doing so. Lubbock was the outlier. Stan Lassiter had convinced managers there to give him a chance this year. The committee's letter asking to void their contract due to "changed circumstances" had been on its way to Prescott's offices before Ty and Mandy had arrived in Lubbock. The committee had agreed, however, to give Prescott a shot at next year's contract if the contract included the sweetener Ty had given Abilene and there were no complaints from other rodeos over Prescott's performance this year. And this time, Mandy had offered the sweetener.

Ty had admired how she had handled the negotiations, needing little assistance from him. It was true Ty's presence had helped ease some tension from the traditionalists, but hardly reason enough for JM to turn so much control over to him. Made a guy wonder why JM had been so concerned about the business. Guess he was a man used to being in control and couldn't imagine things going on without him. Ty could relate. That's how he'd felt when he'd left the ranch. And when he'd left the land development company. Both seemed to be getting along okay without him, though the ranch was probably less successful. Still, it humbled a guy to think he wasn't quite as crucial as he thought.

As for Prescott, Ty had made one significant contribution on the trip. He'd been able to meet with the AFBR's livestock director and secure a promise to visit the ranch and assess Prescott's bulls for participation in an upcoming Touring Division Event. He'd decided to wait until he knew for certain Cody Lane would keep that promise before giving Mandy the good news.

No, it was strictly on a personal level that this trip had been a failure, starting with Abilene.

He'd come on too strong, pushed too fast, too hard. Mandy had made clear that it was separate beds and separate lives. But they were sharing a room, and he'd seen her checking him out. Fight it all she could, reality was they were going to end up in bed together.

His ears popped, signaling a change in air pressure even before he saw the thick gray clouds swirling up ahead. This was going to be a rough ride. Weather report had not been good over the plains. Well, this wouldn't be the first time—but it was probably the first time for Mandy.

The plane rose and fell and rose again. Mandy clutched her seat as the battleship-gray clouds smothered the plane and rain pelted the windows like tiny bullets.

"What is happening, Ty?" she yelled above the commotion. Fear squeezed her heart as she struggled against panic.

"Weather. We're heading through a storm."

"Wh…what kind of storm." Please let it not be a tornado or something.

"Old-fashioned gully washer. We'll be fine, Mandy,"

His large hand patted her thigh and quickly withdrew. Like heat lightning, a little shimmer of electricity shot through her. That was the first time he'd touched her since Abilene, gratefully. The thought of that first night in the hotel room still brought heat to her cheeks. Each night in every hotel room had been another test of willpower. So far, she'd passed the tests, but barely.

Now here she was, smack-dab in turbulence that mirrored her emotions.

"Can you guarantee that?"

The radio crackled with a string of nonsense words.

"Pretty much. I've clearance to increase altitude. We'll try to ride over it."

"We're going higher?" She felt as pukey as a green-gilled fish.

"Best way to avoid the turbulence. That's what the big jets do. We can't climb as high, but we'll do our best."

The plane shuddered as it bumped and dipped along. Ty had both hands on the steering column, his focus locked on the panel of instruments.

Rain pummeled the glass. Wind thrashed the cabin.

She bit her lip and tried to hold in the shrieks climbing up her throat.

She yelped just as the plane bucked, and her stomach roiled.

"I'm going to be sick," she managed to gasp out.

"Bag's under the seat."

She fumbled, finding it and a square cushion, which she left on the floor.

"You have a parachute with this?" She placed the opened bag under her chin.

"That's a floatation device. Besides, no way you're shooting out of a plane at this altitude, honey. We'll be fine. Trust me."

Trust might be easy to request—but hard to grant as they tossed about.

The plane dipped, then rose again as the pelting rain sent rivulets of water down the glass windshield. No sense looking out the window. She couldn't see anything but the eerie gray darkness of a huge abyss.

"Just a few more miles of this. Hang in there," Ty said.

He was flipping this and that switch on the panel. Did he really know what he was doing? The plane shuddered, and the queasiness in Mandy's stomach ended up in the bag.

The rain ceased as abruptly as it had begun. The shuddering stopped, and with the tick of a clock, they were flying once again through settled clouds and aqua-blue skies.

"You okay?" Ty said, a grin on his face as he peered at her bag.

She crumpled the top closed, hoping it didn't smell too bad. "I will be." It was mortifying enough to have lost her lunch while Ty had remained the model of calmness. She'd never get used to flying in these little planes, she realized. Just like she'd never get used to being with Ty Martin. And yet here she was.

"Good. We're almost home."

Home? Where was that now? The ranch house she couldn't face? Her mother's house, where she no longer lived? Ty's hotel suite, where she'd merely be a guest in a man's room?

Mandy headed for the airport's lounge as soon as she disembarked the plane so she could fix her makeup, do a quick brush of her teeth, rinse her mouth, and try to calm the wings still flapping in her stomach. As she exited the bathroom, however, the queasiness she felt from the plane ride lurched into downright nausea as she watched a willowy blonde tap her high heels across the ragged linoleum floor and fling her arms around Ty's neck as he stood talking to the man behind the counter. Mandy stopped in midstride when the blonde, who looked like the one in the picture on Ty's phone, planted a long, full-mouth kiss on Ty's lips.

"Surprised?" The blonde giggled, her curvy body still wrapped around Ty's. "When you said you were working on a special project and too busy to see me, I thought I'd come down here for the weekend and see if I couldn't coax you into a little time off. But when you weren't at your hotel room this morning, I figured the next best place to find you either coming or going was to check on your plane—and I was right!" She squealed the last words.

Now that was a woman who obviously was used to getting what she wanted. And given the way she was put together, tall, thin, and with a bust measurement unnaturally out of proportion to her narrow hips, she probably wasn't insecure enough to think a man might not be pleased to see her. Dressed in spiked white heels, tight white skinny jeans, and a sleeveless, strapless pink top, even Mandy had to admit she looked like a female version of a sugary confection.

Irritation spiked in her. Not that Mandy was jealous. How could she be jealous when Ty meant nothing to her? But still, the woman had nerve. Legally, Ty was her husband, and they had both agreed to be faithful to their vows for the six months. Miss Sugar was not part of the deal.

Finding her legs, Mandy strode forward. She knew the exact minute Ty spotted her, because his face colored crimson.

"You going to introduce me, Ty?" Mandy said as

167

she drew alongside the two. The man behind the counter had made himself scarce.

Miss Sugar turned her blond head to look at Mandy. Big blue eyes stared at her from over a perfect little nose. A frown creased the woman's once-smooth brow. The pointed chin rose. "Yes, Ty, introduce us," she drawled. She didn't move an inch from her spot melded to Ty's side.

With some awkwardness, Ty set Miss Sugar away from him. "Mandy, this is Kendall Parker. Kendall, this is Mandy…Martin. My wife." He practically choked on the last words.

She would have admitted those words sounded odd to her too, except she was too caught up in gauging Miss Parker's reaction to the news.

"Your wife?" Kendall said the words with obvious skepticism, as if someone were playing a bad joke. "Honey, you don't believe in marriage." She shifted her gaze to Ty.

He held up his hands. "She's my wife, Kendall. We were married a few days ago."

Kendall looked Mandy up and down, obviously trying to gauge what Mandy had that Kendall didn't. The scowl on Kendall's face said she hadn't come up with anything.

Annoyed, Mandy stepped to Ty and twined her arm in his, like the loving couple they weren't.

"I don't understand," Kendall said. "You said you were working on a project, not marrying some strange woman. Did you get drunk in Vegas or something?"

"Mandy. Her name is Mandy. We've known each other for ten years." The twitch in Ty's jaw belied the steadiness in his voice. He rubbed a hand down his face.

Kendall's eyebrows arched. "Just when were you going to tell me?"

"Yes, Ty, when were you going to tell her?"

If eyes could spark fire, Ty's would have burned a hole right through her. "Mandy, I'd like to have a few words with Kendall."

Mandy arched her brows but didn't move. She'd no reason to make this easy for him.

"Alone."

She forced a smile. "Fine. And when you're done, you can have a few words with me. Alone."

Mandy stepped away, crossed her arms, and watched from a distance as her husband tried to explain things to a woman far more beautiful than she was.

Ty could tell by the resolute way Mandy walked to the car that he was in for it.

"So I'm a business project? I thought you were going to tell her we were married."

Ty searched his mind for an explanation she would buy. He came up empty.

"What would I say? I'm married but not really married, so check back with me in six months?" Ty had also texted the same message to the other women in his life. As far as everyone knew, he was on a special project.

"So you intend to go back with her when this is over?"

He shrugged. "I left the door open. She's nice enough." Kendall didn't ask much from a man other than good sex and a nice gift once in a while. Her preference was jewelry.

Anne Carrole

Mandy's mouth had flatlined. "And that's all you require."

It had been. "I suppose." Although being with Mandy, he'd come to enjoy matching wits with her—business-wise and otherwise. Too bad she was so much work. Kendall was no work at all.

"And will she…be around after six months?"

Kendall had not taken the news well. And he hadn't offered any explanation for this change in his circumstances, because there was none he felt anyone would believe, not to mention it was complicated. "Doubtful."

"Well, I'm sorry. I guess."

"No need to be." He'd never had a problem finding willing women.

But was that all he required? Someone who didn't demand anything from him? Who just wanted sex and a gift now and again?

He glanced over at Mandy. She walked with her arms crossed and her body rigid. Could she be upset by Kendall? Could it matter to her? That was an intriguing thought.

* * *

"You've got to put some clothes on," Mandy said as she turned toward the wall to avoid the sight of a naked Ty, towel drying his hair, fresh from the shower. The man apparently had no shame…and a very nice body.

They were ensconced in his hotel suite, the room with just one California king bed. She'd been so distraught over the prospect of staying again in her grandfather's house, she'd failed to ask if they'd have to share a bed if they stayed in his suite. This was the price she paid for that mistake.

Of course, being a mere hotel room, there was no space for her collection of boots or most of her clothes. She'd have to keep her stuff at her mother's and live out of a suitcase. Sounded as temporary as her marriage.

"No, I don't."

"Then I can't stay here. I can't sleep in the same bed."

The wall was decorated with a curlicue patterned paper, and she began to trace the design in her mind to distract her from the hammering of her heart.

"Your choice. But you void the terms of the will and then...well, what was the point of getting hitched?"

She let out a deep breath. That was a question she'd asked herself every day since. "Wrap a towel around yourself then."

"No need. I'm all dried off. What's the big deal? You've seen my junk before." He had the nerve to chuckle.

Yes, she'd seen it that night in Abilene and had tried ever since to avoid seeing it. Because he had nice junk. Very nice junk.

"But I wasn't sleeping next to it. In the same bed." The wallpaper repeated the curlicue pattern every foot or so.

"I'm under the covers. You can turn around."

She turned around and there he was, bare chested, a thin sheet barely covering the lower half of his body, with a wide, mischievous grin covering his face.

Lordy. It was like finding a fantasy man in your bed—all muscle and sinew.

"I'd be fine if you decided to go to bed nude." His grin turned cocky.

"Not happening." Though she was wearing a baggy T-shirt, a memento from one of their rodeos, she still felt overexposed looking into those smoldering, coal-dark eyes of his.

She lifted the covers, careful not to disturb the sheet covering his body, and slid into bed. Tucking the blankets around her, she hoped to create some barrier between them. Unfortunately, there was no barrier that could prevent the pheromones wrapping around her. Her heart was beating fast, and she felt warm, very warm. So warm she wanted to throw the covers right off her.

This was such a bad idea. She couldn't have chosen a better way to torture herself. She closed her eyes, felt a movement on the bed, and opened them only to stare right into his handsome face and those dark eyes. He'd rolled next to her, propping his head on his hand. Gratefully, the sheet still covered the essentials, but that left a lot of flesh and muscle still exposed. Rippling muscle. Tanned flesh. Heaven help her.

"I don't know what you're afraid of, Mandy Martin, but you needn't be. We have an end date, clear terms, and, evidently, your grandfather's consent. I say let's go for it."

That's what scared her. This was merely a distraction for him. She wasn't sure what it would be for her.

"I'm not interested." Her voice sounded thin, reedy, and unconvincing.

He slid up, almost relieving the sheet of its duty. At the last minute he tugged it up, but not before she caught a glimpse.

Every night of their trip, in the intimacy of their hotel room, he'd told her he wanted her. She'd had other men tell her they wanted to have sex with her. But they weren't men she'd once fallen in love with. They weren't men who were willing to steal her company. They weren't men who might also steal her heart.

He stroked his finger down her cheek, sending a little tremor through her. "I can get you interested." His breath puffed against her cheek, and her belly tingled.

She turned her face toward him, realizing too late the mistake she made as he gently cupped her chin. The kiss started sweet but quickly turned hot, very hot. His slick tongue stroked hers, cracking her pitiful attempt at resistance. She wanted him. And he knew it. His passion sent an earthquake-worthy tremor through her and she hung on. Sliding her hands up his neck, she burrowed her fingers in his hair and held him so she could feast on his mouth. He tasted good. He kissed even better.

She felt his warm hand slip under the hem of her T-shirt and slide up her cool flesh to her breast while he pressed his tongue deeper into her mouth. A moan escaped from somewhere in her throat. Her nipples peaked, and her mind turned fuzzy. He kissed her like he was going to devour her, and she wanted to be devoured.

It would just be sex. Just mindless sex. No one would know.

The word *liar* popped into her head. She was lying. To herself. It would never be just sex with Ty. For reasons that at the moment eluded her, he meant something more to her, however mistaken those feelings were. However much she didn't want to own up to them.

It took more willpower than she thought she possessed, but she pulled back. He stared at her through lowered lids, regret in his eyes.

"No," she managed to say.

"It's gonna happen sometime. And soon. You can take that to the bank," he said, his voice husky and his smile assured.

Chapter 11

The following morning, she called Libby and Cat to squeeze in coffee at the café before the dreaded late-morning flight to the Washington rodeo. She hoped Cat and Libby had some good advice to strengthen her quickly fading resolve, because she surely didn't know what to do.

It was a few minutes past ten when Mandy, dressed in a Prescott rodeo T-shirt, jeans, and barn boots, walked into the café, her two friends already situated in a booth and waiting for her. At the last minute, one of Prescott's best broncs had pulled up lame, but it turned out to be only a pebble caught in the hoof. Something Kyle should have checked for before sounding the alarm, but he was still learning.

Mandy slid into the booth just ahead of the waitress heading for their table. It was the same perky blonde from the other night, and they gave her their order before saying their hellos. Not quite ready to talk about herself, Mandy addressed Libby, who was wearing a cute blue-and-white maternity top with her jeans now that she was beginning to show. "So how are you feeling?"

"Good. The second trimester is a lot easier than

the first, thank goodness." The woman was beaming, and Mandy felt an odd sense of emptiness at the thought of never having children. Clearly Libby had found the right man. She wondered if she ever would.

"And, Cat, how are things going with that adverse-possession claim?" Mandy asked.

Cat was dressed in a white tailored shirt, skintight jeans, and a shiny pair of undoubtedly new cowgirl boots. She looked like she stepped out of a fashion magazine rather than a ranch pickup. Cat had always been the girly-girly type when they were growing up, while Mandy had been all tomboy. How her friend was going to run a huge ranch now that her stubborn father had passed away was beyond Mandy, but one thing she could say about Cat, she was determined—a trait they both shared.

"We're still in the discovery phase. Our lawyer said he'll be ready to file in a few weeks. I don't feel right about it, but he keeps telling me it's the law and it involves water rights, so it's not something I can let slide."

Mandy nodded. She understood not feeling right about something that was ostensibly legal.

"And how is Mrs. Martin feeling these days?" Cat asked.

"Confused." And that was the truth.

Mandy elaborated, telling them about almost giving in to her raging hormones back in Abilene, the confrontation with Kendall, and her inability to concentrate, much less sleep, when Ty was in the same bed. "I've never been more attracted to a man, nor trusted one less than I do Ty Martin."

"Maybe it's more than attraction," Libby said as

the waitress set down their coffees, pastries, and the western omelet Libby had ordered. The woman was eating for two, after all.

"That's exactly my fear. I thought being with him twenty-four seven would make me like him less. I hate to admit it, but he actually had some good ideas to help keep business. He's smart, works hard, and doesn't shirk difficult jobs or decisions. Those are traits I'd find attractive in anyone else. But it doesn't change the terms of the will or his quest to sell the place. He's still waiting on financials, which I know will show we are profitable, but I don't know if that's enough to convince him not to sell."

"You're afraid of getting too involved with him if you do have sex, is that it?" Cat leaned in.

"Exactly. I've no doubt that it is going to be great sex, which makes it even more difficult to resist him, but what if I end up caring about him more than is healthy, given he holds the fate of my company in his hands. I mean, I should hate the guy."

"Maybe he'll end up caring about you and won't sell the company." Libby always looked on the bright side.

"Or maybe you could use your feminine wiles to keep him from selling." Cat wiggled her eyebrows.

"Not a chance. Ty is so goddamn objective, it isn't funny. He revels in the fact that he's all business, strictly business."

"Reminds me of my father, and not in a good way," Cat said. "If you want to have sex with him, though, how are you going to resist for six whole months? That's an awfully long time to be in lust."

"That's the problem. He keeps saying that we

have an end point, like that's a good thing. At the end of six months, he could have sold the business and walked away, and I will have been left with nothing."

"Nothing but a pile of cash," Cat said and took a sip of her coffee.

Mandy sighed. "I want more. I want my company." She hesitated a minute before confessing. "And I want a husband and kids. I want it all. And I'm likely to end up with none of it, especially if Ty takes my company."

Libby rubbed her rounded tummy. "I can relate. It almost didn't happen for me."

Cat leaned back. "Well, I have two out of three— the ranch and the kid. Doesn't stop me from hankering for a good man to call my own though. I'm just glad that I have Jake out of the whole sorry mess. I never understood how intense that special love for your child could be until I had my little boy."

"How is it raising him alone?" Mandy asked. It was something she'd been wondering about lately.

"Not difficult, just time consuming. In these first few years, they pretty much need your full attention. I'm lucky to have my mom to help with Jake, and a foreman to run the ranch, though I wish I had more of a handle on what is going on, or at least knew the questions to ask. But as for raising Jake, it's the most fulfilling thing I've ever done."

"That's good to know." Libby's smile was wistful.

"Well, Libby, you have it all. Cat, you have most of it. I, well, I could be left with nothing."

"Question is, would you settle for great memories?" Cat asked.

Libby reached over and patted Mandy's hand just as the food arrived. "It's another dilemma, isn't it?"

* * *

"That one is Painted Glory," she said, talking to Ty as she pointed to a pinto horse on the outside of the band of horses milling in the holding pen of the Washington rodeo. "He likes to whirl to get riders off. The one walking toward us is High Jinks," she said of the bay horse.

Ty had flown her to the rodeo, and the flight had been, gratefully, uneventful. They arrived a few hours before the gates opened so they could touch base with Harold, who had everything under control. Her mother hadn't accompanied Harold this time because she and Mrs. Jenkins were still in the throes of cleaning out the ranch house.

The event committee easily agreed to a contract for next season given Prescott had been putting on the small county rodeo for the last thirty years. Mandy convinced Ty to first check into their room at the nearby hotel so she could reassure herself that the room contained double beds, because she wasn't ready to surrender, even if she was thinking about it—a little too much. They then headed back to the fairgrounds.

As they had time to kill before the traditional kickoff meeting, Ty mentioned he'd like to know more about the livestock, and Mandy obliged.

Reaching the fence, the bay gelding nuzzled Mandy, and she patted the horse on the wide white line that ran down the center of his face. "He's a favorite. Been to the NRF five times and named saddle bronc horse of the year two years ago."

"Most of these are wild horses?" Ty stood beside her, close beside her. He'd taken to wearing one of two options—a white Prescott shirt or black Prescott T-shirt, paired with jeans. Today he'd chosen the white shirt because they likely wouldn't have time to return to the hotel room before the event opened. He'd rolled up the sleeves of his shirt, exposing forearms that were getting tanner with each passing day.

He looked like every other rodeo hand and worked liked one. If she hadn't known he was a lawyer, she'd never have guessed it now.

"Some. Others, like High Jinks here, are just spoiled horses. Owners let them get the upper hand, and now the horses won't let anyone ride them. After High Jinks bucks someone off, he prances around the arena like a prince. He knows he's done his job." She gave him another pat, and the horse, as if cued, moved out.

It was difficult not to think about the finely sculpted body under that shirt, under those jeans. She'd seen all of him, more than once, and unfortunately, his naked image seemed to be burned into the sockets of her eyes, because try as she might, she couldn't stop seeing it.

A stocky black mare nickered as the bay returned to the herd. "That's Black Rum. I'm especially proud of her because she was born and raised at our ranch. Been to the NRF four years in a row. She usually bucks with the rank horses because she's so hard to ride. She's unpredictable in the arena, but around the ranch, she's a gentle soul. Harold may be breeding her next year, which is a tough call since it will take her out for a season. We're still discussing it."

Ty had leaned back against the fence. His Stetson

shaded his eyes from a sun that sat low in the bright-blue sky, and a mild breeze ruffled hair exposed under the brim.

"You love these horses, don't you?"

"Of course I do. They are part of the family." The family Ty was ready to break up. "I would be crushed to lose any of them."

Ty touched her forearm, and heat climbed to her neck. "Let's wait and see what the numbers say," he said.

All he had to do was gather her in his arms and promise not to take Prescott away from her, and she'd be all his. The thought scared her. Because he'd only want her for a while and she...well, she just might want him forever.

"I don't need the numbers—and neither should you. We are profitable. We are happy. End of story." Or it should be.

She glanced at him, but Ty kept his focus on the horses. She wished she knew what he was thinking. Knew if any of it mattered to him. If she mattered to him. At least her happiness.

After Abilene, he'd given her a wide berth until last night. How was she going to sleep, even in her own bed, and not succumb, when a kiss from him made her act like a sex-starved female? Twice she'd come close to having sex with him, and even knowing it wouldn't mean more to him than any one-night stand, she wasn't sure she didn't regret, just a little, the fact they hadn't.

Sex would only complicate things. Sex would magnify every action and reaction. Sex would change everything. Everything except the fact he could still sell her company.

"At the meeting tonight, I'm announcing our marriage to the crew members," Ty said.

She could imagine the speculation that would go on. People wondering what the rush was, if she was pregnant, if JM knew, and how long it would last.

"You okay with that?" Ty pressed.

"It will be all over the circuit then." If it wasn't already. "They'll be taking bets about how long it lasts, you know."

"Does that bother you?" He straightened and pushed off the fence.

She shrugged. "A little. It feels like we are living a lie. Like we are doing something we know is wrong. It doesn't feel...natural."

"Maybe because we haven't consummated it yet. That can be fixed any time you'd like, Mrs. Martin."

Mandy ignored his comment. Being with him twenty-four-seven was getting to be an experiment in self-control she wasn't sure would be successful. "We'd best get set up for the meeting. And I'm thirsty. I'm going to swing by the hospitality tent. You coming?" she asked.

"I'll meet you there."

* * *

Ty walked around the rodeo grounds to try to absorb the atmosphere. Rodeos were lively affairs with vendors of goods and food, local clubs, and attendees, some who looked like they'd stepped right out of the pasture and others who looked like they'd stepped out of an advertisement for western wear.

This was the life that both JM and Mandy were

passionate about. This was the place they wanted to be over 250 days a year. It was a transient life but with one huge difference—the 30,000-acre ranch that anchored them. He was coming to realize, after just a few days, developing that ranch would never happen, regardless of whether he sold the rodeo company or not.

Maybe that was all for the best. He'd find some other property to develop. If the numbers said he should sell Prescott, Mandy would need the ranch and what it represented even more. And with the money from the sale of the company, she'd have the means to keep it going, even if ranching wasn't all that profitable.

He didn't quite know how to play things with Mandy. He knew she was attracted to him. When he had her in his arms, she seemed ready and willing to take it further. Then, out of the blue, she'd stop. She wanted to, but this damn option to sell Prescott kept bringing her up short.

Whether they fooled around or not would have no bearing on selling, so why wouldn't she?

He passed by the trailers of the cowboys and cowgirls who had come to compete, and saw Harold at a makeshift table squeezed between two trailers and ringed by five bales of straw, each holding a cowboy with cards in his hands.

Harold looked up and beckoned Ty over.

"We're just killing some time and taking a break," Harold said by way of explanation.

Ty liked poker. He was pretty good at it.

"Who's winning?" Ty wondered if he should angle for an invitation.

"Not me," Harold said.

The rest of the cowhands concentrated on their cards. Ty wondered if they were purposely ignoring him. None of them said anything to acknowledge him, much less invite him to sit down and play a hand.

Knowing when he wasn't wanted had been a skill he'd honed in his own backyard.

"I'm going to help Mandy set up."

Harold nodded, and the other cowboys continued their stoic impression of wooden soldiers.

It didn't bother him, not being part of things. That's how he'd grown up. That's how he'd spent most of his life. That's where he was most comfortable.

* * *

Mandy looked at the stunned faces of the rodeo workers surrounding her and wondered what was going through their minds. They stood outside the small, empty arena where the rodeo would take place in just two hours. The gates hadn't opened yet, so the only people around were involved in setting up, and most were Prescott employees.

Ty had just announced their marriage at the end of the prerodeo meeting.

Slim Matthews sported a frown when he looked up from the dust he'd been studying on the ground. Doug McClane was staring at Ty as if he'd committed a crime. The rest of the men seemed in similar stages of disbelief.

Harold stepped forward. "I've already celebrated your marriage, but on behalf of the crew, I offer you both our congratulations." He turned to face the men.

"This can only mean good things for Prescott's future."

Mandy could see Ty's face redden, but the men began nodding their heads. It should mean a secure future for Prescott—if the marriage was a real one. Nonetheless, the men started coming forward, shaking Ty's hand, and in turn offering their congratulations to Mandy.

Some of the crew offered her a hug, some a kiss, all their well wishes. She tried to act like a new bride, but that was the problem. It was just an act. She hoped they wouldn't see through it. The last to step forward was Slim Matthews.

"I can't say I'm not surprised," Slim said, wrapping his skinny arms around her for a fatherly hug. "But if you're happy, that's all that matters."

A lump formed in her throat. She hated deceiving these people.

Slim turned his attention to Ty. "Just treat her right. I've known Mandy since she was a babe in her mother's arms. She deserves the best." He extended a weathered and calloused hand to Ty, who shook it and nodded, but he didn't say a word back to the man. Slim ambled away, head down.

"We've had some contestants pull out, so I need to review the horses that are going to be turned out tonight." What she really wanted to do was escape Ty and avoid any more scrutiny from the men.

"Mandy, we had to tell them."

"I know. I'm not suggesting we didn't. It just isn't easy playing a role in front of people who deserve honesty."

"Would you rather we told them the truth—that we married just to fulfill JM's will?"

She raised her chin. "Maybe."

He caught her wrist and raised her hand to his lips, giving her palm a little kiss. "In six months, it will all be worth it."

She tugged her hand away, annoyed at the flush of warmth that filled her. "It better be."

Tomorrow she'd be flying back to Wyoming, sleeping in the same bed with him, fighting biology, and wondering if she really wanted to win.

Chapter 12

Ty swiped the phone closed, feeling an all-too-familiar irritation. He looked out the window at the tarmac puddled with water from the showers that had come through earlier. Mandy had flown back from Washington with him through a late-afternoon shower, and once Ty landed the plane, she'd headed for the ladies' lounge. At least she hadn't lost her lunch this time.

Why his brother had called now, asking to see him after all these years, was a mystery that wouldn't be solved until he went out to the old ranch. It had to be a humdinger of a reason if he'd condescended to call Ty after all this time. Trace Martin was as proud as they came, and asking his little brother to do anything for him meant a heap of swallowing.

"What's wrong?" Mandy asked as soon as she came out of the ladies' room. He must have carried some of his shock on his face. "Kendall isn't here again, is she?" she said, looking around.

The color was back in her cheeks, unless that was some makeup magic. And her eyes were brighter. Given time, he'd bet she'd like flying. And maybe even him.

187

"My brother called." And that in itself should be enough of an explanation.

"Trace?" she asked. It was obviously a rhetorical question since he only had one sibling and Mandy knew it. "Did he find out about our marriage?"

Ty hadn't thought to inform his brother. Not that Trace would care what happened or didn't happen to Ty. They'd long ago realized they didn't see things in the same light, but not before a whole lot of bad feelings had been conjured up.

"No. But he's asked me to come out to the ranch. Today."

Both of her eyebrows peaked.

"I can drop you off at the hotel and then swing by the old place."

"I'd like to go."

Explaining Mandy and his six-month marriage to his brother would just stir up old grievances. Trace had resented Ty's relationship with J. M. Prescott, not to mention the scholarship, since the day Ty had found out he'd won.

"Are you sure you're up for it? Don't you want to relax, take a bath, get the ball rolling for our next rodeo in Utah?"

She shook her head. "I'm fine. Besides, I'm interested in meeting Trace. And seeing where you were raised."

"Why?" he asked, digging for the keys in his pocket.

She shrugged. "Curious, is all. You used to talk about him in the old days."

That was then.

He didn't want her to come, but he didn't have

the stomach to fight over it. Or explain his reluctance. He needed to save all his fortitude for the meeting with his brother. Besides, having her along might serve to keep tempers in check. Or give her a cautionary sample of what was left of his dysfunctional family. He picked up their bags and started walking toward the exit door. "If we don't have to go into the whole will thing with him, you can come."

She skipped a step to catch up to him. "Why? You don't want him to know we are married?"

"I don't mind if he knows we're married. No doubt he's heard it, or will soon enough, given he lives in the same county." Ty pushed the building's door, held it open by the metal rail so she could exit, and then continued walking. The scent of freshly laundered air did nothing to soothe the scrubbed-raw emotions washing over him.

"Then what?"

"It's the six-month part I'd appreciate you not revealing." He spotted his car, hit the starter button on the remote, and strode to the passenger's side as the engine came to life. When he turned to look at her, her cheeks had flushed, and her mouth was open.

"So you want him to think it's permanent."

Ty yanked open the car's back door and threw the bags onto the seat. The air conditioner blasted not-yet-cold air from the vents. "I don't want to explain JM's role in things, is all. Let him think what he wants about us getting married. And divorced." Just like everyone else.

He shut the back door and opened the passenger door for her. She slid into the seat. He walked around to the driver's side and slipped behind the wheel, the leather hot, the car still stuffed with stale air. He hit the button to expose the sunroof and pushed up the air-conditioning. It would cool in a minute. "Deal?"

"Sure," she said with a shrug. "I can play the happy wife."

He put the car in gear. "Just don't overdo. Trace may not have a college degree, but he's sharp as they come."

* * *

The low-slung ranch house, with its weed and dirt-spotted lawn, sat back from the gravel road leading off the main highway. Painted what probably once passed for white but was now a yellowed and stained ivory, the main part of the house might have started out as a bungalow, but the hodgepodge one-story additions gave it a cobbled-together look. The driveway was rutted and mostly dirt, though there were enough stones to attest that it originally held gravel. A black pickup, one fender slightly battered, was parked near a dappled-gray wooden barn, evidence someone was home.

Mandy gave a silent sigh as the car turned in. Somewhere inside of her she'd rooted for Trace to have a prosperous ranch, if only to show Ty there were tangible benefits, instead of merely sentimental ones, to protecting one's heritage. But if the ranch was prosperous, there was no visible sign of it. It wasn't rundown, just weary looking, as if it were ready to retire.

Ty brought the car to a stop, shut off the engine, and stared out the window, not moving.

Mandy wasn't sure what to do, so she sat and waited. How long had it been since Ty had been back? By the intensity of his gaze, she'd guess it had been a while.

A figure appeared in the doorway of the barn. Tall, masculine, and lean. Cowboy hat on head. He walked a few paces before another figure, much smaller and female, followed with hesitant steps.

"He has a daughter?" she asked. Ty had never mentioned a niece.

"Not that I know of."

Ty opened the door and slowly unfolded to stand with the door blocking his body. Mandy exited the car, closing her door behind her.

As Trace lumbered closer, his gate long and rolling, she noted the family resemblance in the color of the hair, the slender but muscular physique, the height, and the long straight nose and chiseled cheekbones. Though a portion of his face was shaded by the hat brim, Trace was a weathered version of his younger brother. Just as handsome but in a rougher, less polished way. Her gaze swept to the little being tailing him. The girl was probably around three or four and had the same dark shade of hair as the Martin boys, cut short and hanging straight in a child's pageboy cut. A lopsided pink bow was stuck on the right side, and the tip of her ear showed through strands of hair. She had on a pair of pink denim pants and a pink T-shirt, with matching pink sneaks, and in her dirt-streaked arms, she held a stuffed brown puppy against her small chest.

"Ty." Trace nodded before shifting his gaze to take in Mandy. "Ma'am," he said in a western drawl.

He was close enough now that she could see his hazel eyes, and though tall, he was probably an inch shorter than his younger brother.

"We were just returning from a business trip to Texas when I got your call. Mandy asked to come with me. Mandy Prescott and I were married this past week." Ty said the words matter of factly, with no display of emotion—not joy, not anger, just a flat voicing of the essential information.

Shock stole across the elder brother's face. He stared at her finger, where no ring resided, and Mandy resisted the impulse to hide her hands behind her back. His gaze shifted to her stomach in a cold appraisal of the situation. An appraisal she resented. "Mandy Prescott Martin," she said, extending her hand. "And no, I'm not pregnant."

His eyes rounded, but he took her hand and shook it, his own hand rough and cold. But still he said nothing in response to the news. Just stared at her.

"Seems we both have some surprises to share," Ty said, looking down at the little girl who hid behind Trace. She didn't cling to Trace, or even touch him. She stood stoically behind him, watching with wide eyes.

"Seems we do," Trace said without offering an explanation. "Let's go in the house."

He didn't say anything to the little girl. She just followed him, like a real-life version of the toy puppy she was holding.

The screen door creaked in protest as Trace opened it. He held it for the little girl, and she toddled in. Ty held the door for Mandy, and they both proceeded into the large kitchen. Neat. Clean.

Surprisingly so. No dishes sat on the white Formica counter or in the sink. No papers lay on the table. But no curtains hung on the window, no placemats on the maple tabletop, nothing that said a woman had ever worked in the kitchen. Yet Ty's mother must have.

The little girl waddled right through the kitchen and into what appeared to be the living room, given the beige carpet and the large green chair Mandy could see from her spot just inside the screen door. She hardly knew where to go.

"See you made some changes to the kitchen," Ty noted.

"Three years ago. It needed work. Lots of things need work," Trace said, his words clipped. "I have to speak to you, Ty. Alone." Trace's pointed gaze left Mandy feeling squirmy. And awkward. Like the odd man out.

"I'll just go in the other room with…" Mandy wanted to at least know what to call the girl.

"Delanie." Trace said the name with reluctance.

Well, if she thought Ty was closed mouthed, it was nothing compared to his brother.

"I'll just be with Delanie then," she said and hoped there were some toys or something to amuse the child. With a brief quizzical look at Ty, she made her way into the living room.

It was plainly furnished with one overstuffed sofa, the large green chair, a scarred coffee table, and a small flat-screen TV sitting on a wood stand. A plastic box of toys was in the corner, and Delanie was standing by it as if deciding what to pull out.

"Toys, how lovely," Mandy said, using her brightest voice. "Will you show me what you have there?" Though there weren't a lot of toys, they all looked rather new. Trace had given the child toys, at least. But where was the mother?

The little girl looked up at Mandy with eyes the same hazel color as Trace's. With the hair color and the eyes, there was little doubt she was looking at Trace's daughter.

"My clock," Delanie said, pointing to a red plastic clock with big numbers and large black hands. The stuffed dog remained tucked in the crook of her little arm. Obviously a favorite. "My baby," she said, pointing to an unclothed baby doll with hair the color of Delanie's. The child proceeded to name each toy as Mandy strained to hear the sound of voices from the other room. But all she heard was the screen door slam shut.

* * *

"You really married J. M. Prescott's granddaughter?" Trace asked as they stepped out into the yard. Trace stayed close to the screen door, no doubt to keep within earshot of the youngster. "Didn't I read he just passed away?"

"Yes. To both questions."

Trace shook his head in that irritating way he had when he didn't want to believe something. "Guess you know what side of the bread is buttered."

"You going to tell me about the child?" Ty said, ignoring the censure in his brother's tone. He was well beyond caring about his brother's opinion. "Do I have a niece?"

Trace stared out over the empty corrals before answering. "Yes."

"You married?" After everything, Ty never thought Trace would marry. He'd been a loner from the moment Ty had become aware of his big brother. It had been rough growing up with a brother who hadn't wanted much to do with you.

"No. But she's mine."

"I could see that just looking at her."

"I had the tests run." Trace looked almost embarrassed by the act. "I knew she was mine, but I needed proof to be able to get custody of her."

"Where's her mother?"

Trace visibly bristled at the question and looked away. His brother had always been private, and Ty imagined answering these questions was painful for him. But Trace was the one who asked him to the ranch. If he didn't want something from Ty, Trace could have kept Ty from ever knowing about Delanie. He suspected whatever was going on had something to do with the little tyke. Question was, what?

"In prison."

Ty might have anticipated a lot of answers to that question, but not prison. Although maybe he should have. "Drugs?"

Trace nodded.

Shit. "I thought you were out of that life."

Trace's eyebrows knitted together as he glowered at Ty. "I am. Delanie is four years old."

Four years. Right at the end, then, Delanie must have happened.

"Did you know about her?" Not that they'd talked much since that time, but Trace might have mentioned something as important as being a father.

"No. Not until her mother came by and dropped

her off. She was going to be sentenced. She had no relatives to leave her with, least none who would have anything to do with her. She'd listed me on the birth certificate. I had to appear before the family court, but I've got temporary custody. Social worker has been assigned."

"And when did this happen?" Ty was still trying to get his head around the fact that he had a niece, that his brother was a father.

"Four weeks ago." Trace ran a splayed hand through his hair. "And I need help." He turned and looked at Ty, and for the first time ever, he saw real fear in his brother's eyes.

Ty took a hard swallow. A child's future was at stake here. Despite what he might feel about his brother, or not feel, he couldn't walk away from a child. From *his niece*.

"I wouldn't ask for myself," Trace began. "But she's just a kid. She's had it rough enough. I don't know much about being a father, but I'm committed to doing the best by her that I can." He stared hard at Ty, the struggle he was going through evident in every line of his weathered face. "I need money. For her."

Ty nodded. No doubt Trace did need money. Ty would guess his brother was barely eking out a living. Selling the small, by Wyoming standards, ranch in this economy probably wouldn't even pay off the mortgage. "How much?"

"She needs to be in preschool. She's bright, but she's had it tough. Her mother, well, she was an addict…"

"What kind of addict?" And dear God let it not be heroin.

"Cocaine, pills. She was sent to prison for dealing. She got fifteen years."

The state was hard on drug dealers, but fifteen years meant it was a whole lot of dope.

"Preschool should be doable, Trace. But you didn't ask me here to lend you money for preschool."

Trace shook his head as his hands dug into the worn pockets of his jeans. "This ain't easy, Ty."

He felt a stab of sympathy. Trace had always had enough pride to fill a 120-foot water tower. "I expect it's not. But we do what we have to do. You've got a child to take care of. I've got a niece to protect. She's a Martin, and we need to do right by her. Both of us. Tell me what you need."

"I guess you think I should sell the ranch. Move into town."

There it was. "A different time, maybe. But truthfully, you wouldn't get much for it now. Developers don't have the money to pick up new projects on this small amount of acreage. Could change in a few years. But not now." Besides, what would Trace do in town? The best he could hope for was to hire on with another ranch, *if* another was hiring, and wages wouldn't be much better, probably, than what he could scratch out here.

A spark of hope jumped into his brother's eyes.

"Just get it out, Trace. It will be painful, but you'll live."

"I need a loan." Trace named a five-figure amount. "I need to build back the herd after the drought last year. I need to hire a housekeeper to mind Delanie when she's not in school and I'm out on the range. I need to get her into the preschool in town so she's ready for kindergarten next year. And I need a lawyer who can assure that I can keep her. Now and, God forbid, if her mother ever gets paroled." His eyes turned flinty. "I'm not giving her back. She's been damaged enough."

"I can loan the money, Trace. That's never been the issue. You cleaning up your act, which it appears you've done, has been the issue. As well as recognizing I'm not the enemy just because I've had opportunities to better myself and took them."

Trace scowled. "No matter that you think you're better than those of us who work with our hands to make a living."

"Spin it however it makes you feel better, brother." Ty wouldn't take the bait. Not this time. Not with a child at risk. "But tell me about Delanie and this damage stuff. How has she been damaged?"

Trace closed his eyes and then opened them as if the hurt cut deep. "She doesn't trust anyone, doesn't trust me. She says her mommy told her not to let a man touch her because they'll do bad things and that she's not supposed to take anything from anyone and she's never to go anywhere with a man. It's been a hell of a few weeks."

Trace had a haunted look as he spoke.

"The mother was probably trying to protect her from the creeps she hung around with."

"Thing is…I don't know if it worked. And that's killing me just as much as Delanie's distrust of me." Trace shook his head. "I need to get her some help…and learn how to deal with this. If I'd known, I'd have sued for custody from the start."

Except four years ago, Trace might not have been

able to make his case. He'd never gotten in serious trouble with the law, but he had hung around with guys who had. He'd been an alcoholic, so bad he had to go through rehab. How much drugs had been part of it, Ty never knew. People may not think drugs made it into ranch country, but no community was immune. Trace had darn near bankrupted the farm during that phase of his life, hence the mortgage. Ty's interference then hadn't been welcomed, but it had been necessary. And Trace resented it to this day and probably forever. The fact he was actually asking for Ty's help now was a testament to how much he was committed to making a good life for Delanie. And Ty had to admire him for swallowing some of that Martin pride for the girl's sake.

"It will take me a few weeks to liquidate some things, but I can set up an account for you to draw on. I can also arrange for a good family-court lawyer for you. I know one of the state judges for that court. And he should be able to direct me to a professional who deals with this sort of thing."

Trace nodded.

It wasn't much in the way of thanks, but then Ty didn't really expect any.

When Ty stepped into the living room, there was Mandy, sitting cross-legged on the floor, providing the voice for the doll she held in her hand. Little Delanie, standing, was telling the baby doll that it was bed time and she mustn't sleep in anyone else's bed.

A shudder went through him. What the hell had his niece had to endure these last four years as a child of a drug addict? He didn't want to imagine.

"Hey, ladies," Ty said, bending down on his haunches so he was eye level with them both. "What a pretty baby you have, Miss Delanie."

"Thank you. But you mustn't touch her. She's afraid of you."

Ty felt his heart squeeze. He shot a look at Mandy. Questions filled her eyes. Questions to which he didn't have the answers. "Is she now? Well, she's not afraid of her uncle, is she?"

She looked so cute and innocent as she stood with her head to the side, thinking. "What's an uncle?"

"An uncle is someone who is related to you, a brother to your daddy. And someone who protects you from harm, just like a daddy does."

"Daddies protect you?"

"Yes, darling, they do. Does your baby have a daddy?"

She shook her head. "But maybe someday we'll find one for her and visit him."

"Then he'll protect her. And she won't have to be afraid of anyone or anything."

He sensed rather than saw Trace enter the room as Delanie shifted her line of sight.

"You have a daddy, Delanie, don't you?" he continued.

She nodded a solemn nod.

"Your daddy is my brother. That makes me your uncle. All three of us are family." Then he remembered Mandy. "And Mandy is my wife, so she's your aunt, and that makes her family too. And aunts and uncles and daddies, they all look out for the children in the family. You're the only child in our family." She looked so vulnerable as she glanced from

Ty's face to Mandy's face up to Trace's face as if she was silently questioning the truth of that statement.

"And my mommy. She looks out for me too, right?"

God, he hoped so.

"Yes, when she's here. But when she's not, your daddy looks out for you. That's how it works." That's how it had worked, however imperfectly, in his life too. "When your daddy was a lot bigger than you, he lost his mother. And his father had to take care of him."

"Really, Daddy?" she looked up, hope overflowing in her eyes, but it didn't quite hide the wariness that also resided there.

"Yes, Delanie."

"But baby doesn't have a daddy. Just me, her mommy. So I'll be looking out for her."

"Why don't you go wash up, Delanie? And we'll have something to eat with your uncle Ty and aunt Mandy." Trace stepped forward, careful not to crowd his daughter. It must be hell, walking on eggshells. "You two will stay for a little bite? One of the neighbors sent over a lasagna. She's been helping me out when she can."

"That okay with you, Mandy?" Ty asked. He hadn't planned on staying long. He was tired and was sure she was, but Trace sounded uncharacteristically needy for some company. He imagined his brother must feel at sea with all this. But at least he was stepping up and doing what was right, what he had to do for his little girl.

Mandy nodded.

"Can baby eat with us, Daddy?" Delanie asked.

"Sure, honey."

"And Buddy?" She nodded at the stuffed dog in her arm.

"As always." Trace sounded almost jovial.

"Okay. I'll take baby, and we'll all wash up." Delanie held out one arm to receive the doll from Mandy and then toddled off toward the bathroom, Buddy in the crook of one arm, the baby doll in the other.

"Shall I go and help her?" Mandy said, rising.

Trace shook his head. "No need. She's an independent sort. I guess she's used to fending for herself."

Ty felt a sudden sadness at that. Robbed of some of her childhood, it seemed. Maybe now she'd have a chance to get it back. Ty would certainly do his part.

Mandy brushed her hands down her jeans, dusting herself off. Watching her simple movements, it struck him like a hammer strikes a nail. She was standing in his house, the house he grew up in. And she didn't look out of place, even though he felt like an alien after all this time.

She raised her head, her expression quizzical. He had a lot to tell her, for sure. Perhaps sensing now was not the time to ask questions, she turned toward Trace.

"Can I help in the kitchen then? Set the table or something?"

"That would be fine, Mandy," Trace said. "Sorry to hear about your grandfather. And sorry I didn't get a chance to say welcome to the family."

With an acknowledging nod, Mandy followed Trace into the kitchen.

He liked that about Mandy. She was always ready

to pitch in. She didn't shirk work or responsibility or just plain helping out. And seeing her playing down on the floor with Delanie brought a whole new dimension to her many facets.

She'd make some guy a wonderful wife.

* * *

"I'm almost afraid to know, but what is Delanie's story?" Mandy asked as the car sped down the road away from Ty's boyhood home.

Ty let go a sigh. He was drained. Seeing his brother after all these years had felt more like a confrontation than a visit. And he didn't kid himself that anything had changed between the two of them. Their issues ran deep, starting with the circumstances surrounding the death of their mother right through the loan Ty would be providing and included a few detours down Trace's alcoholic alleys. And now there was Delaine added to the mix. He wasn't going to allow his brother, however, to shut him out of his niece's life. Ty had never been around kids much, but something about that little girl tugged at him.

"I don't know the details. Neither does Trace, which is eating at him. But I'll tell you what I do know." Ty proceeded to fill Mandy in on the convicted drug-addict mother, Delanie's obvious distrust of men, even Trace's bout with alcoholism. He skipped over the part where he had found his brother passed out in a back alley after learning Trace had mortgaged the ranch to fund his recklessness, and proceeded to beat the crap out of him. As well as the fact that he had thrown his brother into rehab with the threat of turning him over to the authorities if he didn't shape up. Ty had stepped in to cosign so the ranch wouldn't be lost to creditors. The worst investment he'd ever made in terms of payback, but then he didn't do it for a return on his investment. Fact was, he didn't know quite why he had done it. Maybe Delanie would prove the real return.

"At least Trace is being honest with Delanie about her mother. He's told the child that her mother has broken some rules and she has to go someplace to relearn them so she can do better when she gets out. I hope Delanie gives him a chance, because even if that woman gets out before her fifteen years is up, Trace isn't going to give up his daughter to her. Not now that he knows he has one."

"She's a sweet child, Ty. But chatty one minute and so somber the next. Like she's swaying between being a child and an adult. Can we help her, help them both? The ranch doesn't seem all that prosperous."

A quick glance at her showed tears welling in her pretty green eyes. She'd said can *we* help. That surprised him.

"He's asked for help. I'm giving it. I know his asking wasn't easy."

"You're not close?"

"That's an understatement." Ty shifted gears. His relationship with Trace wasn't something he wanted to talk about. It was too complicated. Hell, he didn't even understand it.

"Well, maybe we can have them over or something. Or we could give him a break and take Delanie with us to a rodeo." Ty could see the wheels in her mind turning.

"Given her trust issues, I don't know if taking her away would be the right thing, but we'll stay involved." He turned to her. "I appreciate your support in this, Mandy. Given our situation, can't say I expected you to care much about Trace or Delanie."

"Of course I care. Trace may be a little taciturn, like you—"

"I am nothing like my brother." Ty was surprised at how much he rebelled against that idea.

"Oh, on the contrary. I see a lot of similarities. You both are lone wolves, for one. Neither of you exactly wears your heart on your sleeve. And despite your tough facade, you both are putty in that little girl's hand. I have to say I was pleasantly surprised at how well you handled that whole 'daddies look out for their children' theme."

"Not that I made any progress."

Her smile glowed in the half light. "You never know with kids. It may take some time, but I think you planted a really strong seed in her mind. She was definitely thinking on it. And she seemed pretty relaxed with Trace at dinner. It was kind of cute to see this big cowboy cutting up her meat, fetching her milk. She let him dab her face with the napkin."

"He did look kind of comfortable in father mode. Like he was actually enjoying it." Ty had been amazed at the smiles that little girl could pull from his brother.

"So did you."

Chapter 13

After a few miles of silence, Mandy had given in to exhaustion and slept the rest of the way back to the hotel. Now, as she stood in the hotel room fresh from her shower, clothed in an oversized T-shirt and facing a bare-chested, jean-clad Ty, who had stretched out on the king-sized bed, she felt a tug of desire and an overwhelming need for closeness. Resisting him these last days had required mental discipline and physical restraint.

Here she was only a week in and her resolve was waning. What did that say about her character?

What it said was that her grandfather had purposely rigged the outcome by making them cohabitate in the same bedroom. It was easier, though still hard enough, when they had separate beds. But here she was, in a hotel room with that gigantic king bed containing a lounging *Playgirl* fantasy man.

A man who was so much more complex than she realized. A man whose life had been more difficult than she knew. A man she found herself far more attracted to than she had counted on.

Perfectly relaxed stretched out on the bed, he thumbed through his phone screens, his powerful shoulders resting against the tufted headboard, his jaw shadowed with stubble, his legs hugged by denim pants, and his bare feet crossed casually. And all she wanted to do was snuggle up against all that muscle and let him kiss her senseless.

He lifted his head, and she was caught in the crosshairs of a pair of shining dark eyes. It felt like some internal cyclone was propelling her toward him as his gaze dropped from her eyes to her neck, then to her breasts covered by cotton fabric, where he lingered an extra heartbeat before moving down past the hem to the length of her legs in a slow appraisal that pulled a trail of heat with it.

"You left the seat up, again." It was easier focusing on the toilet seat than on the man sending lust beams from his spot on the bed. She'd found the toilet seat up a few times during their time together, and having a brother, she was used to it. But if they were going to be together for six months, she figured he should at least try to remember.

"Sorry. I'm not accustomed to living with anyone. I'll be more careful." Ty patted the spot next to him. "I won't bite. Unless you ask me to, that is."

Feeling like she was walking on a cliff's edge, she moved toward the bed and settled her bottom on the far side from where he lounged. The cool, shimmery sheets sent a warning shiver through her.

"It was nice to meet Trace. And little Delanie. And see the ranch." Normal conversation, that's all they were having tonight. She hoped she could keep that promise to herself.

"Ranch isn't quite up to Prescott's standards, is it? And the drought has really decimated his herd. He needs to rebuild it, and soon."

She tucked that information away. "At least he's trying. Does that ranch date back before your father?" Seeing where he'd been raised, meeting his brother, had increased her curiosity, made her want to know more.

"My mother's parents owned it."

Mandy turned toward him, stretching out the length of the bed. "Speaking of parents, it must have been tough on you and Trace, losing your mother so young. What did she die from again?"

A car accident had taken Mandy's father. There'd been no time to prepare, no warning that hugging him before he left for that meeting would be the last time she'd ever hug him. She'd often wondered if it was harder or easier knowing the end was near, and she had come to the conclusion that it was rough all the same.

"She killed herself." The deep voice that spoke those words was flat, emotionless. And only added to Mandy's shock.

She remembered he had lost his mother. That was what had her feeling a connection with him way back when. But it hadn't been suicide. She would have remembered that.

He turned toward her. Shadows played across his stoic expression, making him look more rugged, tougher. But it was his eyes, glistening in the low lamp light, that made her feel like she'd just opened a forbidden closet.

"I only found out a few years ago…when I was bailing Trace out of a jam caused by the alcohol." Ty turned his line of sight toward the bedroom door, away from her. "Funny thing is, he thought I knew or at least suspected. I didn't. She'd been staying in bed a lot. I thought that was because she was sick and my daddy hadn't wanted to tell us. She'd cry sometimes. I'd hear her. But I thought that was because she knew she wasn't well and was worried about us. Little did I know she wasn't worried about leaving us at all. She was planning on it."

The pain wasn't covered by the toneless recitation of facts. It was amplified by it.

Mandy thought back to her father's death, so unexpected. The toxicology reports had indicated her father had been drinking that evening. And though her father had never had a drinking problem that she knew of, it had taken a long time for her to forgive him for imbibing that night at the stockowners' association meeting. How long would it have taken her to forgive her father for something like suicide? *Forever.*

Without thought, she reached across and rested her palm on his denim-clad thigh. She felt the muscle flex beneath, but she didn't remove her hand. Even if he didn't want the connection, she did.

"I'm so sorry, Ty," she finally said when she trusted herself to speak. "I know how hard it is to lose a parent regardless of the circumstances, but to learn later it was suicide…that's tough to bear, harder to make sense out of it all."

"I'm not asking for anyone's pity." His tone had sharpened.

"And I'm not offering pity. I got too much of that when my own father passed away. But depression is a disease, Ty. It's an illness. She obviously wasn't thinking straight."

"She was thinking straight enough to take a

whole lot of pills." The bitterness in his voice had the stinging effect of lemon juice on a cut. "As Trace tells it, my daddy found her in the bedroom, passed out. By the time he got her to the hospital, it was too late. She was pronounced dead. All the while I thought she was sick and the doctors just couldn't save her—I thought she had a weak heart. No one told me different."

"Trace knew though?"

"He's four years older. He knew. We never talked about it. My father never said a thing. But knowing it now, I should have seen signs, done something."

Guilt was a heavy burden to carry. Especially when it warred with anger at the very person you felt guilty about. She knew because she had watched JM suffer through it. He'd blamed himself for not going with his son that night. He would have been driving most likely, if he had.

"There's nothing a child can do to save a parent in a state like that, Ty. Even your father couldn't save her. He probably didn't even understand what was happening."

"He took it to his grave. If Trace hadn't slipped, I'd never have known. Part of me wishes I'd never found out that I'd been such a disappointment to both my parents."

"I'm sure that you weren't a disappointment to either of them."

"No? My mother couldn't face being my mother, and my father pretty much cut me out of his life after I took that scholarship. Barely spoke to me." He shifted on the bed. "But I didn't do so bad for myself. Thanks to JM."

"Thanks to your abilities."

Ty was wealthy, independent, self-reliant. Still, she couldn't get the thought of him struggling to understand the actions of a mother bent on leaving him permanently. Or what it must have felt like when he found out the truth.

It was like a damp winter wind had blown over her, over them both. She wanted to hold him, comfort him, wrap her arms around him in a hug, but she settled for resting her hand on his leg to reinforce the fragile bond she felt arcing between them. They had both lost a parent. They had both felt abandoned, felt anger…and betrayal.

She tried to imagine what it must have been like for Ty growing up with a cold father and a distant brother. She'd never been alone in her troubles. She'd always had family around to support her. For all of Ty's lone-wolf nature, he probably could have used some support. Maybe her grandfather knew that. Maybe that was why he'd watched out for Ty.

For the first time, she realized Ty was probably as devastated by the loss of her grandfather as she was and maybe he needed a little support too, given her grandfather had thrown him the same curveball he had thrown her. They were, for better or worse, in this together.

She leaned over and kissed him on the cheek, felt the stubble of his five o'clock shadow. She'd meant it to be just a light caress, but he twisted his face until his mouth met hers. His hand cupped the back of her neck, and his lips swooped over hers. There was nothing light about this kiss. In a heartbeat he was feeding her kisses, and she was returning them, taking them deeper.

Feeling like she was sinking in shifting quicksand, she grabbed his shoulders and hung on. Soft denim brushed against her legs, bare flesh rubbed against her tee shirt. His warm, surprisingly work-roughened fingers brushed up her arm, as if he was checking to make sure she was real. His warm touch brought tingles to her skin.

Ty raised his head and looked into her eyes. "I've wanted you since I first spied you striding through the barn in jeans and a tight pink T-shirt."

He remembered the color of her T-shirt?

"At the creek, you didn't want me." And she'd been desperate for him.

She'd gone after him that summer in the way of a seventeen-year-old starved for attention. She'd sneak up on him and clasp her hands over his eyes, hugging the back of him just so she could feel his body next to hers. He'd turn around, laugh, and hold her hands while he told her that she'd be sorry if she didn't watch it.

She didn't believe she'd be sorry about anything when it came to him.

She'd find him watering the horses and she'd grab the hose and spray him with water. He'd grab it back and spray her. With wet clothes clinging to her body, she'd revel in the appreciation she saw in his eyes.

Each day she found an excuse to be near him and devised ways she could tempt him.

Finally, one day, behind the barn, he grabbed her by the shoulders and kissed her—deep, possessive, with tongue. She'd never been kissed like that before, and it awoke in her a passion so fierce she could barely keep from climbing on top of him.

After that, they took every opportunity to make out. In the tack room, behind the barn, in the hayloft, in the haystack, in an empty stall.

It was bliss, and each day she woke up wondering when and where they'd have their next encounter.

Things progressed from kisses to touching to testing, and Mandy only wanted more. Knowing the summer was ending, and with it Ty's work on the ranch as he headed off to State, she made her move, convincing him that her grandfather wanted him to check out the fencing by the creek. It had been a lie. But Ty hadn't known that.

He dutifully saddled up one of the stable horses and headed out. Mandy saddled up Twinkle, her horse at the time, and cantered after him, taking a short cut through a copse of trees so she could arrive before him.

She stripped naked and waded into the creek near the fence he would be checking and hid behind one of the boulders by the shore.

Riding up, he didn't see her. She waited until he dismounted to check the fence, and then she yelled out to him.

"I'm stuck, Ty. Please help me."

"Mandy, where are you? I can't see you."

"I'm behind the boulder. I'm stuck. Please pull me out."

"Stuck? On what?"

"I don't know. Help me, Ty."

He took off his boots, stripped to his underwear, and dove into the water. As soon as she heard the splash, Mandy emerged from around the boulder. Being the water was only waist high and Mandy was naked, Ty's mouth dropped open at the sight of her—just as she planned.

Before he could react, she ran to him and wrapped her nude, wet body around his. She felt his erection and figured she got what she wanted.

"Mandy, no."

"Why not? There's no one here but us."

"No." He extricated himself from her grasp, turned his back on her, and walked toward the shore.

She'd called after him, told him she wanted him to be the first. Begged him to come back.

Instead, with his back turned, he put on his pants, put on his boots, threw on his shirt, mounted his horse, and rode away without saying another word—leaving her naked and humiliated.

He avoided her for the next two days until he left for college, never saying another word to her. And he never came back to work on the ranch either.

"Make no mistake. I wanted you. But you were just seventeen, Mandy, and I wasn't in any position to do right by you."

Ty shifted his body so he rested on his side, his head propped on his large hand as his dark eyes focused like a laser on her face. She resisted the urge to run her fingers up his chest, to press her body into his. Her heart pumped hard against her ribs as she studied his face, looking for signs he was lying. She didn't find any—but that didn't mean he was telling the truth.

"I know I was just seventeen. I wasn't expecting marriage." Though her fantasies had certainly gone in that direction at the time. She was young. He had been her first love…

"I wasn't ready for any kind of relationship. I had to finish school. Then law school. Knowing that, it wouldn't have been right to take advantage of the situation."

She looked away, taking what little relief that action granted. "I wanted you to be the first." The words came out in a need-filled whisper.

"I didn't feel worthy of the honor. Not when I knew that nothing could come of it."

As it turned out, Chet Voorhees, her first college boyfriend, hadn't been worthy of it either, but that hadn't stopped him.

"And you feel worthy of it now? Or is honor no longer involved?"

His hand cupped the back of her head as his thumb brushed across her cheek.

"Things are different. Clearer. We are much older. There's an end game we've both agreed to. There's an attraction we both have. And a bedroom we've been forced to share. I like you, Mandy. And, maybe more importantly, I respect you. Your business sense, your drive, the way you related to Delanie." Those strokes on her cheek were like zings of electricity jolting through her, softening her from the inside out. "It only increases your attractiveness. And that's the truth."

She wanted to believe him. But believing him would only make it more dangerous for her heart.

His large fingers slid down her cheek and cupped her chin. "Let's finish what was started that summer."

He leaned in. Warm lips brushed across hers in a whisper of a kiss.

"Don't think. Just feel, honey," he murmured against her ear.

That was easy enough to do, given the sensations dancing through her.

He kissed her temple, a sweet and simple gesture. And then covered her mouth as his muscled arms wrapped around her, enclosing her in a Ty-scented cocoon. This kiss was powerful and possessive, spiking passion clear to her toes.

She wanted this. She wanted him. That had never been the question. What she'd risk to have him—that was the problem. But the will to fight desire had drained out of her. She inched her hands around his neck as his tongue delved deep into her mouth and his chest rubbed against her breasts. Pulses of pleasure thrummed through her.

"God, you smell good. Taste good. Feel good." He whispered the words in her ear, and those pulses of pleasure melded into a throbbing ache.

Breathing in his freshly showered scent, she kissed the soft skin of his throat.

He let out a small groan and shifted his body against her. His hips pressed hardened flesh between her legs, and his mouth covered hers, taking her air away.

He was a sensuous kisser, knowing how to play his tongue, how to sweep his lips, how much pressure was needed to tantalize, to possess. His body moved over hers in slow, lazy rhythms that caused a scrumptious friction. How could she resist him when she wanted him so much?

"I've waited a long time, Mandy." Ty's voice was gravely, deep, daunting as he leaned back and looked her in the eye.

She wrapped her legs around his waist, hugging

him to her body. She felt the hard length of his penis through her clothes, and her whole body tightened in response as his mouth curved in an enticing smile. "I'm going to undress you. Slowly."

An involuntary sigh of pure surrender escaped her lips.

He rose up from the bed, his knees astride her hips. She watched as his rough fingers scraped her flesh and fumbled with the fabric of her top. Cool air teased her skin as he lifted her shirt, only to be replaced by the caressing heat of breath and moist lips. A wave of gravity-defying desire lifted her when warm palms stroked across the tender spot of her belly.

In the next breath, his lips brushed across her breast and his tongue circled her nipple. All coherent thought faded. His lips tugged and pulled. Her hunger intensified. He shifted to the other nipple and began the same slow, tortuous dance with his tongue.

She closed her eyes to concentrate on the whirlwind of sensations his wet mouth was provoking just touching her there. She was so focused on what his mouth was doing, she didn't notice his hand until he slid it under the waistband of her underwear. He cupped her crotch and murmured something about how wet she was. She dug her fingers into his hair as she felt the tip of his finger rub against her sensitive spot while his mouth continued to feed on her breasts, and her muscles collapsed.

Ty seemed to know exactly what a woman needed. Exactly what Mandy needed.

"Let me free you of these," he murmured against her tummy, as he slid her undies down her legs, pulling them from under her in one sure motion. Her shirt slid up to her shoulders and then over her head.

She offered no resistance. And little help.

When she felt nothing more—no motion, no touch—she opened her eyes.

He was up on his knees, and pure masculine appreciation stared back at her.

"I've never wanted a woman like I want you, Mandy." His words were matter of fact, but his voice quavered, as if the thought scared him.

She didn't believe him, of course. It had been ten years since that incident at the creek, and he certainly never acted as if he wanted her more than other women. It was lust talking and nothing more. But tonight, lust was enough.

The prominent bulge in his pants, level with her face, beckoned her to explore.

"Strip," she commanded in a voice that had suddenly gone hoarse. She would have done it for him if she had the strength.

She watched, mesmerized, as he did her bidding. Muscles rippled across his chest, bare except for the narrow ribbon of hair arrowing toward the denim waistband. Bronzed flesh glistened in the diffused light. He had a sculpture's dream body of well-defined muscles, smooth skin, and long limbs. On his upper arms, where the muscles were most prominent, the tan lines of a man who worked outdoors were visible, separating the two shades of tan—one with the shirt on, one with the shirt off, all of it cosmically glorious.

He pulled on his belt buckle, the crinkles in his pants attesting to the ever-expanding bulge it protected. Belt ends drooped as he tugged down the jeans zipper, exposing white fabric wrapping a cylindrical object.

He stared at her as he slid the faded denims down his carved and muscled thighs, leaving just the underwear.

Something elemental tripped inside—as if her DNA had flipped an electrifying switch.

"Take it out," he said, his voice gravelly, his tone urgent.

Not needing to be asked twice, she shoved down the waistband of his tighty-whities. His penis sprang free and dangled before her like forbidden fruit on a limb.

She grasped his long, hot shaft in her hand, the skin as smooth as polished marble. His groan was deep as he brushed hair from her face. He wrapped his hands around hers so she couldn't move.

"All you have to do is touch me, and I'm set to go off. I don't want to finish before I get started." He kissed her forehead, and, reluctantly, she released him.

In one motion he dispensed with his clothes and, once again, straddled her, his knees capturing her hips.

From his broad shoulders, to his workout-defined torso, to hair-brushed thighs that supported the substantial symbol of his maleness, he was perfection.

She brushed her hands up his firm thighs, and his muscles bunched. Self-respect, she'd determined, was highly overrated.

"If we're finally going to do this, really do this, Mandy, I need to put on protection," he said, a tinge of regret in his voice as he looked down at her, his eyes so intense and stormy they belied the practical words he'd just spoken.

She nodded, at once glad and irritated he was still so clear headed.

He pulled a condom from the draw on the bed stand and pulled open the foil pouch. She watched as he expertly guided the condom over and down his thick, hard cock. With the condom in place, he slid between her legs. She was beyond caring about business and wills and anything that would keep her from him.

He began trailing kisses down her neck, behind her ear, and at the little indentation at her throat, all the while gently kneading her breast.

"You have beautiful breasts." He was now kissing his way to her nipple. She wondered what made breasts beautiful to a man? After all, hers weren't that large. He teased her nipple with his tongue. "And nice rosy nipples." He suckled and she arched her back. His fingers played with her clitoris. Inside of her, tension coiled and desire engulfed her.

He kissed his way up her chest, past her throat, and stopped short of her lips. "Look at me," he said.

She was looking at him, or at least his body. But she shifted her gaze to stare into his eyes, eyes that were dark, intense, dangerous. Eyes filled with so much heat, they melted her.

He placed his hands under her thighs, lifted them up. "I'm finally going to have you."

One smooth thrust and he plunged deep inside of her as his hands pressed against her thighs. She gasped. He smiled. "I want you to know, to remember, what I feel like when I'm buried in you, Mandy."

She'd never forget this wonderful combination of pressure and tension, this sense of being totally filled.

He slowly withdrew, then thrust again, then again and again. He was building the delicious tension. Too slow. Agonizingly slow. She bucked as he pressed her thighs to her chest, encouraging him to go faster. "More," she gasped out.

The rhythm increased as he kept thrusting. But it was still too controlled.

"Do you want me, Mandy," he growled.

"Yes." She did with every fiber of her being. She'd been denying it so long, she'd almost believed it. But she'd been lying to herself.

"Say you want me. Say the words."

"I want you."

"Say my name."

"I want you, Ty."

He slung her leg over his shoulder, growled her name, and thrust into her so deep she felt it in her belly. And then he was pounding against her. Faster, harder, pounding, pounding, as his hands tightly held her bottom. He slapped against her thighs like a nail gun on speed until the wave of tension broke in a torrential release that zinged within her body like a pinball hitting the jackpot. She trembled as she clenched around him. He growled something and then crumbled on top of her, his ragged breath sounding in her ear.

Chapter 14

Ty wrapped his arms around Mandy, spooning flesh to flesh as she slept, her breathing calm and even.

It had only taken a week for them to tumble into bed together, but it seemed like a lifetime, and he was surprised it had happened at all, given everything. He felt drained yet strangely exhilarated. He pressed a kiss to the silky hair that swept across the pillow

He felt like he'd tumbled over a cliff and was still in free fall. Maybe that's why, all those years ago, he had run from Mandy Prescott. Because he, maverick though he was, would have married her—and not because she was JM's granddaughter. Not just that, anyway.

But because she was a woman he could appreciate. Strong, firm, smart, passionate, loyal. Despite the provisions of JM's will, she hadn't once said a word against her grandfather. She wouldn't, he realized. Because to Mandy, JM was as much a part of her as her leg or her arm. He was family, and that meant everything.

The fact he hadn't had much of a family—not after his mother died, anyway, and not much before, if he was honest—had set him on the path of independence early. He'd taken care of himself and expected the same of everyone else. When Trace had gotten into trouble all those years ago, he'd resented having to step in. After all, Ty had kept up his part of the unspoken bargain. He'd never asked for anything from his father or his brother. And what JM had provided, Ty had earned through hard work that resulted in stellar grades. When he stepped out into the world, he'd used his education to make a good living.

Mandy, on the other hand, had always been surrounded by family—a community of people who wanted the best for her, even if they didn't agree on what that was. And she accepted their doubts along with their support while she made her contribution to the fabric of that community. She didn't whine about Tucker's lack of effort for Prescott, or resent her grandfather's lack of faith in her. She accepted the role of making the family business stronger, even if that meant not leading it. She may have resented Ty's interference, but she'd taken what he offered when she thought it helped the business, the family, the community that made up her company. She didn't resent those family ties—she celebrated them. Because they made her stronger, not weaker.

He'd always been careful not to care too much about anything—or anyone. Keeping his distance allowed him to remain objective and detached, and that enabled him to make tough decisions when needed and walk away when politics got too much. And, if he was honest, it assured he wouldn't risk feeling the pain of loss if things didn't go his way.

That summer he'd come to work for JM, he'd felt like an orphan looking in the window of somebody else's home and wishing he could be part of the family residing there. By then, his father had pretty much washed his hands of a son who thought he was too good for ranching, at least that was his father's version. Maybe Ty had been that orphaned kid too long, had been looking in JM's window these last ten years and unconsciously coveting JM's family—and Mandy.

He closed his eyes.

He wasn't the kind of man who fit anywhere or with anyone. So where was this need to belong coming from? And shouldn't sex with Mandy fill that void instead of adding to it? Why wasn't being alone, dependent on no one and no one dependent on him, satisfying anymore?

Hell, even his individualist-to-a-fault brother had become part of a family the moment Delanie entered his life. Trace was no longer an island, isolated and detached. He was talking about preschool and social workers, for Christ's sake.

He could almost relate because being the other half of a team with Mandy had been surprisingly enjoyable this last week. Self-reliance sounded good, but was it real? After all, JM's connections had smoothed his way, had created trusting relationships earlier and easier than if he'd had to go it totally alone.

He rolled away from her, feeling the chill where her body had warmed him. The fact he wanted to be part of anything with Mandy spooked him. He tucked his hands under his head. He had to get a grip. Being independent, needing no one, should be a good thing. Particularly since it was the only way he knew how to be.

Mandy woke up to sun streaming in the windows and the smell of bacon wafting through the room.

It took her a moment to realize where she was and what had happened the night before. So why wasn't she panicked, she wondered as she stretched. Instead, she felt indulged, lazy, content like a lioness after a huge meal.

Sitting up, she looked around the spacious but empty room. Ty's new boots sat in the corner, the pants he'd flung to the ground lay bunched on the carpet with the pile of her clothes, and a tray of eggs, bacon, toast, and coffee sat on the small side table. She heard water running in the shower and took a deep breath.

Last night had been incredible—and unnerving. Physically satisfying and emotionally upending. Her heart did a flippy-floppy kind of beat. She leaned back against the cushioned headboard for support.

Despite all her attempts to resist him, she was falling for Ty Martin, this man of so many contradictions. How could that be when just a few days ago he'd been her sworn enemy, a man who had duped her grandfather and undermined her role?

She shook her head, hoping for some sense. This was temporary. No commitment. Six months and done. Sex and nothing more.

Reality hadn't changed. Ty was still going to decide the fate of the company based on the numbers. He was still going to walk away at the end of six months. All they'd been doing last night was playing.

Easy as it would be to sentimentalize it, there was no romance here. *Just incredible pleasure.* If she could remember that, if she could keep it strictly physical, maybe she could enjoy the moment and keep the whole business side of their relationship separate. But could she keep the emotional side separate?

Her cell phone jangled, startling her. Scooping it up from the nightstand, she noted the caller was Harold. He'd already be at the Utah rodeo setting up, having headed there directly from Washington. The fact he was calling probably meant problems.

Though Harold was economical with words, it didn't take many to tell her that Stan Lassiter had been brought in as "backup" at the Utah rodeo. Never in all the years her family had been in the rodeo business had someone been brought in to "back up" a Prescott-run rodeo unless Prescott had requested it. And now this rodeo committee had done it.

Just as she finished the call, Ty appeared in the doorway, looking like sex on a stick with nothing but a towel wrapped around his showered body. Playtime was over. Back to reality.

"That was Harold. We've got trouble in Utah."

* * *

She admired the way Ty swung into action even as she resented the command aspect of it. Within the hour he'd *permitted* her for showering, dressing, and a bite to eat, he'd made the calls, filed the flight plan— since they couldn't waste time driving—and packed the bags so they could take off by midmorning.

Mandy had steeled for the flight and given a prayer of thanks when the landing had been uneventful. She'd never get used to flying in such a small aircraft, no matter how often she'd be forced to use it for convenience's sake.

Ty drove the rental car into the parking lot of the arena right after lunchtime, kicking up gravel as he aimed the vehicle toward the horse trailers parked in the distance. There was only one bearing the Rustic Rodeo insignia. Clearly Lassiter hadn't brought the full complement of rodeo stock he'd had at Greenville, making her wonder why Stan had bothered himself for a dozen broncs and bulls.

He wouldn't make a profit on that small amount, so he was likely here for next year's contract, like a buzzard circling a young heifer. But young as she might be in Stan's eyes, she wasn't going to lie down and roll over.

She glanced at Ty, but with those aviator sunglasses on, she couldn't tell what he was thinking. He'd barely mentioned their encounter last night. Maybe a one-night stand was all he was after. Maybe she'd disappointed. Maybe she was still a foolish seventeen-year-old thinking sex would change everything for the better.

Instead, on the flight they'd discussed the cowboys who were likely to show and the stock Harold was bringing. Ty had also asked for a rundown on the rodeo committee.

Though Ty had voiced surprise at the news of Stan's arrival, that didn't mean he hadn't known. Or arranged it. Had the decision been made already? Maybe the roll in the hay had been a means of distraction. No doubt Ty was in a hurry to wrap things up so he could get on with his real life. And the way to do that was to sell the company. And fast. And Stan Lassiter was interested.

Running a rodeo company might be enough for

her, but it would never satisfy a guy like Ty, who was used to big deals—and going it alone. If working with livestock had been for him, wouldn't he have thrown in with Trace and run the family ranch, undoubtedly making it a going concern and giving little Delanie better prospects.

She gave a silent sigh as she thought about Delanie, born into such risky circumstances. If Mandy had a child, even on her own, there would be so many people who would love that child. Her child would want for nothing—except a father.

Which unnervingly brought her thoughts back to Ty and his plans to sell her company.

The night might have been filled with passion for her, but now it was back to reality, harsh reality.

"Have you talked to Stan since the Greenville Rodeo?" she asked.

He glanced in her direction as he maneuvered the car around the gravel potholes, but those sunglasses guarded his eyes. Even without sunglasses, Ty was a study in reticence.

"No. Have you?"

"Hardly." Mandy clenched and unclenched her fingers in an attempt to mitigate the tension she was feeling. "You will let me know when the analysis is done."

He stopped the car alongside the two livestock trailers bearing the Prescott logo and turned off the ignition.

"I'm not going to sneak out and sell the company behind your back, if that is what you're asking."

"That's what I'm asking."

Ty blew out a breath. "I checked in with the

consultants before we left. They are hoping to have some preliminary figures on the business by Tuesday. As soon as they come through, I'll review them with you. Promise."

"You know I'm going to fight you with everything I can if you try to sell. Last night didn't change that." She held her breath, hoping it had for him but knowing by his amused half smile that nothing had changed.

"I didn't think it would, Mandy. And I'm in full agreement on keeping pleasure and business separate."

Of course he was, because he'd have no trouble doing that. If only it would be as easy for her.

"I'm hoping the numbers will make the case all by themselves. One way or the other," he said as he shoved the keys into his jeans pocket.

That was the flaw in his thinking. No amount of accounting could capture the intrinsic value she placed on Prescott Rodeo Company. How could mere numbers reflect the sweat and labor her grandfather and father had spent building up the company that carried their name? Or the joys and triumphs she'd experienced in working with the animals? Or the warm sense of community that had grown with the enterprise? All of this was the legacy she wanted to provide her children. And Tuck's children, even if her brother didn't value it yet as much as she did.

"You could be a rich woman, Mandy. Especially if you decided to develop the ranch land once the company was sold. Rich enough to start your own stock company, if that's really your passion."

Though she'd never willingly sell the ranch, she'd thought about starting another company if

Prescott was sold. But why sell something to buy the same thing. "I wouldn't be able to use the name Prescott Rodeo Company, would I?"

"The name could be part of the company's goodwill value."

"How about Prescott Stock Company?"

He shrugged. "Depends on the type of restrictions the buyer asks for. They could ask for a noncompete clause but only for a set time, generally no more than two years."

Two years. Seemed a lifetime. Six months seemed a lifetime.

"And then I'd be starting over. All the bloodlines my grandfather and Harold took such great pains to preserve in breeding programs would be for the benefit of someone else. No, Ty, I intend to keep what I've got. It may surprise you," she said, grabbing the handle to open the door as a wave of irritation rolled over her, "but some things can't be measured in dollars and cents."

She stepped out of the car as his driver's door clicked shut. She closed her door with a little more gusto, causing a loud clang.

He stared at her from across the top of the car, the sun's rays bouncing off the shiny black surface of his sunglasses.

"Everything has a price, Mandy. And trade-offs. The decision comes in figuring out which trade-offs are worth it." He glanced away, undoubtedly to check out movement across the yard, before focusing back on her. "Just want to be sure starting your own company is something you've given some thought."

"I have thought about it. And I want Prescott."

He walked around the car, heading toward her with deliberate steps, his long legs closing the distance in seconds. He stopped mere inches in front of her, invading her space. She peered up into a face just a breath from her own and silently cursed the mask of glass that guarded his eyes.

She wanted to know what he felt, not just what he said. Did he have any regard for her, for what she wanted?

"So what's the plan?" he said, his question catching her off guard.

"The plan?"

"With the rodeo committee."

He'd changed the topic without apology or explanation.

"I think I should see the rodeo committee. Alone. I know these people. I feel very comfortable requesting an explanation. They'll likely be more honest with just me."

He nodded, surprising her with his acceptance.

"I should probably see Stan, then," he said.

"He's the primary potential buyer, isn't he?"

At that question, he removed his sunglasses to look her square in the eye. "Yes. So far." Unfortunately, his stoic expression didn't reveal anything that gave her hope¬—about her or Prescott.

"You planning on sealing the deal this weekend?" She'd never been good about keeping her thoughts, or opinions, to herself. Under the stress of circumstances, she'd given up trying.

"I owe it to him to hear him out. But as I said, the numbers won't be available until Monday, which I told Stan. I really want to understand what the hell he's doing here."

"If he was asked to come by the committee, I may not like it, but I can't blame him for it."

"I'd still like to talk to him. Find out what he's up to. And tell him we're married."

"I'm sure he already knows. I'm sure everyone knows. News travels fast on the circuit." Whoever thought men didn't gossip likely had never worked with them.

She knew there would be a lot of speculation as to the whys and wherefores. It didn't matter to her what people would think at the moment, but what they would think a few months from now when Ty walked away, owning almost a third of the company—or worse, having sold off the outfit—and she would be left alone, a divorced woman, and perhaps a divorced, unemployed woman. And no happily ever after as her poor, deluded grandfather had hoped.

"Regardless, it's better to get ahead of the rumor mill. Everyone probably thinks we're crazy and will be betting it won't last. In six months, when we divorce, they'll feel vindicated. In the meantime, we get to play house." His smile broadened to a full-blown grin.

This was business, strictly business, to him. And she was just a way to pass the time. She was annoyed at how her heart squeezed at that truth. She blinked back the moisture forming in her eyes

"Any regrets about last night?" he asked, cocking his head to one side.

More than she had earlier that morning. But she didn't believe in regrets. The marriage, last night, may have been mistakes, but she'd made those decisions. Living was moving forward, not looking back. With a shake of her head, she gave him the reassurance of a negative response.

"Me either, Mandy."

Of course not. He had nothing to lose.

He leaned in, tucked his finger under her chin, and turned her mouth to his.

He meant to kiss her.

Heart pounding, she took an irrational step back.

He straightened, his jaw bunched.

Mandy turned and walked toward the arena with her head high, her back straight, and all the Prescott pride she could muster.

Chapter 15

Ty walked back to the holding pens, where the smell was pure manure. Cattle lowed, horses nickered, and bulls snorted their displeasure at being caged. The cattle pens and horse pens were larger because they held the herds, but the bulls usually had individual holding pens, being they weren't the most social of animals. He looked around for Mandy, but all he saw were a few hands going about their set-up duties.

He'd had his talk with Stan. The man claimed the committee had initiated the call, and then pointed out all the things that could ruin a rodeo stock company's reputation, urging Ty to sell immediately and naming a price Ty didn't need an analysis to know was ridiculously low. Poor choice of tactics. Made him distrust the man even more.

Last night had been pretty damn amazing, awakening in him a lust like he'd never known before. It must have been the fact he'd been waiting ten years. That had to be the explanation for the powerful surge of emotion that had rushed through him—still rushed through him.

She'd said she had no regrets about last night, but she'd stepped back from his kiss, and there had been something in her eyes that said otherwise. It hadn't been there last night. No, she'd been all warm and welcoming last night. It hadn't been there early this morning either. He'd swear he'd seen a "come hither" look in her eyes, and if Harold hadn't called, they'd have taken another tumble.

Her frostiness had begun when she'd pressed him about Stan's interest in the company and why Stan had shown up. Her reception to the news that Stan was at the rodeo made him silently bet against a repeat performance of last night. She didn't trust him, and the fact he was trying to play it straight with her only seemed to fuel that distrust. The prospect of selling Prescott stood between them.

So why was selling made an option? He doubted the analysis would show Prescott was in financial trouble. Was the size of the revenue stream more important than the endeavor? A week ago Ty would have said yes. But now being part of Prescott, he was no longer so sure.

Ty looked around the pens and didn't see Mandy. He asked a young hand who had been hired on a temporary basis to fill in for Bradshaw. Ty would never have granted a crew member time off during the busy season, but that had been Mandy's call. The newly hired young man sent Ty to the arena. Still no Mandy.

He wanted to find her. Tell her about the meeting with Stan and allay her fears, given the man's offer had been way too low. In this economy it would be tough to find qualified buyers who could meet the likely price. That would relieve him of the conflict between Mandy's interest and JM's—and make Mandy a happy woman.

He headed back toward the holding pens as he searched in the distance for any sign of a feminine form.

Rounding the corner, Ty heard the yelling even before he reached the pens. The commotion was coming from the parking lot. He glanced at his watch. The gates would have just opened.

With clipped steps, he passed by the corrals and spied a few cowboys running toward the lot. Ty was just about to follow when Harold swung in on his horse, spraying up dirt and gravel.

"Ty," he called. "We've got trouble. A bull got loose."

"Loose?"

Harold nodded. "Bring a rope." He motioned toward a horse tied to fencing, a horse that looked like Willow. A rope was hanging off the saddle.

At least Mandy wasn't on her horse trying to capture the bull. Bulls were dangerous animals. They'd gore a horse or a human—it didn't matter to them. Charging was their way of defending themselves, and anything was fair game.

It had been a while since he'd done any fancy roping, but he'd been good enough to handle his father's herd back in the day. He'd do better though if he was mounted, like Harold.

Willow backed up when Ty's rump settled in the saddle. No doubt she'd been expecting Mandy's weight on her back. But he'd seen the mare in action. She was a trained cutting horse, and she took commands well.

He reined the horse around and headed at a fast trot toward the parking area and the shouting. As he came out into open space, he saw two cowboys fanning hats in the direction of a large black bull. But the bull wasn't paying any mind. He was staring at something or someone up against a cement wall.

Harold, his rope in hand, was yelling for somebody to get one of the bullfighters.

Ty nudged his horse closer. And blood drained from his body.

It wasn't just something or someone that bull had pinned against the wall. It was Mandy. She looked stoically composed for being in the sight line of an angry bull, except her face was as white as bleached cotton.

Like a jackhammer on steroids, Mandy's heart pounded against her ribs as she glanced at the snorting bull pawing the asphalt. *Breathe*, she reminded herself. Careful not to meet the bull's gaze, she didn't dare look away either, settling instead for watching him out of the corner of her eye as she leaned against the rough cement wall for support. Her legs were weakening, and her hands felt like a thousand needles were pricking her.

The rope clutched in her sweaty fingers was the slim hope she had of distracting the beast. She weighed her odds as movement caught her eye, and she forced herself to look up and away—and right at Ty Martin mounted on Willow. Harold came charging in on his horse right behind Ty.

Both men let go a whoop, and as the bull's head swung in Ty's direction, the two men swung their ropes—and missed. Within a heartbeat, Ty had regrouped and swung again, this time catching on the black bull's smallish horns. A flick of the bull's head, and the rope was dislodged. In a blink, the bull's attention refocused on her. And then his head lowered.

"Run right." Ty's voice thundered over the clacking of hooves, and Mandy realized he'd maneuvered Willow between her and the bull.

Her feet felt like lead weights, but she followed his directions, aware that Willow was now blocking the sight of the bull as she ran alongside her horse.

From behind she heard Harold whooping and the clattering of several pairs of hooves against the hard pavement.

She could feel her chest squeeze as her legs continued to propel her. She gasped for breath.

"Stop," called Ty.

Willow pulled up with such abruptness, Mandy was almost past the horse by the time she could come to a halt. Ty leaned over and threw an arm out to encircle her. He freed a stirrup for her use, and she fitted her foot in and grabbed on to him and slung her leg over Willow's rump. Atop her horse, behind the saddle, she wrapped her arms around Ty's warm body clothed in soft cotton and leaned her head against his back while she took a deep, lung-filling breath that pulled in Ty's scent.

"You okay?" Ty called, urging Willow into a trot.

"Yes," she shouted, all too aware there was still danger. "We've got to get him. Before he hurts someone."

Two more mounted cowhands had ridden into the parking lot. The agitated bull was now prancing between some cars. Whatever few people had been out in the lot had scattered for shelter, and one of the cowboys had gone to the lot entrance to stop any additional vehicles from coming in.

It took several attempts and much whooping and circling, but finally Ty and Harold were able to get a rope around the bull's neck. They pulled it taut between them, and the bull stopped in his tracks.

Who knew the man could rope?

"Yes, I can rope," Ty said as he twisted back to look at her as if he'd read her mind.

"You ready, Ty? We can't afford any slack with this one," Harold called.

"Ready."

It took a bit to get the bull back into the pen, but by keeping the animal off balance between the two, the bull had given up fighting and allowed himself to be led. By the time they penned him, he was pretty docile.

Two cowboys stood by, ready to lock the gate.

Once the bull was secure, Mandy slid off Willow and checked the lock herself.

Looking at the two cowboys and the others who had wandered back, she stood with her hands on her hips. Fear had given way to irritation. "I want to know what happened here. Why did this bull get out? I checked these pens myself just a half hour ago. Which means someone had to open it. I want to know who. And why?" She kept her voice calm and even and hoped no one saw the lingering tremor in her hand as she brushed a strand of hair out of her face.

As if for emphasis, the bull, safely behind bars, charged the side of the pen, creating a clatter. Mandy jumped as her heart landed in her throat.

"We were watering the horses, Mandy." Doug

McClane spoke for him and his partner, Slim Matthews. "The bulls were done first. I don't know why anyone would even be over here now."

"That would suggest that someone was up to no good—at Prescott Rodeo's expense," Mandy said, trying to ignore the bull, which once again rattled the pen. "You guys ask around," she told the handful of cowhands who had assembled. "Let me know what you hear.

"Harold, maybe a cowhand should be assigned to watch over these pens. If someone is causing trouble, we need to be prepared." Ty said as he slid off Willow.

Harold leaned forward in his saddle. "Saunders," he called to the tall, thin man who usually worked the livestock gates in the arena. "You're on duty until I relieve you." Harold turned his attention back to Ty. "That was some pretty good cowboying out there, Ty."

Ty acknowledged the compliment with a nod as Harold moved out.

Mandy waited as Ty secured Willow to a post, the mare's coat matted in sweat. He gave the horse a pat on her nose as he whispered words to the animal that she couldn't hear.

Ty's strides were purposeful as he walked toward Mandy.

She could still feel the tension needles pricking her limbs. It no longer felt like her legs would hold her weight. Aftershock was setting in.

"You all right, honey?" Ty asked, stopping a few feet from her as if waiting for some signal from her.

At that moment she needed comfort and his strength, and she walked right into the arms he stretched out to her.

"I've been better," she whispered against his shirt as she leaned on him, no longer trusting her legs. "Thanks for helping. That bull might have hurt someone."

"It might have hurt you. What were you doing out there?"

"Keeping my bull from going after anyone else."

"So you're some kind of bullfighter now?" He sounded beyond annoyed, as if she'd done something wrong.

"I did what I had to do. If It's Nasty had hurt anyone, we wouldn't have a chance of coming back next year. As it is, we may not."

"Didn't it go well with the committee?" He squeezed her tighter.

"We'll be bidding against Stan for next year. The committee is divided."

"You mention the sweetener?"

She brushed another strand of hair from her face. "I did, though we keep giving that sweetener and we'll overwork our premier stock."

"You know you about gave me a heart attack." She felt his moist lips on her forehead.

"Did I? I 'bout gave myself one."

He had been there for her this time. But he wasn't sticking around. And he had the power to ruin her life.

She looked up at him, and his warm brown eyes swept over her.

"I'm going to kiss you. And you're going to let me. Right here, in front of whoever wants to watch, Mandy."

She pulled back, but he didn't give her more than a second before his lips claimed hers in an anything but gentle kiss. It swamped her senses like some hot whirlwind, scrambling her mind and leaving her dizzy.

When he'd finished creating havoc, he stepped back, and all manner of whooping and hollering started as applause erupted. Over the din, Mandy heard her name being called.

"I'm all right, Mom," she shouted as the small crowd dispersed.

Now that was a lie. Her body may have been all right, but her heart was in major trouble. She could lie to herself and blame being off balance on the encounter with the bull. But that wasn't it. Ty was the only male who had done this to her.

"My God, what happened? Harold said a bull got out." Sheila scooped Mandy away from Ty into her loving arms and squeezed her tight.

"I'm fine."

"That bull put away?" Sheila asked, looking around as if she expected the creature to materialize right by her side.

"Yes. Harold and Ty corralled it," Mandy explained as she took a step back. She was embarrassed to be the center of attention for an audience of her rodeo workers. How was she ever to gain their respect if people kept fussing over her? And kissing her?

"Your daughter decided to be a hero," Ty said, shaking his head.

"I did what any responsible owner of an escaped bull would do. What should I have done, let him stampede some poor patron in the parking lot?"

Ty stared at her like she was addlebrained. "Called for backup."

"I did call. Why do you think Harold was already saddled and the other two cowboys rode in?"

Her mother looped her arm around Mandy's. "I'm taking you to the hotel. You need a break."

Mandy didn't protest. She was being bombarded by emotions she couldn't sort out right now, and the cause was standing there frowning.

"Well, I'm glad you're okay, but Ty was right— what were you thinking?" her mother said before she took a sip from the hotel restaurant's ivory mug.

Mandy wrapped her hand around her warm cup of tea. She'd have preferred coffee, but in her mother's book, hot tea was the only thing that helped you through an ordeal.

"I had a duty, as the owner of that bull, to protect people."

Her mother shook her perfectly coiffed blond head, as if her daughter didn't understand the lesson. "That kind of protecting is for a man to do, Mandy. A woman, any woman, is no match for a two-ton bull."

"He's PRC's responsibility. That means he's my responsibility." But she couldn't deny that little tingle low in her stomach and the warmth flowing through her veins knowing Ty had protected her. Like a knight charging, he'd come to rescue her—as if he cared— about her. And then he'd kissed her. And it hadn't been a peck on the cheek but a full-out, tongue-in-mouth, hard-to-breathe kiss.

She didn't know what to make of it. Maybe it was the adrenaline of the moment. That had to be it. She couldn't get her hopes up, because she feared this time the fall would be too far for recovery. Her mother's lips pursed. "You're stubborn, Mandy, just like your grandfather—and not his best quality."

"I won't refute either statement. But I am who I am." And that meant she had to stay grounded and not romanticize a relationship that had no future. He was still going to sell her company if the numbers said so. A man who cared for her would never, ever do that. A man who just wanted sex to pass the time wouldn't hesitate. Ty was definitely the latter.

"Yes, well...I didn't bring you here to talk about PRC." She set her mug down and brushed her fingers across the cream-colored tablecloth as if trying to dismiss the fabric's soft wrinkles. She raised her head and looked straight at Mandy.

"I saw that kiss. Is there something you want to tell me?" Her mother's eyes were wide with interest.

"Like what?" she asked, knowing full well what was on her mother's mind. She just wasn't sure she should share it yet, considering she didn't understand what *it* was. She hadn't a clue how to describe her relationship with Ty. And having sex with him had just muddied things further.

"Have you two...you know?" her mother pressed.

Mandy closed her eyes, knowing there was no escape. She opened them. Sheila leaned in.

"Yes. But it doesn't mean anything."

Shelia shifted back with a way-too-satisfied expression on her face. "That kiss I witnessed sure looked like it meant something."

And it had felt like it meant something. But Mandy knew differently. "To Ty it's just a way to pass the time." Just saying those words sent a pinch to her heart. But it was the truth.

"Really? Could have fooled me. If this is how you two are after just a week or two, I'd place a bet on having a still-married daughter and maybe a grandchild in a year from now."

If her mother only knew how much those words pained her.

"You're whistling in a hail storm. There's a canyon-size gap between what Ty and I have been forced into and a real marriage." And Ty's focus on selling made it an unbridgeable one. Too bad, because if Ty wasn't so damn single minded in his pursuit of the almighty dollar, she'd seen some real promise in him after the visit with Trace and little Delanie. She'd gotten a glimpse, however small, of a man who could care about someone else, of a man capable of tenderness and in need of it.

"I'd like grandchildren, is all."

Mandy leaned back against her chair. Her temple pulsed like a hammer gun popping nails. "And I hope to give you a grandchild someday. *After* I find the right man." Whenever that might be, if that ever might be. What were her odds of finding a man who could share her dream for Prescott? And someone who would be good father material?

What if she never found Mr. Right? Or he turned out to be Mr. Wrong? She might have better luck finding a sperm donor than finding the right man. The pounding in her head got stronger.

Chapter 16

Mandy watched as Tucker prepared to mount his bronc. Running a rodeo where her brother competed was a mixed blessing. She was happy to see him, given he got home infrequently during the rodeo season, which seemed to last longer and longer these days. But she could barely watch him ride for fear he would get injured.

This time he was bucked off before the eight-second buzzer for a no score, which meant he'd be heading out for another rodeo.

"Can you check on the next rider," she said to McClane, who had been helping with the gates. She handed him her roster. "I want to talk with Tucker."

Tucker had headed to the locker room, and Mandy hurried to catch up. Ty was back by the loading pens with Harold, no doubt assuring that no livestock got out.

"Tuck?" she called through the open doorway. Inside the room several cowboys were either getting ready or packing up, depending on their spot on the roster. She spotted Libby's husband, Chance Cochran, among the ones getting ready. Libby had found herself a good one, it appeared. Though their path had been a rocky one, they were now happily married and expecting a child. It didn't get better than that.

"Hey, Chance, good to see you." Chance was already up in the top twenty, giving him a shot at making the NRF by the end of the year. After he missed out last year due to an injury, she knew how important every rodeo was to him.

"Mandy. I was going to look for you. Libby sends her regards. Says she's waiting to hear—only she didn't say about what." He looked at her quizzically with those steel-gray eyes of his. He was a handsome cowboy, a bit tall for a saddle bronc rider, but lean and muscular.

"Tell her I've a lot to say when I get back." Mandy could really use both Libby's and Cat's advice again. "Did you see Tucker?"

Chance nodded toward an interior room. "Think he's in there. He had some tough luck today."

That meant he was probably having a beer with some of the other guys who also didn't make their time.

Chance slipped on his black hat, his smile wide. "Time to saddle up."

"Good luck."

Chance nodded as he strode out of the doorway.

She bustled through the few men in the locker room and glanced in the interior room. Sure enough, there was Tuck and four other guys, beers in hand. Upon spotting her, Tuck sauntered over. "Did you see my ride?"

Of course she had. She was right there. "Better luck next time." It was all she could think to say about it. "I wanted to talk to you about the ranch."

"I told you I would never want to sell, no matter the money." He tipped the bottle back and took a sip.

"I know, but this is about the cattle. I think Ty's brother could use some stock, and I was thinking that, if you were agreeable, we might thin out the Angus cattle a bit and sell him some heifers at a good price. He's got some issues he's dealing with…"

Before she could finish, Tucker laid a hand on her shoulder. "You know I'm good with whatever you decide."

Tucker always seemed to be on the same page with her, and it was a blessing that as siblings they complemented each other rather than competed with each other. "Mom wanted me to remind you to stop by the hospitality tent tonight before you leave." Her mother never watched Tucker ride. It was too stressful, she said.

"I will. But I thought you should know Mitch Lockhart is here. He wanted me to tell you he wants to talk with you."

With all that happened, she'd had little time to think about Mitch—or regret what had happened.

"Think he knows about my marriage?"

"It's the talk of the rodeo."

"I doubt that."

"Well, that and the bull getting loose and you crazy enough to take it on. What the hell were you thinking?"

Mandy inwardly sighed. She didn't want to explain herself yet again, so she ignored his question. "I'll keep an eye out for him, but I'm too busy to go chasing after him."

"I'm just the messenger."

"See Mom," she said and then took her leave. One more aggravation to look forward to on an already aggravating day.

* * *

"Is it true?"

Mandy whipped around, startled by a familiar deep voice. She'd been finishing up feeding the broncs while Ty and Harold checked on the bulls and cattle pens. It was late, and the light from the spotlights provided an overlay of shadows among slices of light in the night as bugs danced under the warmth of the lamps. Most contestants, if they stayed for the next day, were out by the trailers, either sound asleep or shooting the breeze with other entrants. A few lucky cowboys might even share a bed with one of the barrel racers. Rodeo life was a transient one and had its share of casual hook-ups.

Mitch stood before her, a brown cowboy hat covering his dark-blond hair. He was clad in a plaid shirt and denims, fancy cowboy boots on his feet. She'd watched him compete, but there had not been time, gratefully, to say a word to him.

She still resented the way he'd unceremoniously dumped her, and at her grandfather's funeral, no less. She'd once found him handsome, but today he had such a sullen expression on his face, she felt nothing. Absolutely nothing.

"Hello to you too, Mitch." She brushed a strand of hair out of her eyes and steeled herself for the interrogation.

"Is it true?" Mitch glared at her, his fists resting

on his hips. He was husky and tall, all muscle and bone. Not an ounce of fat on him. The build of a tie-down roper. "You pulled my sponsorship?" He practically snarled the accusation.

"My grandfather sponsored you as a favor to me. I no longer wanted the favor."

"I didn't think you'd be that petty. I thought this was a business relationship."

"Based on the premise of a personal relationship—and nothing more. Prescott doesn't sponsor cowboys. We supply them." Given the anger stampeding across his face, she decided to forgo mentioning that his standing had fallen so low that even if Prescott did provide sponsorship money to cowboys, he wouldn't be on the list.

"And not doing a very good job at that, given the incident with the bull today."

"Things happen."

"Like you getting hitched to that guy you called an SOB? Didn't take you long to recover from our breakup, did it? Only I don't see no ring on your finger."

His comment about the ring bothered her more than it should have. "I married Ty Martin."

His gaze roved over her like he was checking for signs of pregnancy. Not the only one who had done so, but it rankled more from him.

"You told me you hated the guy."

At the time she had. Despite everything, she couldn't say that now.

"I've no more intention of explaining my decisions to you than you have of explaining why you dumped me little more than an hour after we put my grandfather's body in the ground." And this was the type of guy who filled too much of the rodeo arena. The type of guy she was likely to meet in her line of work. It didn't bode well for life after Ty.

"Obviously you didn't care that much, because you got married like a week later, so don't go acting like it's a big thing. But I need that sponsorship money. I'm in the middle of the season. It was a bitchy thing to do, Mandy."

"Is there a problem here?"

Mandy jumped at the smooth, cold sound of Ty's voice. He must have come from behind the corrals.

Ty didn't so much as glance at Mandy. His focus was solidly on Mitch as he walked forward, slow and steady, determined and purposeful. The light caught the streaks of dust that accented his jeans. Sweat marked areas of his white Prescott shirt. With his battered Stetson and scuffed boots, he looked the epitome of the working cowboy.

"Mitch Lockhart, my husband, Ty Martin." This time the introduction sounded familiar, normal.

Neither man reached out to shake hands.

"Yeah, I got a problem. The problem is that Prescott Rodeo Company canceled my sponsorship in midseason. That's a piss-poor way to do business."

"I'm heading up Prescott, and I decided to cancel your sponsorship."

"No doubt after instructions from your wife." Mitch's face twisted in an ugly expression. "It's all over the circuit that Prescott is in trouble and going on the auction block. Couldn't happen to a more worthy rodeo supplier. Thanks for screwing me, Mandy— literally and figuratively." He spit on the ground before turning and walking back into the darkness toward the trailer area.

"So that's Mitch Lockhart," Ty said, his eyebrows raised as they both watched Mitch walk away. "He seems like a real dickhead."

Mandy didn't like the description, especially since it reflected on her taste in men, but she couldn't exactly disagree with it.

Ty turned around. "Is that what a trophy boyfriend looks like?"

Mandy didn't mean to laugh, but the edges of her mouth turned up, and it just gurgled out. "Touché, Mr. Martin."

Mandy hesitated at the door to the hotel room as Ty lugged their two suitcases through the entryway. There sat one king-sized bed covered in white bed linens and sporting tons of pillows. It seemed her life these days began and ended with hotel rooms. Unfortunately, these hotel rooms were filled with a man she found increasingly attractive—even if he was so wrong for her.

Sex with Ty had definitely complicated things—at least for her. She'd been hoping she could be like him—take it for what it was and not wish or expect something more. Considering how she'd felt about him just a week ago, that shouldn't have been a problem. But in a short time, things had changed.

And it had her thinking about even bigger changes. Something that would change every aspect of her life, for the better. Something that would give her life meaning beyond Prescott.

Ty turned to look behind him as he set the luggage down. "What's the matter?"

"I'm taking a shower and going right to bed. It's been a long, eventful day." And a confusing one. She needed space and time to think. "Stan, the bull, and then Mitch..." And you, she thought. She let go of the hotel door, and it slammed closed behind her.

Ty frowned as he doubled back to her. He seemed to take up the whole room as he crooked a finger under her chin and stared at her as if he was trying to figure out his own puzzle.

"If it's about selling the company, Stan Lassiter did mention a figure today. But it was so low, Mandy, I told him no."

A seed of hope lodged inside of her. "So you're not selling Prescott?"

"Not at that price. I don't need an analysis to know it's too low. And given the state of the economy, you may be fretting about nothing. A the end of six months, the company could still be yours, and the business, I promise, will be on firm footing."

"If there is even a chance..."

"You know I can't promise, but if the other stock contractors think like Lassiter, you'll have nothing to worry about. I won't surprise you. You'll be kept informed every step of the way. Trust me."

Trust was something she couldn't afford to give—not to Ty. Yet, part of her wanted to. Part of her wanted a happily ever after. Not selling Prescott would be that happily ever after—only now she wanted something more.

How to tell him? And would he even listen?

Chapter 17

"Mandy, we love you, but you've got to stop calling these emergency meetings," Cat said as she looked over at her son sitting next to her at the table in the spacious McKenna ranch house kitchen. "My mom's not always available, and I can't get a sitter on a moment's notice."

A toy truck, a light saber, and several superhero action figures were strewn across the wood floor—all attempts to keep Jake busy while Cat had manned the outdoor grill and put dinner on the table.

Mandy felt the flush in her cheeks. Cat was right. She wasn't being a considerate friend. But she was desperate, and as soon as she'd returned from Utah that Sunday evening, she'd pleaded with her friends to join her for dinner, leaving Ty to eat alone. Because Cat couldn't get a sitter and her mother was at a church meeting, Cat had been nice enough to invite them to her house for grilled hamburgers and hot dogs.

She was grateful because this was something she couldn't or didn't want to decide on her own.

"I apologize to both of you," she said, looking first at Cat and then at Libby, who was tucking into her second hamburger, Mandy and Cat having already finished. "And to you, Jake."

Jake, upon hearing his name, sent Mandy a big smile as he waved a french fry he'd plucked from his plate, leaving behind, momentarily, a hot dog cut up into little pieces. With his big brown eyes, blond hair, and cherub face, he was sure to be a heartbreaker when he grew up—apparently just like his daddy had been.

"Ice cream?" he asked.

"After you eat your dinner," Cat replied with a sigh. "I've become very adept at using bribery," she said unapologetically. "Can you color a picture?" Cat nudged the coloring book and crayons toward him, and Jake dutifully complied, paging through the book and settling on one of the superheroes pictured there. He set about tackling it with a blue crayon. "And using distraction," she said, turning her attention back to her friends.

"I'm taking notes." Libby giggled.

"That's sort of what I wanted to talk to you guys about." Mandy's stomach felt queasy as she considered how she would broach the subject.

"We are all ears. And you better talk fast. When you don't care about coloring in the lines, it doesn't take long to finish your masterpiece." Cat glanced back at Jake.

"Well, first, Ty and I have…"

"Omigod, you didn't last two weeks!" Cat said, her arched eyebrows conveying her lack of surprise.

Libby smiled. "Chance and I didn't last long either."

Relieved she didn't have to get too specific in front of the little one, Mandy nodded.

"And?" Libby asked, even as she blushed.

"Really, you want details?" Mandy jerked her head in Jake's direction.

"Summarize—good or bad?" Cat said.

"Good."

"Just good?" Libby sounded disappointed.

"Incredibly good, okay?"

"So that's not why you called us here, then." Cat looked over at Jake. "What a nice picture you colored."

"It's for Libby's new baby." He smiled, and the room seemed to light up.

Cat tore out the page and handed it to Libby.

"Thank you so much, Jake. I will hang it in the baby's room."

"Can you find another one, maybe do one in red crayon?" Cat asked her son.

Jake nodded and proceeded to explore his other artistic options in the book.

"It's weird between us, given the potential to sell the company, but that's not why I've called you here." Mandy watched Jake page through his book and felt a little squeeze in her heart. "I'm thinking of having a baby with him."

Libby almost choked on her bite of burger, and Cat laughed. So much for support.

"You're serious," Cat said when she stopped laughing.

"Yes. Look, when six months is over, I may be left with nothing. No business, no job, no legacy."

"But rich," Libby reminded.

"I think I need a beer after that news," Cat said, getting up and going to the fridge. She turned back to Mandy. "Want one?"

Mandy shook her head. Cat retrieved the beer and settled back down next to Jake.

"Money isn't everything. At least not to me." For Ty it was everything. "Family, my friends, the people who work at Prescott, those are the reasons the company means so much to me. I will lose that if the company is sold. I want something equally special to replace that."

"But why a baby with a man you don't…" Cat glanced at Jake. "You know."

"Because I may never find a man to marry. Odds haven't been in my favor." She thought back to Mitch and, unfortunately, several others. "If he sells the company, then at least I'll have the baby. And the money to raise the child properly. And if he doesn't sell it, I'll have double the happily ever after."

"And what does Ty say to this?" Libby asked.

"I haven't asked him yet." Mandy let out a sigh. "I wanted to run it by you guys first to see if I am crazy. Cat, you're a single mom, and Libby, you're a mother-to-be. I figured you would know if I'm nuts or not."

"A child is a big step, Mandy. A lifetime commitment." Cat smiled at her son who, at that moment, looked up. His ketchup-smeared face beamed as he held up a picture of some mythical figure of a man with streaks of red crayon running through it. "That's very good. Now eat some of your hot dog."

"I want to give this to Mandy," he said.

Cat dutifully tore the page out of the coloring book, and Jake then handed it to Mandy.

"Thank you, Jake. I'll treasure this picture. It's going up on the refrigerator as soon as I get home." Of course, it would have to be the hotel's mini fridge. At the moment, her life felt very small.

"I'll make you another," he said cheerfully. "Do you like orange?"

"I love orange." Mandy couldn't resist. She reached over and tousled his hair. He beamed again. "And I love you."

"I love you too, Mandy," he said, never losing eye contact with the coloring book.

"That's what I want, Cat. What you have and Libby is going to have. And I can provide for a child. And with Tucker and Harold around, my child will have men who love him or her."

"Babysitters."

"What?" Mandy asked, not sure she heard correctly.

Cat shrugged and took a sip a beer. "That's what you are going to need. Babysitters. Preferably family. I don't think anyone ever tells you just how much time and attention our little folks need. Not that it isn't rewarding. It most definitely is. But relatives willing to babysit—especially if you are going to run the ranch or another stock company—is a must if you are going to be a single mom." She looked over at Libby. "And even if you aren't."

"Chance's mother is ready to move back to Wyoming for this child," Libby said. "And my dad, believe it or not, has offered."

"How does Chance feel about his mother moving?" Chance hadn't been on good terms with his mother until Libby had stepped into the picture.

"He's okay with it. A little concerned given her past, but willing to give it a go."

"My mother has been asking me about grandchildren since I graduated from business school.

Did I tell you that she's going to be marrying Harold soon? They haven't set a date yet. I think they are waiting until this six-month thing is past. Apparently, they have been sneaking around for some time."

"How do you feel about your mother remarrying?" Libby asked.

"I love Harold. He is completely different in temperament from my father but a wonderful man. My mother and Harold are surprisingly cute together."

"Well, they are certainly old enough to make their own decisions, and so are you, Mandy. If you think you can handle a child, go for it. But do you think Ty will agree?" Cat asked.

"That is the million-dollar—or more—question," Mandy said. "That, and how to approach him."

* * *

"You want to have my baby?" Ty felt the air drain out of his lungs like a tire with a massive leak. Mandy sat across from him in the pub-like restaurant near their hotel, looking perfectly normal, and tempting, in a silky red camisole and a pair of washed-out jeans, but she'd just said the darnedest thing.

Ty swiped a hand across his forehead. It had suddenly gotten hot in the busy dining room. He'd anticipated a few different reasons for Mandy asking to have dinner alone with him on that Monday, since the preliminary report on the valuation of the company had just come in. Ty had given the analysis a quick scan. The figures looked reasonable, and unfortunately, there appeared to be a case for selling the business at the right price. He wasn't eager to make that argument to Mandy like he had been just a week ago. It would likely cause a permanent freeze in their relationship, just when things seemed to be heating up.

But a baby wasn't even in the top ten of discussion topics. This had to be a joke, only Mandy looked as serious as a judge about to give out a life sentence.

"Hear me out, is all I ask," Mandy said as she took a sip of sparkling water. The tables were made of the same golden wood as the walls and the bar that squatted at the far end of the dining room packed with families. It was cozy and homey in a most uncomfortable way.

He'd finally gotten her in bed for some pretty spectacular sex, and now she wanted to have a baby together? *Stunned* didn't begin to describe how he felt.

"I'm listening," he said, surprising himself. Was he listening? He shouldn't be. No one knew more than him that he wasn't cut out to be a father. Just like he wasn't cut out to be a husband. Or part of a team. He knew he worked best alone. Hadn't he spent seven years in the land development company pretending to be part of the management team, knowing they didn't want the truth they paid him to uncover? Grappling with corporate politics that forced facts to fit predetermined scenarios had vanquished any qualms he may have had about going into business for himself—by himself. He was an outsider, a maverick. He liked it best when he depended on no one but himself.

And no one depended on him.

"Really? Because the look on your face says

you've already decided no." She cocked her head, those sparkling green eyes full of doubt.

"I'm just surprised, is all."

"Well, actually, so was I when the thought first popped into my head. I mean, it's bad enough that you're part of Prescott now. Having a child together will make you part of my life forever. But when I thought about it some more, the pros outweighed the cons." She leaned back and peered at him from under those thick lashes of hers as if she was still trying to weigh those pros and cons.

"I'm the con, I take it." Why did that thought disturb him so much?

"Well, yes, I guess you could say that." She smiled from her eyes as well as her lips, and the warmth of that smile took some of the sting out of her words. "But you're less of one than I may have thought just a bit ago."

"How so?" Should he be encouraged by that?

Her gaze shifted away from him, toward the wider room. "I guess I see you more as a person."

"What the hell did you see me as before?"

She gave a demure chuckle. "You really don't want me to answer that, do you?"

He was offended. "Of course I want you to answer that."

"I don't want to insult you. The fact I want to have a baby with you now should really be seen as a compliment."

"I want to know. How did you see me before?"

She sighed. Closed her eyes and opened them again. Played with the fork that sat upon the white paper napkin.

He waited. He wanted to know.

"As the devil."

The devil?

She looked up and caught his eye. Shook her head. "Not really, but, well, you seemed so unfeeling. So by the book. So…cold."

Cold. Wasn't the first time a woman had called him that, so why did it slice through him with the sting of a razor blade this time? "And now?"

She cocked her head and shrugged. "Well, when it comes to the business, maybe still." Her brows knitted together, and Ty knew she was thinking about the prospect of selling. No help for that. But then her brows relaxed. "But on a personal level, not as much."

"Why?" Something was driving him to push for a response, in a vague hope she might have some insight into why people always thought of him that way. And why she didn't now—so much.

Her eyes moved about the room as if the answer was on one of the walls. "Maybe knowing more about you. Maybe seeing you in action, working, with your family."

What had she been able to see? At the ranch, she'd spent a few minutes getting acquainted with his niece, meeting his brother, seeing where he'd come from and knowing it wasn't exactly a Norman Rockwell family portrait.

"You are going to help Trace, right? And Delanie." Her tone held both hope and censure.

"I've already set up the account for the money he needs. Should be more than enough to hire a housekeeper, enroll Delanie in preschool, and pay for an attorney. And a psychologist." Ty could only hope there hadn't been any long-term damage. "As I mentioned, Trace could also use some beeves to strengthen his herd. He lost quite a few in the last drought. If you and Tucker agree, I was hoping…" He didn't get the words out of his mouth and she was nodding.

"I already spoke to Tuck, so anything Trace might need."

"I'll make sure it's a decent deal for both sides, if you trust me to make that deal."

She waved her hand as if money, or trust, didn't matter. But Ty knew money and trust always mattered.

"It will probably be about fifty heifers, more or less," he continued, happy for the temporary change in subject to give him time to process exactly what she was asking. "You're running about thirty-five hundred of the Angus on the ranch now, according to the last count." He'd made sure they had taken a count for the ranch analysis, which wouldn't be ready for another few days. They had done the company analysis first, since that was the crucial one.

"He's family, Ty. We help family."

"He's *my* family though."

"Right now, that also makes Trace and Delanie part of my family." She said the words matter of factly, but the sentiment caught him off guard. "We can do the roundup Wednesday, if you like. Tucker will be home because of the Cheyenne rodeo coming up, and there might be a few others who can help. Everyone likes a roundup. We can host a barbeque afterwards."

Sounded like she'd already been thinking about it and had it all planned out. That was Mandy.

"I'll let Trace know and see if that will work for him."

She tucked a strand of hair behind her ear, looking very pleased with herself. "Now about the baby."

The baby? As if it had already been decided?

"Why a baby? Why now? And why me, beyond the notion you see me as a person?"

She shrugged again. Played with the knife this time. Before she answered, the waitress came and deposited before each of them a square white plate piled high with various types of lettuce, some cranberries, walnuts, and other salad fixings for their starter salad. They both waited for the waitress to depart before digging into their food.

"I may not get another chance." Her voice was low and oddly fragile sounding.

"To get married?"

She nodded.

Mandy Prescott? Single forever? "Why would you think that? You're a beautiful woman. You're smart. Ambitious. Determined." She was ten times more interesting, and complicated, than the women he usually dated.

"And I seem attracted to the wrong types of men."

He frowned, hoping she was referring to that no-account tie-down roper.

"How so?" He stabbed some lettuce and savored the tangy flavor of balsamic vinegar that greeted his taste buds.

Her one shoulder slid up. "The men I've dated tend to be good-time Charlies. In it for fun, not commitment." She dipped the fork into the salad but didn't spear anything.

"Date other men." Seemed simple enough. "There must be lots of good men, good ranching types, who'd make fine husbands and fathers. I've seen them at the rodeos." Unfortunately, the thought of Mandy with any of them didn't sit well with him. She deserved someone who would appreciate her.

"They are already married. The good ones anyway. And besides, they aren't looking for wives that are on the road thirty-five weekends a year running a business."

"That's why selling would be a good thing. Free you up to pursue a personal life. Did you know your mother wouldn't object if Prescott was sold? She told me so."

Too late, Ty realized he'd blundered by bringing Prescott into the conversation, as Mandy took a deep breath, and her nostrils flared. He'd poked the bear.

"We've had this conversation. What I want is to run Prescott Rodeo Company. And have a baby. Every stock contractor I know is married and has a family."

And they were all men, though Ty knew he didn't have to say it. The defiant lift of her chin said that was her whole point.

"And if I say no? Because I can tell you, having a family is not something I've thought much about and am not sure I want."

"You didn't want to be married and run a stock company, I'll wager, but here you are."

He took a forkful of salad, buying some time. They ate in silence for a few moments. He needed time to think. What exactly would it mean to become a father, especially since he wouldn't be married to the mother? At least not long enough to see the child born.

"Why haven't you ever wanted a family?" she asked. Mandy was never one to let a comment pass unremarked upon. "It isn't natural, you know."

"Why isn't it natural? Maybe if more people followed their own inclinations instead of what the world expected of them, we'd have a lot fewer dysfunctional families." Like his had been.

"We're hard wired to procreate. That's why the sex drive is so intense. And I can attest that yours is pretty damn strong." She looked at him from across the table, her eyes dancing in the low light.

God, she was flirting with him. And he liked it. His whole body tensed in response to the light in her eye.

He waggled his eyebrows. "So you do admit it was good sex?"

She tilted her head, and the left side of the mouth crooked up in a smile. He liked this flirty Mandy. He liked her a lot.

"Yes. But you knew that. You shouldn't need your ego stroked. It's big enough."

"And with all these faults, you still want me to be the father of your child?"

"Yes. Because you are also smart, ambitious, and surprisingly aren't afraid of hard work. And you are rather nice looking. I'm willing to take the good with the bad."

"Well, thank you. I think. But I feel like I'm being sized up for my genetics, like those bulls you breed." Not that he minded.

"I didn't mean to sound so clinical. But we are

married, so it's convenient. And we are planning to divorce, so that's also convenient."

"You want my sperm, and then that's it? I'm to get out of your life?"

Unfortunately, the waitress came to clear the plates at that moment. She avoided eye contact as she grabbed the dishes and then hurried away.

"If you want to be more involved, of course you can be," Mandy resumed. "But I would have custody of the child. That would have to be agreed to in advance. However, you just said you're not a family man, so I don't want you to feel obligated, is all. I'm perfectly capable of raising a child, and I'll have lots of help. And if it's a boy, there will be plenty of role models around."

A boy. What kind of father would his son need? Or his daughter, for that matter. And shouldn't he be that role model? "What if Prescott is sold?"

"I'm hoping the economy keeps stock contractors from being able to buy it, but if I can't keep you from selling, there is still the ranch. That will never be sold." She shook that pretty head of hair, long silky hair that felt so nice brushing over a man's skin. "Ever."

"The numbers for the company came in late today. I thought we could go over them together tomorrow morning. The numbers on the ranch won't be in for a few more days though."

"I'll hate you if you sell Prescott, you know. Even if we have this child together. But at least by giving me a child, you'd be giving me something precious in return for what you've taken away. Not that you care about my feelings."

Hell. She did think he was the devil. Why couldn't she see that if he did sell Prescott, it would be to protect her and her family? To make sure they were economically taken care of? An even more important factor if they had a child together.

"I'd want to be part of the child's life. And I'd want to make sure the child was financially taken care of. I could set up a trust or something."

He couldn't believe he was actually thinking about it. And neither could she, by the size of the grin on her face.

"That would be fine. But I don't want you to feel you'd have to do any of that."

The waitress appeared with their food. Steak for him. Pasta for Mandy. Given how quickly the waitress took her leave, Ty was pretty sure she'd been appalled by their discussion.

"I'll think about it. It's a big commitment. A lifetime commitment, Mandy."

"I'm aware of that. And I'm all about big commitments, Ty. Prescott. The baby. The ranch. It's the kind of person I am."

The obvious and unsaid implication was it was the exact opposite of who he was.

"Am I to assume no sex if I say no." And that would be a shame.

"Don't make it sound like I'm using sex to blackmail you. I'm not. We do have a physical attraction to each other, but trying for a baby would change the dynamic, for the better."

"Attraction isn't enough for you?"

"I want more."

Did he want more?

"I'll think about it." It was the best he could promise.

She bit her lip. "I hope you will give what I asked serious thought, Ty."

He'd give it nothing but serious thought.

Chapter 18

The next day Ty watched as Mandy scanned the figures on the sheet he'd presented to her as they sat in the office formerly used by JM. Karen had packed up all signs of JM except the leather saddle that still sat on its stand in the corner, like the finely embossed and polished piece of art that it was.

Mandy had already questioned the amount that had been calculated for "goodwill," declaring it hadn't been high enough, and scoffed at the value assigned to the horses and bulls, arguing that both figures were too low.

He felt tense and exhausted, having been up half the night thinking about the prospect of having a baby with Mandy while she slept inches from him, their discussion earlier that evening having placed a momentary chill on things. He thought by getting married he'd have several months of guilt-free sex, and now here he was contemplating having a baby with her, making them some sort of family.

It certainly wouldn't be a traditional one, but he would be a father to any child he brought into this world. What that meant he wasn't sure, but oddly, he was curious to find out. He wouldn't be an absentee father either. He had taken some time this morning to research the custody laws of the state, and he would make sure that he would be involved in raising the child. If he agreed to this, he wanted to do it *with* Mandy, not separated from her. Trouble was, it wasn't clear what that arrangement would look like.

If it wasn't for circumstances that seemed to pit them against each other, he could almost see himself married to her, raising a family with her, and running Prescott Rodeo Company. It would mean belonging somewhere and to someone he had begun to care about.

But reality was, it would never happen. Not now. Not with the figures that showed the Prescott family would be better off investing their money in stocks and bonds than in horses and bulls.

"You say Stan Lassiter offered you only eighty percent of *this* figure?" she said, looking up from the paper and casting her cool, green-eyed gaze on him.

Ty nodded.

He wanted more than to do right by her. He wanted her to *agree* he was doing right by her. He wanted her approval—and understanding. He was working to make her a wealthy woman—not to rob her.

But the frostiness in her eyes said she was having none of it.

"And you have had no other offers?"

"I haven't officially announced yet that PRC is for sale. I wanted to wait until I had good numbers. Stan just jumped the gun. I think he wanted to see how desperate we were."

Mandy straightened. "*I* am not desperate. *I* don't want to sell."

"If we could get an AFBR contract, we'd be able to increase the value of the company considerably as well as make it even more attractive to buyers."

"I'm only interested in making it more attractive to keep. You acknowledge PRC is profitable?"

"The profit margins aren't big enough, Mandy. Especially when you take into account the tenuous nature of things. Take this herpes virus that was afflicting horses last year. Rodeos get cancelled, stock gets sick. Suddenly you have a bad year. You'd get more with less risk by selling and leaving the money invested."

"I see you calculated an eight percent return on the proceeds from the sale. Think you can get that these days, because I'd like to know where?"

"I assumed some of the money would be invested in the stock market, and in that case, the estimate is conservative."

"Invest so bankers and gambling Wall Street types can loot it? And you have the nerve to talk about risk?"

"Recent events keep me from arguing that point, but let's hope that was an aberration."

She snorted.

"I should have the figures for the development of the ranch in the next day or two. I'd like to go over them with you."

"You have not been listening. We are not selling the ranch. That's nonnegotiable."

"All I'm asking is for you to look at the figures. Just want you to know what you're turning down."

Mandy sighed. "After the roundup and barbeque."

Ty had wasted no time in getting Trace's agreement to a deal on the cattle, and Ty had arranged for the roundup to take place near the end of the week. Mandy had decided to throw a good old-fashioned barbeque for all the hands who participated, and she'd invited two of her friends to join them, one who had a son near Delanie's age and the other who had a rodeo bronc rider for a husband, who was also supposed to be a decent roper. Since it was happening right before the Cheyenne rodeo, even Tucker promised to be there.

Trace would bring Delanie when he selected his cattle, and Mandy had agreed to watch the tyke while she set up and her mother and Mrs. Jenkins handled the cooking chores. It was damn decent of her. She kept saying that Trace was family, but they both knew differently.

"When will you give me an answer to my question? About having a baby?"

Ty fiddled with his pen. He owed her an answer—one way or another. "Same day you look at the figures for the ranch."

"So if I say no to the deal, you'll say no to the baby."

"Only one way to find out."

* * *

A soft breeze wrapped around Mandy as she grabbed Delanie, dressed in her tiny denim jeans, T-shirt, and cowgirl boots, from Trace's arms and settled the little girl in front of her on the saddle. Willow had stood still, as if sensing the precious cargo entrusted to her. The psychologist Trace had found with Ty's help

273

must have made some difference, as Delanie now allowed her father to hold her. Such a simple thing, yet so complicated for one so young.

Trace touched the brim of his hat and whirled around the quarter horse he'd brought over in a much-used trailer, to face the herd milling in the open field. The cattle swirled up dust as they moved, and their lowing filled the air.

Trace had insisted on paying the going rate, but Mandy and Tucker had agreed that Trace should get a discount. As if they really were family.

She wished it were so. But Ty's inability to see beyond the dollar signs on a page made any happily ever after unlikely, however much she was attracted to him physically, however much she admired his business acumen—though not when it came to Prescott Rodeo. Of course, if he agreed to a child, he would be part of her life, part of her child's family forever.

It was a risk. She'd seen glimpses of promise in Ty—but the substance remained elusive.

She was looking forward to this mini roundup, watching Delanie, and hosting a barbeque for those helping out. She was happy the occasion had coincided close to the start of the Cheyenne rodeo occurring that weekend. It meant Tucker could participate. And Libby's husband, Chance, had offered to help when Mandy had invited them to the midweek barbeque. Libby would meet up with her husband at the barbeque, after the dealership she managed closed. Cat would be coming also, with Jake. She was anxious for both her friends to meet Ty, and little Jake might prove to be the perfect playmate for Delanie.

She nuzzled Delanie's hair, breathing in the fresh baby-shampoo scent, careful not to crush the cowgirl hat hanging off the back of the child's head by the chin strap. Mandy had bought it for her along with a cute little sundress for later. She hadn't been able to resist.

Delanie waved as Ty maneuvered his new horse, Paddy, toward them.

She'd been amazed at what he'd paid for the horse, whose full name was Paddy's Four Leaf Clover. It was sired by a champion cutting horse out of Texas. It was the kind of horse that would have been home in the arena. But Ty had wanted the best for his work horse, and he'd paid top dollar for it. Since he wouldn't be staying for good, Mandy could only imagine he would use the animal as an investment, eventually leasing it out to some lucky rider.

"Unky Ty," Delanie called.

The smile that lit her husband's face at the title touched Mandy's heart. Who would have thought this calculated businessman would go soft for a little girl.

"Hey, peanut," he called affectionately. "You watching?"

She nodded as Ty waved and then rode away.

"Where is he going, Aunt Mandy?"

She could get used to being this little girl's aunt for real.

"Your father and Uncle Ty are going to go into the herd, and when they see a heifer your father likes, they are going to bring it out of the herd. It's called cutting, but it has nothing to do with anything sharp. They are just going to maneuver the animal to the edge of the circle, and then the cowboys, with the help of their horses, will get it to that pen over there." She motioned to one of the holding pens. "Whatever heifers they put in that holding pen will be delivered in trailers to your house tomorrow."

"They need all these cowboys to do that?" she asked, sitting up straighter, as if on alert. There were about a half-dozen mounted men who ringed the herd, including Chance Cochran and her brother. A few more sat on the railings of the holding pen, watching. Delanie was tense, a reminder that the little girl still had a ways to go in the trust department.

"Those cowboys are there to keep the rest of the herd together," she explained, hoping to ease any worries. "See," she said, pointing to Ty, who had moved toward one of the cows. "Uncle Ty's on one side, and your daddy is on the other side. Let's see if they can do it."

Mandy frequently applauded with Delanie as the brothers worked rather deftly together for two men who hadn't been in the same pasture for years. Only if she looked closely could she spot a bit of sibling rivalry. Though Ty worked his horse expertly, Trace showed more experience in maneuvering the cattle.

A half hour later, Delanie was getting fidgety, so Mandy headed her horse back to the ranch house, where her mother could fuss over the little girl.

"This may be the closest I'll get to a grandchild," Sheila grumbled as she helped the child change into the new pink polka-dot sundress. "I'm going to enjoy her while I can."

And this may be the closest I get to having a child, Mandy thought ruefully.

As Mandy helped her mother and Mrs. Jenkins get the picnic table set and the meal ready, Delanie helped in the best way a four-year-old could, by playing her own version of house with the small set of plastic pots and pans Sheila had fished out of the basement and set in the yard. Seeing those old, familiar childhood items sent a pang of regret through Mandy. Those had been lovingly saved for her children. Not that she begrudged using them to amuse Delanie. On the contrary. It just served to remind her of what she wanted and might never have.

* * *

After traipsing through the line that formed for beef, burgers, and assorted salads, Ty took the seat at the head of the set of long wooden tables decked out with plastic checkered cloth. Surveying the friendly mob of cowhands and family who had gathered under the grove of trees to the side of the ranch house, an unfamiliar emotion filled him. Happiness.

"Great job out there. You two look like you're born ranchers," Doug McClane said as he sat down the table from Ty and Trace.

Ty nodded his acknowledgment and hoped the praise was sincere.

"Seriously, that was some real cowboy work. Guess you do know a thing or two about livestock," Harold, who was sitting on the opposite side of the table, chimed in.

"Glad I got home to see it. Next, you'll be taking on a bronc," said Tucker, who had sat next to Harold, with a huge pile of food on his plate.

This was a man's life. Running his own operation, working out in the elements with his herd.

Doing something purposeful. Ty turned his back on ranching once. But it had been a certain ranch and for specific reasons.

He glanced over at Mandy, who was helping cut up Delanie's burger into small pieces. Watching Mandy mother Delanie, he felt an uncomfortable twinge.

He wanted to give her that. To leave her with something. Something of his. The thought scared the living bejeezus out of him. He wasn't sure what was happening, but he knew it wasn't anything familiar. And it all centered around the woman hovering over his niece.

If they brought a child into the world, would that bring them closer or make the gulf wider?

"That's some horse you bought," Trace said, interrupting Ty's thoughts.

"Should be. I paid enough for him." Ty took a chomp of his burger, enjoying the juicy taste, glad for some distraction. He didn't yet have the rapport with the horse that Trace had with his horse. But that would come. Paddy was so well trained, any rider could get a decent performance out of him.

"So you really are going to be a rodeo stockman as well as run horses and cattle?" Trace shook his head. "Never thought you'd come to this after all that fancy education."

As if she'd overhead Trace's comment, Mandy turned her head toward them briefly before Delanie recaptured her attention.

"I enjoy ranching, working with the animals. I always did." Aware he was playing a role in front of his brother, Ty was startled at the truth of it all.

Trace snorted. "You always had your nose in a book, as I recall. Dad and I could never figure you out."

Ty had studied hard in order to better himself. And he'd succeeded at that, money-wise, at least. But it didn't mean he hadn't wanted to ranch. He just hadn't wanted to be part of the Martin ranch.

Or family.

Deep down he must have blamed his father for his mother's death even before he'd known it was a suicide. Maybe on some level he had guessed. He'd turned against his father—not outwardly, but inwardly. He'd turned against everything his father was.

"I still like learning. Just working with Mandy and the Prescott outfit reminded me of what else I like." He sent a wink to his wife and felt a tender pressure on his heart when she blushed.

"Guess J. M. Prescott got back that son he lost."

Ty met his brother's hard stare. He knew Trace and his father had resented JM's interest. But he'd never presumed he could take a son's place in JM's heart. JM had been generous and tough, supportive and demanding. His father had only been demanding. "Care to explain that comment?"

"Well, seems he found a man who wanted to follow in his footsteps. Marrying Mandy keeps it all in the family. All worked out damn convenient for you."

Ty swiped his hand across his chin. Of course he'd never admit to Trace the circumstances of his marriage. How would he explain it and not have it sound like he married for profit? And now she'd thrown him a curveball, and he wasn't sure he could catch it.

"Life sometimes takes surprising turns."

"That's for sure," Trace said as he looked over at his daughter. "Some good, some not so good. Delanie has been a great gift, and that compensates for a lot."

"Glad you see it that way," Ty said.

"Why wouldn't I?"

"A child is a lot of work, Trace. I was trying to by sympathetic."

Trace grunted. "You don't know the half of it. But I'm not complaining. I've just got to make sure she stays with me—always."

* * *

"So that is the notorious Ty Martin," Cat said as she stood with Mandy watching Jake and Delanie play on the large hill of hay by the side of the barn. Mandy and Tucker had played on similar mounds when they were that age. And Ty had kissed her behind one many times that one youthful summer.

Mandy thought it would be a good place for the kids to work off their energy and figured Delanie might be more comfortable away from all the men crowding the picnic table.

"That's him."

Before getting Cat's full feedback, Mandy wanted to wait for Libby, who was standing off to the side talking to her husband. She watched as Chance patted Libby's stomach and Libby reached up on tippy-toes to give him a kiss before walking toward them. She wanted that—or at least as much of that as she could have.

"So, what do you guys think?"

"About what?" Libby asked as she joined them.

"Ty."

"He's hot," Libby offered. She wore a blousy maternity top over a pair of cropped leggings, the glow of pregnancy on her face.

"Yumm," added Cat.

"Did you ask him about having a baby?" Libby patted her stomach.

"He's thinking about it."

"It looks like it would be pure pleasure making a baby with him," Cat said with a sigh.

It had been pleasurable, but Mandy wanted something more than pleasure. "It's a big step," Mandy said.

"The biggest," Cat agreed.

"What do you think of Trace, Cat?" Leave it to Libby to ask what Mandy had been wondering.

"He's as handsome as his brother but a bit taciturn for my taste. The only time he smiles is when he looks at his daughter. I guess that's something in his favor."

"Still looking in Cody Taylor's direction?" Mandy teased.

Cat shook her head. "Once we file that adverse-possession suit, that man will be after my hide. That was just a schoolgirl crush from long ago that's going to go very wrong in a few more weeks."

"Like Ty and me in four more months."

The air filled with kid giggles from Jake and Delanie as they tumbled down the side of the haystack.

"So enjoy those four months, baby or not."

Mandy hadn't figured out what she should or would do if Ty turned her down. But one thing was certain—it would be one more wedge between them. There were only so many things one man could disappoint on.

* * *

The guys had wondered over to the corrals where the heifers were circling. At the insistence of some of the hands, Tucker in particular, Chance Cochran was recounting his ride on Bad Medicine, a top bronc from a rival company. Ty watched as every man, including his brother, gave Chance their full attention. Ty had to admit, it took guts to get into the arena night after night for a wild ride—and a little bit of crazy.

After some jawing about rodeos past, a few of the guys called it a day. Tucker headed back for some more food, and Trace went in search of Delanie. Ty wandered over to Chance, whom Mandy had introduced to him when the bronc rider had arrived. He'd only just met Chance's pregnant wife, Libby, since she had come separately.

"Guess you have to love rodeo to do what you do," Ty said.

Chance grinned. "And the money isn't bad either, leastwise now."

"It takes quite a bit to make the top fifteen for the NRF."

"It doesn't come easy."

Ty was wondering about something else that didn't come easy. "You excited about being a father?"

Chance tugged on the brim of his hat. "And scared, I don't mind admitting."

Ty had to laugh. "You get in an arena with a

horse that weighs more than a ton, and you're scared of becoming a father?" Though Ty laughed, he was sympathetic.

"I didn't have the easiest upbringing. I'm not sure how to do it."

"But you're doing it."

"Not much to life if you can't pass something on to someone else who matters. I intend to pass something good on." Chance glanced around. "I was with Libby yesterday when she had an ultrasound. I tell you, seeing our child growing inside of her was a humbling thing."

Ty could only imagine.

"You and Mandy considering children?" Chance asked.

"Considering. Not yet decided."

"Well, you two just got married. Guess you've got time."

Ty wished that was true.

* * *

Ty and Mandy had said their good-byes to pretty much everyone before they headed back to the picnic table, where Trace and Shelia were helping Delanie finish up the last piece of a blueberry pie someone had brought.

Ty reached for Mandy, and they walked back hand in hand. He liked the feel of her smooth skin against his. And for a moment, he enjoyed the fantasy of being a couple.

If someone had told him he'd one day be entertaining his brother and niece as well as hosting a barbeque for a passel of people, he'd have thought them loco. Yet here he was, and it didn't feel all that strange. He'd enjoyed cutting cattle. He'd enjoyed meeting Mandy's friends. Mandy had told him the women knew the truth about their marriage, but neither of them treated him like anything but Mandy's husband.

And he'd felt like Mandy's husband.

"I'm tired," Delanie announced as Ty sat down beside his brother and Mandy sat on the other side, next to Delanie.

The little peanut had blueberry filling smeared across her face, like someone had used her for a swath of canvass.

"I bet, little one. It's been a long day," Ty said.

The breeze caught a wisp of Mandy's wavy hair, blowing it across her lips. She tucked it behind her ear and glanced at Ty, as if she'd known he'd been watching her, before she turned her attention to Delanie, grabbing a napkin to wipe the little one's face.

Trace dropped his paper napkin on the table. "We'd better head home. Those trailers will be at the ranch bright and early."

"Yup. And after they drop off your cattle, they'll be coming back here to load for the Cheyenne rodeo."

"How about I take Delanie in the house, wash her up a bit before you take her back. Save you some time when you get home, Trace," Mandy offered.

"You sure?" Trace asked, his voice gruff.

Mandy nodded as she brushed a hand down Delanie's hair. The little girl leaned against her.

"I'll come with you," Shelia said, rising as she

wiped her hands with a napkin. "And bring in some of these dishes."

Ty watched the three females walk away, Delanie between the two women. He lingered over the sight of Mandy's swaying derrière. She held little Delanie's hand and was bending low to talk to the tyke.

He caught Trace watching him, an amused expression on his face. Time to change the mental subject matter.

"Seems things have gotten better, you know, with Delanie and the whole trust thing."

"We're working on it," Trace said. He sounded weary. "Social worker is involved. We're seeing that psychologist. I've enrolled her in preschool for the fall. It's falling into place, slowly."

"She was more relaxed around you though. Saw you holding her in the saddle today."

"She likes being on the horse, is all. She'll let me give her a hug now, if I ask. She likes to be warned." Pain shone through Trace's eyes even as he struggled to hide it. "Given I'm not the most demonstrative guy, this has been the hardest thing I've ever dealt with."

"What does the psychologist say?"

"That Delanie's young—she can recover. And that I need to hug her often. Tell her I love her. Make her feel secure." Trace looked almost haunted as he fiddled with the knife on the table. "Of course I do love her. Truth is, I never thought I could love anyone like I love her. But showing it...well, it don't come natural for me. I'm learning though. Have another meeting with the psychologist next week. Half of me wants to know just how bad things were for her. Half of me is damn scared of the truth." Trace shook his head. "'Cause I just might have to kill someone."

Ty would certainly be out for blood if it was his daughter. He doubted Trace was any different. In fact, he knew he wasn't. They were Martins, after all.

"You and Mandy looking to have kids?"

Ty wished he had an answer to that question.

"We're taking it slow. Marriage was kind of sudden. We need some time to adjust."

"The way she was looking at you and you were looking at her, I'd say no adjustments needed." Trace chuckled.

If only that were the truth.

Chapter 19

Mandy tossed and turned and tossed some more. She pounded her pillow, shifted from her back to her side, and opened her eyes to shadowy darkness. The hotel room clock said five thirty, and she was wide awake.

She peeked at Ty. Even in a California King, he took up more than his fair share of space. Why didn't that surprise her? His arms were flung out as he lay on his back. Despite the shadowed light, she could still appreciate his body.

Sleeping in the same bed, mere inches from him, was so much harder now that they'd had sex, spectacular sex. What would happen if he said no to the baby?

Would she, should she, sleep with him anyway? That would certainly be the path of least resistance.

But what would be the purpose? Other than immense satisfaction, of course.

Mandy turned on her side, away from the sight of Ty. She'd have to make a decision. Or give up after little more than a week of being married.

Hadn't been so bad. There were parts that were enjoyable. Sex, of course. And he had galloped in like a white knight to save her from that bull. She'd almost felt as if he'd cared then. The kiss he planted on her

287

could almost make her believe in the fantasy of Mandy and Ty. And at the barbeque it had almost felt like they were an ordinary couple, hosting friends and family at an old-fashioned roundup. But almost only counted in horseshoes.

She glanced over at him. He slept soundly. Like he hadn't a care. Nothing to do but get up. Ty promised the financials for the ranch today—and his answer about the baby. If she hurried, she could be out the door before he even woke. She could use the time to brace for the coming disappointment.

Mandy stood in Ty's office, looking over the report submitted by the analysts. She could hardly believe the seven-figure number she was viewing.

So much money made her a little shaky about turning down the offer.

She looked up from the paper, and the eyes that followed her were serious and somber. He undoubtedly knew that the amount would make it tough to walk away. He was counting on it.

"That dollar figure guaranteed?"

"There are no guarantees, but I was conservative. I do know a little about real estate development." And, no doubt, this deal would be a feather in his cap.

"Even in this market?"

"Even in this market."

She folded the paper and shook her head. "The ranch is off the table regardless of the money. I'm half owner, so you can't do it without me." She prayed Tucker would stay the course and money wouldn't lure him. After all, Tucker had walked away from Prescott even though it cost him some stock.

"You wouldn't just be well off—you'd be rich. As would Tucker." He hesitated a breath before adding, "And so would the baby."

Mandy wasn't sure she could trust her ears. "The baby? Does that mean you agree? To having a baby?"

Her heart was thumping, and she felt like her blood pressure had just shot up. Could it be true? She might almost forgive him for pursuing a sale— almost.

"Yes."

Mandy felt the burn of tears in her eyes as she released a breath she hadn't realized she'd been holding. "You sure?"

His smile was surprisingly broad as he rose.

She scrambled from her chair, her mind whirling and her heart bobbing in her chest like a buoy on a breaking wave. He'd agreed. He wanted a baby. With her. She'd always been attracted to him, but at that moment, he was like the most powerful magnet in the world drawing her to his outstretched arms.

Coming around to his side of the desk, she flung her arms around his neck and planted a kiss on his lips. He seemed prepared for her, because he scooped her up and held her tight against his hard chest. She fed him kisses like a gambler feeds quarters to a slot machine. She was relieved. Happy. Bliss filled.

His hands cupped her rear end, and, coming up for air, he tilted his head back. "Does this mean we are having sex?" he said, barely above a growl.

The giggle bubbled in her throat. "Unless you know of a better way to make a baby."

He nuzzled her neck, and tiny little pricks of lust zinged through her.

"I mean right now, here, in the office."

That had her straightening up. "Noooo."

"Why not?"

"What would we tell our child?"

"Who tells a child how they were conceived?" He nipped her shoulder and then covered her mouth with his lips. He kissed her like a she was the last woman on earth—engulfing her in a siege of pheromones. She slid her hands down his shoulders, down his back, beneath the waistband of his pants until she felt warm flesh. Then she worked her fingers back up his bare skin and pressed his back, holding him to her. His mouth pressed deeper, and her tongue teased his. She felt his muscles tighten under her hands. He pulled her hips closer to his, and she felt him swell against her belly. Feminine satisfaction filled her.

He stepped back and, without a word, walked toward the door. Was he leaving?

She heard the lock click.

"No one to bother us," he said, sauntering back.

"Karen's right outside the door," she reminded as she sucked air back into her lungs.

"We'll be quiet." He pulled her against his hard body She felt him, long and hard.

College dorms had given Mandy some practice at being quiet.

Ty feathered kisses down her neck while his hand massaged her breast. It had only been a few days, but it had seemed like a few years since he'd made love to her.

"You want a baby, right?" His hand slid lower, brushing the denim of her jeans against her skin.

She nodded, having a hard time finding her voice when he cupped her crotch.

"No better time to get started. Skin to skin. Flesh to flesh. No condom."

She swallowed, her mouth suddenly dry. He was moving against her through the denim fabric, and she could feel the wetness between her legs.

He shifted so that he sat on the front edge of the desk, capturing her between his legs. With a swipe, he unfastened the button of her jeans and pulled down the zipper, his fingers brushing against sensitive areas.

She groaned.

"Shhhh," he said as he nuzzled her ear.

Oh God, she had to be quiet. So quiet.

He unfastened the button at the top of her jeans, and with both hands, pulled down the zipper, his hand brushing against her silky underwear. Little shimmers of sensation danced inside of her.

He pushed down her jeans and undies so that they pooled around her ankles. "Boots," she whispered.

He reached for the side chair, pulled it forward, and gently pushed her onto it. Her body collapsed into it like a tent without its poles. He bent on one knee and pulled the right boot off, then the left, before tugging the jeans, undies, and socks off each leg. She was naked from the waist down.

He kissed her inner thigh and then kissed the same spot on the other thigh. His thumb touched where she was slick, and Mandy had to bite her lip to keep in the moan that had climbed up her throat. His hands slid under her backside, and he lifted her to his mouth. Mandy fisted her hands in his hair, astonished that he was doing this where he was doing it. She'd never been more aroused.

When his hot mouth touched, her back arched as

his tongue caressed her. Pure pleasure swirled around her, dragging her into a vortex of sensation.

"Ty," she whispered. Tension coiled inside of her. With each swirl, each flick of his tongue, the tension pulled tighter. He draped a leg over his shoulder while he pressed his hand under the thigh of the other leg. She held his head, and he worked his tongue so each lick took the tension up a notch, then another, then another. She bit her lip and wondered if it was bloody from biting down so hard to keep from calling out his name. When she thought she couldn't stand it any longer, she dropped over the edge in a shuddering climax, the contractions racking through her like the aftershocks of an earthquake.

Ty rose and unbuckled his belt. Within a heartbeat his boots were off, his socks and pants thrown to the side, and he stood there, half naked, with a wonderful, full erection. He pulled her to her feet and leaned his butt against the edge of the desk.

"Climb aboard, Mrs. Martin," he growled. "We're making a baby."

Mandy didn't have to be asked twice. He held her at her hips, and she propped a knee against the hard surface of the desk and slung a leg around his waist. The engorged head of his hot erection nudged against her opening. He pressed her hips down as he thrust up. He stretched her, but she was slick and he buried himself inside her, deep inside her. A moan escaped.

"Shhh, honey. You said you'd be quiet."

But he didn't tell her how erotic this would be. How aroused she would feel.

"Wrap your legs tight around me," he commanded.

She did as he asked, and he lifted her as he rose off the desk. He flipped around, and her bare butt slapped the smooth surface of the desktop.

"Hold on tight," he whispered through the sexual fog engulfing her mind.

His hands moved to her back, and he pressed her to him. Then his hips moved back, and he was hammering into her, again and again, faster, harder, pushing against her as his large hands held her in place. His chest heaved, and his breathing was ragged. Still he pounded, and she was caught in a sexual swirl that sent her, finally, over the edge, the contraction hard and powerful, and it shook her like an earthquake splitting the earth. She wanted to shout, but somewhere through the haze, she remembered she had to be quiet, and instead she bit into the soft fabric of his shirt to hold it in. The aftershocks rippled through her, and she tightened her grip on his shirt. His groan rumbled out like plains thunder, and his knees bent for a second before he crushed her to his chest. So much for being quiet.

* * *

Ty had just had the best sex of his life, in an office, on a desk. He fastened his belt and helped Mandy find a sock. Clearly it wasn't due to the surroundings.

Mandy, still breathing a little heavy, sat on the same chair where he'd made her come minutes before and pulled on a gray python boot with a pointed toe. He'd never realized how many different types of boots there were until he'd met Mandy.

293

"If you'd be okay with it, I'd like to move back to the ranch house. I think, given one life ended there, it would be fitting to begin a new life there." She looked at him from under those beautiful thick lashes of hers, and he felt a zing of lust. Hell.

"You want to?" He wasn't sure that going back to her grandfather's would be good for her, but if that's what she wanted, he had no problem.

"I know you wanted to have a place to work out and all."

"I haven't used the facilities since we've been married. I'm too exhausted at the end of the day, and there's too much to do at the beginning of the day." He leaned over and nipped her ear. She smelled like him. "Seems my muscles are getting enough of a workout the old-fashioned way."

She kissed his cheek. "I'll ask Mrs. Jenkins to fix up the bedroom and tell her we are coming back. I think she'll be relieved."

His smile crooked up. "As long as it's the bedroom with the king-size bed."

* * *

Mandy sat on the sofa in the ranch house library and as her heart hammered against her ribs, the clock ticking the seconds away while she waited for Ty. He was in the kitchen, having insisted on fixing them coffee after the wonderful dinner of ribs and sweet potatoes Mrs. Jenkins had made before she'd headed out at her designated time of three o'clock. Mrs. Jenkins had seemed quite cheered by the news that Ty and Mandy would be coming back to the house and appeared relieved when Mandy had asked her to make up the guest room with the king bed. Mandy imagined she'd been a tad worried about her job, despite reassurances.

Talk over dinner had been about the preparations for the Cheyenne rodeo. Yet all she could think about was Ty's mouth on her crotch and her straddling him on his desk. She flushed just remembering. And they might have made a baby. Right there.

Ty strode into the library, tray in hand. "Here you go," he said, lifting the steaming cup of coffee from the tray. "Just the way you like it, strong, diluted with sugar and lots of cream."

He'd remembered.

"Thanks." She sipped the coffee. It had been so unlike her, having sex in the office. Oh, she'd had her share of sex in cars, sex in the living room, once even in the kitchen. But an office was a somewhat public space, and she'd never had sex in a public space, unless a campsite in Yellowstone qualified.

The coffee was strong, yet mellow. Just the way she liked it. "Good coffee."

"Thanks. I'm actually pretty handy in the kitchen. Had to be if I wanted to eat, given I've been on my own all these years."

"Really." She tried to imagine him bustling about the kitchen, and failed. The man was full of surprises.

"If we ever find a weekend when we are at home, I'll cook you something. I make a sausage and pasta dish that's garnered a few accolades."

She set her coffee down on the tray that graced the square walnut table in front of the overstuffed sofa. Ty sat on the edge of the cushion within arm's length of her.

"You okay being here, in the ranch house?" Ty asked.

Her mother and Mrs. Jenkins had done a good job of clearing out the little things of her grandfather's—framed pictures, many of his books, much of his private papers—as well as his bedroom. But all the awards the company and its livestock had earned over the thirty-plus years still hung on the wall or sat on a shelf. The overstuffed furniture covered in saddle leather, the worn rug, and the bookshelves that lined the wall and framed the big-screen TV were comfortingly familiar. It felt like home, in a good way.

"I think it was just the day, the funeral being so recent. It actually feels good to be here. And there's more room for my boots." Mandy had moved about half of them in already. She'd had to commandeer one whole closet in another bedroom to accommodate them. She'd have to get one of those closet companies to come in and organize them all.

"I never knew there were so many types of boots. How many do you have?"

She shrugged. "Have never counted them. But a lot."

Ty chuckled. "You have enough inventory to start a business."

"Speaking of business, how do you like it so far? Certainly not a nine-to-five lifestyle."

He took a gulp of coffee before answering. "I never did work nine to five, so the hours aren't much of a change. But I'm finding I enjoy it. I like working with livestock again. I like the business end too. Negotiating contracts, putting together budgets, looking at strategies to grow the business. Those are things I think I'm pretty good at. Seems it's the best of both worlds. What makes you so committed to the rodeo business?"

"I like working with the animals and the people, establishing relationships with the committees. I think I'm pretty good at those things."

Ty raised his cup in a toast. "Seems we make a good team. You know we'll have to keep on trying until we get it right?"

"Get what right?"

"Making a baby." His grin exposed his set of very white, very straight teeth.

A flush of heat washed over her.

"I suppose we will have to do it more than once." She tried to keep her tone casual, but the thought of more sex with Ty had her pulse rat-a-tatting.

He lifted his cup in a mock toast and waggled his eyebrows. "I'm counting on it. I've something to show you," he said and stretched out his hand.

Clasping it, a warm cozy feeling enveloped her. They rose together, and he led her out of the library and down the hall toward the bedrooms. He walked through the house as if it was the most natural thing for them to be there, together. And heading for bed.

They passed the closed door of her grandfather's cleared-out bedroom, passed the guestroom where the king-sized bed had been made up, and stopped at the guest room where they had spent their first night in separate twin beds. The door was closed, and she wondered if he'd made a mistake.

"This isn't our room," she said. "Least not anymore."

His chuckle was warm and knowing, and he looked down at her with a wide smile on his face. He kissed the tip of her nose. "I should hope not." Still holding her hand, he opened the door and gave it a little push so it swung wide.

There stood a crib in place of the twin beds. A beautiful walnut-tone crib with a curved backboard. Against the wall next to it was a matching dresser, and on top of it was a toy airplane.

He looked at her expectantly. She was literally speechless.

He frowned. "Did I get the wrong color or something?"

"No," she said, finding her voice. "It's just…when did you get this?"

"I went out today after…after we decided to have a kid. I took one of the ranch's pick-up trucks. Only I didn't realize you needed to put this stuff together. Took me the better part of two hours." He walked over and touched the railing and gave a little shake. He turned to her. "See, it's sturdy. It's convertible too."

"I see." She was still amazed that he had done such a thing. She walked forward and touched the rail. It was real wood and looked expensive—and complicated to put together. She looked up into his eager face. "It's beautiful."

She didn't have the heart to tell him that it might be considered bad luck to buy things for a baby that was not yet conceived, much less born.

"I put the twin beds in storage in the basement and sealed up the mattresses in plastic covers."

"And you bought a toy airplane."

He nodded, obviously pleased with himself. "Boy or girl, I figure they'll enjoy it. It has a remote control."

The grin on his face was downright boyish. But when he turned to look at her, his expression had turned serious.

He cupped her chin. His hands were warm. His thumb brushed over her cheek, and he rested his forehead against hers, blocking out everything else, engulfing her and sucking up all the oxygen in the room. "I want everything to be perfect for our baby, Mandy. For as long as it lasts, I'd like everything to be perfect for us as well."

Her heart swelled, and she tried to breathe, as it seemed her heart was pressed against her lungs. His mouth swept over hers. She wanted him. She wanted all of him. And she wanted more from him than she knew he was willing to give.

The kiss was deep, full, and with a tongue that performed a sensuous dance with hers. She wrapped her arms around his neck and hung on, giving as much as she could. There was no reason to hold back. They had successfully negotiated an agreement that would be a win for both of them, regardless of what he did to the company. She could finally let herself go, enjoy the guilty pleasure he conjured up every time she looked him.

While his one hand cupped her chin, his other wrapped around her and tugged her tight against him. She gave herself over to the sensuous pleasure of having a man make love with his mouth.

When he broke the kiss, he leaned back to gauge her reaction. She wasn't sure what he saw, but his half-cocked smile said he was pleased. So did the hard rod tenting his jeans.

"You kiss like a fucking goddess."

She flushed. He was to blame for making her feel sensual and wanton and wild.

"Hopefully you're tempted," she said.

"Tempted? I'm goddamn addicted."

This time she initiated the kiss, caressing him with her lips, enticing him with her tongue, and wrapping her arms around him like a python hugging its meal.

His hands brushed down her back, pressing her closer, against his hard body, sending little shivers of anticipation through her. She wanted him. She wanted him inside of her. She wanted him deep inside of her.

Before she realized what he was doing, he'd lifted her off the ground, cradling her in his muscular arms.

"We're going to bed," he said, heading for the hallway. "We've got a crib to fill."

Chapter 20

Mandy stepped out of the office building and into the bright sunshine of a late September morning. Ty was off doing god-knew-what, and so it was left to her to decide what bulls would be used for next weekend's rodeo. She headed toward the pens. This next rodeo was a big one, and they would be expecting Prescott's best.

The days had melded into weeks, and the weeks into months, and she still wasn't pregnant. The sex, however, was mighty incredible. The attraction she felt for Ty had grown stronger with the knowledge that each time could be the moment they conceived their child. She had tried not to get too hyper about the ebb and flow of her cycle. Her doctor had warned her to simply relax and let it happen, as it surely would, given they were both healthy and everything was working.

She had tried to push from her mind any idea Ty would sell her company. He'd promised to advise her if any realistic offer came their way, and so far, none had. And she'd asked. Though it was known on the circuit that Prescott might be for sale, apparently tight credit and a struggling economy were giving any serious buyer pause. And Mandy didn't consider Stan Lassiter a serious buyer, given his lowball offer.

It was true that negotiations on future contracts had been hampered by the rumors, since the rodeo circuit was a small community. But in just two more months, it would be over, and Prescott would be hers, free and clear. She could endure until she could announce with certainty that Prescott was *not* for sale, was off the block, was staying in the family for good.

Surprisingly, Ty had thrown himself into running Prescott like it would always be his, and it had been weeks since he'd brought up the prospect of selling. He'd worked every rodeo, like he promised, and he actually seemed to enjoy it. While they both worked on contract negotiations, she had become the front person, building up the relationships with the rodeo committees and managing the crew at the site, while Ty did the backroom stuff, such as drawing up the contracts, working out the logistics, developing the budgets, and setting up the schedule, freeing Harold to concentrate on the breeding program and the quality of the stock for each event. Once the responsibilities had been sorted, Mandy was surprised at how well they worked together. When Ty left, she would miss his contribution. Who was she kidding? She'd miss him.

That knowledge had been creeping up on her for weeks now.

A fly buzzed around her head, and she swatted at the air, hoping the insect would move on.

She liked being married. She liked having someone to share the day with, having someone who cared about her, someone who noticed.

She liked being married to Ty. The fringe benefits were amazing. But he also understood the business, more than she expected from a mere lawyer. She could talk to him about everything and anything, and he was interested, knowledgeable, and helpful. And the crew seemed more accepting of him. He'd even been invited to one of their poker games.

It was all too easy to imagine they were really married. Really running Prescott Rodeo Company together.

He acted married. He'd take her out to dinner on a whim, just to give her a lift after a particularly hard day. When they weren't on the road, he'd make coffee for them in the evening, and they'd sit together sipping their coffee in the library as they watched some silly show on TV. And almost always, he'd find some excuse to lean over and give her a sweet kiss. That kiss would lead to more kisses, and before the next commercial she'd be gathered in his arms and they'd be helping each other unwind.

A smile crept across her face as she ambled along the gravel path, past the small arena they used for exhibitions, to the horse paddocks and corrals where the bulls were kept. She waved away the horseflies in a vain attempt to keep them from biting her bare arms, since she had on a sleeveless top. There was a mild breeze today, a reprieve from the recent heat that made denims cling to clammy legs.

Life was surprisingly good. And she wanted it to continue, but how was that going to happen? Ty hadn't said anything about the future. He hadn't talked about his job, whether his condo had sold or even if it was still on the market.

And she hadn't asked. She was too afraid of the answers.

Rounding the corner of one of the barns, she shaded her eyes against the sun and focused on the pens holding some of Prescott's prize bulls. Standing at the corral gate was Ty with a man she didn't recognize.

Why would a strange man be looking over her premier bull stock? Rodeo committeemen didn't routinely visit rodeo suppliers. Her stomach did a somersault. What if Ty hadn't given up on selling Prescott?

She marched toward the two. Watching them appraise her bulls caused an ache deep within her, as if someone had driven a blade into her stomach and was pushing on the heel of the knife, making sure it went in deep.

Engrossed in conversation, neither man noticed her until she was within a yard of them. Then they turned.

The stranger was probably midforties, if the lines on his face were an indicator, handsome in a boy-next-door kind of way, and wearing the denims and plaid shirt that marked him as a rancher—or rodeo supplier.

"Mandy? What are you doing here?" Ty asked. He sounded like she had just caught him up to no good. Her heart sank. Ty wore a black Prescott Rodeo Company T-shirt and a pair of leather chaps over dusty denims, with a cowboy hat covering his thick head of hair. The chaps were something new.

He might look the part of a PRC cowboy, but that was just an illusion. Just like their marriage. Ty was no more part of PRC than the stranger. Not if Ty could sell the company.

"I could ask you the same," she said. "Hi, I'm Mandy Prescott...Martin." She thrust out her hand. She still hadn't gotten used to her full name.

Ty straightened. "My wife. Mandy, this is Cody Lane, livestock director for the AFBR."

A rush of relief pulsed through her. The AFBR. Not a rodeo contractor. Someone who contracts *for* rodeos.

She shook his hand, the man's grip firm and reassuring. "Pleased to meet you."

As relief subsided, guilt took over. She'd actually thought Ty would sell her company—after all they'd done together these last four months. Only he wasn't going to sell it. He was working to strengthen it.

"What brings you to Prescott, Mr. Lane?"

"Cody." The cowboy smiled, showing a pair of fine white teeth. "Ty asked us to come by and take a look a while back, and since I was in Cheyenne at one of the tour stops, I thought I'd swing by."

"Ty has rounded up some of our finest."

"I was just giving Cody the rundown on some of these bulls, Mandy, but you know them as well as anyone." Ty shot her an encouraging smile. Dusty boots, dusty chaps, dusty hat. Her cowboy husband. Just seconds ago, she'd been ready to believe the worst. Now she felt a warm glow suffuse through her. Was this love she'd been feeling lately? Was she falling in love with him?

The thought sparked along some invisible electric wire.

It took a beat before she could shift her gaze to Cody. Hoping the man hadn't noticed and wondering if Ty had, she began to fill Cody in on each of the bulls, its pedigree, its bucking prowess, its stats, and its idiosyncrasies. As if cued, a few bulls started prancing around their pens, eager to put on a show.

"I wonder if someone's around who'd be willing to give me a demonstration of these bulls' abilities," Cody asked when she'd finished.

"When you called this morning, I started rounding up some of the hands, just in case," Ty responded. "We can stroll to the exhibition arena, and I'll have the bulls moved over."

Why hadn't he told her someone from the AFBR was coming if he knew this morning? She supposed the important thing was they had an opportunity to showcase Prescott bulls for the AFBR. The fact Ty still operated, on occasion, like a lone wolf, well, that was a small price to pay.

Because if they got the AFBR contract, there could be no reason they'd have to sell, should sell. The fact Ty had pushed for this warmed her in ways that made her want to run into his arms and kiss him silly. But that would have to wait until after Mr. Lane took his leave. Still, she couldn't keep her heart from floating.

It didn't take long for the bulls to be shifted to the chutes in the small arena they used for bucking schools. Several cowhands, having heard about the demonstration, had wandered over to participate and watch. Mandy and Cody Lane hung by the back fence where they could get a good view of the action.

One by one the hands took a turn, and the bulls showed off, landing most cowboys in the dirt. Never one to miss a rodeo opportunity, Tucker was one of the last to ride. A bronc rider by trade, it took four seconds before he was unceremoniously dumped. Gratefully, Tucker had on his helmet, a safety measure insisted on by her mother if and when Tucker rode bulls.

One more bull left to ride, and it was the whirling dervish that had pinned her in the parking lot. Straining her neck to see who was getting set to ride him, her stomach lurched to her throat.

Donning Tucker's helmet, Ty was taking instructions from the hands as he eased his strong chap-clad legs down and around the snorting bull.

Panicked, Mandy was set to run toward the gate and stop the craziness, when, with a terse nod from Ty, the chute gate opened and Mandy's throat closed. Eight seconds was an eternity, as any rough-stock rider could attest.

The bull whirled to the right and then jumped, kicking its back legs out. Ty was still on, barely, as the bull switched direction and bucked hard and high. Ty flew through the air like a missile, landing with a thud on the hard ground. Things seemed to move in slow motion as Mandy tried to scramble up the fence. Any thoughts of the bull and the danger it represented had evaporated as soon as she'd heard the thud of Ty's body hitting the ground. One of the cowboys distracted the bull as Mandy climbed toward the top rail. Her focus was on the heap that was Ty. But she stalled at the top. She saw a leg bend, then a torso lift, and Ty was on his feet. He unbuckled the helmet and swung it off, a big old grin on his dirt-streaked face.

The thin crowd of cowboys hooted and whistled. And that, Mandy realized, was the reason Ty had done it. To show the men he was one of them, that he had the true grit of a cowboy and wasn't just some interfering suit. It was a lot to risk just to prove a point.

Mandy jumped back off the fence, no longer needing to enter the arena. Instead, she headed for the gate without waiting for Cody. The thump of footsteps behind her said he was following. In seconds she was within arm's reach of Ty, who was getting congratulatory slaps on the back, while from behind her, Cody heartily declared the bull a contender and the rider not.

"I hung on as long as I could," Ty said, shaking his head now covered by his Stetson. "Unfortunately, it wasn't all that long." The dirt on his clothes couldn't take the shine off his smile. Damn if she wasn't proud of him, crazy as he had been for getting on a bull.

"No, but all you thrown riders showcased just how well those bulls move. I'd like to see at least three of those bulls at our next Touring Division event being held in Casper in another two weeks. If they show well in the Touring Division, they'll eventually graduate to the top AFBR series. That's serious money," he said, turning to look directly at Mandy.

She knew just how serious that money was. A good bull team could earn out six figures in the AFBR, even with the steep entry fees. She'd been trying to get on the AFBR's radar for the last three years. Ty apparently did it with a phone call. And she thought he was selling her out.

It didn't take long to sort out what bulls Lane wanted. After Cody refused an offer for lunch, saying he had to get on the road, Mandy hung back as Ty walked him to his truck. There was so much she wanted to say to Ty, and little of it she would say. No matter what she was feeling, in two months Ty would be leaving. As they'd agreed. As she had insisted. Baby or no baby.

She took a deep breath as she watched him amble back. He had a slight hitch to his gate.

"You all right?" she asked as he drew near.

He smiled, more of a grimace, as dust kicked up behind him from the departing truck. "Other than being sore as hell?"

She gave a laugh to cover up her relief. "That wasn't the smartest thing you've ever done, or your finest hour, cowboy."

He stared at her, looking at once sheepish and pleased. "I know. I've been practicing on that mechanical bull we have for classes. Thought it was an opportunity to give the real thing a try."

She took in that news, rolled it around in her mind. This man was full of surprises and contradictions. "But why?"

"I wanted to prove something."

"To those cowboys?" she asked, startled he would care about anyone else's opinion.

"No. To myself." He tipped his hat back, revealing a serious set of dark eyes. "That I'm good enough."

"For what?"

He shrugged and looked over the fences to the mountains in the distance.

She was touched by the fact that a man like Ty, who always seemed so confident, so in control, would be insecure about anything. She walked to him, sliding her hand down his face in a caress.

His attention was on her now, those dark eyes

drilling into her, asking her some silent question she couldn't quite decipher, but which she knew was important to him.

"I've never felt like I'm good enough."

Mandy touched his arm. "Believe me, you're good enough, cowboy. You don't have to prove it to anyone." And she meant it. Ty had worked each rodeo alongside the men, alongside her. He pulled long hours in the saddle during an event and even longer hours before and after to assure that Prescott presented the best rodeo for the money.

"Neither do you, Mrs. Martin."

She kissed him. She meant it to be a sweet, comforting kiss, but the moment their lips touched, it took on a fire-fueled passion. Her arms wrapped around his neck, his hand cupped her chin, and their tongues did a sensual dance, deeper and deeper, more and more until there was no one else, nothing else in the whole universe but the two of them, body pressed to body, mouth devouring mouth.

When they finally broke, he stared at her as if he was searching for the answer to his silent question from before.

"I want to take you back home, strip you naked, and make love to you, Mandy Martin. Make that baby."

"It will have to wait until tonight. We've work to do."

"Later then. That's a promise." He kissed the tip of her nose. She felt like she could dance on air.

* * *

Ty wanted to urge Paddy into a full-out run, but he held back. He could use the time to work out what he was going to say, and riding in companionable silence next to Mandy mounted on Willow would give him that time. It was a bright fall afternoon in Wyoming, and the breeze was cool, the air mild, and the grasses lush.

He had convinced Mandy to take a horseback ride and have a picnic dinner. He had things to discuss. They hadn't had many chances to ride during the hectic summer season, but now that the circuit had calmed down as fall arrived, they didn't have a rodeo every weekend.

Which meant they had time to start planning for next year—when he would no longer be with Prescott Rodeo, with Mandy. Unless…

He'd been trying for days to figure out what to say and how to say it and if he should say it. This would be the biggest commitment of his life. And if she said yes, he'd be taking on the responsibility of someone else's happiness, and that scared the crap out of him. Of the few people whose life had once intersected with his, he hadn't made any of them happy. And he wondered if he could make her happy.

Didn't look like they would have to sell Prescott, given they were only six weeks from the six-month finish line and he hadn't had any offers except for Stan's early lowball bid. It was a relief knowing he had done his best, but he would be leaving Prescott in Mandy's hands, and with the AFBR potential, PRC would be in better shape for her. That would make her happy.

Maybe she'd want him to move on so she could

run PRC all by herself. She didn't need him. She was fully capable of handling it herself. And so what was the value to her of being married to him?

Nothing.

So far, he hadn't even been able to give her a child. That had been surprisingly disappointing. The doctor had said everything was working, and he was relieved he wasn't shooting blanks, but shouldn't she be pregnant by now? Because it wasn't for lack of trying.

Yeah, the only thing he could offer her was sex. And he knew from experience that wasn't enough.

Up ahead the creek was coming into view. He wondered how she'd feel about the spot he'd chosen. He wanted her to know that he was willing to make a fresh start and put the past, their past, behind them.

He glanced over at Mandy, her horse keeping pace with his. He loved the easy way she sat a horse, her cute butt glued to the saddle like the horsewoman she was.

She had twined the reins around her long, elegant fingers. Those slender fingers were at odds with the type of work she often did. He'd told her to let the hired help clean out the barn or curry the horses, but he'd often find her working side by side with one of the hands just to get the job done. She always comported herself like a lady, but she didn't think twice about doing tasks most "ladies" would never touch.

He still didn't know what he would say to her or if he would have the courage to ask her. Maybe he should just get to the creek and wing it. He padded his breast pocket to assure himself the rings were still there and then checked behind him to make sure the picnic basket was securely strapped to the back of his saddle, giving the basket a firm tug for reassurance.

"Race you," he called out, and gave Paddy a gentle kick. The sorrel lurched into action, apparently happy to be given rein to run. Air whipped across his face as he urged Paddy forward. A quick glance behind confirmed that Mandy had followed at a pounding pace.

Ty headed for the copse of trees in the distance, the beating of hooves in time with the rapid beating of his heart. Anything was possible, he reminded himself, and nothing was certain.

Mandy pulled Willow up at the edge of the bank that gently sloped into the creek. The familiar rock she'd once hidden behind loomed over the water. She'd lost the race. Willow had given it her all, but the prized cutting horse from Texas was too much for her. Mandy could relate, but she wondered why Ty had chosen this spot for their picnic.

He'd already tied Paddy to a tree limb and was unbuckling the straps that secured the picnic basket and blanket, his large fingers working the knots.

She'd been surprised when he'd suggested a picnic dinner and even more surprised that Mrs. Jenkins had apparently known about it since, when they arrived home, fried chicken, biscuits, and corn on the cob were already packed in a hamper. Ty had pulled out a bottle of wine from the fridge, and they had set off.

It had seemed romantic of Ty and out of character. But this place, of all places?

Ty lost no time in setting up while Mandy secured Willow to one of the trees. The sun was low in the sky but still above the mountain peaks in the distance, flooding the bank with afternoon light. Ty was laying the Navajo-style blanket under a tree opposite to where the horses were secured.

"Didn't beat me this time, did you?" he said, grinning up at her as he knelt on the ground, smoothing the fabric.

"Paddy proved too much—today. Never know about tomorrow."

He looked at her from under his hat brim and nodded. "I brought bug spray," he said as he rose and held up a plastic bottle.

"You had this all planned," she said, feeling complimented by his efforts. He'd gone to some trouble to get her here. "I'm just surprised at your choice of location."

He came over to her and rested his large hands on her shoulders. His touch was warm and heavy, and he seemed to take up the whole landscape as he stood before her.

"I thought it appropriate."

She wanted to ask him why it was appropriate, since it had been the sight of her greatest humiliation, but he slid his hand up to her face and grazed a thumb across her cheek, and all thought vanished as a pleasant little shiver cascaded through her. He did this to her every time they were together. Made her want him. What would happen in a few weeks when he walked away?

She pushed that thought from her mind. She'd surely be pregnant by then, considering how frequently they made love. She'd have a child. He'd be in her life. Though that had once been a negative, his being in her life now sat squarely in the positive column, at least for the moment. Only she wondered how long it would be positive. What would happen when he took up with another woman and brought her to their child's birthday party?

She'd fantasized about raising her child, and he'd always been in the picture—as her husband. He was all the things she shouldn't want—arrogant, by the book, a loner—but he'd also been surprisingly tender and caring and protective. He'd been generous with his time, his knowledge, and his contacts. He'd respected her knowledge of the industry and had backed her decisions, even if he didn't agree with them. He'd been a talented lover—and a good friend. She'd fallen in love with him, and she wasn't sure she could take his leaving. It seemed, one way or another, the men in her life left her, and she didn't know what to do about it.

"Let's eat first, and then we should talk." He cupped her chin and lightly kissed her on the mouth.

The pit of her stomach felt funny.

Isn't that what guys said when they had something bad to tell you?

He took her hand and pulled her toward the blanket. Sitting down, she opened the latch of the basket and lifted the lid. The smell of fried chicken filled her nostrils as she peered at a tangle of plastic plates, linen napkins, a wineglass and bottle, a water bottle, plasticware, and lidded tubs filled with food. She began unpacking as Ty grabbed the wine and poured it into a glass.

She was aware when he took a sip of wine, when he settled on his knees, when he reached in and pulled open the tub with the corn. She took out the still-warm tub with the fried chicken and set it on the blanket. At the bottom of the basket were salt and pepper shakers. Mrs. Jenkins and Ty had thought of everything.

She settled on her rump and tucked her legs under her. The top of the basket made a small table, and Mandy began setting it. She'd been aware of Ty watching her even as he placed an ear of corn on each of their plates. He opened the larger tub that contained the chicken and placed a golden-fried breast next to each ear of corn. He took the bag with the biscuits and set one next to the chicken. He was playing host, and she wondered if he had a part in mind for her—beyond guest.

"Time to eat," he said, looking at his plate. "I'm starved."

She took her lead from him. As they ate, she listened to the water tumbling over the rocks, the birds tweeting among the trees, and her own breathing. The chicken was the perfect blend of crispy on the outside and moist on the inside, and the biscuit was tasty.

It seemed perfect and romantic, and she couldn't fathom what Ty wanted to talk about that wouldn't ruin the mood. She took a sip of bottled water and wished she could have had wine to suppress the anxious feeling filling her. But she might be pregnant, and she wasn't about to take a chance.

"We're having a school in next week. Promise me you won't be tempted to ride a bull again?" she asked. He was working his way down the ear of corn, getting a kernel or two on his lower cheek. Ty had a hearty appetite—for many things.

"Little ibuprofen and I'm as good as new," he said when he came to the end of the row of kernels.

"You had me worried there for a second." More like several seconds. Or a minute. It had taken her some time to erase the image of him in a heap from her mind.

Ty shook his head. "I now get how addictive that rush of adrenaline is. If I was younger, I just might compete. On broncs, though, not bulls."

"Well then, I'm glad you are older and wiser." She took an ear of corn and bit into it, enjoying the sweet kernels.

"I am older. Not sure about wiser." He chuckled and took another sip of wine. More like a gulp. He grabbed the bottle and poured some more, topping off his glass. One thing about riding a horse after drinking, if you weren't drunk enough to fall off, the horse would likely get you home in one piece. But she had to wonder why Ty was drinking so quickly.

Stripping her ear of kernels and having made a solid attempt to finish her chicken breast, she began to pack up the remnants while Ty finished off another breast. Clearly her appetite wasn't that of a pregnant woman, but it would be a few weeks before her next cycle, before she would know for sure. There was still time. She needn't panic—yet.

Ty's pieces of chicken were now nothing but bone. She watched as he swiped a napkin across his chin, a satisfied grin on his face. He threw the trash into the large tub, closed it up, and packed it away. She followed, putting everything back except the water bottle. Ty poured more wine into his glass and took a long draw, his eyes looking her over from head to toe and back again. Any other place, and she'd be up for some spectacular sex, but here she felt on edge, as if any second he was going to tell her he had to leave.

She was no longer worried about the company. If no one, including Lassiter, had made an offer by now, it wasn't likely any other stock contractor would step forward at this late date. Just securing financing could take a while. No, it wasn't the company she was worried about. It was her heart.

He settled behind her, his big body sliding against hers as he wrapped his arms around her waist and tugged her into his lap. Was he holding her in case she fell apart?

He felt warm and hard, and she should feel secure in his embrace. She didn't.

He nuzzled her neck, and she detected the scent of liquor, which was probably responsible for the intimate moment.

He kissed the side of her neck. A little tingle spread within her. "My condo sold," he said.

"That's good. Right?" She wasn't sure. If he put his house on the market when he thought he'd be working at Prescott for two years, he might not be so happy that it sold.

"I think so. Do you?" He nibbled her ear.

She twisted a little so she could see him. He'd opened the top button of his shirt, exposing his clavicle and the base of his throat "Yes." She guessed she was happy. For him. She didn't know what it meant for them.

"So I won't have a place to go to when the six months are up." His tongue trailed down the side of her throat.

"No. I don't suppose you will," she said, wondering where he was taking this and trying not to let her imagination fill her with hope.

"So I was thinking…"

She wanted to know what he was thinking. And whom he was thinking about.

"Maybe I could stay on. With you. For a while longer." He feathered kisses down her neck, and his hands cupped her breasts.

"How much longer?" she wasn't sure what he was asking, but it didn't sound like a marriage proposal. Not that she expected one, but she'd definitely imagined one.

She felt one of his shoulders raise and lower. "I don't know. For as long as it feels right."

That sounded very open ended…and vague. "Feels right for whom?"

"For both of us."

It would relieve some of the anxiety that had been building inside of her, dreading the day he'd leave and wondering what would happen if she wasn't pregnant. But putting off the inevitable wasn't a commitment or a declaration of love. Once again it was simply convenient for him.

He kneaded her breasts as he kissed the base of her neck, and she involuntarily leaned back. "There's no hurry…right?" he asked. His tongue tickled her ear, and desire pulsed inside of her.

"What about your job? Don't you have to get back to it?"

Behind her he took a breath. "I quit my job six months ago, before I agreed to help Prescott."

She'd tried to process what he said, but she

couldn't understand what would make him do it. "Why?"

"They wanted me to ignore some things, and I couldn't. So I don't have a job or a home." He squeezed her tightly against his chest, and she could feel the buttons on his shirt. "If I stay on, you'd be running things, of course. You pretty much do now. But I could still help out until I figured out what to do. We could continue together. No hurry about divorcing, or anything." His hand softly cupped the side of her face and turned her toward him. "If you're okay with that."

She hadn't expected a commitment from him. She should be happy that he agreed to a child with her, right? And since she wasn't pregnant yet, continuing on would be convenient for her as well. She shouldn't expect more from him.

"I'm okay with it."

He shifted, and his hand supported her back as he bent her down to lie upon the blanket. The ground was hard, the blanket itchy, and all she wanted was him. He'd been all she ever wanted. He sidled up beside her and stared down into her eyes. "Let's make a memory, Mandy. A good one."

Expecting more than a memory was just asking for heartache. Her head knew that. Too bad her heart hadn't listened.

Chapter 21

Ty stared at the offer letter and then looked back at the resolute man sitting across from him in the office that used to be JM's. Stan Lassiter settled back into the folds of his chair. The offer was 50 percent more than Stan had offered the first time. A fair offer, even considering the AFBR opportunity. Prescott bulls had just finished another good weekend on the tour, bucking off contestants to pull strong scores. How Stan had gotten wind of it so fast was amazing, though Ty shouldn't have been surprised. The rodeo stock community was a small one, as industries go.

"It's a legitimate offer. A damn good one and you know it. You have the bank's statement saying they'd approve the line of credit." Stan had read Ty's pause as concern.

He guessed he was concerned. Things had been going so well, and there had been no serious nibbles in quite a while. Ty had been so sure he wouldn't have to sell Prescott, wouldn't have to disappoint Mandy. The AFBR opportunity meant Prescott Rodeo Company was in better shape, and he'd fulfilled his promise to JM.

He'd even allowed himself to hope that he could make things permanent with Mandy.

The months he'd spent with her had shown him a woman he didn't know existed, didn't know he wanted. He'd begun to think JM had outfoxed them, though he couldn't be certain Mandy felt the same way. At the creek, he'd intended to ask her to stay married to him, but she'd seemed so surprised he'd sold his condo, surprised he'd given up his job, the words got caught in his throat. Instead, he'd asked to stay on longer, and given she hadn't conceived yet, she'd agreed. He may have fallen for her, but he couldn't be sure he wasn't just a convenient sperm donor.

He'd decided to wait and take the opportunity to show her what she meant to him now that he'd negotiated more time together and, when the time seemed right, pop the question, maybe at their six-month anniversary.

He'd bought rings, taking one of her rings she'd left on the dresser to the jewelers for size. The engagement ring was a large diamond set in platinum, and the matching wedding band had several smaller diamonds because that's what Mandy was—a diamond surrounded by others.

He'd been thinking about different ways he could propose. Like having Jace Parrish announce Ty during the rodeo parade and handing Ty the mike, taking her for a plane ride and engaging the autopilot so he could propose, hiring a skywriting plane to write it in the sky, or handing her a gift for the baby, with the ring tied to the ribbon.

Now, mere weeks from the six-month deadline, he held a lucrative deal in his hand. One he couldn't walk away from, however much it would break Mandy's heart.

"I'm just surprised. This is quite a bit more than your original offer, Stan."

"I've tried for years to crack the AFBR. You've done it in a matter of months." He steepled his fingers, resting his hands on the chambray shirt covering his rounded belly. "I won't admit this in public, but your bulls have really come into their own. And the AFBR saw that. Breeding them to my stock and running them in the AFBR, well, it will set me apart."

Just as it could set Prescott apart. Except that hadn't been his charge. His charge was to financially secure the future of the Prescott family.

Ty ran his fingers through his hair, wishing he could make the offer and its complications vanish, but he couldn't.

"I need to review this with the other stockholders." And particularly Mandy.

"I know you can okay this deal on your own. Hear tell JM set it up that way so the decision could be objective and not emotional. I doubt your wife," he said with a sneer, "would ever agree. So I need to know if I'm doing business with the right person."

"I'm the right person." For a few more weeks anyway. "But that doesn't mean I will move without discussion."

"I have thirty days to access this line of credit. That's all, Ty."

"Believe me, this will get the highest priority." Ty rubbed his hand across his chin. "Let me ask you something. Did you let that bull out?"

Stan pressed his hand across his heart. "I don't do stuff like that, Ty. Now whether one of my men may have gotten carried away, I couldn't say. But I suspect there are more than a few people who wouldn't want to see Prescott succeed."

Ty didn't believe that Stan couldn't say…but it was water under the proverbial bridge. There had been some local publicity, but Harold had made sure that it hadn't happened again, and there hadn't been any additional fallout from it.

Stan rose and extended his hand. Ty shook it.

"Man's handshake is as good as his word, I expect. Even with you, Martin." Stan gave him a nod and then ambled out of the room with an uneven gait.

Ty slunk back in his chair and swiveled to look out of the window, across the grounds to the corrals, where Mandy was no doubt checking on the horses for the weekend rodeo.

He could show the offer to Mandy but tell her he was saying no.

That would be the easy way out.

A few more weeks and it wouldn't even be his decision anymore. He could simply delay Stan until the six months were up and not even bring it up.

But that was a coward's way, and Ty was not a coward. Besides, Ty felt a fiduciary responsibility to present the offer.

Even knowing that showing Mandy the offer, much less accepting it, would ruin everything.

What exactly was "everything?" His role in her life was nebulous at best. He didn't know where things stood between them, even though she'd agreed they'd stay married for a while longer. She hadn't gotten pregnant yet, to his knowledge anyway, and it sure wasn't for lack of trying. A smile formed on his lips. No, it wasn't for lack of trying.

Thing was, he wanted to stay married. He wanted to stay with Mandy.

He'd fallen in love with his wife.

* * *

"It is a good offer," Brian said as he held the paper in his hand.

Being a lawyer himself and conversant in contract law, Ty had already made that assessment. He hadn't come to the Prescott family lawyer for legal advice. He needed objectivity. Every fiber in his being said to reject it, while every inch of his brain said to accept it. He'd never had such conflicting feelings about a deal before. He'd always prided himself on making the *right* decision. That was easy when the only consideration had been to maximize the investment.

Come to find out, that hadn't been the only consideration his partners had wanted. And he had walked away precisely because he felt his partners had lost their objectivity.

Now he found himself in the same circumstance. He didn't want a cool, detached, unemotional decision. He wanted one that took into account Mandy's dreams and hopes and aspirations. One that included him in those dreams of hers. But he was at a loss of how to value that versus the hard, cold facts of a good financial deal.

"That's the problem." Ty paced the window-lined office, hoping it would relieve the pressure building in his chest.

Was he being selfish by putting his desire to be part of her life ahead of making her a wealthy woman? One who would never want for anything?

Right now she'd resent him for selling her company. But she would have enough money to start her own enterprise, albeit on a smaller scale, considering she'd have to split the proceeds with her brother, and her mother would be entitled to a stipend. Twenty years from now, when who knew where the rodeo industry and the economy were headed, she might thank him.

"Mandy's not going to want to sell, regardless of the size of the offer." Brian laid down the paper on his neat and organized desk and looked at Ty over the rim of his glasses.

"I know. But that's why JM didn't leave the decision to her. He asked me to do it. Hell, he made me promise I'd look after the family's future."

Brian eased back in his chair. He was without his suit jacket, but with his neatly pressed white shirt and a red tie choking his neck, he didn't look comfortable.

That used to be me. Trussed up like a Christmas turkey.

Now Ty wore the clothes of a rancher and a cowboy, and few would be able to tell by looking at him if he was the owner or a hand. And in the community he now inhabited, it didn't matter. What mattered was character, hard work, and grit, and Ty found he enjoyed that yardstick better than the size of his bank account.

"So what have you come to me for, Ty?"

Ty wished he knew. "Support, maybe."

"You have it." Removing his glasses, Brian leaned forward. "But it's not my support you want, is it?"

Ty's stomach soured. He slumped into the chair

in front of Brian's desk. "So how do I convince Mandy that it is the right thing to do?"

"That is a much harder issue."

Ty rubbed his hand across his face. "We're trying to have a baby, you know."

Brian's eyebrows arched. "No, I didn't know. Are you saying that you two are intending to stay married?"

Ty heaved a breath. He wished he could say that. It was what he'd been hoping for, planning on, dreaming about. But this offer would raze that hope like a giant wrecking ball.

"No. I'm just the sperm donor." That wrecking ball slammed right into his heart.

"Your child would be quite well-off once this deal goes through."

"I would have made sure of that, regardless."

Brian nodded. "You planning on resuming your work with the land development company?"

"I left the partnership about a month before JM passed."

Brian, being the lawyer he was and undoubtedly used to hearing family-type secrets, held his face expressionless except for the arched eyebrows. "I wondered how you could just take a leave of absence like that. So what will you do? This deal will enrich you too, though not to the same degree as Mandy."

"I don't know."

"Were you planning on getting Mandy and Tuck's agreement to develop the ranch now that the business will be sold?"

"That had been the plan once. It's not now."

"You know it's unlikely she'll ever speak to you

again. Awkward, seeing you two will parent a child together. Congratulations, by the way. I assume she's pregnant by now."

Ty shook his head. He hadn't even been able to give her that. He'd take everything from her and leave her with nothing. "No congratulations. She's not pregnant, at least not yet that I know."

Brian harrumphed "Once you tell her you are selling her company, I'm pretty sure that will end any trying. But you're within a few weeks of the end anyway."

Why did it feel like someone had taken an egg beater to his brain? He wanted to do the right thing—if he could just figure out what the hell that was. If it was up to him, he'd choose Mandy over anything else. But that was being selfish. That was making the decision with his heart, not his head, the very thing he'd been critical of others doing. The very thing he'd always been so proud of not doing.

"So what's next for you?"

"Start my own development firm, I guess." What had once been his dream seemed more like a jail sentence now. A sentence of isolation and separation from the woman he'd grown to love. With all his heart.

"No interest in the rodeo stock business, huh?" Brian grinned as if sure of his answer.

"Actually, I've enjoyed it." *A lot.* "I can see why JM loved it." *And why Mandy does.*

"Really? I'd never take you for a man who worked with livestock."

Yet for the majority of Ty's life, he'd been a ranch kid, working alongside his father and brother, scratching out a living.

Ty thought of Trace, of what his brother had been going through these past years. Working hard and getting nowhere but still persisting. Because he loved it. Ty had never understood that type of drive. Now he did.

"Me either," Ty confessed.

"You want me there? When you tell Mandy?"

Ty nodded. She might be more controlled if there were other people around, though he doubted it. Still, it couldn't hurt. "Can you do it this afternoon? Tucker's at the ranch now. I'm sure I can track down Sheila and Harold. I know where Mandy is. We can meet in the library at the ranch house at say…two o'clock?"

Brian glanced at his calendar. "I'll move some things around and see you there."

Ty unfurled from the chair. His muscles stiff, his heart sore like it had been pummeled in a boxing match. "I just hope she doesn't shoot me."

* * *

Ty leaned against the doorjamb of what was to have been the baby's room and stared at a barren crib set against the faded yellow walls. Here he was again, looking in at something that could never be his. He hadn't been able to give her a baby or give himself a family. The crib was as empty as his life was about to become, made worse by the realization of how full it could have been. Like a tree being hollowed out by a swarm of termites, his life was being destroyed by events he could not control.

When Mandy had agreed to extend their time

together, he'd been certain he could make her happy. She'd be able to keep the company. He'd be able to give her a child. She already had claimed his heart and he hoped she'd see him as good enough to claim hers.

Now, he would lose everything…and give her nothing. That crib and all it represented would be abandoned. Might never be filled…and certainly not by him.

Empty crib, empty life, empty future.

"No. No. No." Mandy blasted out the one-syllable word like she was firing bullets.

Ty could see the moisture collecting in her eyes, the horror on her face as she realized her dreams had died. And he had yielded the murder weapon.

"Mandy, it's a good offer." But he knew the futility of those words.

She rose from the overstuffed library chair and looked at her mother, Tucker, Harold, and Brian in turn, but not at Ty. "Don't let him do this. Don't let him destroy everything JM built. There must be some other way."

Her voice cracked. Her body visibly trembled with anger. Ty wished he could have spared her this. But that would have entailed breaking his promise to the old man—a man who had trusted him to make the hard decisions.

When she finally turned her face toward him, it was blotched with red like someone had punched her. "All this time you made it seem like you were building Prescott into something *with* me. But you were just getting it fattened up so you could sell it. The AFBR…" She waved her arm. "The contract sweeteners, they were just to make it more attractive to a buyer. And you found him. The one you've been courting since day one—Stan Lassiter." She practically growled out the name like a caged dog sighting the warden.

"You're a cold, calculating coward," she seethed. "Afraid to give life a chance. I can hardly believe I wanted to have a child with you."

Tucker choked, Harold blew out a breath, and Sheila gasped, her expression torn between delight and sorrow at the realization it wouldn't happen now.

"How could you? After everything." A sob escaped from Mandy and the chain her words had been wrapping around his heart tightened.

She stalked across the oriental carpet toward the double French doors of the library. Reaching them, she yanked open the door. They weren't done, but apparently Mandy was.

She stopped, turned around. "You get your stuff and move out. Now," she said, directing her comments at Ty.

"If he does that, Mandy, the six-month deal is void," Brian said.

Though Ty knew this outcome was a possibility, he'd had a modicum of hope that Mandy would see reason once she heard the deal. But instead, this was it. The end.

"It doesn't matter now. He's selling the damn place. Stan has the financing. I only agreed to this ludicrous arrangement to keep Prescott from being sold. If you tell me I can delay this deal a couple of weeks so I can turn it down, I'll reconsider."

"Anything can happen." Brian said. "But it's unlikely."

"I hate you, Ty Martin," she hissed. The doors slammed shut behind her.

She had reached into the cavity holding his heart and pulled on that chain, ripping it from his body, leaving nothing but blood and guts.

Chapter 22

Mandy stared at the white plastic stick through watery eyes. Three other plastic sticks sat on the bathroom counter. They all said the same thing. She was pregnant. It should be the happiest moment of her life. It was certainly what she wanted. But the knowledge only deepened the pain of Ty's betrayal.

The man she'd now have to see for the rest of her life. At holidays. During summer vacations. On weekends. And at birthdays. The last thought lifted the corners of her mouth into a weak smile. Her child's birthdays.

Mandy sat on the lid of the toilet, trying to make sense of everything. Of the changes about to occur in her life. She would be a single mother. Raising the child on the ranch, in JM's house. There would be no rodeos to gear up for. She wouldn't have to be away from home on weekends, working from dawn to past midnight to set up and break down an event.

Maybe things happened for a reason.

She could take care of the baby. Take care of herself. And when the baby was a little older, she could start another rodeo company.

But she could have raised the baby and still run

Prescott. Especially if Ty had been by her side. If he had stayed. Been a husband to her.

Only he'd had no intention of doing so even though he'd asked to extend their marriage. She'd been a fool to think there was any hope to do otherwise. To think he enjoyed running Prescott with her. Wanted to be married to her. Raise a family. A fool to think he had any real feelings for her. Like love.

She had forgotten this was Ty Martin— businessman extraordinaire. All business. No pleasure. Well, that wasn't totally true. There had been pleasure. At night, in his arms.

How could a man make such intense love to her and not feel anything?

And here she'd allowed hope to blossom when he'd said he wanted to stay with her longer. Wanted to stay at Prescott.

And all the while he'd been scheming behind her back. Charging after the almighty dollar like it was his salvation.

Grandfather, is this truly who you wanted me to marry?

It was so unlike JM to be such a poor judge of character.

I wish you had been right.

She rose from the seat. Happy as she was with the result of the pregnancy test, her heart felt like it had been dropped into a rock tumbler.

Squaring her shoulders, Mandy walked out into the bedroom. Its emptiness struck her. No cowboy boots by the bed. No comb on the dresser. Half the closet bare.

He was gone.

From her bed, but not from her life.

* * *

Ty looked out on the horses munching grass in the corral as Slim walked by without saying a word to him. Kyle seemed to go out of his way to circle around the other side of the pasture to avoid him. The cowhands were loading the trailers for the next rodeo, and they were making it clear that Ty was persona non grata.

Ty hadn't felt this kind of loneliness since he was a kid.

By the tenets of the will, he was still in charge. But no one spoke to him. No one looked to him for direction or guidance.

He watched Mandy, clipboard in hand, wave each cowboy with a bronc toward this or that trailer. Watched the men mount up and trot their horses over to bull pens, ready to load the animals when Harold gave the word.

They all had heard the rumor that Prescott had a buyer. And they all hated him for it.

No one could hate him more than he hated himself. Even if selling was the right thing, the rational thing. Doing the right thing wasn't always easy. A truth he'd learned courtesy of the land development company.

And it sure didn't get you friends. Or the woman you loved.

Ty didn't hear Harold until the old cowboy had pressed a boot to the fence rail.

"How you holding up?" Harold said in his typical blunt fashion.

"I didn't come here to win any popularity contest." The words sounded churlish, even to him.

"They say it's lonely at the top," Harold offered. The crusty cowboy was dressed for work with his Prescott T-shirt and jeans and the black Stetson that rarely left his head. "I wouldn't know though. Never wanted to find out. I prefer working with the men."

"Never thought you cared much about being around people, Harold. You always seemed to go your own way."

A rare smile curled Harold's mouth. "I don't care about being around just anyone, that's true. But this here stock company is my family—literally and figuratively. They understand me, let me be. But most of all they care about me. And I care about them. Every one of them."

"I care. And getting the best deal is how I showed it. Stan will be taking on every wrangler that chooses to move to Colorado."

Harold nodded. "Working for Stan will never be the same as working for JM, or anyone associated with Prescott."

"Stan pays same wages we do." Ty had checked into that.

"Ranch hands don't do it for the pay. They do it for the way of life and to feel valued. By those you do it for. See Kyle over there?"

Harold motioned toward the shorter young cowboy who had avoided Ty. "He's grown up around rodeo. His father was a bull rider. His mother a barrel racer. Getting a college degree in equine studies with the help of a scholarship from us. The same scholarship that helped you. Works here so he can learn about breeding broncs and bulls. I can ask him to do anything. Muck out stalls, wash down the horses. He loves what he does. He knows I not only appreciate it, I value when he takes extra care with my brood mares, when he checks the fencing to make sure the bull I'm breeding is secure. He's a quiet sort, but he's humming just about all the time. I doubt he'll be humming around Stan if he decides to go."

"I'm sure Stan will value him too, Harold. Or he'll find another outfit that will." Ty refused to feel bad for making the Prescott family a bunch of money.

"Maybe. But Davis over there has been working here since high school. First summers and then full time after he graduated. JM knew his father, his mother, knew his sisters, attended his father's wedding. It's a family here. An extended family. You were once part of it. Even after you got your fancy education. JM made you part of Prescott."

"He also gave me the duty of securing the family's future."

"And the only way you've seen fit to do that is to break up the community JM built by selling the damn thing, is that right? And breaking that girl's heart in the process."

"She'll start another stock company. She'll have the money to do it." And she'd do it without him.

"It's not losing the company that will break Mandy's heart, Ty. Because you're right. She probably will start another company. But it won't give her what JM wanted for her, for the family. I knew my uncle just about as well as anybody could know another. He wanted to secure his family's future, all right, but it wasn't by selling the company. And the fact you haven't figured that out yet, well, I guess I underestimated you."

Ty met Harold's gaze. And realized what a fool he'd been.

* * *

Mandy was bone weary as she hung her hat on the peg inside the ranch house's side door. It was past midnight. The last rodeo of the regular season was over. The last rodeo maybe forever. The thought made her insides ache.

It had been all over the fairgrounds. Every committee person had come up to ask why she was selling the company. And she didn't have an answer. She'd have told them to see Ty, but he hadn't come. And she was glad he hadn't.

Tears clouded her sight. She wondered if she was so emotional because of the baby. The thought made her smile, bittersweet as it was. Of course she was thrilled, beyond rational measure, at the thought of being pregnant. She hadn't told anyone yet, not even her mother. Not until it was confirmed. She carried her secret close to her heart, though right now it was so hard to focus on what should be the happiest moment of her life.

She was losing Prescott. And it was more than a business. She was losing the place where she belonged and the families who had touched her life since she was a little girl. Fathers, sons, mothers, sisters. She knew them all, and they knew her.

As she walked into the white and granite kitchen, lighted only by the nightlight Mrs. Jenkins had undoubtedly left on for her, she felt empty, abandoned, betrayed. Ty should be sharing this moment with her. They should be planning for the NRF. For next season. Instead, her horses and bulls would be going to the NRF under the name of another contractor. And she would not.

How could she go as a mere spectator when she'd always been an integral part of the fabric of the ten-day event? She had never missed an NRF. Not even after her father had passed away and it was especially difficult. The Prescott community, the rodeo community, had gotten her through it. People had come together and held a special dinner in her father's honor. The stories they had told… She couldn't help but smile at the memory of it.

She spied the blinking light on the answering machine and, hoping it wasn't another call from Ty she'd have to delete, hit the button. She was surprised when she heard Trace's deep voice asking her to call him tomorrow because he wanted to talk to her about a housekeeper for Delanie. Last Ty had said, Delanie was settling into preschool and, aside from asking after her mother, seemed to be accepting Trace as her father. The psychologist thought that Delanie had trust issues but nothing more, and that had been a small blessing. Of course Mandy would call tomorrow. Even though Ty was a double-dealing hypocrite, she would do everything she could for his niece.

She walked down the hall and past her bedroom, right to the baby's room. She flicked on the overhead fixture, and the crib and dresser Ty had bought were

339

bathed in light. The toy airplane still sat on the dresser. Nothing had been disturbed since he'd put it together, and yet everything in her life had been disturbed. She leaned against the wall.

Despite her exhaustion, sleep would elude her tonight, she knew, as it had for the past few nights since Ty's announcement. Tomorrow she had an appointment with the doctor. If he confirmed the pregnancy, she would tell her mother.

And then she would have to tell Ty. She'd have to speak to him. To be in the same room with the man who had betrayed her and everything she stood for.

And why did her traitorous heart speed up at the thought of seeing him? Maybe it was just the baby sending her a signal of some sort.

"What kind of daddy will he be to you?" she wondered aloud as she swept a hand gently over her tummy. "You will always have me, baby, to lean on. I promise you that."

* * *

It went against every rational argument. And still Ty did it.

"Now what?" Brian asked as he looked over the papers set before him.

"Now I tell Mandy."

Brian leaned forward on the desk, his hands pressing down on the polished surface as if bracing for the worst.

"Will she even speak to you?"

Ty shook his head. "Hasn't since she stormed out of the meeting. Hasn't returned my calls. Hasn't come into the office. Hell, it's like a morgue in there. No one wants to get within ten feet of me, it seems. Karen, JM's former assistant, is as frosty as a freezer. Guess they are all waiting for the official ax to fall."

"You know, given you voided the provision by not sleeping in the same room with your wife, you would have had another six months at least as head of Prescott if you hadn't done this. You might have been able to work it out with Mandy and avoided taking this step. It's a lot of money just to make a point."

Ty braved a smile. "It's the right point to make. And I'm hoping for more than just her agreement."

"JM has a letter he wants read to both you and Mandy at the end of the six-month period. I could call a meeting about it, and you can tell her the news then?"

Ty shook his head. "I think I'd best do this in private. If I have any hope of getting through to her, of convincing her to stay married to me, I think it has to be just her and me."

"You thought about how you are going to get her to meet with you? She's stubborn. Like her grandfather."

How well Ty knew. He'd already tried every way he could think of to get her to see him, but she'd refused to acknowledge he even existed. He realized he needed to enlist some help. Not an easy thing when everyone treated him like a leper.

"I think I've got it covered. If I don't, you can be the backup plan."

Ty picked up his hat from its resting place on Brian's desk and secured it on his head. If everything went as he hoped, maybe he could have it all.

* * *

Mandy turned into the sparsely graveled driveway and noted the house looked as tired as it had before, despite the money Ty had reportedly made available to Trace. But at least the barns looked repaired, and there were cattle in the nearby pasture and two cowboys on horses trailing behind a bunch being moved to another corral.

The place didn't exactly look prosperous, but it did look like it was moving in that direction.

She'd been surprised to get Trace's call asking her for help in interviewing a housekeeper and caregiver for Delanie. He wanted a woman's perspective, and his neighbor, it seemed, was out of town. How could she say no? Or tell him she and Ty were no longer a couple, since Ty had obviously not spoken to his brother, yet.

In fact, if not in deed, she was still married. Mandy had been determined not to file the divorce papers until she knew for certain she was pregnant, and her pregnancy had only been confirmed that morning. And, then she would have to tell Ty first.

Not that she wanted to face Ty. If she could have kept it from him and still looked herself in the mirror, she would have. But her child deserved to know its father.

Something to deal with another day.

As she closed the car door, a little figure came running out of the house, letting the screen door slam behind her.

"Aunt Mandy," the little girl called as she ran toward her, the child's lissome legs, clad in denims, moving at the full throttle of four-year-old speed.

Mandy's heart crumbled into little pieces like a dried leaf under a tire. How and when would she tell this special little girl she was no longer *Aunt* Mandy? At least Delanie would have a cousin. Mandy could give the little girl that.

Mandy scooped Delanie into her arms and gave her a hug, breathing in the sweet scent of baby shampoo as she nuzzled her. "What a wonderful greeting," Mandy said as she kissed the little one's cheek.

And so unlike their first encounter. That psychologist Trace had found through Ty's connections was surely working wonders.

"The meeting is there." Delanie pointed to the house. "Daddy's going to take me riding while you talk."

Odd, Mandy thought. She had expected to interview the applicants with Trace there.

"Where's Daddy now?" she asked.

"Inside. They both are."

Mandy looked around for another car, but there was none visible. Perhaps Trace had picked up the candidate in town and brought the woman out to the ranch house. And was there only to be one? Trace had made it sound like there would be several applicants lined up.

Mandy set the squirming child down on the ground and, holding Delanie's sticky little hand, walked to the house. Delanie held the screen door open as Mandy stepped inside. She blinked as her eyes adjusted from the bright sunlight of a fall day to the relative darkness of the unlit kitchen.

It took her a moment to make out Trace.

Shifting her gaze, she found another figure sitting off to the side of the kitchen table, a single sheet of paper lying on the table before him.

Heat climbed up her throat. Moisture collected under her arms. Ty had some nerve. She didn't lose sight, however, that Delanie was watching her, a smile on the little girl's precious face.

Trace had moved to the screen door. To block it or exit quickly, she wasn't sure. She swung her gaze toward him. He shrugged in a sheepish way. "You two need to talk."

And then he was out the door, Delanie grabbing his hand. That psychologist *had* made progress.

The door slammed behind them.

Now what?

Mandy turned to study Ty. She hadn't seen him since the meeting in the library. He looked a little haggard around the edges, dressed in a pair of wrinkled denims and flannel shirt. Soon he could go back to his suits and ties, content that he had once again made a lot of money and not at all bothered about the good people whose lives he had disrupted.

She could feel a vein pulse at her temple like a drum thumping out a funereal melody. She wanted to turn around and go home. But she had to tell him about the baby. And now was as good a time as any.

"You went to a lot of trouble to get me out here. Yet I can't think of a single reason why. There is nothing, absolutely nothing, you can tell me that I want to hear. And if it is to announce that the papers to sell Prescott have been signed, believe me when I tell you, this is the worst way you could have communicated it to me."

344

Ty rose from his seat, his six-foot frame unfurling before her as he ran his fingers through his dark hair. He stared at her. Just stared at her. Looked her up and down. It wasn't a sexual appraisal. It made her more uncomfortable than that. It was more like a caress. As if he needed to assure she was really standing before him.

"I'd appreciate it if you could you sit down, Mandy. I've something to say that doesn't involve selling Prescott."

Mandy's heart was racing, and her legs did feel a little weak. She pulled back the kitchen chair from the table and perched on the edge of the seat, primed to make a quick exit if need be.

Ty followed, sitting back down on the wood slat chair.

"How are you?"

Mandy could feel her blood steam at the question. Why should he care after what he had done to make her miserable? "I'm doing as well as can be expected for a woman who has lost her company. Not to mention her extended family—because that's what Prescott is to me. Something you'd never understand, and even if you did, you wouldn't care."

Ty dropped his eyes down to the sheet of paper before him, looking beleaguered, but if he was, it was of his own making. He'd never been a part of Prescott, as it turned out. He'd been planning its demise from the first day. She thought he had changed, had maybe found his place—by her side—but she was wrong. He didn't want to be there. He didn't want anything to do with her, or he wouldn't have done this. She and Prescott Rodeo Company had just been a convenient way to pass time. Anger stampeded through her like horses running from fire.

"You look…" Whatever he was going to say died on his lips.

She pressed her cold palms on the table, steadying herself. "I'm not here for a chat, Ty. Say what you have to say. Then I've got something to tell you."

"You can say your piece first." Ty could only imagine the names she wanted to call him. Best to let her vent now. Maybe she'd be in a better frame of mind for the news. Maybe, just maybe, she'd give him a second chance.

"No, you are the one who went to all this trouble to get me here. To trick me." Her eyebrows arched as she labeled his maneuver. "You first."

Ty had thought about telling her all the whys and wherefores he had used to justify his original decision to sell and what had caused his opinion to change, but every time he had rehearsed it in his head, it had sounded lame. Like why hadn't he seen it from the very beginning? He didn't know how to explain that he had been looking through a different lens, one that didn't focus on people or relationships or the satisfaction of the work, but only on the value measured by the dollar.

In the end he opted for shooting straight and keeping it simple.

"I didn't sell Prescott."

She blinked once and then again, as if shutting off one screen and opening another. "What do you mean? You didn't sell Prescott to Lassiter?"

"That's exactly what I mean."

Tears glistened in her eyes and streamed silently down her cheeks. Mandy's body began to tremble, like she was shivering. Watching her absorb the news, Ty's stomach lurched as if he'd just plummeted down a roller coaster's hill.

He thought she would be happy, pleased, maybe grateful. But she reacted more like someone who had been badly frightened.

"Mandy?" Ty leaned forward, concerned.

She shook her head in response.

He moved from his seat to crouch on his haunches by her chair. She looked as confused as he was by whatever emotion had propelled her to tears. He gathered her in his arms, placing a hand gently behind her to press her head onto his shoulder, anchoring her.

It would have felt good to hold her again after days of denial, except for the sobs that now racked through her.

After a minute or two, it was over. The sobs vanished, and the shaking stopped. Her warm breath upon his shoulder came in small, even puffs.

"I'm all right," she said, pulling back from his embrace. "I don't know what came over me." She swiped a hand under her eyes, spreading the dampness over her cheek.

Ty remained on his haunches as he searched her face for some clue as to what she was thinking. In the kitchen of his family home, her tears should have been a painful reminder of his mother's crying, as she had done so often in his young life. But these tears were different. More emotional, yet happier. And totally unexpected.

"Why did you change your mind?" She sniffled. The woman could probably use a tissue. Ty rose, scoped out the napkin holder on the counter, retrieved a textured sheet, and handed it to her. She promptly blew her nose.

He waited until she was done, wondering just how he would answer her question. It was an important question because the reasons he gave would have to change how she felt about him. She needed to understand that he saw things differently, or there would be no hope for them.

"I finally realized that I can fulfill JM's wishes in another way."

She squared her shoulders and lifted her chin. The tension had returned as if a rattler had slithered into the room.

"If you think I'll sit by idly while you run Prescott for another year and a half just to look for a better offer and put me through this all over again, you can forget it. I'll take you to court. I don't care what Brian says. I'll fight you even if I have no chance of winning, just to mess things up. I'll…" She didn't finish, having either run out of steam or threats. Instead, she glared, apparently too furious to speak.

This wasn't going at all like he'd planned. She really did think he was the devil. The thought pained him so much more now. After they had made love, shared dreams, worked together.

"No. That won't be necessary." Ty slid the paper on the table toward her.

She snatched it. He watched as her eyes darted right then left. Like a football receiver who knows he's going to get hit as he goes up for the ball, Ty steeled himself for the blow. This was his last chance and it was either going to be a touchdown or an incomplete pass.

It took several moments for her to lift her head. The accusations that had filled her eyes were gone, replaced by amazement. "You granted me your personal shares? Why?" Her voice was but a whisper.

If only he could make her understand.

"You now have forty percent of the company—all with voting rights. Along with Tucker and Harold's share, you have more than enough to form a majority. No one can sell Prescott without all three of you agreeing to it."

"I don't understand. How can I accept this? This represents a lot of money, Ty."

He knew how much to the penny. And for once in his life, it didn't matter. "Consider it something I owe you. For putting you through all of this."

Her smile was wobbly, just like her voice. "Does this mean you think Prescott is the better bet for the future?"

For a split second he thought about lying, but that had never been his way. Ty shook his head. "No. I still think accepting Stan's offer is the best financial deal for future security."

Her eyes widened, and her fragile smile vanished. "Then why didn't you accept it? Like grandfather wanted?"

"Because I realized it wasn't what your grandfather wanted. He wanted to make something work between us. He knew either way the family couldn't lose. But he pinned his hope for the future on us, both of us."

Mandy's body heaved as she took a deep breath. "You mean you and I married, living happily ever after?"

"Yes."

His throat constricted as if a piece of food was lodged there and he was on the verge of choking. He still had a kernel of hope that his initial decision to sell hadn't totally decimated what they had been building, but it was just a kernel. Her emotion-packed reaction to his news had driven home how deeply his actions had hurt her.

"She looked down at the paper. "I have something to tell you too, Ty. I hardly know where to start."

"If it is that you hate me, I already know that."

She smiled, a sweet, delicate turn of the lips as if he'd said something clever. Was that a good sign? He wasn't in any position to interpret.

"No. Although I did up until a few seconds ago."

"I guess I don't blame you. I'd hoped…" Ty took a deep breath to calm the erratic beats of his heart. "Mandy, I have one more thing to tell you before you tell me your news."

"I will pay you back. For the stock," she said.

"I don't care about the stock or the money. If I did, I wouldn't have given you the shares."

"But you always said it was about the money. I don't understand." She cocked her head, her gorgeous green eyes quizzical.

This time he'd say it and let things fall where they may. He bent down on one knee. Pulling out the jeweler's box from his shirt pocket, he opened it. The rings, studded in diamonds, sparkled even in the dim light.

He took a bracing breath. "Mandy, I have fallen in love with you. I want to be with you, and only you.

Life isn't worth anything without the right person to share it with. And these months together have proven to me you are the right person, the only person. I'm hoping you'll give me another chance to show you that I'm the right person for you. I haven't done a very good job of making you happy. But if you'll take another chance on me, I promise I will give everything I have to make you happy because I love you."

Mandy tried to process Ty's declaration as he knelt before her, his outstretched hand holding a box with a pair of shimmering rings, but her mind was swamped with a dizzying array of emotions from joy to disbelief, to gratefulness. But the strongest emotion, the one that was swelling her heart like an air pump stuck in overdrive, was love.

"Did you hear what I said? I said I love you."

She had heard. And it had sent her reeling like a lightweight boxer in a heavyweight fight.

His roughened finger grazed her chin, lifting it so he could peer into her eyes.

"If you can find it in your heart to forgive me, to love me, marry me all over again. This time for real. And this time because we both love each other."

He'd given her back her company, her family, her legacy. He'd given her a child. And now he'd given her everything.

"Please," he pleaded, still holding the box in his outstretched hand.

"I'm pregnant."

His kiss was deep, soul scorching, passionate, and persuasive. She wrapped her arms around his neck. She had no intention of letting go.

Chapter 23

Mandy glided across the polished dance floor secure in Ty's arms while the strains of "Bless the Broken Road" streamed from the house speakers of the private room at the Cattleman's Club. With all eyes on her and Ty, she stole a glance at her handsome husband, looking darn attractive in his black tuxedo. Just as she sported a pair of white embossed leather and gold-studded cowgirl boots under her gown, Ty had insisted on wearing Caiman boots with his tux in true cowboy style.

It was their first dance together as husband and wife, even if they had been technically married for six months already. This, she felt, was the start of their real marriage. One based on love, not convenience or contrivance.

They'd been lucky the Cattleman's Club could host the reception on such short notice with some persuading from Libby Cochran's father and his Cheyenne connections. It helped that it was a Tuesday, the same day of the week six months earlier that they had first said wedding vows.

Today the vows had been handwritten, filled with meaning, and recited before a minister. Friends, relatives, and Prescott employees and their families had been invited to celebrate the occasion. Mandy looked down at her Cinderella wedding dress and the diamond-studded platinum wedding band and engagement ring that now graced her finger, and then into the dark, soulful eyes of the man she loved. And who loved her.

How it had happened, how it had all come out right in the end, she couldn't understand. But that it had filled her with happiness…and contentment.

After a few stanzas where they danced alone, the floor filled, and two little persons on the edge of the crowd caught her eye.

"Look," Mandy whispered in her husband's ear. He turned his head in the direction she was staring.

An impish Jake in a dark suit was squiring little Delanie in pink tulle in a rough approximation of dancing. Actually it looked more akin to a slow skip. They'd been ring bearer and flower girl in the ceremony.

"Now that's the definition of a cute couple," Mandy said.

"You know if we have a daughter, she's not going to be able to date until she's like, thirty." Ty broke into a smile that was becoming a more frequent feature of his face these days. In fact, he hadn't stopped smiling since that day at Trace's house, almost two weeks ago. And that smile got especially broad when he told someone he was going to be a father. And he had told everyone.

"Good luck with that."

He chuckled. "I'm going to need it if she's as headstrong as her mother."

"Or stubborn as her father."

Mandy spotted Libby, with her ever-expanding waistline and her handsome bronc-riding husband, Chance, slow dancing in a half embrace. Libby smiled in their direction. She was due any day but had insisted she would make the wedding. Naturally, Libby and Cat had been the bridesmaids. Libby wore the only maternity dress she owned—a blue empire-waisted, cocktail-length dress. Cat happened to also have a fitted blue dress available, though Mandy wouldn't have been surprised if Cat had secretly bought it just for the wedding.

"I like Chance," Ty said: "He's a down-to-earth kind of guy. And clearly in love with your girlfriend. We should spend more time with them. We can learn from their experiences with the baby."

"I'd like that. What did you think of Cat?"

Cat was sitting alone at her table, keeping a watchful eye on her son.

"She's a strong woman. Raising a son as a single mother and running a ranch operation. I was thinking maybe Trace and she might find common ground, but I think she's too much for him to handle."

Mandy shook her head. "I had someone in mind for her too, but I think events are going to keep it from working out." Over some land dispute, Cat was taking to court the only man she ever talked about these days, and that was a whole other story.

"You never know. Stranger things have happened." Ty kissed her on the nose.

They certainly had.

Harold and her mother waltzed by. Harold wore his only suit. Her mother had insisted on buying an eggplant-colored mother-of-the-bride dress that she found online, and she had located a seamstress who guaranteed she would hem it in time.

"Now those two look almost as happy as we do," Ty noted. "Can't wait for their wedding next month."

"That's because my mother was worried I would never marry and she'd never be a grandma. And now we've given her both. And I didn't have to give up Prescott to do it."

She felt the squeeze of Ty's hand. "We are very lucky, Mandy."

The song ended, and dancers dispersed to their respective tables. Except little Jake and Delanie, who decided to run across the dance floor and out of the room, their respective parent in pursuit.

As Mandy and Ty settled on the dais, Brian approached, a grin on his face.

"I can't tell you how happy I am to be attending this wedding," Brian said as he looked around the chandelier-lit ballroom filled with guests. "Or should I say re-wedding."

"Call it a do-over," Ty said as he gave Mandy's knee a pat.

"Well, I have one more thing to do." Brian reached into the interior pocket of his suit jacket. He pulled out an envelope and laid it on the linen-clad table before them. "A note from your grandfather." With a nod he walked away.

"Should we read it here?" Mandy asked, feeling a little apprehensive at the prospect. After all, her grandfather's will had caused quite a bit of havoc in her life, good intentions aside. Not that it hadn't been worth it all in the end. Or that she hadn't learned a thing or two about herself along the way.

"I think it only fitting that we read it here, today, don't you?"

Mandy handed it over to him. "Whatever it says, I still love you."

She felt the brush of Ty's lips across her cheek. "And I, you, Mandy Martin."

Ty opened the envelope and withdrew a single sheet of manila paper. Her eyes welled up at the sight of her grandfather's handwriting. All that had been missing to make this day truly perfect was his presence. She missed him still. Would always miss him, despite his meddling ways—or maybe because of them.

Mandy leaned against Ty's shoulder as they read the letter together.

Dear Ty and Amanda:

If you are reading this letter, it means that the biggest bet I ever made has paid off. You two are married, planning on staying married, and Prescott Rodeo Company continues on in good hands.

I know neither of you is probably thrilled with how I went about things. My excuse is that, as your elder, I did what I thought was best. I knew I was running out of time. Death would come too soon for me to play matchmaker and get you both to see you would be perfect for one another. Especially considering before that could take place, I had to teach you both what was important in life.

Mandy, you had to learn to believe in yourself, even when others doubt you—as every stock contractor in the industry undoubtedly did. You also had to recognize that there is more to life than the company—something I learned a little too late. I didn't want my only granddaughter to make the same mistake I did. And your father did. Tucker, bless him, is right about that.

That was the lesson Ty had to learn too. Using the yardstick of the almighty dollar isn't a good measure of a successful life. As good a businessman as you had become, Ty, there was nothing else in your life. Hopefully, you have learned there is value in letting someone into your heart, someone who will appreciate you as my granddaughter will and as I expect you will appreciate her.

Have a wonderful life. Give me lots of grandkids to watch over, and always remember what really matters in life.

Your loving grandfather,
J.M. Prescott

Dear Readers,

I hope you enjoyed this book as much as I enjoyed writing Ty and Mandy's story. Please consider leaving a review on the book's page on Amazon's website. This helps increase visibility of the book so other readers can find it. All you need to write is a sentence or two. It means the world to authors to know what readers think of their books.

If you haven't read it yet, **Loving a Cowboy** is Libby and Chance's story and the first book in the Hearts of Wyoming series, though you do not need to read these books in order. **The Rancher's Heart** will be coming out in 2016, where Cat will finally find love with a man she thought she never had a chance with.

And you can weigh in on whose story you would like to see in subsequent books by sending me an e-mail or commenting on Facebook. Would you like Trace to find a wife and a mother for little Delanie? What about that heartbreaker Tucker Prescott? Or Doug Brennan, Libby's brother from **Loving a Cowboy**?

There are lots of characters who need a second chance at finding their true love in the Hearts of Wyoming series!

Hugs,

Anne

About the Author

I have been creating stories since I first wondered where Sally was running to in those early reader books. Besides reading and writing romances, you might find me researching western history, at the rodeo, watching football, in the garden, or on the tennis court. Married to my own suburban cowboy, I'm the mother of a twentysomething cowgirl. I'm also the founder of the western romance fan page http://www.facebook.com/lovewesternromances.com.

I love hearing from readers. You can friend, follow, or find me on

Facebook: http://www.facebook.com/annecarrole
Twitter: http://twitter.com/annecarrole
Web: http://www.annecarrole.com (Where you can also sign up for my newsletter.)

Titles by Anne Carrole
Falling for a Cowboy
Saving Cole Turner

Hearts of Wyoming Series
Loving a Cowboy
The Maverick Meets His Match
The Rancher's Heart (coming 2016)